EVERYMAN,

I WILL GO WITH THEE,

AND BE THY GUIDE,

IN THY MOST NEED

TO GO BY THY SIDE

HORSE STORIES

EDITED BY DIANA SECKER TESDELL

EVERYMAN'S POCKET CLASSICS
Alfred A. Knopf New York London Toronto

THIS IS A BORZOI BOOK
PUBLISHED BY ALFRED A. KNOPF

This selection by Diana Secker Tesdell first published in
Everyman's Library, 2012
Copyright © 2012 by Everyman's Library
A list of acknowledgments to copyright owners appears at the back
of this volume.

US website: www.randomhouse.com/everymans

ISBN: 978-0-307-96145-7 (US)
978-1-84159-612-9 (UK)

A CIP catalogue reference for this book is available from the
British Library

Library of Congress Cataloging-in-Publication Data
Horse stories / edited by Diana Secker Tesdell.
      p.   cm.—(Everyman's pocket classics)
         "This is a Borzoi book."
Includes bibliographical references and index.
ISBN 978-0-307-96145-7 (hardcover: alk. paper)
 1. Horses—Fiction.   2. Short stories, American.   3. Short stories,
          English.   I. Tesdell, Diana Secker.
PN6120.95.H73H67   2012   2012025286
823'.010836296655—dc23   CIP

Typography by Peter B. Willberg

Typeset in the UK by AccComputing, North Barrow, Somerset

Printed and bound in Germany by GGP Media GmbH, Pössneck

HORSE
STORIES

Contents

BERYL MARKHAM

THE SPLENDID
OUTCAST

THE STALLION WAS named after a star, and when he fell from his particular heaven, it was easy enough for people to say that he had been named too well. People like to see stars fall, but in the case of Rigel, it was of greater importance to me. To me and to one other – to a little man with shabby cuffs and a wilted cap that rested over eyes made mild by something more than time.

It was at Newmarket, in England, where, since Charles I instituted the first cup race, a kind of court has been held for the royalty of the turf. Men of all classes come to Newmarket for the races and for the December sales. They come from everywhere – some to bet, some to buy or sell, and some merely to offer homage to the resplendent peers of the Stud Book, for the sport of kings may, after all, be the pleasure of every man.

December can be bitterly cold in England, and this December was. There was frozen sleet on buildings and on trees, and I remember that the huge Newmarket track lay on the downs below the village like a noose of diamonds on a tarnished mat. There was a festive spirit everywhere, but it was somehow lost on me. I had come to buy new blood for my stable in Kenya, and since my stable was my living, I came as serious buyers do, with figures in my mind and caution in my heart. Horses are hard to judge at best, and the thought of putting your hoarded pounds behind that judgment makes it harder still.

I sat close on the edge of the auction ring and held my breath from time to time as the bidding soared. I held it because the casual mention of ten thousand guineas in payment for a horse or for anything else seemed to me wildly beyond the realm of probable things. For myself, I had five hundred pounds to spend and, as I waited for Rigel to be shown, I remember that I felt uncommonly maternal about each pound. I waited for Rigel because I had come six thousand miles to buy him, nor was I apprehensive lest anyone should take him from me; he was an outcast.

Rigel had a pedigree that looked backward and beyond the pedigrees of many Englishmen – and Rigel had a brilliant record. By all odds, he should have brought ten thousand guineas at the sale, but I knew he wouldn't, for he had killed a man.

He had killed a man – not fallen upon him, nor thrown him in a playful moment from the saddle, but killed him dead with his hooves and with his teeth in a stable. And that was not all, though it was the greatest thing. Rigel had crippled other men and, so the story went, would cripple or kill still more, so long as he lived. He was savage, people said, and while he could not be hanged for his crimes, like a man, he could be shunned as criminals are. He could be offered for sale. And yet, under the implacable rules of racing, he had been warned off the turf for life – so who would buy?

Well, I for one – and I had supposed there would not be two. I would buy if the price were low enough, because I had youth then, and a corresponding contempt for failure. It seemed probable that in time and with luck and with skill, the stallion might be made manageable again, if only for breeding – especially for breeding. He could be gentled, I thought. But I found it hard to believe what I saw that day.

I had not known that the mere touch of a hand could, in an instant, extinguish the long-burning anger of an angry heart.

I first noticed the little man when the sale was already well on its way, and he caught my attention at once, because he was incongruous there. He sat a few benches from me and held his lean, interwoven fingers upon his knees. He stared down upon the arena as each horse was led into it, and he listened to the dignified encomiums of the auctioneer with the humble attention of a parishioner at mass. He never moved. He was surrounded by men and women who, by their impeccable clothes and by their somewhat bored familiarity with pounds and guineas, made him conspicuous. He was like a stone of granite in a jeweler's window, motionless and grey against the glitter.

You could see in his face that he loved horses – just as you could see, in some of the faces of those around him, that they loved the idea of horses. They were the cultists, he the votary, and there were, in fact, about his grey eyes and his slender lips, the deep, tense lines so often etched in the faces of zealots and of lonely men. It was the cast of his shoulders, I think, the devotion of his manner that told me he had once been a jockey.

A yearling came into the ring and was bought, and then another, while the pages of catalogues were quietly turned. The auctioneer's voice, clear but scarcely lifted, intoned the virtues of his magnificent merchandise as other voices, responding to this magic, spoke reservedly of figures: 'A thousand guineas ... two thousand ... three ... four! ...'

The scene at the auction comes to me clearly now, as if once again it were happening before my eyes.

'Five, perhaps?' The auctioneer scans the audience expectantly as a groom parades a dancing colt around the arena. There is a moment of near silence, a burly voice calls, 'Five!'

and the colt is sold while a murmur of polite approval swells and dies.

And so they go, one after another, until the list is small; the audience thins, and my finger traces the name, Rigel, on the last page of the catalogue. I straighten on my bench and hold my breath a little, forgetting the crowd, the little man, and a part of myself. I know this horse. I know he is by Hurry On out of Bounty – the sire unbeaten, the dam a great steeplechaser – and there is no better blood than that. Killer or not, Rigel has won races, and won them clean. If God and Barclays Bank stay with me, he will return to Africa when I do.

And there, at last, he stands. In the broad entrance to the ring, two powerful men appear with the stallion between them. The men are not grooms of ordinary size; they have been picked for strength, and in the clenched fist of each is the end of a chain. Between the chain and the bit there is on the near side a short rod of steel, close to the stallion's mouth – a rod of steel, easy to grasp, easy to use. Clenched around the great girth of the horse, and fitted with metal rings, there is a strap of thick leather that brings to mind the restraining harness of a madman.

Together, the two men edge the stallion forward. Tall as they are, they move like midgets beside his massive shoulders. He is the biggest thoroughbred I have ever seen. He is the most beautiful. His coat is chestnut, flecked with white, and his mane and tail are close to gold. There is a blaze on his face – wide and straight and forthright, as if by this marking he proclaims that he is none other than Rigel, for all his sins, for all the hush that falls over the crowd.

He is Rigel and he looks upon the men who hold his chains as a captured king may look upon his captors. He is not tamed. Nothing about him promises that he will be tamed. Stiffly, on reluctant hooves, he enters the ring and flares his crimson nostrils at the crowd, and the crowd is still. The crowd whose pleasure is the docile beast of pretty paddocks, the gainly horse of cherished prints that hang upon the finest walls, the willing winner of the race – upon the rebel this crowd stares, and the rebel stares back.

His eyes are lit with anger or with hate. His head is held disdainfully and high, his neck an arc of arrogance. He prances now – impatience in the thudding of his hooves upon the tanbark, defiance in his manner – and the chains jerk tight. The long stallion reins are tightly held – apprehensively held – and the men who hold them glance at the auctioneer, an urgent question in their eyes.

The auctioneer raises his arm for silence, but there is silence. No one speaks. The story of Rigel is known – his breeding, his brilliant victories, and finally his insurgence and his crimes. Who will buy the outcast? The auctioneer shakes his head as if to say that this is a trick beyond his magic. But he will try. He is an imposing man, an experienced man, and now he clears his throat and confronts the crowd, a kind of pleading in his face.

'This splendid animal –' he begins – and does not finish. He cannot finish.

Rigel has scanned the silent audience and smelled the unmoving air, and he – a creature of the wind – knows the indignity of this skyless temple. He seems aware at last of the chains that hold him, of the men who cling forlornly to the heavy reins. He rears from the tanbark, higher and higher still, until his golden mane is lifted like a flag unfurled and defiant. He beats the air. He trembles in his rising anger, and the crowd leans forward.

A groom clings like a monkey to the tightened chain. He is swept from his feet while his partner, a less tenacious man, sprawls ignobly below, and men – a dozen men – rush to the ring, some shouting, some waving their arms. They run and swear in lowered voices; they grasp reins, chains, rings, and swarm upon their towering Gulliver. And he subsides.

With something like contempt for this hysteria, Rigel touches his forehooves to the tanbark once more. He has killed no one, hurt no one, but they are jabbing at his mouth now, they are surrounding him, adding fuel to his fiery reputation, and the auctioneer is a wilted man.

He sighs, and you can almost hear it. He raises both arms and forgoes his speech. 'What,' he asks with weariness, 'am I offered?' And there is a ripple of laughter from the crowd. Smug in its wisdom, it offers nothing.

But I do, and my voice is like an echo in a cave. Still there is triumph in it. I will have what I have come so far to get – I will have Rigel.

'A hundred guineas!' I stand as I call my price, and the auctioneer is plainly shocked – not by the meagerness of the offer, but by the offer itself. He stares upward from the ring, incredulity in his eyes.

He lifts a hand and slowly repeats the price. 'I am offered,' he says, 'one hundred guineas.'

There is a hush, and I feel the eyes of the crowd and watch the hand of the auctioneer. When it goes down, the stallion will be mine.

But it does not go down. It is still poised in midair, white, expectant, compelling, when the soft voice, the gently challenging voice is lifted. 'Two hundred!' the voice says, and I do not have to turn to know that the little jockey has bid against me. But I do turn.

He has not risen from the bench, and he does not look at me. In his hand he holds a sheaf of bank notes. I can tell by their color that they are of small denomination, by their rumpled condition that they have been hoarded long. People near him are staring – horrified, I think – at the vulgar spectacle of cash at a Newmarket auction.

I am not horrified, nor sympathetic. Suddenly I am aware that I have a competitor, and I am cautious. I am here for a purpose that has little to do with sentiment, and I will not be beaten. I think of my stable in Kenya, of the feed bills to come, of the syces to be paid, of the races that are yet to be won if I am to survive in this unpredictable business. No, I cannot now yield an inch. I have little money, but so has he. No more, I think, but perhaps as much.

I hesitate a moment and glance at the little man, and he returns my glance. We are like two gamblers bidding each against the other's unseen cards. Our eyes meet for a sharp instant – a cold instant.

I straighten and my catalogue is crumpled in my hand. I moisten my lips and call, 'Three hundred!' I call it firmly, steadily, hoping to undo my opponent at a stroke. It is a wishful thought.

He looks directly at me now, but does not smile. He looks at me as a man might look at one who bears false witness against him, then soundlessly he counts his money and bids again, 'Three fifty!'

The interest of the crowd is suddenly aroused. All these people are at once conscious of being witnesses, not only before an auction, but before a contest, a rivalry of wills. They shift in their seats and stare as they might stare at a pair of duelists, rapiers in hand.

But money is the weapon, Rigel the prize. And prize enough, I think, as does my adversary.

I ponder and think hard, then decide to bid a hundred more. Not twenty, not fifty, but a hundred. Perhaps by that I can take him in my stride. He need not know there is little

17

more to follow. He may assume that I am one of the casual ones, impatient of small figures. He may hesitate, he may withdraw. He may be cowed.

Still standing, I utter, as indifferently as I can, the words, 'Four fifty!' and the auctioneer, at ease in his element of contention, brightens visibly.

I am aware that the gathered people are now fascinated by this battle of pounds and shillings over a stallion that not one of them would care to own. I only hope that in the heat of it some third person does not begin to bid. But I need not worry; Rigel takes care of that.

The little jockey has listened to my last offer, and I can see that he is already beaten – or almost, at least. He has counted his money a dozen times, but now he counts it again, swiftly, with agile fingers, as if hoping his previous counts had been wrong.

I feel a momentary surge of sympathy, then smother it. Horse training is not my hobby. It is my living. I wait for what I am sure will be his last bid, and it comes. For the first time, he rises from his bench. He is small and alone in spirit, for the glances of the well-dressed people about him lend him nothing. He does not care. His eyes are on the stallion and I can see that there is a kind of passion in them. I have seen that expression before – in the eyes of sailors appraising a comely ship, in the eyes of pilots sweeping the clean, sweet contours of a plane. There is reverence in it, desire – and even hope.

The little man turns slightly to face the expectant auctioneer, then clears his throat and makes his bid. 'Four eighty!' he calls, and the slight note of desperation in his voice is unmistakable, but I force myself to ignore it. Now, at last, I tell myself, the prize is mine.

The auctioneer receives the bid and looks at me, as do a

hundred people. Some of them, no doubt, think I am quite mad or wholly inexperienced, but they watch while the words 'Five hundred' form upon my lips. They are never uttered.

Throughout the bidding for Rigel, Rigel has been ignored. He has stood quietly enough after his first brief effort at freedom; he has scarcely moved. But now, at the climax of the sale, his impatience overflows, his spirit flares like fire, his anger bursts through the circle of men who guard him. Suddenly, there are cries, shouts of warning, the ringing of chains and the cracking of leather, and the crowd leaps to its feet. Rigel is loose. Rigel has hurled his captors from him and he stands alone.

It is a beautiful thing to see, but there is terror in it. A thoroughbred stallion with anger in his eye is not a sight to entrance anyone but a novice. If you are aware of the power and the speed and the intelligence in that towering symmetrical body, you will hold your breath as you watch it. You will know that the teeth of a horse can crush a bone, that hooves can crush a man. And Rigel's hooves have crushed a man.

He stands alone, his neck curved, his golden tail a battle plume, and he turns, slowly, deliberately, and faces the men he has flung away. They are not without courage, but they are without resource. Horses are not tamed by whips or by blows. The strength of ten men is not so strong as a single stroke of a hoof; the experience of ten men is not enough, for this is the unexpected, the unpredictable. No one is prepared. No one is ready.

The words 'Five hundred' die upon my lips as I watch, as I listen. For the stallion is not voiceless now. His challenging scream is shrill as the cry of winter wind. It is bleak and heartless. His forehooves stir the tanbark. The auction is forgotten.

A man stands before him – a man braver than most.

He holds nothing in his hands save an exercise bat; it looks a feeble thing, and is. It is a thin stick bound with leather – enough only to enrage Rigel, for he has seen such things in men's hands before. He knows their meaning. Such a thing as this bat, slight as it is, enrages him because it is a symbol that stands for other things. It stands, perhaps, for the confining walls of a darkened stable, for the bit of steel, foreign, but almost everpresent in his mouth, for the tightened girth, the command to gallop, to walk, to stop, to parade before the swelling crowd of gathered people, to accept the measured food gleaned from forbidden fields. It stands for life no closer to the earth than the sterile smell of satin on a jockey's back or the dead wreath hung upon a winner. It stands for servitude. And Rigel has broken with his overlords.

He lunges quickly, and the man with a bat is not so quick. He lifts the pathetic stick and waves it in desperation. He cries out, and the voice of the crowd drowns his cry. Rigel's neck is outstretched and straight as a sabre. There is dust and the shouting of men and the screaming of women, for the stallion's teeth have closed on the shoulder of his forlorn enemy.

The man struggles and drops his bat, and his eyes are sharp with terror, perhaps with pain. Blood leaves the flesh of his face, and it is a face grey and pleading, as must be the faces of those to whom retribution is unexpected and swift. He beats against the golden head while the excitement of the crowd mounts against the fury of Rigel. Then reason vanishes. Clubs, whips, and chains appear like magic in the ring, and a regiment of men advance upon the stallion. They are angry men, brave in their anger, righteous and justified in it. They advance, and the stallion drops the man he has attacked, and the man runs for cover, clutching his shoulder.

I am standing, as is everyone. It is a strange and unreal thing to see this trapped and frustrated creature, magnificent

20

and alone, away from his kind, remote from the things he understands, face the punishment of his minuscule masters. He is, of course, terrified, and the terror is a mounting madness. If he could run, he would leave this place, abandoning his fear and his hatred to do it. But he cannot run. The walls of the arena are high. The doors are shut, and the trap makes him blind with anger. He will fight, and the blows will fall with heaviness upon his spirit, for his body is a rock before these petty weapons.

The men edge closer, ropes and chains and whips in determined hands. The whips are lifted, the chains are ready; the battle line is formed, and Rigel does not retreat. He comes forward, the whites of his eyes exposed and rimmed with carnelian fire, his nostrils crimson.

There is a breathless silence, and the little jockey slips like a ghost into the ring. His eyes are fixed on the embattled stallion. He begins to run across the tanbark and breaks through the circle of advancing men and does not stop. Someone clutches at his coat, but he breaks loose without turning, then slows to an almost casual walk and approaches Rigel alone. The men do not follow him. He waves them back. He goes forward, steadily, easily and happily, without caution, without fear, and Rigel whirls angrily to face him.

Rigel stands close to the wall of the arena. He cannot retreat. He does not propose to. Now he can focus his fury on this insignificant David who has come to meet him, and he does. He lunges at once as only a stallion can – swiftly, invincibly, as if escape and freedom can be found only in the destruction of all that is human, all that smells human, and all that humans have made.

He lunges and the jockey stops. He does not turn or lift a hand or otherwise move. He stops, he stands, and there is silence everywhere. No one speaks; no one seems to breathe.

Only Rigel is motion. No special hypnotic power emanates from the jockey's eyes; he has no magic. The stallion's teeth are bared and close, his hooves are a swelling sound when the jockey turns. Like a matador of nerveless skill and studied insolence, the jockey turns his back on Rigel and does not walk away, and the stallion pauses.

Rigel rears high at the back of the little man, screaming his defiant scream, but he does not strike. His hooves are close to the jockey's head, but do not touch him. His teeth are sheathed. He hesitates, trembles, roars wind from his massive lungs. He shakes his head, his golden mane, and beats the ground. It is frustration – but of a new kind. It is a thing he does not know – a man who neither cringes in fear nor threatens with whips or chains. It is a thing beyond his memory perhaps – as far beyond it as the understanding of the mare that bore him.

Rigel is suddenly motionless, rigid, suspicious. He waits, and the grey-eyed jockey turns to face him. The little man is calm and smiling. We hear him speak, but cannot understand his words. They are low and they are lost to us – an incantation. But the stallion seems to understand at least the spirit if not the sense of them. He snorts, but does not move. And now the jockey's hand goes forward to the golden mane – neither hurriedly nor with hesitance, but unconcernedly, as if it had rested there a thousand times. And there it stays.

There is a murmur from the crowd, then silence. People look at one another and stir in their seats – a strange self-consciousness in their stirring, for people are uneasy before the proved worth of their inferiors, unbelieving of the virtue of simplicity. They watch with open mouths as the giant Rigel, the killer Rigel, with no harness save a head collar, follows his Lilliputian master, his new friend, across the ring.

All has happened in so little time – in moments. The

audience begins to stand, to leave. But they pause at the lift of the auctioneer's hand. He waves it and they pause. It is all very well, his gestures say, but business is, after all, business, and Rigel has not been sold. He looks up at me, knowing that I have a bid to make – the last bid. And I look down into the ring at the stallion I have come so far to buy. His head is low and close to the shoulder of the man who would take him from me. He is not prancing now, not moving. For this hour, at least, he is changed.

I straighten, and then shake my head. I need only say, 'Five hundred,' but the words won't come. I can't get them out. I am angry with myself – a sentimental fool – and I am disappointed. But I cannot bid. It is too easy – twenty pounds too little, and yet too great an advantage.

No. I shake my head again, the auctioneer shrugs and turns to seal his bargain with the jockey.

On the way out, an old friend jostles me. 'You didn't really want him then,' he says.

'Want him? No. No, I didn't really want him.'

'It was wise,' he says. 'What good is a horse that's warned off every course in the Empire? You wouldn't want a horse like that.'

'That's right. I wouldn't want a horse like that.'

We move to the exit, and when we are out in the bright cold air of Newmarket, I turn to my friend and mention the little jockey. 'But he wanted Rigel,' I say.

And my old friend laughs. 'He would,' he says. 'That man has himself been barred from racing for fifteen years. Why, I can't remember. But it's two of a kind, you see – Rigel and Sparrow. Outlaws, both. He loves and knows horses as no man does, but that's what we call him around the tracks – the Fallen Sparrow.'

JANE SMILEY

JUSTA QUARTER CRACK

IN REVIEWING HIS life after he developed a painful quarter crack in his right front hoof wall, Justa Bob could find no precedents for either the place he now found himself or the people he found himself with. There was indeed a fence, though it was low and mostly made of vertical slats. The space it ran around was small and contained no grass. Rather, there was a house that people of all sizes went into and out of, there was another small house, containing chickens, and there were several unusual objects that the smaller denizens of the house ran to every day and climbed about on. Justa Bob's corner of this compound contained his buckets of water and feed and his mound of hay. It was divided from the rest by only some slender boards. He remained inside it more out of courtesy than anything else. Every day, though, a very small old human who appeared to be female came to him four times, fed and watered him. Twice a day, she snapped a shank onto his halter and led him carefully around the compound, scattering the children and chickens if she had to. All of this was quite different from the racetrack and from the studfarm where he was born and the training center where he received his education. Other than this woman, there were two men who attended to his foot. They touched it, looked at it, nodded at it, smiled at it, talked to it, put something into it that was rather soothing for a moment. Justa Bob did not have the sense that they recognized him except insofar as he was attached to his foot.

As odd as it was, Justa Bob had no complaints about this place. The feed was sweet and wholesome, the hay was rich, the water was quite nice, no off tastes, and the old woman always treated him kindly and tactfully. She adhered to a strict schedule, and in gratitude for that, he held off manuring in his water bucket. When the children ran under his feet, as they sometimes did, he stood still, though occasionally he aimed a stray kick at one of those damned chickens.

Lin Jay 'the Pisser' Hwang was eager to get the gelding Justa Bob back to Golden Gate, but there was no reason to pay a fifty-dollar-a-day fee to his trainer just to have the horse stand in the stall. You never knew with a quarter crack. It could grow down and disappear, it could linger for as long as the horse lived. There were various techniques, old and new, for treating it, but it was slow, rather like growing out a damaged fingernail or a bad haircut. Even so, you had a chance. The Pisser, who had an affinity for making odds, since he had started out as a math-genius Red Guard handicapper just off the boat from China back in 1983, often tried to specify the odds on a quarter crack or a bowed tendon or a condylar fracture or an ankle chip, but too many horses had defied the odds one way or another. The odds, he finally realized, had to be reserved for a reasonably sized statistical population, say the eight or ten horses in one race. One horse could not help defying the odds.

This horse, Justa Bob, or, as his mother called the animal in Chinese, 'The Iron Plum,' had 'odds-defier' written all over him. He didn't look like much, just a brown horse, but after forty-two starts, eight wins, six seconds, four thirds, and a handful of fourths, he seemed unchanged by his experiences – that is, unchangeable by experience. 'Good horse' was what his mother said, in her usual oracular fashion. The Pisser was himself fifty-five, so that made his mother near eighty. She knew a good horse when she saw one, and since she herself was unchangeable by experience, she recognized a kinship with the animal. She hadn't liked one of the Pisser's claimers this well in years. That was why she took care of the Iron Plum herself. The Pisser was reasonably sure that she was slipping some herbs into his feed. That was okay, too. In fact, everything his mother did was okay with the Pisser.

The Pisser was much changed by experience, even though he had always, since his school days in a small city in Hupei Province, been known as the Pisser. At first he had gained this name because in schoolboy pissing contests he had been able to go twice as long as the other boys. After that, it was just a name. When he got to America, he found out that a 'pisser' seemed to be something especially strong or interesting or unpleasant. That was what he aspired to be, and so he translated his name and kept it. Americans were shocked and put off by it, just a little. That was fine with the Pisser. The way he had gotten to the racetrack, Golden Gate Fields and Bay Meadows, was that, when he couldn't find a job in his field, which was teaching algebra, and, as a result of his experiences in the Cultural Revolution, when he had spent several years planting paddy in Guangzhou Province, he had chosen not to repeat his experiences with menial work, but to try gambling. As a mathematician, he preferred variables to pure chance, and so he had ended up at the racetrack rather than playing the numbers or visiting poker rooms. He probably hadn't actually lifted his eyes from the *Form* to look at a horse for the first year or more, but when he did, he liked what he saw. Another thing that he saw was that if you owned and claimed horses you could play both ends, sort of like raising crops and playing the commodities market at the same time, so he always had a couple of horses with a couple of trainers. He was always out in the a.m., watching works, and he went to just about every race. His wife was resigned to all of this, even though she would have preferred to live among other Chinese people in the middle of San Francisco rather than out in Pleasanton with the whites, where they could keep a horse who happened to be on the DL. She herself had a job she liked, selling designer dresses at Saks. Her customers, whom she called 'clients,' often spent more for a dress than the Pisser spent for a horse.

The Pisser's mother had lived a life that the Pisser had witnessed much of but still could not imagine. Waves of history and death had passed over her as rhythmically as surf. The thing about her that the Pisser found the most intriguing was that she had named herself, because her own parents, peasant farmers in Fukien Province, had not valued their seventh daughter enough to do so. His mother's name, in English, meant Round Pebble, a name unlike that of any Chinese female he had ever heard of. It was possible that she had never seen a horse before the Pisser brought home his first project. Certainly on that occasion she had walked and walked around the animal, a nice filly named Ladidah who won three races for him before being claimed away. Anyway, maybe his mother was four feet six, maybe not. Maybe she liked him, maybe not, maybe she liked his wife, maybe not, maybe she liked his children and grandchildren who came around, maybe not. His mother seemed to have no desires, no wishes, no hopes, no fears, no illnesses, no complaints; in fact, she seemed to be just what she called herself, a round pebble.

The thing the Iron Plum found most intriguing about the Round Pebble was her fragrance. He often put his nose up to her face and snuffled her in. She let him. After her face, he would sometimes work his way down her shoulder, or over her back, or down her chest, or into her hair. She let him. Her hand never came up to touch him or pet him, she never looked at him or spoke to him, but she was available for investigation, and the Iron Plum investigated. She was endlessly fascinating to him. If he wanted to lick the front of her dress, as he did a couple of times, or lick her hands, or even nip her on the cheek, she made no reaction, not even a contained startled reaction of the sort any observant horse could sense. The Iron Plum recognized that the Round Pebble was absolute stillness, a space there in the clutter of the house and the chicken house and the garden and the tools and equipment and vehicles and trailers and noise and chatter and wishes and frustrations and dreams and dissatisfactions. Such a space was unique in his experience, so he snuffled and nosed and probed and pushed her gently with his head and dropped his manure in one spot in the corner of the pen, where it was easy for her to pick it up. Track grooms, perhaps, did not think this sort of choice could be a part of a horse's repertoire, but, then, there was no track groom like the Round Pebble. When she led him around on his scheduled program, he watched her and smelled her. It was a complete change of pace.

It was the Pisser's mother who held in check the natural sense of superiority that a dialectical education had given him. He often caught himself looking around at the Americans he knew and saw and marveling at their foolishness, loudness, carelessness. Even their largeness seemed, sometimes, to be somehow their own fault, as if they didn't know the proper moment to stop doing anything, including to stop growing. And his fellow workers, the bettors at the chosen scene of his operations, seemed even less controlled, if possible, than most. They were always whooping, shouting, lamenting. If they hit a long shot, they thought it was meaningful in terms of their personal glory. If they lost a big race, they screamed as if the jockey, or even the horse, had designed the loss just for them. Even his best American friends, the ones who had shockproof systems, who never looked once at a horse, who took into account all sorts of extraneous factors, like where the turf rail was placed, and the direction and speed of the wind, even these Americans were tempted regularly by the notion of personal salvation – that the numbers were going to look *right at them* and take mercy upon them. At such times, the Pisser felt himself fill, molecule by molecule, with contempt, and then he drove home, and looked at his family and his house and his life, and he felt the contempt he had for others surge back over himself a thousandfold. It was then that he looked at his mother, creeping along in front of the horse, the horse staring at her, his ears pricked, his nose just inches from her neck, and he was so mystified by this sight that he decided that he knew nothing after all, and he decamped from the high ground of his contempt, and went in the house and had a glass of water, and felt better.

On the day when the Iron Plum was to go back to Golden Gate Fields and resume training, the Pisser got up earlier even than usual, way before dawn. The Iron Plum was still asleep in his pen, flat out on his side, his ankles relaxed, his toes almost pointed, his ribs rising in single heaves, his ears flopped. The Pisser had already hitched the trailer to his old truck and set out the horse's wraps by the time the animal sighed and rolled up onto his breastbone, then put a lazy foot out and levered himself to his feet. The Pisser performed his tasks in orderly quiet, and soon enough the horse was on the trailer, his nose in his hay net, and the trailer ramp was latched up. One last check of the hitch and the lights and the Pisser was ready to go. He picked his cup of coffee up off the railing of the Iron Plum's pen, and went around and got in the truck. When he opened the door, the overhead light revealed the small figure of his mother in the passenger's seat. The Pisser contained his astonishment – the Round Pebble had never gone to the track with him before – let out the parking brake, and drove out into the street. He could feel all of his expectations for the day, and they had been utterly routine, slip away. He smiled.

The fact was, when you had your mother settled in one spot, and she did the same things all day, day after day, you didn't have to think about her much, but when you got her out on the road, driving through the neighborhood and then onto the highway, and you could see that she was looking out the window, everything, from the truck cab itself to the highway on-ramp to the passing semi-trucks, looked big, fast, and amazing. Sometimes the Pisser himself was reminded, especially by his dreams, that he had passed through several universes to get to this moment. It was intimidating in retrospect, especially if one dream held objects or persons from different universes. The Pisser sometimes thought of the old topology problem, the four-color problem, which stated that only four shapes in a two-dimensional space could actually touch each other, and that therefore a mapmaker needed only five colors to make his map. Only in a nightmare, then, could teachers from his childhood, his father's death during the Great Leap Forward, a beating he got just after leaving his university and going into the countryside during the Cultural Revolution, the first man he had ever met who had gone to America and come back (a math colleague at the school where he taught), and his wife in a black suit and high heels, standing in front of a row of dresses, seem to squirm together like snakes, all touching in an impossible way.

33

He had to wake himself up and remember all the steps he had taken in between, every step working out the manageable and credible distance between individual universes. And there was time, too. In dreams, time and distance collapsed, but in life, time and distance were one and the same; walking and waiting, having to make your slow and deliberate way, prevented the special terror of having to be in two or three universes at once.

How much stranger things must be for his mother, sitting there, a cipher, a curl against the door (he checked to be sure it was locked), her hand on the dashboard, her eyes on the road, her feet barely touching the floor under the seat. She wore loose, khaki-green-colored pants, a white shirt with buttons, and a pair of child's sneakers; her hair, gray, coarse, and thick, made a ball at the nape of her neck. She could not read. She had never been taught to read Chinese, of course, and reading English had been out of the question at her age. He wasn't really sure how many children she had borne. He and his wife had figured out seven, but there could have been more. Formerly, the Round Pebble had had a fair amount to say, mostly instructions and admonitions, not much about herself or her life, though. But now for years she had said very little. There was an American expression that no American children seemed to abide by, that children should be seen and not heard. That was his mother, in her second childhood – doing this, doing that, busy all day long, always in evidence, but never more than a word or two, and those always in English.

For her part, the Round Pebble knew perfectly well that Hwang Lin, her son, continued to think of her as his mother, even though she herself had grown out of motherhood years ago. It was like all those other things about her that she had once thought were her, but had left behind – her parents' daughter, her brothers' sister, a wife to the man her parents had sold her to, a wife to the man she had chosen on her own after the first one was killed in Hunan Province by some thieves, it was said. A mother a mother a mother a mother, over and over, a woman who swept, a woman who cooked, a woman who carried nightsoil, a woman who minded other women's children, a woman who changed beds in a hospital and washed the bloody sheets by hand, a woman who planted gardens and killed chickens and bled hogs out and carried water and waited to be told what else she was to do, a woman. All of these things she had shed like husks, one after another. Now she called herself nothing but the Round Pebble. Work found itself done after she had passed through it, but she no longer felt herself work any more than she felt herself breathe. Soon enough, she would shed the final husk. Sometimes she wondered what she might find out then, but wondering was something she also did little of anymore, since it made no difference of any kind what you wondered about, what you wished for, or even what you got. At this point, what the Round Pebble knew was that just about everything there was was larger than she was. Even her great-grandchildren were larger than she was, for the most part. But it wasn't as if this hadn't always been true. Her mother, her father, her brothers and sisters, her husbands, her sons and their wives, wars, revolutions, famines, epidemics, the sum of money her parents had sold her for, the work she was put to, the orders she was given, now these horses. You name it. But her feelings about that had changed, too. Largeness had once been frightening to her; now it was not. Now that she wondered nothing, wished for nothing, and cared nothing about what she got, the largeness of everything outside of her carried her along smoothly, the steady deep current of a broad river passing through a spacious valley under a generous sky. She was only a small pebble after all; she required no violent force of nature to lift her to her destination. She sighed as she looked around. The sun rose before her in the windshield of the truck, and she shaded her eyes. When they came to a stoplight, the Iron Plum stamped a bit, and she could feel the truck beneath her shiver with the vibrations. Hwang Lin looked around, but the Round Pebble knew it was only the horse making his music.

The Pisser was glad to get to the track, where everything was familiar business. For sheer activity, you couldn't beat the backside of a racetrack at seven in the morning. Horses looked over the doors of their stalls. Other horses cooled out on their walkers. Others were being mounted and ridden out to the track. Still others, steaming in the sunlight, were being sponged and scraped. No horse was ugly on the backside. All lifted their heads, turned their bodies, swished their tails, pricked their ears, tossed their manes in an endless series of graceful gestures. The Pisser had seen lots of horses in his day, of all breeds and ages. Horses in general, he felt, were good. But Thoroughbreds in general, he felt, were more than good. Beauty flowed through their bodies like a steady ocean breeze, sometimes seeming, if he was in the mood, to pass from one to another in an exchange of energy that netted them all together, and all their humans with them, their genetic tie become nearly visible to the naked eye as the body electric, a single body electric repeated everywhere you turned your head. Those were good days. But driving with his mother had filled him with longing, made him think how little he could do for her. If she wanted something, he would surely give it to her, but it didn't do a bit of good to ask. There was never anything she wanted. He had come along too late to give her anything, and it made him, just now, feel useless. He drove the trailer carefully to Barn C, where his trainer was already mounted to go out with his third set. That was okay, though. The Pisser knew what to do, and the stall was bedded deep in yellow straw. The horse's hay net was hanging by the door.

The horses left for their exercise, and the Pisser got out of his truck. He closed the door carefully and went around to the trailer. He opened the side doors and untied the gelding, then went around to the back and let down the ramp. The Iron Plum stood calmly until the Pisser said, 'Okay, fella.' Then the Iron Plum stepped carefully backward, his hooves feeling for the ramp. The Pisser reached for the leadshank, but there was his mother, before him, her hand scooping it delicately from his. The horse looked around.

Here he was again, Justa Bob, justa racehorse. Justa Bob flared his nostrils and snorted in the familiar smells, yes. Pivoted his ears like satellite dishes, yes. Turned his head this way and that to focus his big eyes on the scene he was born to see, yes. His skin shivered over his muscles as if flies were landing on him, but it wasn't only the excitement. He hadn't seen another horse in a long time, and now he was among them, signals flying everywhere. He whinnied a single loud greeting, and other whinnies answered him immediately, Hello, hello, hello, I'm here, I'm here, too, hello, a ripple of whinnies spreading from Barn C out over the backside, until, far away, they had nothing to do with Justa Bob at all, only to do with Hello, I am here, where are you, I'm here, too.

While his mother held the horse, the Pisser squatted beneath him and unwrapped his legs, throwing the wraps off to the side. Then he ran his hands down where the wraps had been. Cool and tight. The quarter crack had grown out nicely,

37

ready for a patch, and the coronary band was smooth and whole. He was a stable system, this Justa Bob horse. Not the fastest thing in the world, or the prettiest, but his architecture was damn good. The foundation sat square under the rest of him, and the rest of him moved squarely upon the foundation. He was indeed a plum, and he was indeed made of iron. The Pisser said, 'Okay, Ma. Let's walk him around a little, then put him in his stall.'

He did not take the horse away from her, as he was tempted to do. It wasn't so easy to walk around here on the backside of Golden Gate. Conditions were crowded, and the footing was uneven. All he needed at this point was to see his child-mother stumble and fall underneath the horse, even for the horse to step on her. As little as she looked at home, she looked even littler here, smaller than the smallest jockey. And the horse was clearly excited to be back, arching his neck, picking up his feet. So the Pisser turned away and busied himself with cleaning out and closing up the trailer so as not to interfere, so as not to let her see that he had tears in his eyes. His mother was passing through his life. The speed of her passage was accelerating. He had nothing to give her, no going-away present. All he could do was watch her for a moment, watch her with that horse, who, for all the distractions around him, still followed the Round Pebble attentively, his nose inches behind her neck, his ears pricked, his steps careful. Oddest thing he ever saw.

The round pebble led the Iron Plum into his stall and turned him around so that he was facing outward. She reached up and undid the buckle of his halter and slipped it off his head. Meanwhile, the Pisser adjusted the animal's blanket. The groom would come around about noon and wrap the horse's legs for the night. Light training would begin tomorrow.

If they were lucky, the horse would run again in six or eight weeks. Whatever, thought the Pisser. His mother preceded him out of the stall, and after he did the latch, he paused to give the horse a piece of carrot that he had in his pocket. His mother did not look back. It was impossible to tell if she felt affection for the horse. She headed down the shedrow. The horse looked after her, his ears as far forward as a horse's ears could be. And then he started in again, whinnying and whinnying. He beat his knees against the stall door, turned and plunged and whinnied and turned and plunged. The Round Pebble did not look back. The horse's distress grew. The Round Pebble opened the door of the truck and got in, then shut the door. The Iron Plum watched, whinnied again. The Pisser had never seen anything like it. He shook his head, then he closed the top half of Justa Bob's stall door and latched it, then he himself walked to the truck. Sometimes you just had to leave a horse in the dark in his stall to figure it out and get over it.

BRET HARTE

CHU CHU

I DO NOT BELIEVE that the most enthusiastic lover of that 'useful and noble animal,' the horse, will claim for him the charm of geniality, humor, or expansive confidence. Any creature who will not look you squarely in the eye – whose only oblique glances are inspired by fear, distrust, or a view to attack; who has no way of returning caresses, and whose favorite expression is one of head-lifting disdain, may be 'noble' or 'useful,' but can be hardly said to add to the gayety of nations. Indeed it may be broadly stated that, with the single exception of gold-fish, of all animals kept for the recreation of mankind the horse is alone capable of exciting a passion that shall be absolutely hopeless. I deem these general remarks necessary to prove that my unreciprocated affection for Chu Chu was not purely individual or singular. And I may add that to these general characteristics she brought the waywardness of her capricious sex.

She came to me out of the rolling dust of an emigrant wagon, behind whose tail-board she was gravely trotting. She was a half-broken filly – in which character she had at different times unseated everybody in the train – and, although covered with dust, she had a beautiful coat, and the most lambent gazelle-like eyes I had ever seen. I think she kept these latter organs purely for ornament – apparently looking at things with her nose, her sensitive ears, and, some-times, even a slight lifting of her slim near foreleg. On our first interview I thought she favored me with a coy glance, but as it was accompanied by an irrelevant 'Look out!' from her owner, the teamster, I was not certain. I only know that after some conversation, a good deal of mental reservation, and the disbursement of considerable coin, I found myself standing in the dust of the departing emigrant wagon with one end of a forty-foot riata in my hand, and Chu Chu at the other.

I pulled invitingly at my own end, and even advanced a step or two toward her. She then broke into a long disdainful pace, and began to circle round me at the extreme limit of her tether. I stood admiring her free action for some moments – not always turning with her, which was tiring – until I found that she was gradually winding herself up *on me*! Her frantic astonishment when she suddenly found herself thus brought up against me was one of the most remarkable things I ever saw, and nearly took me off my legs. Then, when she had pulled against the riata until her narrow head and prettily arched neck were on a perfectly straight line with it, she as suddenly slackened the tension and condescended to follow me, at an angle of her own choosing. Sometimes it was on one side of me, sometimes on the other. Even then the sense of my dreadful contiguity apparently would come upon her like a fresh discovery, and she would become hysterical. But I do not think that she really *saw* me. She looked at the riata and sniffed it disparagingly; she pawed some pebbles that were near me tentatively with her small hoof; she started back with a Robinson Crusoe-like horror of my footprints in the wet gully, but my actual personal presence she ignored. She would sometimes pause, with her head thoughtfully between her forelegs, and apparently say: 'There is some extraordinary presence here: animal, vegetable, or mineral – I can't make out which – but it's not good to eat, and I loathe and detest it.'

When I reached my house in the suburbs, before entering the 'fifty vara' lot inclosure, I deemed it prudent to leave her outside while I informed the household of my purchase; and with this object I tethered her by the long riata to a solitary sycamore which stood in the centre of the road, the crossing of two frequented thoroughfares. It was not long, however, before I was interrupted by shouts and screams from that vicinity, and on returning thither I found that Chu Chu, with the assistance of her riata, had securely wound up two of my neighbors to the tree, where they presented the appearance of early Christian martyrs. When I released them it appeared that they had been attracted by Chu Chu's graces, and had offered her overtures of affection, to which she had characteristically rotated with this miserable result. I led her, with some difficulty, warily keeping clear of the riata, to the inclosure, from whose fence I had previously removed several bars. Although the space was wide enough to have admitted a troop of cavalry she affected not to notice it, and managed to kick away part of another section on entering. She resisted the stable for some time, but after carefully examining it with her hoofs, and an affectedly meek outstretching of her nose, she consented to recognize some oats in the feed-box – without looking at them – and was formally installed. All this while she had resolutely ignored my presence. As I stood watching her she suddenly stopped eating; the same reflective look came over her. 'Surely I am not mistaken, but that same obnoxious creature is somewhere about here!' she seemed to say, and shivered at the possibility.

It was probably this which made me confide my unreciprocated affection to one of my neighbors – a man supposed to be an authority on horses, and particularly of that wild species to which Chu Chu belonged. It was he who, leaning over the edge of the stall where she was complacently and, as usual, obliviously munching, absolutely dared to toy with a pet lock of hair which she wore over the pretty star on her forehead.

'Ye see, captain,' he said, with jaunty easiness, 'hosses is like wimmen; ye don't want ter use any standoffishness or shyness with *them*; a stiddy but keerless sort o' familiarity, a kind o' free but firm handlin', jess like this, to let her see who's master' –

We never clearly knew *how* it happened; but when I picked up my neighbor from the doorway, amid the broken splinters of the stall rail, and a quantity of oats that mysteriously filled his hair and pockets, Chu Chu was found to have faced around the other way, and was contemplating her forelegs, with her hind ones in the other stall. My neighbor spoke of damages while he was in the stall, and of physical coercion when he was out of it again. But here Chu Chu, in some marvelous way, righted herself, and my neighbor departed hurriedly with a brimless hat and an unfinished sentence.

My next intermediary was Enriquez Saltello – a youth of my own age, and the brother of Consuelo Saltello, whom I adored. As a Spanish Californian he was presumed, on account of Chu Chu's half-Spanish origin, to have superior knowledge of her character, and I even vaguely believed that his language and accent would fall familiarly on her ear. There was the drawback, however, that he always preferred to talk in a marvelous English, combining Castilian precision with what he fondly believed to be Californian slang.

'To confer then as to thees horse, which is not – observe me – a Mexican plug! Ah, no! You can your boots bet on that. She is of Castilian stock – believe me and strike me dead! I will myself at different times overlook and affront her in the stable, examine her as to the assault, and why she should do thees thing. When she is of the exercise I will also accost and restrain her. Remain tranquil, my friend! When a few days shall pass much shall be changed, and she will be as another. Trust your oncle to do thees thing! Comprehend me? Everything shall be lovely, and the goose hang high!'

Conformably with this he 'overlooked' her the next day, with a cigarette between his yellow-stained fingertips, which made her sneeze in a silent pantomimic way, and certain Spanish blandishments of speech which she received with more complacency. But I don't think she ever even looked at him. In vain he protested that she was the 'dearest' and 'littlest' of his 'little loves' – in vain he asserted that she was his patron saint, and that it was his soul's delight to pray to her; she accepted the compliment with her eyes fixed upon the manger. When he had exhausted his whole stock of endearing diminutives, adding a few playful and more audacious sallies, she remained with her head down, as if inclined to meditate upon them. This he declared was at least an improvement on her former performances. It may have been my own jealousy, but I fancied she was only saying to herself, 'Gracious! can there be two of them?'

'Courage and patience, my friend,' he said, as we were slowly quitting the stable. 'Thees horse is yonge, and has not yet the habitude of the person. Tomorrow, at another season, I shall give to her a foundling' ('fondling,' I have reason to believe, was the word intended by Enriquez) – 'and we shall see. It shall be as easy as to fall away from a log. A leetle more of this chin music which your friend Enriquez possesses, and some tapping of the head and neck, and you are there. You are ever the right side up. Houp la! But let us not precipitate this thing. The more haste, we do not so much accelerate ourselves.'

He appeared to be suiting the action to the word as he lingered in the doorway of the stable. 'Come on,' I said.

'Pardon,' he returned, with a bow that was both elaborate and evasive, 'but you shall yourself precede me – the stable is *yours*.'

'Oh, come along!' I continued impatiently. To my surprise he seemed to dodge back into the stable again. After an instant he reappeared.

'Pardon! but I am re-strain! Of a truth, in this instant I am grasp by the mouth of thees horse in the coattail of my dress! She will that I should remain. It would seem' – he disappeared again – 'that' – he was out once more – 'the experiment is a sooccess! She reciprocate! She is, of a truth, gone on me. It is lofe!' – a stronger pull from Chu Chu here sent him in again – 'but' – he was out now triumphantly with half his garment torn away – 'I shall coquet.'

Nothing daunted, however, the gallant fellow was back next day with a Mexican saddle, and attired in the complete outfit of a vaquero. Overcome though *he* was by heavy deerskin trousers, open at the side from the knees down, and fringed with bullion buttons, an enormous flat sombrero, and a stiff, short embroidered velvet jacket, I was more concerned at the ponderous saddle and equipments intended for the slim Chu Chu. That these would hide and conceal her beautiful curves and contour, as well as overweight her, seemed certain; that she would resist them all to the last seemed equally clear. Nevertheless, to my surprise, when she was led out, and the saddle thrown deftly across her back, she was passive. Was it possible that some drop of her old Spanish blood responded to its clinging embrace? She did not either look at it or smell it. But when Enriquez began to tighten the cinch or girth a more singular thing occurred. Chu Chu visibly distended her slender barrel to twice its dimensions; the more he pulled the more she swelled, until I was actually ashamed of her. Not so

Enriquez. He smiled at us, and complacently stroked his thin mustache.

'Eet is ever so! She is the child of her grandmother! Even when you shall make saddle thees old Castilian stock, it will make large – it will become a balloon! Eet is a trick – eet is a leetle game – believe me. For why?'

I had not listened, as I was at that moment astonished to see the saddle slowly slide under Chu Chu's belly, and her figure resume, as if by magic, its former slim proportions. Enriquez followed my eyes, lifted his shoulders, shrugged them, and said smilingly, 'Ah, you see!'

When the girths were drawn in again with an extra pull or two from the indefatigable Enriquez, I fancied that Chu Chu nevertheless secretly enjoyed it, as her sex is said to appreciate tight lacing. She drew a deep sigh, possibly of satisfaction, turned her neck, and apparently tried to glance at her own figure – Enriquez promptly withdrawing to enable her to do so easily. Then the dread moment arrived. Enriquez, with his hand on her mane, suddenly paused and, with exaggerated courtesy, lifted his hat and made an inviting gesture.

'You will honor me to precede.'

I shook my head laughingly.

'I see,' responded Enriquez gravely. 'You have to attend the obsequies of your aunt who is dead, at two of the clock. You have to meet your broker who has bought you feefty share of the Comstock lode – at thees moment – or you are loss! You are excuse! Attend! Gentlemen, make your bets! The band has arrived to play! 'Ere we are!'

With a quick movement the alert young fellow had vaulted into the saddle. But, to the astonishment of both of us, the mare remained perfectly still. There was Enriquez bolt upright in the stirrups, completely overshadowing by his

49

saddle-flaps, leggings, and gigantic spurs the fine proportions of Chu Chu, until she might have been a placid Rosinante, bestridden by some youthful Quixote. She closed her eyes, she was going to sleep! We were dreadfully disappointed. This clearly would not do. Enriquez lifted the reins cautiously! Chu Chu moved forward slowly – then stopped, apparently lost in reflection.

'Affront her on thees side.'

I approached her gently. She shot suddenly into the air, coming down again on perfectly stiff legs with a springless jolt. This she instantly followed by a succession of other rocket-like propulsions, utterly unlike a leap, all over the inclosure. The movements of the unfortunate Enriquez were equally unlike any equitation I ever saw. He appeared occasionally over Chu Chu's head, astride of her neck and tail, or in the free air, but never *in* the saddle. His rigid legs, however, never lost the stirrups, but came down regularly, accentuating her springless hops. More than that, the disproportionate excess of rider, saddle, and accoutrements was so great that he had, at times, the appearance of lifting Chu Chu forcibly from the ground by superior strength, and of actually contributing to her exercise! As they came toward me, a wild tossing and flying mass of hoofs and spurs, it was not only difficult to distinguish them apart, but to ascertain how much of the jumping was done by Enriquez separately. At last Chu Chu brought matters to a close by making for the low-stretching branches of an oak-tree which stood at the corner of the lot. In a few moments she emerged from it – but without Enriquez.

I found the gallant fellow disengaging himself from the fork of a branch in which he had been firmly wedged, but still smiling and confident, and his cigarette between his teeth. Then for the first time he removed it, and seating himself easily on the branch with his legs dangling down, he blandly waved aside my anxious queries with a gentle reassuring gesture.

'Remain tranquil, my friend. Thees does not count! I have conquer – you observe – for why? I have *never* for once *arrive at the ground*! Consequent she is disappoint! She will ever that I *should*! But I have got her when the hair is not long! Your oncle Henry' – with an angelic wink – 'is fly! He is ever a bully boy, with the eye of glass! Believe me. Behold! I am here! Big Injun! Whoop!'

He leaped lightly to the ground. Chu Chu, standing watchfully at a little distance, was evidently astonished at his appearance. She threw out her hind hoofs violently, shot up into the air until the stirrups crossed each other high above the saddle, and made for the stable in a succession of rabbit-like bounds – taking the precaution to remove the saddle, on entering, by striking it against the lintel of the door.

'You observe,' said Enriquez blandly, 'she would make that thing of *me*. Not having the good occasion, she ees dissatisfied. Where are you now?'

Two or three days afterwards he rode her again with the same result – accepted by him with the same heroic complacency. As we did not, for certain reasons, care to use the open road for this exercise, and as it was impossible to remove the tree, we were obliged to submit to the inevitable. On the following day I mounted her – undergoing the same experience as Enriquez, with the individual sensation of falling from a third-story window on top of a countinghouse stool, and the variation of being projected over the fence. When I found that Chu Chu had not accompanied me, I saw Enriquez at my side.

'More than ever it is become necessary that we should do thees things again,' he said gravely, as he assisted me to my feet. 'Courage, my noble General! God and Liberty! Once more on to the breach! Charge, Chestare, charge! Come on, Don Stanley! 'Ere we are!'

He helped me none too quickly to catch my seat again, for it apparently had the effect of the turned peg on the enchanted horse in the Arabian Nights, and Chu Chu instantly rose into the air. But she came down this time before the open window of the kitchen, and I alighted easily on the dresser. The indefatigable Enriquez followed me.

'Won't this do?' I asked meekly.

'It ees *better* – for you arrive *not* on the ground,' he said cheerfully; 'but you should not once but a thousand times make trial! Ha! Go and win! Nevare die and say so! 'Eave ahead! 'Eave! There you are!'

Luckily, this time I managed to lock the rowels of my long spurs under her girth, and she could not unseat me. She seemed to recognize the fact after one or two plunges, when, to my great surprise, she suddenly sank to the ground and quietly rolled over me. The action disengaged my spurs, but, righting herself without getting up, she turned her beautiful head and absolutely *looked* at me! – still in the saddle. I felt myself blushing! But the voice of Enriquez was at my side.

'Errise, my friend; you have conquer! It is *she* who has arrive at the ground! *You* are all right. It is done; believe me, it is feenish! No more shall she make thees thing. From thees instant you shall ride her as the cow – as the rail of thees fence – and remain tranquil. For she is a-broke! Ta-ta! Regain your hats, gentlemen! Pass in your checks! It is ovar! How are you now?' He lit a fresh cigarette, put his hands in his pockets, and smiled at me blandly.

For all that, I ventured to point out that the habit of alighting in the fork of a tree, or the disengaging of one's self from the saddle on the ground, was attended with inconvenience, and even ostentatious display. But Enriquez swept the objections away with a single gesture. 'It is the *preencipal* – the bottom fact – at which you arrive. The next come of himself! Many horse have achieve to mount the rider by the knees, and relinquish after thees same fashion. My grandfather had a barb of thees kind – but she has gone dead, and so have my grandfather. Which is sad and strange! Otherwise I shall make of them both an instant example!'

I ought to have said that although these performances were never actually witnessed by Enriquez's sister – for reasons which he and I thought sufficient – the dear girl displayed the greatest interest in them, and, perhaps aided by our mutually complimentary accounts of each other, looked upon us both as invincible heroes. It is possible also that she overestimated our success, for she suddenly demanded that I should *ride* Chu Chu to her house, that she might see her. It was not far; by going through a back lane I could avoid the trees which exercised such a fatal fascination for Chu Chu. There was a pleading, childlike entreaty in Consuelo's voice that I could not resist, with a slight flash from her lustrous dark eyes that I did not care to encourage. So I resolved to try it at all hazards.

My equipment for the performance was modeled after Enriquez's previous costume, with the addition of a few fripperies of silver and stamped leather out of compliment to Consuelo, and even with a faint hope that it might appease Chu Chu. *She* certainly looked beautiful in her glittering accoutrements, set off by her jet-black shining coat. With an air of demure abstraction she permitted me to mount her, and even for a hundred yards or so indulged in a mincing maidenly amble that was not without a touch of coquetry. Encouraged by this, I addressed a few terms of endearment to her, and in the exuberance of my youthful enthusiasm I even confided to her my love for Consuelo, and begged her to be 'good' and not disgrace herself and me before my Dulcinea. In my foolish trustfulness I was rash enough to add a caress, and to pat her soft neck. She stopped instantly with an hysteric shudder. I knew what was passing through her mind: she had suddenly become aware of my baleful existence.

The saddle and bridle Chu Chu was becoming accustomed to, but who was this living, breathing object that had actually touched her? Presently her oblique vision was attracted by the fluttering movement of a fallen oak-leaf in the road before her. She had probably seen many oak-leaves many times before; her ancestors had no doubt been familiar with them on the trackless hills and in field and paddock, but this did not alter her profound conviction that I and the leaf were identical, that our baleful touch was something indissolubly connected. She reared before that innocent leaf, she revolved round it, and then fled from it at the top of her speed.

The lane passed before the rear wall of Saltellos' garden. Unfortunately, at the angle of the fence stood a beautiful madroño-tree, brilliant with its scarlet berries, and endeared to me as Consuelo's favorite haunt, under whose protecting shade I had more than once avowed my youthful passion. By the irony of fate Chu Chu caught sight of it, and with a succession of spirited bounds instantly made for it. In another moment I was beneath it, and Chu Chu shot like a rocket into the air. I had barely time to withdraw my feet from the stirrups, to throw up one arm to protect my glazed sombrero and grasp an overhanging branch with the other, before Chu Chu darted off. But to my consternation, as I gained a secure perch on the tree, and looked about me,

I saw her – instead of running away – quietly trot through the open gate into Saltellos' garden.

Need I say that it was to the beneficent Enriquez that I again owed my salvation? Scarcely a moment elapsed before his bland voice rose in a concentrated whisper from the corner of the garden below me. He had divined the dreadful truth!

'For the love of God, collect to yourself many kinds of thees berry! All you can! Your full arms round! Rest tranquil. Leave to your ole oncle to make for you a delicate exposure. At the instant!'

He was gone again. I gathered, wonderingly, a few of the larger clusters of parti-colored fruit, and patiently waited. Presently he reappeared, and with him the lovely Consuelo – her dear eyes filled with an adorable anxiety.

'Yes,' continued Enriquez to his sister, with a confidential lowering of tone but great distinctness of utterance, 'it is ever so with the American! He will ever make *first* the salutation of the flower or the fruit, picked to himself by his own hand, to the lady where he call. It is the custom of the American hidalgo! My God – what will you? *I* make it not – it is so! Without doubt he is in this instant doing thees thing. That is why he have let go his horse to precede him here; it is always the etiquette to offer these things on the feet. Ah! behold! it is he! – Don Francisco! Even now he will descend from thees tree! Ah! You make the blush, little sister (archly)! I will retire! I am discreet; two is not company for the one! I make tracks! I make tracks! I am gone!'

How far Consuelo entirely believed and trusted her ingenious brother I do not know, nor even then cared to inquire. For there was a pretty mantling of her olive cheek, as I came forward with my offering, and a certain significant shyness in her manner that were enough to throw me into a state of hopeless imbecility. And I was always miserably conscious that Consuelo possessed an exalted sentimentality, and a predilection for the highest mediæval romance, in which I knew I was lamentably deficient. Even in our most confidential moments I was always aware that I weakly lagged behind this daughter of a gloomily distinguished ancestry, in her frequent incursions into a vague but poetic past. There was something of the dignity of the Spanish châtelaine in the sweetly grave little figure that advanced to accept my specious offering. I think I should have fallen on my knees to present it, but for the presence of the all-seeing Enriquez. But why did I even at that moment remember that he had early bestowed upon her the nickname of 'Pomposa'? This, as Enriquez himself might have observed, was 'sad and strange.'

I managed to stammer out something about the madroño berries being at her 'disposicion' (the tree was in her own garden!), and she took the branches in her little brown hand with a soft response to my unutterable glances.

But here Chu Chu, momentarily forgotten, executed a happy diversion. To our astonishment she gravely walked up to Consuelo and, stretching out her long slim neck, not only sniffed curiously at the berries, but even protruded a black under lip towards the young girl herself. In another instant Consuelo's dignity melted. Throwing her arms around Chu Chu's neck she embraced and kissed her. Young as I was, I understood the divine significance of a girl's vicarious effusiveness at such a moment, and felt delighted. But I was the more astonished that the usually sensitive horse not only submitted to these caresses, but actually responded to the extent of affecting to nip my mistress's little right ear.

This was enough for the impulsive Consuelo. She ran hastily into the house, and in a few moments reappeared in a bewitching riding-skirt gathered round her jimp waist.

In vain Enriquez and myself joined in earnest entreaty: the horse was hardly broken for even a man's riding yet; the saints alone could tell what the nervous creature might do with a woman's skirt flapping at her side! We begged for delay, for reflection, for at least time to change the saddle – but with no avail! Consuelo was determined, indignant, distressingly reproachful! Ah, well! if Don Pancho (an ingenious diminutive of my Christian name) valued his horse so highly – if he were jealous of the evident devotion of the animal to herself, he would – But here I succumbed! And then I had the felicity of holding that little foot for one brief moment in the hollow of my hand, of readjusting the skirt as she threw her knee over the saddle-horn, of clasping her tightly – only half in fear – as I surrendered the reins to her grasp. And to tell the truth, as Enriquez and I fell back, although I had insisted upon still keeping hold of the end of the riata, it was a picture to admire. The petite figure of the young girl, and the graceful folds of her skirt, admirably harmonized with Chu Chu's lithe contour, and as the mare arched her slim neck and raised her slender head under the pressure of the reins, it was so like the lifted velvet-capped toreador crest of Consuelo herself, that they seemed of one race.

'I would not that you should hold the riata,' said Consuelo petulantly.

I hesitated – Chu Chu looked certainly very amiable – I let go. She began to amble towards the gate, not mincingly as before, but with a freer and fuller stride. In spite of the incongruous saddle the young girl's seat was admirable. As they neared the gate she cast a single mischievous glance at me, jerked at the rein, and Chu Chu sprang into the road at a rapid canter. I watched them fearfully and breathlessly, until at the end of the lane I saw Consuelo rein in slightly, wheel easily, and come flying back. There was no doubt about it;

the horse was under perfect control. Her second subjugation was complete and final!

Overjoyed and bewildered, I overwhelmed them with congratulations; Enriquez alone retaining the usual brotherly attitude of criticism, and a superior toleration of a lover's enthusiasm. I ventured to hint to Consuelo (in what I believed was a safe whisper) that Chu Chu only showed my own feelings towards her.

'Without doubt,' responded Enriquez gravely. 'She have of herself assist you to climb to the tree to pull to yourself the berry for my sister.'

But I felt Consuelo's little hand return my pressure, and I forgave and even pitied him.

From that day forward, Chu Chu and Consuelo were not only firm friends but daily companions. In my devotion I would have presented the horse to the young girl, but with flattering delicacy she preferred to call it mine.

'I shall erride it for you, Pancho,' she said. 'I shall feel,' she continued, with exalted although somewhat vague poetry, 'that it is of *you*! You lofe the beast – it is therefore of a necessity *you*, my Pancho! It is *your* soul I shall erride like the wings of the wind – your lofe in this beast shall be my only cavalier forever.'

I would have preferred something whose vicarious qualities were less uncertain than I still felt Chu Chu's to be, but I kissed the girl's hand submissively. It was only when I attempted to accompany her in the flesh, on another horse, that I felt the full truth of my instinctive fears. Chu Chu would not permit any one to approach her mistress's side. My mounted presence revived in her all her old blind astonishment and disbelief in my existence; she would start suddenly, face about, and back away from me in utter amazement as if I had been only recently created, or with an affected modesty as if I had been just guilty of some grave indecorum towards her sex which she really could not stand. The frequency of these exhibitions in the public highway were not only distressing to me as a simple escort, but as it had the effect on the casual spectators of making Consuelo seem to participate in Chu Chu's objections, I felt that, as a lover, it could not be borne. Any attempt to coerce Chu Chu ended in her running away. And my frantic pursuit of her was open to equal misconstruction.

'Go it, miss, the little dude is gainin' on you!' shouted by a drunken teamster to the frightened Consuelo, once checked me in mid-career.

Even the dear girl herself saw the uselessness of my real presence, and after a while was content to ride with 'my soul.'

Notwithstanding this, I am not ashamed to say that it was my custom, whenever she rode out, to keep a slinking and distant surveillance of Chu Chu on another horse, until she had fairly settled down to her pace. A little nod of Consuelo's round black-and-red toreador hat, or a kiss tossed from her riding-whip, was reward enough!

I remember a pleasant afternoon when I was thus awaiting her in the outskirts of the village. The eternal smile of the Californian summer had begun to waver and grow less fixed; dust lay thick on leaf and blade; the dry hills were clothed in russet leather; the trade-winds were shifting to the south with an ominous warm humidity; a few days longer and the rains would be here. It so chanced that this afternoon my seclusion on the roadside was accidentally invaded by a village belle – a Western young lady somewhat older than myself, and of flirtatious reputation. As she persistently and – as I now have reason to believe – mischievously lingered, I had only a passing glimpse of Consuelo riding past at an unaccustomed speed which surprised me at the moment. But as I reasoned later that she was only trying to avoid a merely formal meeting, I thought no more about it. It was not until I called at the house to fetch Chu Chu at the usual hour, and found that Consuelo had not yet returned, that a recollection of Chu Chu's furious pace again troubled me. An hour passed – it was getting towards sunset, but there were no signs of Chu Chu or her mistress. I became seriously alarmed. I did not care to reveal my fears to the family, for I felt myself responsible for Chu Chu. At last I desperately saddled my horse, and galloped off in the direction she had taken. It was the road to Rosario and the hacienda of one of her relations, where she sometimes halted.

The road was a very unfrequented one, twisting like a mountain river; indeed, it was the bed of an old watercourse, between brown hills of wild oats, and debouching at last into a broad blue lake-like expanse of alfalfa meadows. In vain I strained my eyes over the monotonous level; nothing appeared to rise above or move across it. In the faint hope that she might have lingered at the hacienda, I was spurring on again when I heard a slight splashing on my left. I looked around. A broad patch of fresher-colored herbage and a cluster of dwarfed alders indicated a hidden spring. I cautiously approached its quaggy edges, when I was shocked by what appeared to be a sudden vision! Mid-leg deep in the centre of a greenish pool stood Chu Chu! But without a strap or buckle of harness upon her – as naked as when she was foaled!

For a moment I could only stare at her in bewildered terror. Far from recognizing me, she seemed to be absorbed in a nymph-like contemplation of her own graces in the pool. Then I called, 'Consuelo!' and galloped frantically around the spring. But there was no response, nor was there anything to be seen but the all-unconscious Chu Chu. The pool, thank Heaven! was not deep enough to have drowned any one; there were no signs of a struggle on its quaggy edges. The horse might have come from a distance! I galloped on, still calling. A few hundred yards further I detected the vivid glow of Chu Chu's scarlet saddle-blanket, in the brush near the trail. My heart leaped – I was on the track. I called again; this time a faint reply, in accents I knew too well, came from the field beside me!

Consuelo was there! reclining beside a manzanita bush which screened her from the road, in what struck me, even at that supreme moment, as a judicious and picturesquely selected couch of scented Indian grass and dry tussocks. The velvet hat with its balls of scarlet plush was laid carefully aside; her lovely blue-black hair retained its tight coils undisheveled, her eyes were luminous and tender. Shocked as I was at her apparent helplessness, I remember being impressed with the fact that it gave so little indication of violent usage or disaster.

I threw myself frantically on the ground beside her.

'You are hurt, Consita! For Heaven's sake, what has happened?'

She pushed my hat back with her little hand, and tumbled my hair gently.

'Nothing. *You* are here, Pancho – eet is enofe! What shall come after thees – when I am perhaps gone among the grave – make nothing! *You* are here – I am happy. For a little, perhaps – not mooch.'

'But,' I went on desperately, 'was it an accident? Were you thrown? Was it Chu Chu?' – for somehow, in spite of her languid posture and voice, I could not, even in my fears, believe her seriously hurt.

'Beat not the poor beast, Pancho. It is not from *her* comes thees thing. She have make nothing – believe me! I have

61

come upon your assignation with Miss Essmith! I make but to pass you – to fly – to never come back! I have say to Chu Chu, "Fly!" We fly many miles. Sometimes together, sometimes not so mooch! Sometimes in the saddle, sometimes on the neck! Many things remain in the road; at the end, I myself remain! I have say, "Courage, Pancho will come!" Then I say, "No, he is talk with Miss Essmith!" I remember not more. I have creep here on the hands. Eet is feenish!'

I looked at her distractedly. She smiled tenderly, and slightly smoothed down and rearranged a fold of her dress to cover her delicate little boot.

'But,' I protested, 'you are not much hurt, dearest. You have broken no bones. Perhaps,' I added, looking at the boot, 'only a slight sprain. Let me carry you to my horse; I will walk beside you, home. Do, dearest Consita!'

She turned her lovely eyes towards me sadly.

'You comprehend not, my poor Pancho! It is not of the foot, the ankle, the arm, or the head that I can say, "She is broke!" I would it were even so. But' – she lifted her sweet lashes slowly – 'I have derrange my inside. It is an affair of my family. My grandfather have once toomble over the bull at a rodeo. He speak no more; he is dead. For why? He has derrange his inside. Believe me, it is of the family. You comprehend? The Saltellos are not as the other peoples for this. When I am gone, you will bring to me the berry to grow upon my tomb, Pancho; the berry you have picked for me. The little flower will come too, the little star will arrive, but Consuelo, who lofe you, she will come not more! When you are happy and talk in the road to the Essmith, you will not think of me. You will not see my eyes, Pancho; thees little grass' – she ran her plump little fingers through a tussock – 'will hide them; and the small animals in the black coats that lif here will have sorrow – but you will not. It ees better so!

My father will not that I, a Catholique, should marry into a camp-meeting, and lif in a tent, and make howl like the coyote.' (It was one of Consuelo's bewildering beliefs that there was only one form of dissent, – Methodism!) 'He will not that I should marry a man who possess not the many horses, ox, and cow, like him. But *I* care not. *You* are my only religion, Pancho! I have enofe of the horse, and ox, and cow when *you* are with me! Kiss me, Pancho. Perhaps it is for the last time – the feenish! Who knows?'

There were tears in her lovely eyes; I felt that my own were growing dim; the sun was sinking over the dreary plain to the slow rising of the wind; an infinite loneliness had fallen upon us, and yet I was miserably conscious of some dreadful unreality in it all. A desire to laugh, which I felt must be hysterical, was creeping over me; I dared not speak. But her dear head was on my shoulder, and the situation was not unpleasant.

Nevertheless, something must be done! This was the more difficult as it was by no means clear what had already been done. Even while I supported her drooping figure I was straining my eyes across her shoulder for succor of some kind. Suddenly the figure of a rapid rider appeared upon the road. It seemed familiar. I looked again – it was the blessed Enriquez! A sense of deep relief came over me. I loved Consuelo; but never before had lover ever hailed the irruption of one of his beloved's family with such complacency.

'You are safe, dearest; it is Enriquez!'

I thought she received the information coldly. Suddenly she turned upon me her eyes, now bright and glittering.

'Swear to me at the instant, Pancho, that you will not again look upon Miss Essmith, even for once.'

I was simple and literal. Miss Smith was my nearest neighbor, and, unless I was stricken with blindness, compliance was impossible. I hesitated – but swore.

'Enofe – you have hesitate – I will no more.'

She rose to her feet with grave deliberation. For an instant, with the recollection of the delicate internal organization of the Saltellos on my mind, I was in agony lest she should totter and fall, even then, yielding up her gentle spirit on the spot. But when I looked again she had a hairpin between her white teeth, and was carefully adjusting her toreador hat. And beside us was Enriquez – cheerful, alert, voluble, and undaunted.

'Eureka! I have found! We are all here! Eet is a leetle public – eh? a leetle to much of a front seat for a tête-à-tête, my yonge friends,' he said, glancing at the remains of Consuelo's bower, 'but for the accounting of taste there is none. What will you? The meat of the one man shall envenom the meat of the other. But' (in a whisper to me) 'as to thees horse – thees Chu Chu, which I have just pass – why is she undress? Surely you would not make an exposition of her to the traveler to suspect! And if not, why so?'

I tried to explain, looking at Consuelo, that Chu Chu had run away, that Consuelo had met with a terrible accident, had been thrown, and I feared had suffered serious internal injury. But to my embarrassment Consuelo maintained a half-scornful silence, and an inconsistent freshness of healthful indifference, as Enriquez approached her with an engaging smile.

'Ah, yes, she have the headache, and the molligrubs. She will sit on the damp stone when the gentle dew is falling. I comprehend. Meet me in the lane when the clock strike nine! But,' in a lower voice, 'of thees undress horse I comprehend nothing! Look you – it is sad and strange.'

He went off to fetch Chu Chu, leaving me and Consuelo alone. I do not think I ever felt so utterly abject and bewildered before in my life. Without knowing why, I was miserably conscious of having in some way offended the girl for whom I believed I would have given my life, and I had made her and myself ridiculous in the eyes of her brother. I had again failed in my slower Western nature to understand her high romantic Spanish soul! Meantime she was smoothing out her riding-habit, and looking as fresh and pretty as when she first left her house.

'Consita,' I said hesitatingly, 'you are not angry with me?'

'Angry?' she repeated haughtily, without looking at me. 'Oh, no! Of a possibility eet is Mees Essmith who is angry that I have interroopt her tête-à-tête with you, and have send here my brother to make the same with me.'

'But,' I said eagerly, 'Miss Smith does not even know Enriquez!'

Consuelo turned on me a glance of unutterable significance.

'Ah!' she said darkly, 'you *tink*!'

Indeed I *knew*. But here I believed I understood Consuelo, and was relieved. I even ventured to say gently, 'And you are better?'

She drew herself up to her full height, which was not much.

'Of my health, what is it? A nothing. Yes! Of my soul let us not speak.'

Nevertheless, when Enriquez appeared with Chu Chu she ran towards her with outstretched arms. Chu Chu protruded about six inches of upper lip in response – apparently under the impression, which I could quite understand, that her mistress was edible. And, I may have been mistaken, but their beautiful eyes met in an absolute and distinct glance of intelligence!

During the home journey Consuelo recovered her spirits, and parted from me with a magnanimous and forgiving pressure of the hand. I do not know what explanation of Chu Chu's original escape was given to Enriquez and the rest of the family; the inscrutable forgiveness extended to me by Consuelo precluded any further inquiry on my part. I was willing to leave it a secret between her and Chu Chu. But, strange to say, it seemed to complete our own understanding, and precipitated, not only our love-making, but the final catastrophe which culminated that romance. For we had resolved to elope. I do not know that this heroic remedy was absolutely necessary from the attitude of either Consuelo's family or my own; I am inclined to think we preferred it, because it involved no previous explanation or advice. Need I say that our confidant and firm ally was Consuelo's brother – the alert, the linguistic, the ever happy, ever ready Enriquez! It was understood that his presence would not only give a certain mature respectability to our performance – but I do not think we would have contemplated this step without it. During one of our riding excursions we were to secure the services of a Methodist minister in the adjoining county, and later, that of the mission padre – when the secret was out.

'I will gif her away,' said Enriquez confidently; 'it will on the instant propitiate the old shadbelly who shall perform the affair, and withhold his jaw. A little chin music from your oncle 'Arry shall finish it! Remain tranquil and forget not a ring! One does not always, in the agony and dissatisfaction of the moment, a ring remember. I shall bring two in the pocket of my dress.'

If I did not entirely participate in this roseate view it may have been because Enriquez, although a few years my senior, was much younger-looking, and with his demure deviltry of eye, and his upper lip close shaven for this occasion, he suggested a depraved acolyte rather than a responsible member of a family. Consuelo had also confided to me that her father

66

– possibly owing to some rumors of our previous escapade – had forbidden any further excursions with me alone. The innocent man did not know that Chu Chu had forbidden it also, and that even on this momentous occasion both Enriquez and myself were obliged to ride in opposite fields like out-flankers. But we nevertheless felt the full guilt of disobedience added to our desperate enterprise. Meanwhile, although pressed for time, and subject to discovery at any moment, I managed at certain points of the road to dismount and walk beside Chu Chu (who did not seem to recognize me on foot), holding Consuelo's hand in my own, with the discreet Enriquez leading my horse in the distant field. I retain a very vivid picture of that walk – the ascent of a gentle slope towards a prospect as yet unknown, but full of glorious possibilities; the tender dropping light of an autumn sky, slightly filmed with the promise of the future rains, like foreshadowed tears, and the half-frightened, half-serious talk into which Consuelo and I had insensibly fallen. And then, I don't know how it happened, but as we reached the summit Chu Chu suddenly reared, wheeled, and the next moment was flying back along the road we had just traveled, at the top of her speed! It might have been that, after her abstracted fashion, she only at that moment detected my presence; but so sudden and complete was her evolution that before I could regain my horse from the astonished Enriquez she was already a quarter of a mile on the homeward stretch, with the frantic Consuelo pulling hopelessly at the bridle. We started in pursuit. But a horrible despair seized us. To attempt to overtake her, to even follow at the same rate of speed, would only excite Chu Chu and endanger Consuelo's life. There was absolutely no help for it, nothing could be done; the mare had taken her determined long, continuous stride; the road was a straight, steady descent all the way back to the village; Chu Chu had the bit between her teeth, and there was no prospect of swerving her. We could only follow hopelessly, idiotically, furiously, until Chu Chu dashed triumphantly into the Saltellos' courtyard, carrying the half-fainting Consuelo back to the arms of her assembled and astonished family.

It was our last ride together. It was the last I ever saw of Consuelo before her transfer to the safe seclusion of a convent in Southern California. It was the last I ever saw of Chu Chu, who in the confusion of that rencontre was overlooked in her half-loosed harness, and allowed to escape through the back gate to the fields. Months afterwards it was said that she had been identified among a band of wild horses in the Coast Range, as a strange and beautiful creature who had escaped the brand of the rodeo and had become a myth. There was another legend that she had been seen, sleek, fat, and gorgeously caparisoned, issuing from the gateway of the Rosario patio, before a lumbering Spanish cabriolé in which a short, stout matron was seated – but I will have none of it. For there are days when she still lives, and I can see her plainly still climbing the gentle slope towards the summit, with Consuelo on her back, and myself at her side, pressing eagerly forward towards the illimitable prospect that opens in the distance.

MARY E. WILKINS FREEMAN

THE DOCTOR'S HORSE

THE HORSE WAS a colt when he was purchased with the money paid by the heirs of one of the doctor's patients, and those were his days of fire. At first it was opined that the horse would never do for the doctor: he was too nervous, and his nerves beyond the reach of the doctor's drugs. He shied at every wayside bush and stone; he ran away several times; he was loath to stand, and many a time the doctor in those days was forced to rush from the bedsides of patients to seize his refractory horse by the bridle and soothe and compel him to quiet. The horse in that untamed youth of his was like a furnace of fierce animal fire; when he was given rein on a frosty morning the pound of his ironbound hoofs on the rigid roads cleared them of the slow-plodding country teams. A current as of the very freedom and invincibility of life seemed to pass through the taut reins to the doctor's hands. But the doctor was the master of his horse, as of all other things with which he came in contact. He was a firm and hard man in the pursuance of his duty, never yielding to it with love, but unswervingly staunch. He was never cruel to his horse; he seldom whipped him, but he never petted him; he simply mastered him, and after a while the fiery animal began to go the doctor's gait, and not his own.

When the doctor was sent for in a hurry, to an emergency case, the horse stretched his legs at a gallop, no matter how little inclined he felt for it, on a burning day of summer, perhaps. When there was no haste, and the doctor disposed to take his time, the horse went at a gentle amble, even though the frosts of a winter morning were firing his blood, and every one of his iron nerves and muscles was strained with that awful strain of repressed motion. Even on those mornings the horse would stand at the door of the patient who was ill with old-fashioned consumption or chronic liver disease, his four legs planted widely, his head and neck describing a long downward curve, so expressive of submission and dejection that it might have served as a hieroglyphic for them, and no more thought of letting those bounding impulses of his have their way than if the doctor's will had verily bound his every foot to the ground with unbreakable chains of servitude. He had become the doctor's horse. He was the will of the doctor, embodied in a perfect compliance of action and motion. People remarked how the horse had sobered down, what a splendid animal he was for the doctor, and they had thought that he would never be able to keep him and employ him in his profession.

Now and then the horse used to look around at the empty buggy as he stood at the gate of a patient's house, to see if the doctor were there, but the will which held the reins, being still evident to his consciousness even when its owner was absent, kept him in his place. He would have no thought of taking advantage of his freedom; he would turn his head, and droop it in that curve of utter submission, shift his weight slightly to another foot, make a sound which was like a human sigh of patience, and wait again. When the doctor, carrying his little medicine chest, came forth, he would sometimes look at him, sometimes not; but he would set every muscle into an attitude of readiness for progress at the feel of the taut lines and the sound of the masterly human voice behind him.

Then he would proceed to the house of the next patient,

and the story would be repeated. The horse seemed to live his life in a perfect monotony of identical chapters. His waiting was scarcely cheered or stimulated by the vision and anticipation of his stall and his supper, so unvarying was it. The same stall, the same measure of oats, the same allotment of hay. He was never put out to pasture, for the doctor was a poor man, and unable to buy another horse and to spare him. All the variation which came to his experience was the uncertainty as to the night calls. Sometimes he would feel a slight revival of spirit and rebellion when led forth on a bitter winter night from his stolidity of repose, broken only by the shifting of his weight for bodily comfort, never by any perturbation of his inner life. The horse had no disturbing memories, and no anticipations, but he was still somewhat sensitive to surprises. When the flare of the lantern came athwart his stall and he felt the doctor's hand at his halter in the deep silence of a midnight, he would sometimes feel himself as a separate consciousness from the doctor, and experience the individualizing of contrary desires.

Now and then he pulled back, planting his four feet firmly, but he always yielded in a second before the masterly will of the man. Sometimes he started with a vicious emphasis, but it was never more than momentary. In the end he fell back into his lost state of utter submission. The horse was not unhappy. He was well cared for. His work, though considerable, was not beyond his strength. He had lost something undoubtedly in this complete surrender of his own will, but a loss of which one is unconscious tends only to the degradation of an animal, not to his misery.

The doctor often remarked with pride that his horse was a well-broken animal, somewhat stupid, but faithful. All the timid womenfolk in the village looked upon him with favor; the doctor's wife, who was nervous, loved to drive with her husband behind this docile horse, and was not afraid even to sit, while the doctor was visiting his patients, with the reins over the animal's back. The horse had become to her a piece of mechanism absolutely under the control of her husband, and he was in truth little more. Still, a furnace is a furnace, even when the fire runs low, and there is always the possibility of a blaze.

The doctor had owned the horse several years, though he was still young, when the young woman came to live in the family. She was the doctor's niece, a fragile thing, so exposed as to her network of supersensitive nerves to all the winds of life that she was always in a quiver of reciprocation or repulsion. She feared everything unknown, and all strength. She was innately suspicious of the latter. She knew its power to work her harm, and believed in its desire to do so. Especially was she afraid of that rampant and uncertain strength of a horse. Never did she ride behind one but she watched his every motion; she herself shied in spirit at every wayside stone. She watched for him to do his worst. She had no faith when she was told by her uncle that this horse was so steady that she herself could drive him. She had been told that so many times, and her confidence had been betrayed. But the doctor, since she was like a pale weed grown in the shade, with no stimulus of life except that given at its birth, prescribed fresh air and, to her consternation, daily drives with him. Day after day she went. She dared not refuse, for she was as compliant in her way to a stronger will as the horse. But she went in an agony of terror, of which the doctor had no conception. She sat in the buggy all alone while the doctor visited his patients, and she watched every motion of the horse. If he turned to look at her, her heart stood still.

And at last it came to pass that the horse began in a curious fashion to regain something of his lost spirit, and met her fear of him, and became that which she dreaded. One day as he stood before a gate in late autumn, with a burning gold of maple branches over his head and the wine of the frost in his nostrils, and this timorous thing seated behind him, anticipating that which he could but had forgotten that he could do, the knowledge and the memory of it awoke in him. There was a stiff northwester blowing. The girl was huddled in shawls and robes; her little pale face looked forth from the midst with wide eyes, with a prospectus of infinite danger from all life in them; her little thin hands clutched the reins with that consciousness of helplessness and conviction of the horse's power of mischief which is sometimes like an electric current firing the blood of a beast.

Suddenly a piece of paper blew under the horse's nose. He had been unmoved by firecrackers before, but today, with that current of terror behind him firing his blood, that paper put him in a sudden fury of panic, of self-assertion, of rage, of all three combined. He snorted; the girl screamed wildly. He started; the girl gave the reins a frantic pull. He stopped. Then the paper blew under his nose again, and he started again. The girl fairly gasped with terror; she pulled the reins, and the terror in her hands was like a whip of stimulus to the evil freedom in the horse. She screamed, and the sound of that scream was the climax. The horse knew all at once what he was – not the doctor, but a horse, with a great power of blood and muscle which made him not only his own master, but the master of all weaker things. He gave a great plunge that was rapture, the assertion of freedom, freedom itself, and was off. The faint screams of the frightened creature behind him stimulated him to madder progress. At last he knew, by her terrified recognition of it, his own sovereignty of liberty.

He thundered along the road; he had no more thought of his pitiful encumbrance of servitude, the buggy, than a free soul of its mortal coil. The country road was cleared before him; plodding teams were pulled frantically to the side; women scuttled into dooryards; pale faces peered after him from windows. Now and then an adventurous man rushed into his path with wild halloos and a mad swinging of arms, then fled precipitately before his resistless might of advance. At first the horse had heard the doctor's shouts behind him, and had laughed within himself, then he left them far behind. He leaped, he plunged, his iron-shod heels touched the dashboard of the buggy. He heard splintering wood. He gave another lunging plunge. Then he swerved, and leaped a wall. Finally he had cleared himself of everything except a remnant of his harness. The buggy was a wreck, strewn piecemeal over a meadow. The girl was lying unhurt, but as still as if she were dead; but the horse which her fear had fired to new life was away in a mad gallop over the autumn fields, and his youth had returned. He was again himself – what he had been when he first awoke to a consciousness of existence and the joy of bounding motion in his mighty nerves and muscles. He was no longer the doctor's horse, but his own.

The doctor had to sell him. After that his reputation was gone, and indeed he was never safe. He ran with the doctor. He would not stand a moment unless tied, and then pawed and pulled madly at the halter, and rent the air with impatient whinnies. So the doctor sold him, and made a good bargain. The horse was formed for speed, and his lapse from virtue had increased his financial value. The man who bought him had a good eye for horseflesh, and had no wish to stand at doors on his road to success, but to take a beeline for the winning post. The horse was well cared for, but for the first time he felt the lash and heard curses; however, they only served to stimulate to a fiercer glow the fire which had awakened within him. He was never his new master's horse as he had been the doctor's. He gained the reputation of speed, but also of vicious nervousness. He was put on the racecourse. He made a record at the county fair. Once he killed his jockey. He used to speed along the road drawing a man crouched in a tilting gig. Few other horses could pass him. Then he began to grow old.

At last when the horse was old he came into his first master's hands again. The doctor had grown old, older than the horse, and he did not know him at first, though he did say to his old wife that he looked something like that horse which he had owned which ran away and nearly killed his niece. After he said that, nothing could induce the doctor's wife to ride behind him; but the doctor, even in his feeble old age, had no fear, and the sidelong fire in the old horse's eye, and the proud cant of his neck, and haughty resentment at unfamiliar sights on the road, pleased him. He felt a confidence in his ability to tame this untamed thing, and the old man seemed to grow younger after he had bought the horse. He had given up his practice after a severe illness, and a young man had taken it, but he began to have dreams of work again. But he never knew that he had bought his own old horse until after he had owned him some weeks. He was driving him along the country road one day in October when the oaks were a ruddy blaze, and the sumacs like torches along the walls, and the air like wine with the smell of grapes and apples. Then suddenly, while the doctor was sitting in the buggy with loose reins, speeding along the familiar road, the horse stopped. And he stopped before the house where had used to dwell the man afflicted with old-fashioned consumption, and the window which had once framed his haggard, coughing visage reflected the western sunlight like a blank page of gold. There the horse stood, his head and long neck bent in the old curve. He was ready to wait until the consumptive arose from his grave in the churchyard, if so ordered. The doctor stared at him. Then he got out and went to the animal's head, and man and horse recognized each other. The light of youth was again in the man's eyes as he looked at his own spiritual handiwork. He was once more the master, in the presence of that which he had mastered. But the horse was expressed in body and spirit only by the lines of utter yielding and patience and submission. He was again the doctor's horse.

RUDYARD KIPLING

THE MALTESE CAT

THEY HAD GOOD reason to be proud, and better reason to be afraid, all twelve of them; for though they had fought their way, game by game, up the teams entered for the polo tournament, they were meeting the Archangels that afternoon in the final match; and the Archangels men were playing with half a dozen ponies apiece. As the game was divided into six quarters of eight minutes each, that meant a fresh pony after every halt. The Skidars' team, even supposing there were no accidents, could only supply one pony for every other change; and two to one is heavy odds. Again, as Shiraz, the grey Syrian, pointed out, they were meeting the pink and pick of the polo-ponies of Upper India, ponies that had cost from a thousand rupees each, while they themselves were a cheap lot gathered, often from country-carts, by their masters, who belonged to a poor but honest native infantry regiment.

'Money means pace and weight,' said Shiraz, rubbing his black-silk nose dolefully along his neat-fitting boot, 'and by the maxims of the game as I know it –'

'Ah, but we aren't playing the maxims,' said The Maltese Cat. 'We're playing the game; and we've the great advantage of knowing the game. Just think a stride, Shiraz! We've pulled up from bottom to second place in two weeks against all those fellows on the ground here. That's because we play with our heads as well as our feet.'

'It makes me feel undersized and unhappy all the same,'

said Kittiwynk, a mouse-coloured mare with a red brow-band and the cleanest pair of legs that ever an aged pony owned. 'They've twice our style, these others.'

Kittiwynk looked at the gathering and sighed. The hard, dusty polo-ground was lined with thousands of soldiers, black and white, not counting hundreds and hundreds of carriages and drags and dog-carts, and ladies with brilliant-coloured parasols, and officers in uniform and out of it, and crowds of natives behind them; and orderlies on camels, who had halted to watch the game, instead of carrying letters up and down the station; and native horse-dealers running about on thin-eared Biluchi mares, looking for a chance to sell a few first-class polo-ponies. Then there were the ponies of thirty teams that had entered for the Upper India Free-for-All Cup – nearly every pony of worth and dignity, from Mhow to Peshawur, from Allahabad to Multan; prize ponies, Arabs, Syrian, Barb, country-bred, Deccanee, Waziri, and Kabul ponies of every colour and shape and temper that you could imagine. Some of them were in mat-roofed stables, close to the polo-ground, but most were under saddle, while their masters, who had been defeated in the earlier games, trotted in and out and told the world exactly how the game should be played.

It was a glorious sight, and the come and go of the little, quick hooves, and the incessant salutations of ponies that had met before on other polo-grounds or race-courses, were enough to drive a four-footed thing wild.

But the Skidars' team were careful not to know their neighbours, though half the ponies on the ground were anxious to scrape acquaintance with the little fellows that had come from the North, and, so far, had swept the board.

'Let's see,' said a soft gold-coloured Arab, who had been playing very badly the day before, to The Maltese Cat;

'didn't we meet in Abdul Rahman's stable in Bombay, four seasons ago? I won the Paikpattan Cup next season, you may remember?'

'Not me,' said The Maltese Cat, politely. 'I was at Malta then, pulling a vegetable-cart. I don't race. I play the game.'

'Oh!' said the Arab, cocking his tail and swaggering off.

'Keep yourselves to yourselves,' said The Maltese Cat to his companions. 'We don't want to rub noses with all those goose-rumped half-breeds of Upper India. When we've won this Cup they'll give their shoes to know *us*.'

'We sha'n't win the Cup,' said Shiraz. 'How do you feel?'

'Stale as last night's feed when a muskrat has run over it,' said Polaris, a rather heavy-shouldered grey; and the rest of the team agreed with him.

'The sooner you forget that the better,' said The Maltese Cat, cheerfully. 'They've finished tiffin in the big tent. We shall be wanted now. If your saddles are not comfy, kick. If your bits aren't easy, rear, and let the *saises* know whether your boots are tight.'

Each pony had his *sais*, his groom, who lived and ate and slept with the animal, and had betted a good deal more than he could afford on the result of the game. There was no chance of anything going wrong, but to make sure, each *sais* was shampooing the legs of his pony to the last minute. Behind the *saises* sat as many of the Skidars' regiment as had leave to attend the match – about half the native officers, and a hundred or two dark, black-bearded men, with the regimental pipers nervously fingering the big, beribboned bagpipes. The Skidars were what they call a Pioneer regiment, and the bagpipes made the national music of half their men. The native officers held bundles of polo-sticks, long cane-handled mallets, and as the grand stand filled after lunch they arranged themselves by ones and twos at different points

83

round the ground, so that if a stick were broken the player would not have far to ride for a new one. An impatient British Cavalry Band struck up 'If you want to know the time, ask a p'leeceman!' and the two umpires in light dust-coats danced out on two little excited ponies. The four players of the Archangels' team followed, and the sight of their beautiful mounts made Shiraz groan again.

'Wait till we know,' said The Maltese Cat. 'Two of 'em are playing in blinkers, and that means they can't see to get out the way of their own side, or they *may* shy at the umpires' ponies. They've *all* got white web-reins that are sure to stretch or slip!'

'And,' said Kittiwynk, dancing to take the stiffness out of her, 'they carry their whips in their hands instead of on their wrists. Hah!'

'True enough. No man can manage his stick and his reins and his whip that way,' said The Maltese Cat. 'I've fallen over every square yard of the Malta ground, and I ought to know.'

He quivered his little, flea-bitten withers just to show how satisfied he felt; but his heart was not so light. Ever since he had drifted into India on a troop-ship, taken, with an old rifle, as part payment for a racing debt, The Maltese Cat had played and preached polo to the Skidars' team on the Skidars' stony polo-ground. Now a polo-pony is like a poet. If he is born with a love for the game, he can be made. The Maltese Cat knew that bamboos grew solely in order that polo-balls might be turned from their roots, that grain was given to ponies to keep them in hard condition, and that ponies were shod to prevent them slipping on a turn. But, besides all these things, he knew every trick and device of the finest game in the world, and for two seasons had been teaching the others all he knew or guessed.

'Remember,' he said for the hundredth time, as the riders

came up, 'you *must* play together, and you *must* play with your heads. Whatever happens, follow the ball. Who goes out first?'

Kittiwynk, Shiraz, Polaris, and a short high little bay fellow with tremendous hocks and no withers worth speaking of (he was called Corks) were being girthed up, and the soldiers in the background stared with all their eyes.

'I want you men to keep quiet,' said Lutyens, the captain of the team, 'and especially not to blow your pipes.'

'Not if we win, Captain Sahib?' asked the piper.

'If we win you can do what you please,' said Lutyens, with a smile, as he slipped the loop of his stick over his wrist, and wheeled to canter to his place. The Archangels' ponies were a little bit above themselves on account of the many-coloured crowd so close to the ground. Their riders were excellent players, but they were a team of crack players instead of a crack team; and that made all the difference in the world. They honestly meant to play together, but it is very hard for four men, each the best of the team he is picked from, to remember that in polo no brilliancy in hitting or riding makes up for playing alone. Their captain shouted his orders to them by name, and it is a curious thing that if you call his name aloud in public after an Englishman you make him hot and fretty. Lutyens said nothing to his men, because it had all been said before. He pulled up Shiraz, for he was playing 'back,' to guard the goal. Powell on Polaris was half-back, and Macnamara and Hughes on Corks and Kittiwynk were forwards. The tough, bamboo ball was set in the middle of the ground, one hundred and fifty yards from the ends, and Hughes crossed sticks, heads up, with the Captain of the Archangels, who saw fit to play forward; that is a place from which you cannot easily control your team. The little click as the cane-shafts met was heard all over the ground, and

85

then Hughes made some sort of quick wrist-stroke that just dribbled the ball a few yards. Kittiwynk knew that stroke of old, and followed as a cat follows a mouse. While the Captain of the Archangels was wrenching his pony round, Hughes struck with all his strength, and next instant Kittiwynk was away, Corks following close behind her, their little feet pattering like raindrops on glass.

'Pull out to the left,' said Kittiwynk between her teeth; 'it's coming your way, Corks!'

The back and half-back of the Archangels were tearing down on her just as she was within reach of the ball. Hughes leaned forward with a loose rein, and cut it away to the left almost under Kittiwynk's foot, and it hopped and skipped off to Corks, who saw that if he was not quick it would run beyond the boundaries. That long bouncing drive gave the Archangels time to wheel and send three men across the ground to head off Corks. Kittiwynk stayed where she was; for she knew the game. Corks was on the ball half a fraction of a second before the others came up, and Macnamara, with a backhanded stroke, sent it back across the ground to Hughes, who saw the way clear to the Archangels' goal, and smacked the ball in before any one quite knew what had happened.

'That's luck,' said Corks, as they changed ends. 'A goal in three minutes for three hits, and no riding to speak of.'

'Don't know,' said Polaris. 'We've made 'em angry too soon. 'Shouldn't wonder if they tried to rush us off our feet next time.'

'Keep the ball hanging, then,' said Shiraz. 'That wears out every pony that is not used to it.'

Next time there was no easy galloping across the ground. All the Archangels closed up as one man, but there they stayed, for Corks, Kittiwynk, and Polaris were somewhere on

86

the top of the ball, marking time among the rattling sticks, while Shiraz circled about outside, waiting for a chance.

'We can do this all day,' said Polaris, ramming his quarters into the side of another pony. 'Where do you think you're shoving to?'

'I'll – I'll be driven in an *ekka* if I know,' was the gasping reply, 'and I'd give a week's feed to get my blinkers off. I can't see anything.'

'The dust is rather bad. Whew! That was one for my off-hock. Where's the ball, Corks?'

'Under my tail. At least, the man's looking for it there! This is beautiful. They can't use their sticks, and it's driving 'em wild. Give old Blinkers a push and then he'll go over.'

'Here, don't touch me! I can't see. I'll – I'll back out, I think,' said the pony in blinkers, who knew that if you can't see all round your head, you cannot prop yourself against the shock.

Corks was watching the ball where it lay in the dust, close to his near fore-leg, with Macnamara's shortened stick tap-tapping it from time to time. Kittiwynk was edging her way out of the scrimmage, whisking her stump of a tail with nervous excitement.

'Ho! They've got it,' she snorted. 'Let me out!' and she galloped like a rifle-bullet just behind a tall lanky pony of the Archangels, whose rider was swinging up his stick for a stroke.

'Not today, thank you,' said Hughes, as the blow slid off his raised stick, and Kittiwynk laid her shoulder to the tall pony's quarters, and shoved him aside just as Lutyens on Shiraz sent the ball where it had come from, and the tall pony went skating and slipping away to the left. Kittiwynk, seeing that Polaris had joined Corks in the chase for the ball up the ground, dropped into Polaris' place, and then 'time' was called.

The Skidars' ponies wasted no time in kicking or fuming. They knew that each minute's rest meant so much gain, and trotted off to the rails, and their *saises* began to scrape and blanket and rub them at once.

'Whew!' said Corks, stiffening up to get all the tickle of the big vulcanite scraper. 'If we were playing pony for pony, we would bend those Archangels double in half an hour. But they'll bring up fresh ones and fresh ones and fresh ones after that – you see.'

'Who cares?' said Polaris. 'We've drawn first blood. Is my hock swelling?'

''Looks puffy,' said Corks. 'You must have had rather a wipe. Don't let it stiffen. You'll be wanted again in half an hour.'

'What's the game like?' said The Maltese Cat.

''Ground's like your shoe, except where they put too much water on it,' said Kittiwynk. 'Then it's slippery. Don't play in the centre. There's a bog there. I don't know how their next four are going to behave, but we kept the ball hanging, and made 'em lather for nothing. Who goes out? Two Arabs and a couple of country-breds! That's bad. What a comfort it is to wash your mouth out!'

Kitty was talking with a neck of a lather-covered soda-water bottle between her teeth, and trying to look over her withers at the same time. This gave her a very coquettish air.

'What's bad?' said Grey Dawn, giving to the girth and admiring his well-set shoulders.

'You Arabs can't gallop fast enough to keep yourselves warm – that's what Kitty means,' said Polaris, limping to show that his hock needed attention. 'Are you playing back, Grey Dawn?'

''Looks like it,' said Grey Dawn, as Lutyens swung himself up. Powell mounted The Rabbit, a plain bay country-bred much like Corks, but with mulish ears. Macnamara took Faiz-Ullah, a handy, short-backed little red Arab with a long tail, and Hughes mounted Benami, an old and sullen brown beast, who stood over in front more than a polo-pony should.

'Benami looks like business,' said Shiraz. 'How's your temper, Ben?' The old campaigner hobbled off without answering, and The Maltese Cat looked at the new Arch-angel ponies prancing about on the ground. They were four beautiful blacks, and they saddled big enough and strong enough to eat the Skidars' team and gallop away with the meal inside them.

'Blinkers again,' said The Maltese Cat. 'Good enough!'

'They're chargers – cavalry chargers!' said Kittiwynk, indignantly. '*They'll* never see thirteen three again.'

'They've all been fairly measured, and they've all got their certificates,' said The Maltese Cat, 'or they wouldn't be here. We must take things as they come along, and keep your eyes on the ball.'

The game began, but this time the Skidars were penned to their own end of the ground, and the watching ponies did not approve of that.

'Faiz-Ullah is shirking – as usual,' said Polaris, with a scornful grunt.

'Faiz-Ullah is eating whip,' said Corks. They could hear the leather-thonged polo-quirt lacing the little fellow's well-rounded barrel. Then The Rabbit's shrill neigh came across the ground.

'I can't do all the work,' he cried desperately.

'Play the game – don't talk,' The Maltese Cat whickered; and all the ponies wriggled with excitement, and the soldiers and the grooms gripped the railings and shouted. A black pony with blinkers had singled out old Benami, and was interfering with him in every possible way. They could see Benami shaking his head up and down, and flapping his underlip.

'There'll be a fall in a minute,' said Polaris. 'Benami is getting stuffy.'

The game flickered up and down between goal-post and goal-post, and the black ponies were getting more confident as they felt they had the legs of the others. The ball was hit out of a little scrimmage, and Benami and The Rabbit followed it, Faiz-Ullah only too glad to be quiet for an instant.

The blinkered black pony came up like a hawk, with two of his own side behind him, and Benami's eye glittered as he raced. The question was which pony should make way for the other, for each rider was perfectly willing to risk a fall in a good cause. The black, who had been driven nearly crazy by his blinkers, trusted to his weight and his temper; but Benami knew how to apply his weight and how to keep his temper. They met, and there was a cloud of dust. The black was lying on his side, all the breath knocked out of his body. The Rabbit was a hundred yards up the ground with the ball, and Benami was sitting down. He had slid nearly ten yards on his tail, but he had had his revenge, and sat cracking his nostrils till the black pony rose.

'That's what you get for interfering. Do you want any more?' said Benami, and he plunged into the game. Nothing was done that quarter, because Faiz-Ullah would not gallop, though Macnamara beat him whenever he could spare a second. The fall of the black pony had impressed his companions tremendously, and so the Archangels could not profit by Faiz-Ullah's bad behaviour.

But as The Maltese Cat said when 'time' was called, and the four came back blowing and dripping, Faiz-Ullah ought to have been kicked all round Umballa. If he did not behave better next time The Maltese Cat promised to pull out his Arab tail by the roots and – eat it.

There was no time to talk, for the third four were ordered out.

The third quarter of a game is generally the hottest, for each side thinks that the others must be pumped; and most of the winning play in a game is made about that time.

Lutyens took over The Maltese Cat with a pat and a hug, for Lutyens valued him more than anything else in the world; Powell had Shikast, a little grey rat with no pedigree and no manners outside polo; Macnamara mounted Bamboo, the largest of the team; and Hughes Who's Who, alias The Animal. He was supposed to have Australian blood in his veins, but he looked like a clothes-horse, and you could whack his legs with an iron crowbar without hurting him.

They went out to meet the very flower of the Archangels' team; and when Who's Who saw their elegantly booted legs and their beautiful satin skins, he grinned a grin through his light, well-worn bridle.

'My word!' said Who's Who. 'We must give 'em a little football. These gentlemen need a rubbing down.'

'No biting,' said The Maltese Cat, warningly; for once or twice in his career Who's Who had been known to forget himself in that way.

'Who said anything about biting? I'm not playing tiddly-winks. I'm playing the game.'

The Archangels came down like a wolf on the fold, for they were tired of football, and they wanted polo. They got it more and more. Just after the game began, Lutyens hit a ball that was coming towards him rapidly, and it rolled in the air, as a ball sometimes will, with the whirl of a frightened part-ridge. Shikast heard, but could not see it for the minute, though he looked everywhere and up into the air as The

Maltese Cat had taught him. When he saw it ahead and over-head he went forward with Powell as fast as he could put foot to ground. It was then that Powell, a quiet and level-headed man, as a rule, became inspired, and played a stroke that sometimes comes off successfully after long practice. He took his stick in both hands, and, standing up in his stirrups, swiped at the ball in the air, Munipore fashion. There was one second of paralysed astonishment, and then all four sides of the ground went up in a yell of applause and delight as the ball flew true (you could see the amazed Archangels ducking in their saddles to dodge the line of flight, and looking at it with open mouths), and the regimental pipes of the Skidars squealed from the railings as long as the pipers had breath.

Shikast heard the stroke; but he heard the head of the stick fly off at the same time. Nine hundred and ninety-nine ponies out of a thousand would have gone tearing on after the ball with a useless player pulling at their heads; but Powell knew him, and he knew Powell; and the instant he felt Powell's right leg shift a trifle on the saddle-flap, he headed to the boundary, where a native officer was frantically waving a new stick. Before the shouts had ended, Powell was armed again.

Once before in his life The Maltese Cat had heard that very same stroke played off his own back, and had profited by the confusion it wrought. This time he acted on experience, and leaving Bamboo to guard the goal in case of accidents, came through the others like a flash, head and tail low – Lutyens standing up to ease him – swept on and on before the other side knew what was the matter, and nearly pitched on his head between the Archangels' goal-post as Lutyens kicked the ball in after a straight scurry of a hundred and fifty yards. If there was one thing more than another upon which The Maltese Cat prided himself, it was on this quick, streaking kind of run half across the ground. He did not believe in taking balls round the field unless you were clearly over-matched. After this they gave the Archangels five-minuted football; and an expensive fast pony hates football because it rumples his temper.

Who's Who showed himself even better than Polaris in this game. He did not permit any wriggling away, but bored joyfully into the scrimmage as if he had his nose in a feed-box and was looking for something nice. Little Shikast jumped on the ball the minute it got clear, and every time an Archangel pony followed it, he found Shikast standing over it, asking what was the matter.

'If we can live through this quarter,' said The Maltese Cat, 'I sha'n't care. Don't take it out of yourselves. Let them do the lathering.'

So the ponies, as their riders explained afterwards, 'shut-up.' The Archangels kept them tied fast in front of their goal, but it cost the Archangels' ponies all that was left of their tempers; and ponies began to kick, and men began to repeat compliments, and they chopped at the legs of Who's Who, and he set his teeth and stayed where he was, and the dust stood up like a tree over the scrimmage until that hot quarter ended.

They found the ponies very excited and confident when they went to their *saises*; and The Maltese Cat had to warn them that the worst of the game was coming.

'Now *we* are all going in for the second time,' said he, 'and *they* are trotting out fresh ponies. You think you can gallop, but you'll find you can't; and then you'll be sorry.'

'But two goals to nothing is a halter-long lead,' said Kittiwynk, prancing.

'How long does it take to get a goal?' The Maltese Cat answered. 'For pity's sake, don't run away with a notion that the game is half-won just because we happen to be in luck

93

now! They'll ride you into the grand stand, if they can; you must not give 'em a chance. Follow the ball.'

'Football, as usual?' said Polaris. 'My hock's half as big as a nose-bag.'

'Don't let them have a look at the ball, if you can help it, Now leave me alone. I must get all the rest I can before the last quarter.'

He hung down his head and let all his muscles go slack, Shikast, Bamboo, and Who's Who copying his example.

'Better not watch the game,' he said. 'We aren't playing, and we shall only take it out of ourselves if we grow anxious. Look at the ground and pretend it's fly-time.'

They did their best, but it was hard advice to follow. The hooves were drumming and the sticks were rattling all up and down the ground, and yells of applause from the English troops told that the Archangels were pressing the Skidars hard. The native soldiers behind the ponies groaned and grunted, and said things in undertones, and presently they heard a long-drawn shout and a clatter of hurrahs!

'One to the Archangels,' said Shikast, without raising his head. 'Time's nearly up. Oh, my sire – and *dam*!'

'Faiz-Ullah,' said The Maltese Cat, 'if you don't play to the last nail in your shoes this time, I'll kick you on the ground before all the other ponies.'

'I'll do my best when my time comes,' said the little Arab, sturdily.

The *saises* looked at each other gravely as they rubbed their ponies' legs. This was the time when long purses began to tell, and everybody knew it. Kittiwynk and the others came back, the sweat dripping over their hooves and their tails telling sad stories.

'They're better than we are,' said Shiraz. 'I knew how it would be.'

'Shut your big head,' said The Maltese Cat; 'we've one goal to the good yet.'

'Yes; but it's two Arabs and two country-breds to play now,' said Corks. 'Faiz-Ullah, remember!' He spoke in a biting voice.

As Lutyens mounted Grey Dawn he looked at his men, and they did not look pretty. They were covered with dust and sweat in streaks. Their yellow boots were almost black, their wrists were red and lumpy, and their eyes seemed two inches deep in their heads; but the expression in the eyes was satisfactory.

'Did you take anything at tiffin?' said Lutyens; and the team shook their heads. They were too dry to talk.

'All right. The Archangels did. They are worse pumped than we are.'

'They've got the better ponies,' said Powell. 'I sha'n't be sorry when this business is over.'

That fifth quarter was a painful one in every way. Faiz-Ullah played like a little red demon, and The Rabbit seemed to be everywhere at once, and Benami rode straight at anything and everything that came in his way; while the umpires on their ponies wheeled like gulls outside the shifting game. But the Archangels had the better mounts, – they had kept their racers till late in the game, – and never allowed the Skidars to play football. They hit the ball up and down the width of the ground till Benami and the rest were outpaced. Then they went forward, and time and again Lutyens and Grey Dawn were just, and only just, able to send the ball away with a long, spitting backhander. Grey Dawn forgot that he was an Arab, and turned from grey to blue as he galloped. Indeed, he forgot too well, for he did not keep his eyes on the ground as an Arab should, but stuck out his nose and scuttled for the dear honour of the game. They had watered the ground once or twice between the quarters, and a careless waterman had emptied the last of his skinful all in one place near the Skidars' goal. It was close to the end of the play, and for the tenth time Grey Dawn was bolting after the ball, when his near hind foot slipped on the greasy mud, and he rolled over and over, pitching Lutyens just clear of the goal-post; and the triumphant Archangels made their goal. Then 'time' was called – two goals all; but Lutyens had to be helped up, and Grey Dawn rose with his near hind leg strained somewhere.

'What's the damage?' said Powell, his arm around Lutyens.

'Collar-bone, *of* course,' said Lutyens, between his teeth. It was the third time he had broken it in two years, and it hurt him.

Powell and the others whistled.

''Games' up,' said Hughes.

'Hold on. We've five good minutes yet, and it isn't my right hand. We'll stick it out.'

'I say,' said the Captain of the Archangels, trotting up, 'are you hurt, Lutyens? We'll wait if you care to put in a substitute. I wish – I mean – the fact is, you fellows deserve this game if any team does. 'Wish we could give you a man, or some of our ponies – or something.'

'You're awfully good, but we'll play it to a finish, I think.'

The Captain of the Archangels stared for a little. 'That's not half bad,' he said, and went back to his own side, while Lutyens borrowed a scarf from one of his native officers and made a sling of it. Then an Archangel galloped up with a big bath-sponge, and advised Lutyens to put it under his armpit to ease his shoulder, and between them they tied up his left arm scientifically; and one of the native officers leaped forward with four long glasses that fizzed and bubbled.

The team looked at Lutyens piteously, and he nodded.

96

It was the last quarter, and nothing would matter after that. They drank out the dark golden drink, and wiped their moustaches, and things looked more hopeful.

The Maltese Cat had put his nose into the front of Lutyens' shirt and was trying to say how sorry he was.

'He knows,' said Lutyens, proudly. 'The beggar knows. I've played him without a bridle before now – for fun.'

'It's no fun now,' said Powell. 'But we haven't a decent substitute.'

'No,' said Lutyens. 'It's the last quarter, and we've got to make our goal and win. I'll trust The Cat.'

'If you fall this time, you'll suffer a little,' said Macnamara.

'I'll trust The Cat,' said Lutyens.

'You hear that?' said The Maltese Cat, proudly, to the others. 'It's worth while playing polo for ten years to have that said of you. Now then, my sons, come along. We'll kick up a little bit, just to show the Archangels this team haven't suffered.'

And, sure enough, as they went on to the ground, The Maltese Cat, after satisfying himself that Lutyens was home in the saddle, kicked out three or four times, and Lutyens laughed. The reins were caught up anyhow in the tips of his strapped left hand, and he never pretended to rely on them. He knew The Cat would answer to the least pressure of the leg, and by way of showing off – for his shoulder hurt him very much – he bent the little fellow in a close figure-of-eight in and out between the goal-posts. There was a roar from the native officers and men, who dearly loved a piece of *duga-bashi* (horse-trick work), as they called it, and the pipes very quietly and scornfully droned out the first bars of a common bazar tune called 'Freshly Fresh and Newly New,' just as a warning to the other regiments that the Skidars were fit. All the natives laughed.

'And now,' said The Maltese Cat, as they took their place, 'remember that this is the last quarter, and follow the ball!'

'Don't need to be told,' said Who's Who.

'Let me go on. All those people on all four sides will begin to crowd in – just as they did at Malta. You'll hear people calling out, and moving forward and being pushed back; and that is going to make the Archangel ponies very unhappy. But if a ball is struck to the boundary, you go after it, and let the people get out of your way. I went over the pole of a four-in-hand once, and picked a game out of the dust by it. Back me up when I run, and follow the ball.'

There was a sort of an all-round sound of sympathy and wonder as the last quarter opened, and then there began exactly what The Maltese Cat had foreseen. People crowded in close to the boundaries, and the Archangels' ponies kept looking sideways at the narrowing space. If you know how a man feels to be cramped at tennis – not because he wants to run out of the court, but because he likes to know that he can at a pinch – you will guess how ponies must feel when they are playing in a box of human beings.

'I'll bend some of those men if I can get away,' said Who's Who, as he rocketed behind the ball; and Bamboo nodded without speaking. They were playing the last ounce in them, and The Maltese Cat had left the goal undefended to join them. Lutyens gave him every order that he could to bring him back, but this was the first time in his career that the little wise grey had ever played polo on his own responsibility, and he was going to make the most of it.

'What are you doing here?' said Hughes, as The Cat crossed in front of him and rode off an Archangel.

'The Cat's in charge – mind the goal!' shouted Lutyens, and bowing forward hit the ball full, and followed on, forcing the Archangels towards their own goal.

'No football,' said The Maltese Cat. 'Keep the ball by the boundaries and cramp 'em. Play open order, and drive 'em to the boundaries.'

Across and across the ground in big diagonals flew the ball, and whenever it came to a flying rush and a stroke close to the boundaries the Archangel ponies moved stiffly. They did not care to go headlong at a wall of men and carriages, though if the ground had been open they could have turned on a sixpence.

'Wriggle her up the sides,' said The Cat. 'Keep her close to the crowd. They hate the carriages. Shikast, keep her up this side.'

Shikast and Powell lay left and right behind the uneasy scuffle of an open scrimmage, and every time the ball was hit away Shikast galloped on it at such an angle that Powell was forced to hit it towards the boundary; and when the crowd had been driven away from that side, Lutyens would send the ball over to the other, and Shikast would slide desperately after it till his friends came down to help. It was billiards, and no football, this time – billiards in a corner pocket; and the cues were not well chalked.

'If they get us out in the middle of the ground they'll walk away from us. Dribble her along the sides,' cried The Maltese Cat.

So they dribbled all along the boundary, where a pony could not come on their right-hand side; and the Archangels were furious, and the umpires had to neglect the game to shout at the people to get back, and several blundering mounted policemen tried to restore order, all close to the scrimmage, and the nerves of the Archangels' ponies stretched and broke like cobwebs.

Five or six times an Archangel hit the ball up into the middle of the ground, and each time the watchful Shikast gave Powell his chance to send it back, and after each return when the dust had settled, men could see that the Skidars had gained a few yards.

Every now and again there were shouts of 'Side! Off side!' from the spectators; but the teams were too busy to care, and the umpires had all they could do to keep their maddened ponies clear of the scuffle.

At last Lutyens missed a short easy stroke, and the Skidars had to fly back helter-skelter to protect their own goal, Shikast leading. Powell stopped the ball with a backhander when it was not fifty yards from the goal-posts, and Shikast spun round with a wrench that nearly hoisted Powell out of his saddle.

'Now's our last chance,' said The Cat, wheeling like a cockchafer on a pin. 'We've got to ride it out. Come along.'

Lutyens felt the little chap take a deep breath, and, as it were, crouch under his rider. The ball was hopping towards the right-hand boundary, an Archangel riding for it with both spurs and a whip; but neither spur nor whip would make his pony stretch himself as he neared the crowd. The Maltese Cat glided under his very nose, picking up his hind legs sharp, for there was not a foot to spare between his quarters and the other pony's bit. It was as neat an exhibition as fancy figure-skating. Lutyens hit with all the strength he had left, but the stick slipped a little in his hand, and the ball flew off to the left instead of keeping close to the boundary. Who's Who was far across the ground, thinking hard as he galloped. He repeated stride for stride The Cat's manœuvres with another Archangel pony, nipping the ball away from under his bridle, and clearing his opponent by half a fraction of an inch, for Who's Who was clumsy behind. Then he drove away towards the right as The Maltese Cat came up from the left; and Bamboo held a middle course exactly between them. The three were making a sort of Government-broad-arrow-shaped attack; and there was only the Archangels' back to guard the goal; but immediately behind them were three Archangels racing all they knew, and mixed up with them was Powell sending Shikast along on what he felt was their last hope. It takes a very good man to stand up to the rush of seven crazy ponies in the last quarters of a Cup game, when men are riding with their necks for sale, and the ponies are delirious. The Archangels' back missed his stroke and pulled aside just in time to let the rush go by. Bamboo and Who's Who shortened stride to give The Cat room, and Lutyens got the goal with a clean, smooth, smacking stroke that was heard all over the field. But there was no stopping the ponies. They poured through the goal-posts in one mixed mob, winners and losers together, for the pace had been terrific. The Maltese Cat knew by experience what would happen, and, to save Lutyens, turned to the right with one last effort, that strained a back-sinew beyond hope of repair. As he did so he heard the right-hand goal-post crack as a pony cannoned into it – crack, splinter, and fall like a mast. It had been sawed three parts through in case of accidents, but it upset the pony nevertheless, and he blundered into another, who blundered into the left-hand post, and then there was confusion and dust and wood. Bamboo was lying on the ground, seeing stars; an Archangel pony rolled beside him, breathless and angry; Shikast had sat down dog-fashion to avoid falling over the others, and was sliding along on his little bobtail in a cloud of dust; and Powell was sitting on the ground, hammering with his stick and trying to cheer. All the others were shouting at the top of what was left of their voices, and the men who had been split were shouting too. As soon as the people saw no one was hurt, ten thousand native and English shouted and clapped and yelled, and before any one could stop them the pipers of the Skidars broke onto the ground, with all the native officers and men behind them, and marched up and down, playing a wild Northern tune called 'Zakhme Bagán,' and through the insolent blaring of the pipes and the high-pitched native yells you could hear the Archangels' band hammering, 'For they are all jolly good fellows,' and then reproachfully to the losing team, 'Ooh, Kafoozalum! Kafoozalum! Kafoozalum!'

Besides all these things and many more, there was a Commander-in-chief, and an Inspector-General of Cavalry, and the principal veterinary officer of all India standing on the top of a regimental coach, yelling like school-boys; and brigadiers and colonels and commissioners, and hundreds of pretty ladies joined the chorus. But The Maltese Cat stood with his head down, wondering how many legs were left to him; and Lutyens watched the men and ponies pick themselves out of the wreck of the two goal-posts, and he patted The Maltese Cat very tenderly.

'I say,' said the Captain of the Archangels, spitting a pebble out of his mouth, 'will you take three thousand for that pony – as he stands?'

'No, thank you. I've an idea he's saved my life,' said Lutyens, getting off and lying down at full length. Both teams were on the ground too, waving their boots in the air, and coughing and drawing deep breaths, as the *saises* ran up to take away the ponies, and an officious water-carrier sprinkled the players with dirty water till they sat up.

'My aunt!' said Powell, rubbing his back, and looking at the stumps of the goal-posts, 'that was a game!'

They played it over again, every stroke of it, that night at the big dinner, when the Free-for-All Cup was filled and passed down the table, and emptied and filled again, and everybody made most eloquent speeches. About two in the morning, when there might have been some singing, a wise little, plain little, grey little head looked in through the open door.

'Hurrah! Bring him in,' said the Archangels; and his *sais*, who was very happy indeed, patted The Maltese Cat on the flank, and he limped in to the blaze of light and the glittering uniforms, looking for Lutyens. He was used to messes, and men's bedrooms, and places where ponies are not usually encouraged, and in his youth had jumped on and off a mess-table for a bet. So he behaved himself very politely, and ate bread dipped in salt, and was petted all round the table, moving gingerly; and they drank his health, because he had done more to win the Cup than any man or horse on the ground.

That was glory and honour enough for the rest of his days, and The Maltese Cat did not complain much when the veterinary surgeon said that he would be no good for polo any more. When Lutyens married, his wife did not allow him to play, so he was forced to be an umpire; and his pony on these occasions was a flea-bitten grey with a neat polo-tail, lame all round, but desperately quick on his feet, and, as everybody knew, Past Pluperfect Prestissimo Player of the Game.

SAKI

THE BROGUE

THE HUNTING SEASON had come to an end, and the Mullets had not succeeded in selling the Brogue. There had been a kind of tradition in the family for the past three or four years, a sort of fatalistic hope, that the Brogue would find a purchaser before the hunting was over; but seasons came and went without anything happening to justify such ill-founded optimism. The animal had been named Berserker in the earlier stages of its career; it had been rechristened the Brogue later on, in recognition of the fact that, once acquired, it was extremely difficult to get rid of. The unkinder wits of the neighbourhood had been known to suggest that the first letter of its name was superfluous. The Brogue had been variously described in sale catalogues as a light-weight hunter, a lady's hack, and, more simply, but still with a touch of imagination, as a useful brown gelding, standing 15.1. Toby Mullet had ridden him for four seasons with the West Wessex; you can ride almost any sort of horse with the West Wessex as long as it is an animal that knows the country. The Brogue knew the country intimately, having personally created most of the gaps that were to be met with in banks and hedges for many miles round. His manners and characteristics were not ideal in the hunting field, but he was probably rather safer to ride to hounds than he was as a hack on country roads. According to the Mullet family, he was not really road-shy, but there were one or two objects of dislike that brought on sudden attacks of what Toby called swerving sickness. Motors and cycles he treated with tolerant disregard, but pigs, wheelbarrows, piles of stones by the roadside, perambulators in a village street, gates painted too aggressively white, and sometimes, but not always, the newer kind of beehives, turned him aside from his tracks in vivid imitation of the zigzag course of forked lightning. If a pheasant rose noisily from the other side of a hedgerow the Brogue would spring into the air at the same moment, but this may have been due to a desire to be companionable. The Mullet family contradicted the widely prevalent report that the horse was a confirmed crib-biter.

It was about the third week in May that Mrs Mullet, relict of the late Sylvester Mullet, and mother of Toby and a bunch of daughters, assailed Clovis Sangrail on the outskirts of the village with a breathless catalogue of local happenings.

'You know our new neighbour, Mr Penricarde?' she vociferated; 'awfully rich, owns tin mines in Cornwall, middle-aged and rather quiet. He's taken the Red House on a long lease and spent a lot of money on alterations and improvements. Well, Toby's sold him the Brogue!'

Clovis spent a moment or two in assimilating the astonishing news; then he broke out into unstinted congratulation. If he had belonged to a more emotional race he would probably have kissed Mrs Mullet.

'How wonderful lucky to have pulled it off at last! Now you can buy a decent animal. I've always said that Toby was clever. Ever so many congratulations.'

'Don't congratulate me. It's the most unfortunate thing that could have happened!' said Mrs Mullet dramatically.

Clovis stared at her in amazement.

'Mr Penricarde,' said Mrs Mullet, sinking her voice to what she imagined to be an impressive whisper, though it rather resembled a hoarse, excited squeak, 'Mr Penricarde has just begun to pay attentions to Jessie. Slight at first, but now unmistakable. I was a fool not to have seen it sooner: Yesterday, at the Rectory garden party, he asked her what her favourite flowers were, and she told him carnations, and today a whole stack of carnations has arrived, clove and malmaison and lovely dark red ones, regular exhibition blooms, and a box of chocolates that he must have got on purpose from London. And he's asked her to go round the links with him tomorrow. And now, just at this critical moment, Toby has sold him that animal. It's a calamity!'

'But you've been trying to get the horse off your hands for years,' said Clovis.

'I've got a houseful of daughters,' said Mrs Mullet, 'and I've been trying – well, not to get them off my hands, of course, but a husband or two wouldn't be amiss among the lot of them; there are six of them, you know.'

'I don't know,' said Clovis, 'I've never counted, but I expect you're right as to the number; mothers generally know these things.'

'And now,' continued Mrs Mullet, in her tragic whisper, 'when there's a rich husband-in-prospect imminent on the horizon Toby goes and sells him that miserable animal. It will probably kill him if he tries to ride it; anyway it will kill any affection he might have felt towards any member of our family. What is to be done? We can't very well ask to have the horse back; you see, we praised it up like anything when we thought there was a chance of his buying it, and said it was just the animal to suit him.'

'Couldn't you steal it out of his stable and send it to grass at some farm miles away?' suggested Clovis. 'Write "Votes for Women" on the stable door, and the thing would pass for a Suffragette outrage. No one who knew the horse could possibly suspect you of wanting to get it back again.'

'Every newspaper in the country would ring with the affair,' said Mrs Mullet; 'can't you imagine the headline, "Valuable Hunter Stolen by Suffragettes"? The police would scour the countryside till they found the animal.'

'Well, Jessie must try and get it back from Penricarde on the plea that it's an old favourite. She can say it was only sold because the stable had to be pulled down under the terms of an old repairing lease, and that now it has been arranged that the stable is to stand for a couple of years longer.'

'It sounds a queer proceeding to ask for a horse back when you've just sold him,' said Mrs Mullet, 'but something must be done, and done at once. The man is not used to horses, and I believe I told him it was as quiet as a lamb. After all, lambs go kicking and twisting about as if they were demented, don't they?'

'The lamb has an entirely unmerited character for sedateness,' agreed Clovis.

Jessie came back from the golf links next day in a state of mingled elation and concern.

'It's all right about the proposal,' she announced, 'he came out with it at the sixth hole. I said I must have time to think it over. I accepted him at the seventh.'

'My dear,' said her mother, 'I think a little more maidenly reserve and hesitation would have been advisable, as you've known him so short a time. You might have waited till the ninth hole.'

'The seventh is a very long hole,' said Jessie; 'besides, the tension was putting us both off our game. By the time we'd got to the ninth hole we'd settled lots of things. The honeymoon is to be spent in Corsica, with perhaps a flying visit to Naples if we feel like it, and a week in London to wind up with. Two of his nieces are to be asked to be bridesmaids, so with our lot there will be seven, which is rather a lucky number. You are to wear your pearl grey, with any amount of Honiton lace jabbed into it. By the way, he's coming over this evening to ask your consent to the whole affair. So far all's well, but about the Brogue it's a different matter. I told him the legend about the stable, and how keen we were about buying the horse back, but he seems equally keen on keeping it. He said he must have horse exercise now that he's living in the country, and he's going to start riding tomorrow. He's ridden a few times in the Row on an animal that was accustomed to carry octogenarians and people undergoing rest cures, and that's about all his experience in the saddle – oh, and he rode a pony once in Norfolk, when he was fifteen and the pony twenty-four; and tomorrow he's going to ride the Brogue! I shall be a widow before I'm married, and I do so want to see what Corsica's like; it looks so silly on the map.'

Clovis was sent for in haste, and the developments of the situation put before him.

'Nobody can ride that animal with any safety,' said Mrs Mullet, 'except Toby, and he knows by long experience what it is going to shy at, and manages to swerve at the same time.'

'I did hint to Mr Penricarde – to Vincent, I should say – that the Brogue didn't like white gates,' said Jessie.

'White gates!' exclaimed Mrs Mullet; 'did you mention what effect a pig has on him? He'll have to go past Lockyer's farm to get to the high road, and there's sure to be a pig or two grunting about in the lane.'

'He's taken rather a dislike to turkeys lately,' said Toby.

'It's obvious that Penricarde mustn't be allowed to go out on that animal,' said Clovis, 'at least not till Jessie has married him, and tired of him. I tell you what: ask him to a picnic tomorrow, starting at an early hour; he's not the sort to go out for a ride before breakfast. The day after I'll get the rector to drive him over to Crowleigh before lunch, to see the new cottage hospital they're building there. The Brogue will be standing idle in the stable and Toby can offer to exercise it; then it can pick up a stone or something of the sort and go conveniently lame. If you hurry on the wedding a bit the lameness fiction can be kept up till the ceremony is safely over.'

Mrs Mullet belonged to an emotional race, and she kissed Clovis.

It was nobody's fault that the rain came down in torrents the next morning, making a picnic a fantastic impossibility. It was also nobody's fault, but sheer ill-luck, that the weather cleared up sufficiently in the afternoon to tempt Mr Penricarde to make his first essay with the Brogue. They did not get as far as the pigs at Lockyer's farm; the rectory gate was painted a dull unobtrusive green, but it had been white a year or two ago, and the Brogue never forgot that he had been in the habit of making a violent curtsey, a back-pedal and a swerve at this particular point of the road. Subsequently, there being apparently no further call on his services, he broke his way into the rectory orchard, where he found a hen turkey in a coop; later visitors to the orchard found the coop almost intact, but very little left of the turkey.

Mr Penricarde, a little stunned and shaken, and suffering from a bruised knee and some minor damages, good-naturedly ascribed the accident to his own inexperience with horses and country roads, and allowed Jessie to nurse him back into complete recovery and golf-fitness within something less than a week.

In the list of wedding presents which the local newspaper published a fortnight or so later appeared the following item:

'Brown saddle-horse, "The Brogue," bridegroom's gift to bride.'

'Which shows,' said Toby Mullet, 'that he knew nothing.'

'Or else,' said Clovis, 'that he has a very pleasing wit.'

MARK TWAIN

A GENUINE
MEXICAN PLUG

I RESOLVED TO have a horse to ride. I had never seen such wild, free magnificent horsemanship outside of a circus as these picturesquely-clad Mexicans, Californians and Mexicanized Americans displayed in Carson streets every day. How they rode! Leaning just gently forward out of the perpendicular, easy and nonchalant, with broad slough-hat brim blown square up in front, and long riata swinging above the head, they swept through the town like the wind! The next minute they were only a sailing puff of dust on the far desert. If they trotted, they sat up gallantly and gracefully, and seemed part of the horse; did not go jiggering up and down after the silly Miss-Nancy fashion of the riding schools. I had quickly learned to tell a horse from a cow, and was full of anxiety to learn more. I was resolved to buy a horse.

While the thought was rankling in my mind, the auctioneer came scurrying through the plaza on a black beast that had as many humps and corners on him as a dromedary, and was necessarily uncomely; but he was 'going, going, at twenty two! – horse, saddle and bridle at twenty-two dollars, gentlemen!' and I could hardly resist.

A man whom I did not know (he turned out to be the auctioneer's brother) noticed the wistful look in my eye, and observed that that was a very remarkable horse to be going at such a price; and added that the saddle alone was worth the money. It was a Spanish saddle, with ponderous *tapidoros*, and furnished with the ungainly sole-leather covering with the unspellable name. I said I had half a notion to bid. Then this keen-eyed person appeared to me to be 'taking my measure'; but I dismissed the suspicion when he spoke, for his manner was full of guileless candor and truthfulness. Said he:

'I know that horse – know him well. You are a stranger, I take it, and so you might think he was an American horse, maybe, but I assure you he is not. He is nothing of the kind; but – excuse my speaking in a low voice, other people being near – he is, without the shadow of a doubt, a Genuine Mexican Plug!'

I did not know what a Genuine Mexican Plug was, but there was something about this man's way of saying it, that made me swear inwardly that I would own a Genuine Mexican Plug, or die.

'Has he any other – er – advantages?' I inquired, suppressing what eagerness I could.

He hooked his forefinger in the pocket of my army-shirt, led me to one side, and breathed in my ear impressively these words:

'He can out-buck anything in America!'

'Going, going, going – at *twent-ty*-four dollars and a half, gen-'

'Twenty-seven!' I shouted, in a frenzy.

'And sold!' said the auctioneer, and passed over the Genuine Mexican Plug to me.

I could scarcely contain my exultation. I paid the money and put the animal in a neighboring livery-stable to dine and rest himself.

In the afternoon I brought the creature into the plaza, and certain citizens held him by the head, and others by the tail, while I mounted him. As soon as they let go, he placed all his feet in a bunch together, lowered his back, and then suddenly arched it upward, and shot me straight into the air a matter of three or four feet! I came straight down again, lit in the saddle, went instantly up again, came down almost on the high pommel, shot up again, and came down on the horse's neck – all in the space of three or four seconds. Then he rose and stood almost straight up on his hind feet, and I, clasping his lean neck desperately, slid back into the saddle, and held on. He came down, and immediately hoisted his heels into the air, delivering a vicious kick at the sky, and stood on his forefeet. And then down he came once more, and began the original exercise of shooting me straight up again. The third time I went up I heard a stranger say:

'Oh, *don't* he buck, though!'

While I was up, somebody struck the horse a sounding thwack with a leathern strap, and when I arrived again the Genuine Mexican Plug was not there. A Californian youth chased him up and caught him, and asked if he might have a ride. I granted him that luxury. He mounted the Genuine, got lifted into the air once, but sent his spurs home as he descended, and the horse darted away like a telegram. He soared over three fences like a bird, and disappeared down the road toward the Washoe Valley.

I sat down on a stone, with a sigh, and by a natural impulse one of my hands sought my forehead, and the other the base of my stomach. I believe I never appreciated, till then, the poverty of the human machinery – for I still needed a hand or two to place elsewhere. Pen cannot describe how I was jolted up. Imagination cannot conceive how disjointed I was – how internally, externally and universally I was un-settled, mixed up and ruptured. There was a sympathetic crowd around me, though.

One elderly-looking comforter said:

'Stranger, you've been taken in. Everybody in this camp knows that horse. Any child, any Injun, could have told you that he'd buck; his is the very worst devil to buck on the continent of America. You hear *me*. I'm old Curry. *Old* Curry. Old *Abe* Curry. And moreover, he is a simon-pure, out-and-out genuine d—d Mexican plug, and an uncommon mean one at that, too. Why, you turnip, if you had laid low and kept dark, there's chances to buy an *American* horse for mighty little more than you paid for that bloody old foreign relic.'

ANNIE PROULX

THE BLOOD BAY

THE WINTER OF 1886–87 was terrible. Every goddamn history of the high plains says so. There were great stocks of cattle on overgrazed land during the droughty summer. Early wet snow froze hard so the cattle could not break through the crust to the grass. Blizzards and freeze-eye cold followed, the gant bodies of cattle piling up in draws and coulees.

A young Montana cowboy, somewhat vain, had skimped on coat and mittens and put all his wages into a fine pair of handmade boots. He crossed into Wyoming Territory thinking it would be warmer, for it was south of where he was. That night he froze to death on Powder River's bitter west bank, that stream of famous dimensions and direction – an inch deep, a mile wide and she flows uphill from Texas.

The next afternoon three cowpunchers from the Box Spring outfit near Suggs rode past his corpse, blue as a whetstone and half-buried in snow. They were savvy and salty. They wore blanket coats, woolly chaps, grease-wool scarves tied over their hats and under their bristled chins, sheepskin mitts and two of them were fortunate enough to park their feet in good boots and heavy socks. The third, Dirt Sheets, a cross-eyed drinker of hair-oil, was all right on top but his luck was running muddy near the bottom, no socks and curl-toe boots cracked and holed.

'That can a corn beef's wearin my size boots,' Sheets said and got off his horse for the first time that day. He pulled at the Montana cowboy's left boot but it was frozen on. The right one didn't come off any easier.

'Son of a sick steer in a snowbank,' he said, 'I'll cut em off and thaw em after supper.' Sheets pulled out a Bowie knife and sawed through Montana's shins just above the boot tops, put the booted feet in his saddlebags, admiring the tooled leather and topstitched hearts and clubs. They rode on down the river looking for strays, found a dozen bogged in deep drifts and lost most of the daylight getting them out.

'Too late to try for the bunkhouse. Old man Grice's shack is somewheres up along. He's bound a have dried prunes or other dainties or at least a hot stove.' The temperature was dropping, so cold that spit crackled in the air and a man didn't dare to piss for fear he'd be rooted fast until spring. They agreed it must be forty below and more, the wind scything up a nice Wyoming howler.

They found the shack four miles north. Old man Grice opened the door a crack.

'Come on in, puncher or rustler, I don't care.'

'We'll put our horses up. Where's the barn.'

'Barn. Never had one. There's a lean-to out there behind the woodpile should keep em from blowin away or maybe freezin. I got my two horses in here beside the dish cupboard. I pamper them babies somethin terrible. Sleep where you can find a space, but I'm tellin you don't bother that blood bay none, he will mull you up and spit you out. He's a spirited steed. Pull up a chair and have some a this son-of-a-bitch stew. And I got plenty conversation juice a wash it down. Hot biscuits just comin out a the oven.'

It was a fine evening, eating, drinking and playing cards, swapping lies, the stove kicking out heat, old man Grice's spoiled horses sighing in comfort. The only disagreeable tone to the evening from the waddies' point of view was the fact that their host cleaned them out, took them for three dollars and four bits. Around midnight Grice blew out the lamp and got in his bunk and the three punchers stretched out on the floor. Sheets set his trophies behind the stove, laid his head on his saddle and went to sleep.

He woke half an hour before daylight, recalled it was his mother's birthday and if he wanted to telegraph a filial sentiment to her he would have to ride faster than chain lightning with the links snapped, for the Overland office closed at noon. He checked his grisly trophies, found them thawed and pulled the boots and socks off the originals, drew them onto his own pedal extremities. He threw the bare Montana feet and his old boots in the corner near the dish cupboard, slipped out like a falling feather, saddled his horse and rode away. The wind was low and the fine cold air refreshed him.

Old man Grice was up with the sun grinding coffee beans and frying bacon. He glanced down at his rolled-up guests and said, 'Coffee's ready.' The blood bay stamped and kicked at something that looked like a man's foot. Old man Grice took a closer look.

'There's a bad start to the day,' he said, 'it is a man's foot and there's the other.' He counted the sleeping guests. There were only two of them.

'Wake up, survivors, for god's sake wake up and get up.'

The two punchers rolled out, stared wild-eyed at the old man who was fairly frothing, pointing at the feet on the floor behind the blood bay.

'He's ate Sheets. Ah, I knew he was a hard horse, but to eat a man whole. You savage bugger,' he screamed at the blood bay and drove him out into the scorching cold. 'You'll never eat human meat again. You'll sleep out with the blizzards and wolves, you hell-bound fiend.' Secretly he was pleased to own a horse with the sand to eat a raw cowboy.

The leftover Box Spring riders were up and drinking

coffee. They squinted at old man Grice, hitched at their gun belts.

'Ah, boys, for god's sake, it was a terrible accident. I didn't know what a brute of a animal was that blood bay. Let's keep this to ourselves. Sheets was no prize and I've got forty gold dollars says so and the three and four bits I took off a you last night. Eat your bacon, don't make no trouble. There's enough trouble in the world without no more.'

No, they wouldn't make trouble and they put the heavy money in their saddlebags, drank a last cup of hot coffee, saddled up and rode out into the grinning morning.

When they saw Sheets that night at the bunkhouse they nodded, congratulated him on his mother's birthday but said nothing about blood bays or forty-three dollars and four bits. The arithmetic stood comfortable.

ISAAC BABEL

THE STORY OF
A HORSE

ONE DAY SAVITSKY, our division commander, took for himself a white stallion belonging to Khlebnikov, the commander of the First Squadron. It was a horse of imposing stature, but with a somewhat raw build, which always seemed a little heavy to me. Khlebnikov was given a black mare of pretty good stock and good trot. But he mistreated the mare, hankered for revenge, waited for an opportunity, and when it came, pounced on it.

After the unsuccessful battles of July, when Savitsky was dismissed from his duties and sent to the command personnel reserves, Khlebnikov wrote to army headquarters requesting that his horse be returned to him. On the letter, the chief of staff penned the decision: 'Aforementioned stallion is to be returned to primordial owner.' And Khlebnikov, rejoicing, rode a hundred versts to find Savitsky, who was living at the time in Radzivillov, a mangled little town that looked like a tattered old whore. The dismissed division commander was living alone, the fawning lackeys at headquarters no longer knew him. The fawning lackeys at headquarters were busy angling for roasted chickens in the army commander's smiles, and, vying to outgrovel each other, had turned their backs on the glorious division commander.

Drenched in perfume, looking like Peter the Great, he had fallen out of favor. He lived with a Cossack woman by the name of Pavla, whom he had snatched away from a

Jewish quartermaster, and twenty thoroughbreds which, word had it, were his own. In his yard, the sun was tense and tortured with the blindness of its rays. The foals were wildly suckling on their mothers, and stableboys with drenched backs were sifting oats on faded winnowing floors. Khlebnikov, wounded by the injustice and fired by revenge, marched straight over to the barricaded yard.

'Are you familiar with my person?' he asked Savitsky, who was lying on some hay.

'Something tells me I've seen you somewhere before,' Savitsky said to him with a yawn.

'In that case, here is the chief of staff's decision,' Khlebnikov said gruffly. 'And I would be obliged, Comrade of the reserve, if you would look at me with an official eye!'

'Why not?' Savitsky mumbled appeasingly. He took the document and began reading it for an unusually long time. He suddenly called over the Cossack woman, who was combing her hair in the coolness under the awning.

'Pavla!' he yelled. 'As the Lord's my witness, you've been combing your hair since this morning! How about heating a samovar for us!'

The Cossack woman put down her comb, took her hair in both hands, and flung it behind her back.

'You've done nothing but bicker all day, Konstantin Vasilevich,' she said with a lazy, condescending smile. 'First you want this, then you want that!'

And she came over to Savitsky; her breasts, bobbing on her high heels, squirmed like an animal in a sack.

'You've done nothing but bicker all day,' the woman repeated, beaming, and she buttoned up the division commander's shirt.

'First I want this, then I want that,' the division commander said, laughing, and he got up, clasped Pavla's acquiescing shoulders, and suddenly turned his face, deathly white, to Khlebnikov.

'I am still alive, Khlebnikov,' he said, embracing the Cossack woman tighter. 'My legs can still walk, my horses can still gallop, my hands can still get hold of you, and my gun is warming next to my skin.'

He drew his revolver, which had lain against his bare stomach, and stepped closer to the commander of the First Squadron.

The commander turned on his heels, his spurs yelped, he left the yard like an orderly who has received an urgent dispatch, and once again rode a hundred versts to find the chief of staff – but the chief of staff sent him packing.

'I have already dealt with your matter, Commander!' the chief of staff said. 'I ordered that your stallion be returned to you, and I have quite a few other things to deal with!'

The chief of staff refused to listen, and finally ordered the errant commander back to his squadron. Khlebnikov had been away a whole week. During that time we had been transferred to the Dubno forest to set up camp. We had pitched our tents and were living it up. Khlebnikov, from what I remember, returned on the twelfth, a Sunday morning. He asked me for some paper, a good thirty sheets, and for some ink. The Cossacks planed a tree stump smooth for him, he placed his revolver and the paper on it, and wrote till sundown, filling many sheets with his smudgy scrawl.

'You're a real Karl Marx, you are!' the squadron's military commissar said to him in the evening. 'What the hell are you writing there?'

'I am describing various thoughts in accordance with the oath I have taken,' Khlebnikov answered, and handed the military commissar his petition to withdraw from the Communist Party of the Bolsheviks.

'The Communist Party,' his petition went, 'was, it is my belief, founded for the promotioning of happiness and true justice with no restrictings, and thus must also keep an eye out for the rights of the little man. Here I would like to touch on the matter of the white stallion who I seized from some indescribably counterrevolutionary peasants, and who was in a horrifying condition, and many comrades laughed brazenly at that condition, but I was strong enough to withstand that laughing of theirs, and gritting my teeth for the Common Cause, I nursed the stallion back to the desired shape, because, let it be said, Comrades, I am a white-stallion enthusiast and have dedicated to white stallions the little energy that the Imperial War and the Civil War have left me with, and all these stallions respond to my touch as I respond to his silent wants and needs! But that unjust black mare I can neither respond to, nor do I need her, nor can I stand her, and, as all my comrades will testify, there's bound to be trouble! And yet the Party is unable to return to me, according to the chief of staff's decision, that which is my very own, handing me no option but to write this here petition with tears that do not befit a fighter, but which flow endlessly, ripping my blood-drenched heart to pieces!'

This and much more was written in Khlebnikov's petition. He spent the whole day writing it, and it was very long. It took me and the military commissar more than an hour to struggle through it.

'What a fool you are!' the military commissar said to him, and tore it up. 'Come back after dinner and you and I will have a little talk.'

'I don't need your little talk!' Khlebnikov answered, trembling. 'You and I are finished!'

He stood at attention, shivering, not moving, his eyes darting from one side to the other as if he were desperately trying to decide which way to run. The military commissar came up to him but couldn't grab hold of him in time. Khlebnikov lunged forward and ran with all his might.

'We're finished!' he yelled wildly, jumped onto the tree stump, and began ripping his jacket and tearing at his chest.

'Go on, Savitsky!' he shouted, throwing himself onto the ground. 'Kill me!'

We dragged him to a tent, the Cossacks helped us. We boiled some tea for him, and rolled him some cigarettes. He smoked, his whole body shivering. And it was only late in the evening that our commander calmed down. He no longer spoke about his deranged petition, but within a week he went to Rovno, presented himself for an examination by the Medical Commission, and was discharged from the army as an invalid on account of having six wounds.

That's how we lost Khlebnikov. I was very upset about this because Khlebnikov had been a quiet man, very similar to me in character. He was the only one in the squadron who owned a samovar. On days when there was a break in the fighting, the two of us drank hot tea. We were rattled by the same passions. Both of us looked upon the world as a meadow in May over which women and horses wander.

DAMON RUNYON

OLD EM'S
KENTUCKY HOME

ALL THIS REALLY begins the April day at the Jamaica race track when an assistant starter by the name of Plumbuff puts a twitch on Itchky Ironhat's fourteen-year-old race mare, Emaleen, who is known to one and all as Em for short.

A twitch is nothing but a rope loop that they wrap around a horse's upper lip and keep twisting with a stick to make the horse stand quiet at the starting gate and while I never have a twitch on my own lip and hope and trust that I never have same, I do not see anything wrong with putting twitches on horses' lips, especially the ones I am betting against as it generally keeps them so busy thinking of how it hurts that they sometimes forget about running.

However, it seems that Itchky Ironhat not only considers a twitch very painful to horses, but he also considers it undignified for such a horse as old Em, because while everybody else regards Em as strictly a porcupine, Itchky thinks she is the best horse in the world and loves her so dearly he cannot bear to see her in pain or made to look undignified. To tell the truth, it is common gossip that Itchky loves old Em more than he loves anything else whatever including his ever-loving wife, Mousie.

In fact, when Mousie tells him one day that the time comes for a show down and that it is either her or old Em and Itchky says well, he guesses it is old Em, and Mousie packs up on him at once and returns to her trade as an artists' model many citizens who remember Mousie's shape think

Itchky makes a bad deal, although some claim that the real reason Itchky decides in favour of Em against Mousie is not so much love as it is that Em never wishes for any large thick sirloin steaks such as Mousie adores.

Anyway, it seems that Itchky always goes to the trouble of personally requesting the assistant starters not to place twitches on Em's lip, even though he knows very well that she is by no means a bargain at the post and that she greatly enjoys nibbling assistant starters' ears off and when Plumbuff ignores his request it vexes Itchky no little.

The night after the race he calls on Plumbuff at his home in Jackson Heights and chides him quite some and he also gives him such a going-over that Plumbuff is compelled to take to his bed slightly indisposed for several weeks.

When the racing officials learn of the incident they call Itchky before them and address him in very severe terms. They ask him if he thinks old Em is Mrs Man o' War, or what, that he expects great courtesy for her from assistant starters and they say they have half a mind to rule Itchky off the turf for life and old Em along with him. But Itchky states that he only acts in self-defence and that he can produce twenty witnesses who will testify that Plumbuff pulls a blunt instrument on him first.

The chances are Itchky can produce these witnesses, at that, as all he will have to do is go down to Mindy's restaurant on Broadway and summon the first twenty horse players he sees. Horse players hate and despise assistant starters because they feel that the assistants are always giving the horses they bet on the worst of the starts and naturally these horse players will deem it a privilege and a pleasure to perjure themselves in a case of this nature, especially for Itchky Ironhat, who is a popular character.

His right name is something in twelve letters, but he is

called Itchky Ironhat because he always wears a black derby hat and generally he has it pulled down on his head until the brim is resting on his ears and as Itchky is a short, roly-poly guy with a fat puss he really looks a great deal like a corked jug.

Finally the racing officials say they will not rule Itchky or old Em off this time but that he must remove Em from the New York tracks and run her elsewhere and this is wonderful news to the assistant starters, who are awaiting the decision with interest.

They feel that they are all sure to wind up daffy if they have to always be deciding on whether to cater to old Em at the post or take a going-over from Itchky Ironhat and in fact they say the only thing that keeps them from going daffy on account of old Em long before this is that she does not go to the post often.

She is entered in more races than any horse that ever lives, but just before a race comes up Itchky generally starts figuring that maybe the track will not suit her, or that the race is too long, or maybe too short, or that it is not the right time of day, or that old Em will not feel just like running that day, so he usually withdraws her at the last minute.

Sometimes the racing officials are a little tough with owners who wish to scratch horses from a race at the last minute, but they never argue a second with Itchky Ironhat. In fact, they often give three cheers when Em is taken out of a race, not only because she is so cross at the post but because she is so slow that she is always getting in the way of other horses and inconveniencing them more than somewhat.

It is the way Itchky thinks old Em feels that figures with him in taking her out of a race more than anything else, and to hear him talk you will think she comes right out and informs him how she feels every day. Indeed, Itchky converses with old Em as if she is a human being and he claims she can understand everything he says, though personally I do not believe any horse can understand a slightly Yiddish dialect such as Itchky employs.

She is a big bay mare with a sway-back and of course she is quite elderly for a horse, and especially a race horse, but Itchky says she does not look her years. She is as fat as a goose what with him feeding her candy, apples, cakes and ice cream, besides a little hay and grain, and she is wind-broken and a bleeder and has knobs on her knees the size of baseballs.

She has four bad ankles and in fact the only thing that is not the matter with her is tuberculosis and maybe anæmia. It makes some horse owners shudder just to look at her but in Itchky Ironhat's eyes old Em is more beautiful than Seabiscuit.

A guy by the name of Crowbar gives her to Itchky at the Woodbine track in Canada when she is just a two-year-old, rising three. This guy Crowbar buys her as a yearling out of a sale at Saratoga for fifty fish but becomes discouraged about her when he notices that she cannot keep up with a lead pony even when the pony is just walking.

On top of this she bows a tendon, so Crowbar is taking her out to shoot her to save the expense of shipping her and he is pretty sore at having to waste a cartridge on her when he meets up with Itchky Ironhat and Itchky asks what is coming off. When Crowbar explains, Itchky takes a closer look at Em and she gazes at him with such a sorrowful expression that Itchky's heart is touched.

He asks Crowbar to give her to him, although at this time Itchky is just doing the best he can around the tracks and has about as much use for a race horse as he has for a hearse, and naturally Crowbar is pleased to make the saving of a cartridge. So this is how Itchky becomes the owner of old Em and from now on he practically lives with her even after he marries Mousie, which is what starts Mousie to complaining, as it seems she does not care to be excluded from her home life by a horse.

It is no use trying to tell Itchky that Em is nothing but an old buzzard, because he keeps thinking of her as a stake horse and saying she is bound to win a large stake someday and he spends every dime he can get hold of in entering her in big races and on shipping her and feeding her and on jockey fees.

And all this is very surprising to be sure, as Itchky Ironhat is by no means a sucker when it comes to other horses and he makes a pretty good living hustling around the tracks. What is more, the way he can bring old Em back to the races every time she breaks down, which is about every other time she starts in a race, shows that Itchky is either a natural-born horse trainer or a horse hypnotist.

When he is very desperate for a little moolah, he will place Em in a cheap selling race and it is in spots such as this that she occasionally wins. But then Itchky always worries himself sick for fear somebody will claim her, the idea of a claiming race being that another owner can always claim a horse in such a race by putting up the price for which the horse is entered, which may be anywhere from a few hundred dollars on up, according to the conditions of the race and what the owner thinks his horse is worth.

Naturally, Itchky has to run old Em for as cheap a price as horses are ever run for her to win a race, but even then there is really no sense in him worrying about her being claimed as no owner with any brains wants such a lizard as old Em in his barn, and especially after what happens to a character by the name of One Thumb Haverstraw.

This One Thumb is considered quite a joker and one day

in Maryland he claims old Em out of a race for eight hundred boffoes just for a joke on Itchky, although personally I always figure the joke is on One Thumb when he gets her for this price.

Itchky is really greatly dejected over losing old Em and he goes to see One Thumb right after the race and tries to buy her back for two hundred dollars over the claiming price, but One Thumb is so pleased with his joke that he refuses to sell and then the most surprising things begin to occur to him.

A few nights later a ghost in a white sheet appears at his barn and frightens away all the coloured parties who are working for him as stable-hands and turns all of One Thumb's horses out of their stalls except old Em and chases them around the country until they are worn plumb out and are no good for racing for some weeks to come.

What is more, every time One Thumb himself steps into the open at night, a bullet whistles past him and finally one breezes through the seat of his pants and at this he hunts up Itchky Ironhat and returns old Em to him for four hundred less than the claiming price and considers it a great bargain, at that, and nobody ever plays any more jokes on Itchky with old Em.

Now the night of the racing officials' decision, I am sitting in Mindy's restaurant enjoying some choice pot roast with potato pancakes when in comes Itchky Ironhat looking somewhat depressed and, as he takes a seat at my table, naturally I tell him I deeply regret hearing that he will no longer be permitted to run old Em in New York, and Itchky sighs and says:

'Well,' he says, 'it is a great loss to the racing public of this state, but I always wish to do something nice for old Em and this gives me the opportunity of doing it.'

'What will be something nice for her, Itchky?' I say.

'Why,' Itchky says, 'I take her many places the past dozen years, but there is one place I never take her and that is her old home. You see, Em comes from the Bluegrass country of Kentucky and I get to thinking that the nicest thing I can do for her is to take her there and let her see the place where she is born.'

'Itchky,' I say, 'how is the bank roll?'

'It is thin,' Itchky says. 'In fact, if you are thinking of a touch, it is practically invisible.'

'I am not thinking of such a thing,' I say. 'What I am thinking of is it will cost a gob to ship old Em to Kentucky.'

'Oh,' Itchky says, 'I do not intend to ship her. I intend to take her there in person by motor truck and I am wondering if you will not like to go with us for company, Old Em loves company. After we let her see her old home we can drop her in a stake race at Churchill Downs and win a package.'

Then Itchky explains to me that he acquires a truck that very afternoon from a vegetable pedlar for the sum of sixty dollars and that he also gets a couple of wide, strong planks which he figures he can let down from the rear end of the truck like a runway so old Em can walk on them getting on and off the truck and that by driving by day and resting by night he can take her to the Bluegrass of Kentucky this way very nicely.

Now it is coming on time for the Kentucky Derby and if there is one thing I wish to see it is this event, and furthermore I never get around the country much and I figure that such a journey will be most educational to me so I tell Itchky he has a customer. But if I see the truck first I will certainly never think of trying to get anywhere in it, not even to the Polo Grounds.

Of course when Itchky tells me the truck costs him only sixty dollars, I am not looking for a fancy truck, but I have no idea it is going to be older than Henry Ford, or anyway Edsel, and not much bigger than a pushcart and with no top whatever, even over the seat.

The body of the truck is not long enough for old Em to stand in it spraddled out, the way horses love to stand, or her hind legs will be hanging out the rear end, so what Itchky does is to push her front legs back and her hind legs forward, so that all four feet are close together under her like she is standing on a dime.

Personally, I consider this an uncomfortable position all the way around for a horse but when Itchky and I get on the seat and Em finds she can rest her head on Itchky's shoulder, she seems quite happy, especially as Itchky talks to her most of the time.

It is no time after we start that we find old Em makes the truck top-heavy and in fact she almost falls overboard every time we take a curve and Itchky has to choke down to about two miles per hour until all of a sudden Em learns how to lean her weight to one side of the truck or the other on the curves and then Itchky can hit it up to the full speed of the truck, which is about ten miles per hour. I will say one thing for old Em, I never see a brighter horse in my life.

The first time we stop to take her off for the night, we find that the plank runway is all right for loading her because she can run up the boards like a squirrel but they have too much of a pitch for her to walk down them, so finally we drop the tail gate and get hold of the front end of the truck and lift it gently and let her slide down to the ground like she was on a toboggan and I always claim that old Em likes this better than any other part of the trip.

It seems to be a most surprising spectacle to one and all along our route to see a truck going past with a horse leaning this way and that to keep balanced and with forty per cent.

of her sticking out of one end of the truck, and twenty per cent. of her sticking out of the other end, and we often attract many spectators when we stop. This is whenever we have a blow-out, which is every now and then. Sometimes there is much comment among these spectators about old Em and as it is generally comment of an unfavourable nature, I am always having difficulty keeping Itchky from taking pops at spectators.

We sleep at night in the truck with old Em tied to the rear end and we use her spare blankets for covering as Em has more blankets than any other horse in the country and most of them are very fancy blankets, at that. It is not bad sleeping except when it rains and then Itchky takes all the blankets off us and puts them on Em and my overcoat too, and we have to sit up under the truck and the way Itchky worries about Em catching cold is most distressing.

Sometimes when we are rolling along the road and Em is dozing on Itchky's shoulder, he talks to me instead of her, and I ask him if he knows just where to find Em's old home in the Bluegrass country.

'No,' he says, 'I do not know just where, but the record book gives the breeder of Em as the Tucky Farms and it must be a well-known breeding establishment to produce such a horse as Em, so we will have no trouble finding it. By the way,' Itchky says, 'Em comes of a very high-class family. She is by an important stallion by the name of Christofer out of a mare called Love Always, but,' he says, 'the curious thing about it is I am never able to learn of another horse of this breeding in this country, though Christofer is once a good race horse in France.'

Personally, I consider it a great thing for this country that there is only one horse bred like Em but naturally I do not mention such a thought to Itchky Ironhat, not only because

I know it will displease him but because I am afraid old Em may overhear me and be greatly offended.

The road signs state that we are a few miles out of the city of Lexington, Ky., and we know we are now down in the Bluegrass country, when we come upon a tall old guy leaning against a fence in front of a cute little white house. This old guy looks as if he may be a native of these parts as he is wearing a wide-brimmed soft hat and is chewing on a straw, so Itchky stops the truck and puts on a Southern accent and speaks to him as follows:

'Suh,' Itchky says, 'can you all direct me to a place called the Tucky Farms, suh?'

The tall old guy gazes at Itchky and then he gazes at me and finally he gazes at old Em and he never stops chewing on the straw and after a while he smiles and points and says:

'It is about three miles up that road,' he says. 'It is a big red brick house with some burned-down barns in the background, but friend,' he says, 'let me give you a piece of good advice. I do not know what your business is, but keep away from that place with anything that looks like a horse. Although,' he says, 'I am not sure that the object you have on your truck answers such a description.'

Of course Itchky can see from this crack that the old guy is making fun of Em and he starts to sizzle all over and forgets his Southern accent at once and says:

'You do not like my horse?'

'Oh, it is a horse then?' the old guy says. 'Well, the party who owns Tucky Farms is a trifle eccentric about horses. In fact, he is eccentric about everything, but horses most of all. He does not permit them on his premises. It is a sad case. You may meet a disagreeable reception if you go there with your so-called horse.'

Then he turns and walks into the cute little white house

and I have all I can do to keep Itchky from going after him
and reprimanding him for speaking so disrespectfully of old
Em, especially as the old guy keeps looking around at us and
we can see that he is smiling more than somewhat.

Itchky drives on up the road a little ways and, just as the
old guy says, we come upon a big red brick house and there
is no doubt that this is the Tucky Farms because there is a
faded sign over an arched gateway that so states. The house
is all shuttered up and is on a small hill pretty well back from
the road and not far from the house are the remainders of
some buildings that look as if they burned down a long time
ago and are never fixed up again or cleared away.

In fact, the grounds and the house itself all look as if they
can stand a little attention and there is not a soul in sight and
it is rather a dismal scene in every respect. The gate is closed,
so I get down off the truck and open it and Itchky drives the
truck in and right up to the front door of the house under a
sort of porch with white pillars.

Now the truck makes a terrible racket and this racket
seems to stir up a number of coloured parties who appear
from around in back of the house, along with a large white
guy. This large guy is wearing corduroy pants and laced boots
and a black moustache and he is also carrying a double-
barrelled shotgun and he speaks to Itchky in a fierce tone of
voice as follows:

'Pigface,' he says, 'get out of here. Get out of here before
you are hurt. What do you mean by driving in here with a
load of dog meat such as this, anyway?'

He points a finger at old Em who has her head up and is
snuffling the air and gazing about her with great interest, and
right away Itchky climbs down off the seat of the truck and
removes his derby and places it on the ground and takes off
his coat and starts rolling up his sleeves.

'It is the last straw,' Itchky Ironhat says. 'I will first make this big ash can eat that cannon he is lugging and then I will beat his skull in. Nobody can refer to Emaleen as dog meat and live.'

Now the front door of the house opens and out comes a thin character in a soiled white linen suit and at first he seems to be quite an old character as he has long white hair but when he gets closer I can see that he is not so very old at that, but he is very seedy-looking and his eyes have a loose expression. I can also see from the way the large guy and the coloured parties step back that this is a character who packs some weight around here. His voice is low and hard as he speaks to Itchky Ironhat and says:

'What is this?' he says. 'What name do I just hear you pronounce?'

'Emaleen,' Itchky says. 'It is the name of my race mare which you see before you. She is the greatest race mare in the world. The turf records say she is bred right here at this place and I bring her down here to see her old home, and everybody insults her. So this is Southern hospitality?' Itchky says.

The new character steps up to the truck and looks at old Em for quite a spell and all the time he is shaking his head and his lips are moving as if he is talking to himself, and finally he says to the large guy:

'Unload her,' he says. 'Unload her and take good care of her, Dobkins. I suppose you will have to send to one of the neighbours for some feed. Come in gentlemen,' he says to Itchky and me and he holds the front door of the house open. 'My name is Salsbury,' he says. 'I am the owner of Tucky Farms and I apologize for my foreman's behaviour but he is only following orders.'

As we go into the house I can see that it is a very large house and I can also see that it must once be a very grand house because of the way it is furnished, but everything seems to be as run-down inside as it does outside and I can see that what this house needs is a good cleaning and straightening out.

In the meantime, Mr Salsbury keeps asking Itchky Ironhat questions about old Em and when he hears how long Itchky has her and what he thinks of her and all this and that, he starts wiping his eyes with a handkerchief as if the story makes him very sad, especially the part about why Itchky brings her to the Bluegrass.

Finally, Mr Salsbury leads us into a large room that seems to be a library and at one end of this room there is a painting taller than I am of a very beautiful Judy in a white dress and this is the only thing in the house that seems to be kept dusted up a little and Mr Salsbury points to the painting and says:

'My wife, Emaleen, gentlemen. I name the horse you bring here after her long ago, because it is the first foal of her favourite mare and the first foal of a stallion I import from France.'

'By Christofer, out of Love Always,' Itchky Ironhat says.

'Yes,' Mr Salsbury says. 'In those days, Tucky Farms is one of the great breeding and racing establishments of the Bluegrass. In those days, too, my wife is known far and wide for her fondness for horses and her kindness to them. She is the head of the humane society in Kentucky and the Emaleen Salsbury annual award of a thousand dollars for the kindest deed towards a horse brought to the attention of the society each year is famous.

'One night,' Mr Salsbury continues, 'there is a fire in the barns and my wife gets out of bed and before anyone can stop her she rushes into the flames trying to save her beautiful mare, Love Always. They both perish, and,' he says, 'with them perishes the greatest happiness ever given a mortal on this earth.'

By this time, Itchky Ironhat and I are feeling very sad, indeed, and in fact all the creases in Itchky's face are full of tears as Mr Salsbury goes on to state that the only horses on the place that are saved are a few yearlings running in the pastures. He sends them all with a shipment a neighbour is taking to Saratoga to be disposed of there for whatever they will bring.

'Your mare Emaleen is one of those,' he says. 'I forget all about her at the time. Indeed,' he says, 'I forget everything but my unhappiness. I feel I never wish to see or hear of a horse again as long as I live and I withdraw myself completely from the world and all my former activities. But,' he says, 'your bringing the mare here awakens old fond memories and your story of how you cherish her makes me realize that this is exactly what my wife Emaleen will wish me to do. I see where I sadly neglect my duty to her memory. Why,' he says, 'I never even keep up the Emaleen Salsbury award.'

Now he insists that we must remain there a while as his guests and Itchky Ironhat agrees, although I point out that it will be more sensible for us to move on to Louisville and get into action as quickly as possible because we are now practically out of funds. But Itchky takes a look at old Em and he says she is enjoying herself so much running around her old home and devouring grass that it will be a sin and a shame to take her away before it is absolutely necessary.

After a couple of days, I tell Itchky that I think absolutely necessary arrives, but Itchky says Mr Salsbury now wishes to give a dinner in honour of old Em and he will not think of denying her this pleasure. And for the next week the house is overrun with coloured parties, male and female, cleaning up the house and painting and cooking and dusting and I do not know what all else, and furthermore I hear there is a great to-do all through the Bluegrass country when the invitations to the dinner start going around, because this is the first time in over a dozen years that Mr Salsbury has any truck whatever with his neighbours.

On the night of the dinner, one of the male coloured parties tells me that he never before sees such a gathering of the high-toned citizens of the Bluegrass as are assembled in a big dining-hall at a horse-shoe shaped table with an orchestra going and with flowers and flags and racing colours all around and about. In fact, the coloured party says it is just like the old days at Tucky Farms when Mr Salsbury's wife is alive, although he says he does not remember ever seeing such a character sitting alongside Mr Salsbury at the table as Itchky Ironhat.

To tell the truth, Itchky Ironhat seems to puzzle all the guests no little and it is plain to be seen that they are wondering who he is and why he is present, though Itchky is sharpened up with a fresh shave and has on a clean shirt and of course he is not wearing his derby hat. Personally, I am rather proud of Itchky's appearance, but I can see that he seems to be overplaying his knife a little, especially against the mashed potatoes.

Mr Salsbury is dressed in a white dinner jacket and his eyes are quiet and his hair is trimmed and his manner is most genteel in every way and when the guests are seated he gets to his feet and attracts their attention by tapping on a wine-glass with a spoon. Then he speaks to them as follows:

'Friends and neighbours,' he says. 'I know you are all surprised at being invited here but you may be more surprised when you learn the reason. As most of you are aware, I am as one dead for years. Now I live again. I am going to restore Tucky Farms to all its old turf glory in breeding and racing, and,' he says, 'I am going to re-establish the Emaleen Salsbury award, with which you are familiar, and carry on again in every way as I am now certain my late beloved wife will wish.'

Then he tells them the story of old Em and how Itchky Ironhat cares for her and loves her all these years and how he brings her to the Bluegrass just to see her old home, but of course he does not tell them that Itchky also plans to later drop her in a race at Churchill Downs, as it seems Itchky never mentions the matter to him.

Anyway, Mr Salsbury says that the return of old Em awakens him as if from a bad dream and he can suddenly see how he is not doing right with respect to his wife's memory and while he is talking a tall old guy who is sitting next to me, and who turns out to be nobody but the guy who directs us to Tucky Farms, says to me like this:

'It is a miracle,' he says. 'I am his personal physician and I give him up long ago as a hopeless victim of melancholia. In fact, I am always expecting to hear of him dismissing himself from this world entirely. Well,' the old guy says, 'I always say medical science is not everything.'

'My first step towards restoring Tucky Farms,' Mr Salsbury goes on, 'is to purchase the old mare Emaleen from Mr Itchky Ironhat here for the sum of three thousand dollars, which we agree upon this evening as a fair price. I will retire her of course for the rest of her days, which I hope will be many.'

With this he whips out a cheque and hands it to Itchky and naturally I am somewhat surprised at the sum mentioned because I figure if old Em is worth three G's War Admiral must be worth a jillion. However, I am also greatly pleased because I can see where Itchky and I will have a nice taw for the races at Churchill Downs without having to bother about old Em winning one.

'Now,' Mr Salsbury says, 'for our guest of honour.'

Then two big doors at one end of the banquet hall open wide and there seems to be a little confusion outside and a snorting and a stamping as if a herd of wild horses is coming in and all of a sudden who appears in the doorway with her mane and tail braided with ribbons and her coat all slicked up but old Em and who is leading her in but the large guy who insults her and also Itchky on our arrival at Tucky Farms.

The guests begin applauding and the orchestra plays My Old Kentucky Home and it is a pleasant scene to be sure, but old Em seems quite unhappy about something as the large guy pulls her into the hollow of the horseshoe-shaped table, and the next thing anybody knows, Itchky Ironhat climbs over the table, knocking glasses and dishes every which way and flattens the large guy with a neat left hook in the presence of the best people of the Bluegrass country.

Naturally, this incident causes some comment and many of the guests are slightly shocked and there is considerable criticism of Itchky Ironhat for his lack of table manners. But then it is agreed by one and all present that Itchky is undoubtedly entitled to the Emaleen Salsbury kindness to horses award when I explain that what irks him is the fact that the large guy leads old Em in with a twitch on her lip.

Well, this is about all there is to the story, except that Itchky and I go over to the Louisville the next day and remain there awaiting the Kentucky Derby and we have a wonderful time, to be sure, except that we do not seem to be able to win any bets on the horse races at Churchill Downs.

In fact, the day before the Derby, Itchky remarks that the bank roll is now lower than a turtle's vest buttons and when I express surprise that we toss off four G's in such a short period, Itchky says to me like this:

'Oh,' he says, 'it is not four G's. I send the Emaleen

Salsbury kindness-to-horses award of one G to Mousie. I figure she is legally entitled to this for leaving me with Em. Otherwise, we will never get even the three and besides,' Itchky says, 'I love Mousie. In fact, I invite her to join me here and she agrees to come after I promise I will never as much as think of old Em again.

'By the way,' Itchky says, 'I call up Tucky Farms this morning and Mr Salsbury brings old Em into his study and lets her hear my voice over the phone. Mr Salsbury says she is greatly pleased. I give her your love, but of course not as much of yours as I give her of mine,' he says.

'Thanks, Itchky,' I say, and at this moment I am somewhat surprised to notice a metal ash tray removing Itchky's derby hat from his head and, gazing about, who do I observe standing in the doorway and now taking dead aim at Itchky with another tray but his ever-loving wife, Mousie.

ARTHUR CONAN DOYLE

SILVER BLAZE

'I AM AFRAID, Watson, that I shall have to go,' said Holmes, as we sat down together to our breakfast one morning.

'Go! Where to?'

'To Dartmoor – to King's Pyland.'

I was not surprised. Indeed, my only wonder was that he had not already been mixed up in this extraordinary case, which was the one topic of conversation through the length and breadth of England. For a whole day my companion had rambled about the room with his chin upon his chest and his brows knitted, charging and re-charging his pipe with the strongest black tobacco, and absolutely deaf to any of my questions or remarks. Fresh editions of every paper had been sent up by our newsagent only to be glanced over and tossed down into a corner. Yet, silent as he was, I knew perfectly well what it was, over which he was brooding. There was but one problem before the public which could challenge his powers of analysis, and that was the singular disappearance of the favourite for the Wessex Cup and the tragic murder of its trainer. When, therefore, he suddenly announced his intention of setting out for the scene of the drama, it was only what I had both expected and hoped for.

'I should be most happy to go down with you if I should not be in the way,' said I.

'My dear Watson, you would confer a great favour upon me by coming. And I think that your time will not be mis-spent, for there are points about this case which promise to make it an absolutely unique one. We have, I think, just time to catch our train at Paddington, and I will go further into the matter upon our journey. You would oblige me by bringing with you your very excellent field-glass.'

And so it happened that an hour or so later I found myself in the corner of a first-class carriage, flying along, en route for Exeter, while Sherlock Holmes, with his sharp, eager face framed in his earflapped travelling cap, dipped rapidly into the bundle of fresh papers which he had procured at Paddington. We had left Reading far behind us before he thrust the last of them under the seat, and offered me his cigar case.

'We are going well,' said he, looking out of the window, and glancing at his watch. 'Our rate at present is fifty-three and a half miles an hour.'

'I have not observed the quarter-mile posts,' said I.

'Nor have I. But the telegraph posts upon the line are sixty yards apart, and the calculation is a simple one. I presume that you have already looked into this matter of the murder of John Straker and the disappearance of Silver Blaze?'

'I have seen what the *Telegraph* and the *Chronicle* have to say.'

'It is one of those cases where the art of the reasoner should be used rather for the sifting of details than for the acquiring of fresh evidence. The tragedy has been so uncommon, so complete, and of such personal importance to so many people that we are suffering from a plethora of surmise, conjecture, and hypothesis. The difficulty is to detach the framework of fact – of absolute, undeniable fact – from the embellishments of theorists and reporters. Then, having established ourselves upon this sound basis, it is our duty to see what inferences may be drawn, and which are the special points upon which the whole mystery turns. On Tuesday evening I received telegrams, both from Colonel Ross, the owner of the horse, and from Inspector Gregory, who is looking after the case, inviting my co-operation.'

'Tuesday evening!' I exclaimed. 'And this is Thursday morning. Why did you not go down yesterday?'

'Because I made a blunder, my dear Watson – which is, I am afraid, a more common occurrence than anyone would think who only knew me through your memoirs. The fact is that I could not believe it possible that the most remarkable horse in England could long remain concealed, especially in so sparsely inhabited a place as the north of Dartmoor. From hour to hour yesterday I expected to hear that he had been found, and that his abductor was the murderer of John Straker. When, however, another morning had come and I found that, beyond the arrest of young Fitzroy Simpson, nothing had been done, I felt that it was time for me to take action. Yet in some ways I feel that yesterday has not been wasted.'

'You have formed a theory then?'

'At least I have got a grip of the essential facts of the case. I shall enumerate them to you, for nothing clears up a case so much as stating it to another person, and I can hardly expect your co-operation if I do not show you the position from which we start.'

I lay back against the cushions, puffing at my cigar, while Holmes, leaning forward, with his long thin forefinger checking off the points upon the palm of his left hand, gave me a sketch of the events which had led to our journey.

'Silver Blaze,' said he, 'is from the Isonomy stock, and holds as brilliant a record as his famous ancestor. He is now in his fifth year, and has brought in turn each of the prizes of the turf to Colonel Ross, his fortunate owner. Up to the time of the catastrophe he was first favourite for the Wessex Cup, the betting being three to one on. He has always, however, been a prime favourite with the racing public, and has never yet disappointed them, so that even at those odds enormous sums of money have been laid upon him. It is obvious, therefore, that there were many people who had the strongest interest in preventing Silver Blaze from being there at the fall of the flag, next Tuesday.

'This fact was, of course, appreciated at King's Pyland, where the Colonel's training stable is situated. Every precaution was taken to guard the favourite. The trainer, John Straker, is a retired jockey, who rode in Colonel Ross's colours before he became too heavy for the weighing chair. He has served the Colonel for five years as jockey, and for seven as trainer, and has always shown himself to be a zealous and honest servant. Under him were three lads, for the establishment was a small one, containing only four horses in all. One of these lads sat up each night in the stable, while the others slept in the loft. All three bore excellent characters. John Straker, who is a married man, lived in a small villa about two hundred yards from the stables. He has no children, keeps one maid-servant, and is comfortably off. The country round is very lonely, but about half a mile to the north there is a small cluster of villas which have been built by a Tavistock contractor for the use of invalids and others who may wish to enjoy the pure Dartmoor air. Tavistock itself lies two miles to the west, while across the moor, also about two miles distant, is the larger training establishment of Mapleton, which belongs to Lord Backwater, and is managed by Silas Brown. In every other direction the moor is a complete wilderness, inhabited only by a few roaming gipsies. Such was the general situation last Monday night when the catastrophe occurred.

'On that evening the horses had been exercised and watered as usual, and the stables were locked up at nine o'clock. Two of the lads walked up to the trainer's house, where they had supper in the kitchen, while the third, Ned Hunter, remained on guard. At a few minutes after nine the maid, Edith Baxter, carried down to the stables his supper, which consisted of a dish of curried mutton. She took no liquid, as there was a water-tap in the stables, and it was the rule that the lad on duty should drink nothing else. The maid carried a lantern with her, as it was very dark, and the path ran across the open moor.

'Edith Baxter was within thirty yards of the stables when a man appeared out of the darkness and called to her to stop. As he stepped into the circle of yellow light thrown by the lantern she saw that he was a person of gentlemanly bearing, dressed in a grey suit of tweed with a cloth cap. He wore gaiters, and carried a heavy stick with a knob to it. She was most impressed, however, by the extreme pallor of his face and by the nervousness of his manner. His age, she thought, would be rather over thirty than under it.

' "Can you tell me where I am?" he asked. "I had almost made up my mind to sleep on the moor when I saw the light of your lantern."

' "You are close to the King's Pyland training stables," she said.

' "Oh, indeed! What a stroke of luck!" he cried. "I understand that a stable-boy sleeps there alone every night. Perhaps that is his supper which you are carrying to him. Now I am sure that you would not be too proud to earn the price of a new dress, would you?" He took a piece of white paper folded up out of his waistcoat pocket. "See that the boy has this tonight, and you shall have the prettiest frock that money can buy."

'She was frightened by the earnestness of his manner, and ran past him to the window through which she was accustomed to hand the meals. It was already open, and Hunter was seated at the small table inside. She had begun to tell him of what had happened, when the stranger came up again.

' "Good evening," said he, looking through the window, "I wanted to have a word with you." The girl has sworn that as he spoke she noticed the corner of the little paper packet protruding from his closed hand.

' "What business have you here?" asked the lad.

' "It's business that may put something into your pocket," said the other. "You've two horses in for the Wessex Cup – Silver Blaze and Bayard. Let me have the straight tip, and you won't be a loser. Is it a fact that at the weights Bayard could give the other a hundred yards in five furlongs, and that the stable have put their money on him?"

' "So you're one of those damned touts," cried the lad. "I'll show you how we serve them in King's Pyland." He sprang up and rushed across the stable to unloose the dog. The girl fled away to the house, but as she ran she looked back, and saw that the stranger was leaning through the window. A minute later, however, when Hunter rushed out with the hound he was gone, and though the lad ran all round the buildings he failed to find any trace of him.'

'One moment!' I asked. 'Did the stable-boy, when he ran out with the dog, leave the door unlocked behind him?'

'Excellent, Watson; excellent!' murmured my companion. 'The importance of the point struck me so forcibly, that I sent a special wire to Dartmoor yesterday to clear the matter up. The boy locked the door before he left it. The window, I may add, was not large enough for a man to get through.

'Hunter waited until his fellow grooms had returned when he sent a message up to the trainer and told him what had occurred. Straker was excited at hearing the account, although he does not seem to have quite realized its true significance. It left him, however, vaguely uneasy, and Mrs Straker, waking at one in the morning, found that he was dressing. In reply to her inquiries, he said that he could not sleep on account of his anxiety about the horses, and that he intended to walk down to the stables to see that all was well. She begged him to remain at home, as she could hear the rain pattering against the windows, but in spite of her entreaties he pulled on his large mackintosh and left the house.

'Mrs Straker awoke at seven in the morning, to find that her husband had not returned. She dressed herself hastily, called the maid, and set off for the stables. The door was open; inside, huddled together upon a chair, Hunter was sunk in a state of absolute stupor, the favourite's stall was empty, and there were no signs of his trainer.

'The two lads who slept in the chaff-cutting loft above the harness-room were quickly aroused. They had heard nothing during the night, for they are both sound sleepers. Hunter was obviously under the influence of some powerful drug; and, as no sense could be got out of him, he was left to sleep it off while the two lads and the two women ran out in search of the absentees. They still had hopes that the trainer had for some reason taken out the horse for early exercise, but on ascending the knoll near the house, from which all the neighbouring moors were visible, they not only could see no signs of the favourite, but they perceived something which warned them that they were in the presence of a tragedy.

'About a quarter of a mile from the stables, John Straker's overcoat was flapping from a furze bush. Immediately beyond there was a bowl-shaped depression in the moor, and at the bottom of this was found the dead body of the unfortunate trainer. His head had been shattered by a savage blow from some heavy weapon, and he was wounded in the thigh, where there was a long, clean cut, inflicted evidently by some very sharp instrument. It was clear, however, that Straker had defended himself vigorously against his assailants, for in his right hand he held a small knife, which was clotted with blood up to the handle, while in his left he grasped a red and black silk cravat, which was recognized by the maid as having been worn on the preceding evening by the stranger who had visited the stables.

'Hunter, on recovering from his stupor, was also quite positive as to the ownership of the cravat. He was equally certain that the same stranger had, while standing at the window, drugged his curried mutton, and so deprived the stables of their watchman.

'As to the missing horse, there were abundant proofs in the mud which lay at the bottom of the fatal hollow, that he had been there at the time of the struggle. But from that morning he has disappeared; and although a large reward has been offered, and all the gipsies of Dartmoor are on the alert, no news has come of him. Finally an analysis has shown that the remains of his supper, left by the stable-lad, contain an appreciable quantity of powdered opium, while the people at the house partook of the same dish on the same night without any ill effect.

'Those are the main facts of the case, stripped of all surmise and stated as baldly as possible. I shall now recapitulate what the police have done in the matter.

'Inspector Gregory, to whom the case has been committed, is an extremely competent officer. Were he but gifted with imagination he might rise to great heights in his profession. On his arrival he promptly found and arrested the man upon whom suspicion naturally rested. There was little difficulty in finding him, for he inhabited one of those villas which I have mentioned. His name, it appears, was Fitzroy Simpson. He was a man of excellent birth and education, who had squandered a fortune upon the turf, and who lived now by doing a little quiet and genteel bookmaking in the sporting clubs of London. An examination of his betting-book shows that bets to the amount of five thousand pounds had been registered by him against the favourite.

'On being arrested he volunteered the statement that he had come down to Dartmoor in the hope of getting some information about the King's Pyland horses, and also about Desborough, the second favourite, which was in charge of Silas Brown, at the Mapleton stables. He did not attempt to deny that he had acted as described upon the evening before, but declared that he had no sinister designs, and had simply wished to obtain first-hand information. When confronted with his cravat he turned very pale, and was utterly unable to account for its presence in the hand of the murdered man. His wet clothing showed that he had been out in the storm of the night before, and his stick, which was a Penang lawyer, weighted with lead, was just such a weapon as might, by repeated blows, have inflicted the terrible injuries to which the trainer had succumbed.

'On the other hand, there was no wound upon his person, while the state of Straker's knife would show that one, at least, of his assailants must bear his mark upon him. There you have it all in a nutshell, Watson, and if you can give me any light I shall be infinitely obliged to you.'

I had listened with the greatest interest to the statement which Holmes, with characteristic clearness, had laid before me. Though most of the facts were familiar to me, I had not sufficiently appreciated their relative importance, nor their connection to each other.

'Is it not possible,' I suggested, 'that the incised wound

upon Straker may have been caused by his own knife in the convulsive struggles which follow any brain injury?'

'It is more than possible; it is probable,' said Holmes. 'In that case, one of the main points in favour of the accused disappears.'

'And yet,' said I, 'even now I fail to understand what the theory of the police can be.'

'I am afraid that whatever theory we state has very grave objections to it,' returned my companion. 'The police imagine, I take it, that this Fitzroy Simpson, having drugged the lad, and having in some way obtained a duplicated key, opened the stable door, and took out the horse, with the intention, apparently, of kidnapping him altogether. His bridle is missing, so that Simpson must have put this on. Then, having left the door open behind him, he was leading the horse away over the moor, when he was either met or overtaken by the trainer. A row naturally ensued, Simpson beat out the trainer's brains with his heavy stick without receiving any injury from the small knife which Straker used in self-defence, and then the thief either led the horse on to some secret hiding-place, or else it may have bolted during the struggle, and be now wandering out on the moors. That is the case as it appears to the police, and improbable as it is, all other explanations are more improbable still. However, I shall very quickly test the matter when I am once upon the spot, and until then I really cannot see how we can get much further than our present position.'

It was evening before we reached the little town of Tavistock, which lies, like the boss of a shield, in the middle of the huge circle of Dartmoor. Two gentlemen were awaiting us at the station; the one a tall fair man with lion-like hair and beard, and curiously penetrating light blue eyes, the other a small alert person, very neat and dapper, in a frock-coat and gaiters, with trim little side-whiskers and an eye-glass. The latter was Colonel Ross, the well-known sportsman, the other Inspector Gregory, a man who was rapidly making his name in the English detective service.

'I am delighted that you have come down, Mr Holmes,' said the Colonel. 'The Inspector here has done all that could possibly be suggested; but I wish to leave no stone unturned in trying to avenge poor Straker, and in recovering my horse.'

'Have there been any fresh developments?' asked Holmes.

'I am sorry to say that we have made very little progress,' said the Inspector. 'We have an open carriage outside, and as you would no doubt like to see the place before the light fails, we might talk it over as we drive.'

A minute later we were all seated in a comfortable landau and were rattling through the quaint old Devonshire town. Inspector Gregory was full of his case, and poured out a stream of remarks, while Holmes threw in an occasional question or interjection. Colonel Ross leaned back with his arms folded and his hat tilted over his eyes, while I listened with interest to the dialogue of the two detectives. Gregory was formulating his theory, which was almost exactly what Holmes had foretold in the train.

'The net is drawn pretty close round Fitzroy Simpson,' he remarked, 'and I believe myself that he is our man. At the same time, I recognize that the evidence is purely circum-stantial, and that some new development may upset it.'

'How about Straker's knife?'

'We have quite come to the conclusion that he wounded himself in his fall.'

'My friend Dr Watson made that suggestion to me as we came down. If so, it would tell against this man Simpson.'

'Undoubtedly. He has neither a knife nor any sign of a wound. The evidence against him is certainly very strong.

He had a great interest in the disappearance of the favourite, he lies under the suspicion of having poisoned the stable-boy, he was undoubtedly out in the storm, he was armed with a heavy stick, and his cravat was found in the dead man's hand. I really think we have enough to go before a jury.'

Holmes shook his head. 'A clever counsel would tear it all to rags,' said he. 'Why should he take the horse out of the stable? If he wished to injure it, why could he not do it there? Has a duplicate key been found in his possession? What chemist sold him the powdered opium? Above all, where could he, a stranger to the district, hide a horse, and such a horse as this? What is his own explanation as to the paper which he wished the maid to give to the stable-boy?'

'He says that it was a ten-pound note. One was found in his purse. But your other difficulties are not so formidable as they seem. He is not a stranger to the district. He has twice lodged at Tavistock in the summer. The opium was probably brought from London. The key, having served its purpose, would be hurled away. The horse may lie at the bottom of one of the pits or old mines upon the moor.'

'What does he say about the cravat?'

'He acknowledges that it is his, and declares that he had lost it. But a new element has been introduced into the case which may account for his leading the horse from the stable.'

Holmes pricked up his ears.

'We have found traces which show that a party of gipsies encamped on Monday night within a mile of the spot where the murder took place. On Tuesday they were gone. Now, presuming that there was some understanding between Simpson and these gipsies, might he not have been leading the horse to them when he was overtaken, and may they not have him now?'

'It is certainly possible.'

'The moor is being scoured for these gipsies. I have also examined every stable and outhouse in Tavistock, and for a radius of ten miles.'

'There is another training stable quite close, I understand?'

'Yes, and that is a factor which we must certainly not neglect. As Desborough, their horse, was second in the betting, they had an interest in the disappearance of the favourite. Silas Brown, the trainer, is known to have had large bets upon the event, and he was no friend to poor Straker. We have, however, examined the stables, and there is nothing to connect him with the affair.'

'And nothing to connect this man Simpson with the interests of the Mapleton stables?'

'Nothing at all.'

Holmes leaned back in the carriage and the conversation ceased. A few minutes later our driver pulled up at a neat little red-brick villa with overhanging eaves, which stood by the road. Some distance off, across a paddock, lay a long grey-tiled outbuilding. In every other direction the low curves of the moor, bronze-coloured from the fading ferns, stretched away to the sky-line, broken only by the steeples of Tavistock, and by a cluster of houses away to the westward, which marked the Mapleton stables. We all sprang out with the exception of Holmes, who continued to lean back with his eyes fixed upon the sky in front of him, entirely absorbed in his own thoughts. It was only when I touched his arm that he roused himself with a violent start and stepped out of the carriage.

'Excuse me,' said he, turning to Colonel Ross, who had looked at him in some surprise. 'I was daydreaming.' There was a gleam in his eyes and a suppressed excitement in his manner which convinced me, used as I was to his ways, that his hand was upon a clue, though I could not imagine where he had found it.

'Perhaps you would prefer at once to go on to the scene of the crime, Mr Holmes?' said Gregory.

'I think that I should prefer to stay here a little and go into one or two questions of detail. Straker was brought back here, I presume?'

'Yes, he lies upstairs. The inquest is tomorrow.'

'He has been in your service some years, Colonel Ross?'

'I have always found him an excellent servant.'

'I presume that you made an inventory of what he had in his pockets at the time of his death, Inspector?'

'I have the things themselves in the sitting-room if you would care to see them.'

'I should be very glad.'

We all filed into the front room and sat round the central table, while the Inspector unlocked a square tin box and laid a small heap of things before us. There was a box of vestas, two inches of tallow candle, an A.D.P. briar-root pipe, a pouch of sealskin with half an ounce of long-cut Cavendish, a silver watch with a gold chain, five sovereigns in gold, an aluminium pencil-case, a few papers, and an ivory-handled knife with a very delicate inflexible blade marked Weiss and Co., London.

'This is a very singular knife,' said Holmes, lifting it up and examining it minutely. 'I presume, as I see bloodstains upon it, that it is the one which was found in the dead man's grasp. Watson, this knife is surely in your line.'

'It is what we call a cataract knife,' said I.

'I thought so. A very delicate blade devised for very delicate work. A strange thing for a man to carry with him upon a rough expedition, especially as it would not shut in his pocket.'

'The tip was guarded by a disc of cork which we found beside his body,' said the Inspector. 'His wife tells us that the knife had lain for some days upon the dressing-table, and that he had picked it up as he left the room. It was a poor weapon, but perhaps the best that he could lay his hand on at the moment.'

'Very possibly. How about these papers?'

'Three of them are receipted hay-dealers' accounts. One of them is a letter of instructions from Colonel Ross. This other is a milliner's account for thirty-seven pounds fifteen, made out by Madame Lesurier, of Bond Street, to William Darbyshire. Mrs Straker tells us that Darbyshire was a friend of her husband's, and that occasionally his letters were addressed here.'

'Madame Darbyshire had somewhat expensive tastes,' remarked Holmes, glancing down the account. 'Twenty-two guineas is rather heavy for a single costume. However, there appears to be nothing more to learn, and we may now go down to the scene of the crime.'

As we emerged from the sitting-room a woman who had been waiting in the passage took a step forward and laid her hand upon the Inspector's sleeve. Her face was haggard, and thin, and eager; stamped with the print of a recent horror.

'Have you got them? Have you found them?' she panted.

'No, Mrs Straker; but Mr Holmes, here, has come from London to help us, and we shall do all that is possible.'

'Surely I met you in Plymouth, at a garden party, some little time ago, Mrs Straker,' said Holmes.

'No, sir; you are mistaken.'

'Dear me; why, I could have sworn to it. You wore a costume of dove-coloured silk, with ostrich feather trimming.'

'I never had such a dress, sir,' answered the lady.

'Ah; that quite settles it,' said Holmes: and, with an apology, he followed the Inspector outside. A short walk across the moor took us to the hollow in which the body had been found. At the brink of it was the furze bush upon which the coat had been hung.

'There was no wind that night, I understand,' said Holmes.

'None, but very heavy rain.'

'In that case the overcoat was not blown against the furze bushes, but placed there.'

'Yes, it was laid across the bush.'

'You fill me with interest. I perceive that the ground has been trampled up a good deal. No doubt many feet have been there since Monday night.'

'A piece of matting has been laid here at the side, and we have all stood upon that.'

'Excellent.'

'In this bag I have one of the boots which Straker wore, one of Fitzroy Simpson's shoes, and a cast horseshoe of Silver Blaze.'

'My dear Inspector, you surpass yourself!' Holmes took the bag, and descending into the hollow he pushed the matting into a more central position. Then stretching himself upon his face and leaning his chin upon his hands he made a careful study of the trampled mud in front of him.

'Halloa!' said he, suddenly, 'what's this?'

It was a wax vesta, half burned, which was so coated with mud that it looked at first like a little chip of wood.

'I cannot think how I came to overlook it,' said the Inspector, with an expression of annoyance.

'It was invisible, buried in the mud. I only saw it because I was looking for it.'

'What! You expected to find it?'

'I thought it not unlikely.' He took the boots from the bag and compared the impressions of each of them with marks upon the ground. Then he clambered up to the rim of the hollow and crawled about among the ferns and bushes.

'I am afraid that there are no more tracks,' said the Inspector. 'I have examined the ground very carefully for a hundred yards in each direction.'

'Indeed!' said Holmes, rising, 'I should not have the impertinence to do it again after what you say. But I should like to take a little walk over the moor before it grows dark, that I may know my ground tomorrow, and I think that I shall put this horseshoe into my pocket for luck.'

Colonel Ross, who had shown some signs of impatience at my companion's quiet and systematic method of work, glanced at his watch.

'I wish you would come back with me, Inspector,' said he. 'There are several points on which I should like your advice, and especially as to whether we do not owe it to the public to remove our horse's name from the entries for the Cup.'

'Certainly not,' cried Holmes, with decision: 'I should let the name stand.'

The Colonel bowed. 'I am very glad to have had your opinion, sir,' said he. 'You will find us at poor Straker's house when you have finished your walk, and we can drive together into Tavistock.'

He turned back with the Inspector, while Holmes and I walked slowly across the moor. The sun was beginning to sink behind the stables of Mapleton, and the long sloping plain in front of us was tinged with gold, deepening into rich, ruddy brown where the faded ferns and brambles caught the evening light. But the glories of the landscape were all wasted upon my companion, who was sunk in the deepest thought.

'It's this way, Watson,' he said at last. 'We may leave the

question of who killed John Straker for the instant, and confine ourselves to finding out what has become of the horse. Now, supposing that he broke away during or after the tragedy, where could he have gone to? The horse is a very gregarious creature. If left to himself his instincts would have been either to return to King's Pyland, or go over to Mapleton. Why should he run wild upon the moor? He would surely have been seen by now. And why should gipsies kidnap him? These people always clear out when they hear of trouble, for they do not wish to be pestered by the police. They could not hope to sell such a horse. They would run a great risk and gain nothing by taking him. Surely that is clear.'

'Where is he, then?'

'I have already said that he must have gone to King's Pyland or to Mapleton. He is not at King's Pyland, therefore he is at Mapleton. Let us take that as a working hypothesis and see what it leads us to. This part of the moor, as the Inspector remarked, is very hard and dry. But it falls away towards Mapleton, and you can see from here that there is a long hollow over yonder, which must have been very wet on Monday night. If our supposition is correct, then the horse must have crossed that, and there is the point where we should look for his tracks.'

We had been walking briskly during this conversation, and a few more minutes brought us to the hollow in question. At Holmes' request I walked down the bank to the right and he to the left, but I had not taken fifty paces before I heard him give a shout, and saw him waving his hand to me. The track of a horse was plainly outlined in the soft earth in front of him, and the shoe which he took from his pocket exactly fitted the impression.

'See the value of imagination,' said Holmes. 'It is the one quality which Gregory lacks. We imagined what might have happened, acted upon the supposition, and find ourselves justified. Let us proceed.'

We crossed the marshy bottom and passed over a quarter of a mile of dry, hard turf. Again the ground sloped and again we came on the tracks. Then we lost them for half a mile, but only to pick them up once more quite close to Mapleton. It was Holmes who saw them first, and he stood pointing with a look of triumph upon his face. A man's track was visible beside the horse's.

'The horse was alone before,' I cried.

'Quite so. It was alone before. Halloa, what is this?'

The double track turned sharp off and took the direction of King's Pyland. Holmes whistled, and we both followed along after it. His eyes were on the trail, but I happened to look a little to one side, and saw to my surprise the same tracks coming back again in the opposite direction.

'One for you, Watson,' said Holmes, when I pointed it out; 'you have saved us a long walk which would have brought us back on our own traces. Let us follow the return track.'

We had not to go far. It ended at the paving of asphalt which led up to the gates of the Mapleton stables. As we approached a groom ran out from them.

'We don't want any loiterers about here,' said he.

'I only wished to ask a question,' said Holmes, with his finger and thumb in waistcoat pocket. 'Should I be too early to see your master, Mr Silas Brown, if I were to call at five o'clock tomorrow morning?'

'Bless you, sir, if anyone is about he will be, for he is always the first stirring. But here he is, sir, to answer your questions for himself. No, sir, no; it's as much as my place is worth to let him see me touch your money. Afterwards, if you like.'

As Sherlock Holmes replaced the half-crown which he had drawn from his pocket, a fierce-looking, elderly man strode out from the gate with a hunting-crop swinging in his hand.

'What's this, Dawson?' he cried. 'No gossiping! Go about your business! And you – what the devil do you want here?'

'Ten minutes' talk with you, my good sir,' said Holmes, in the sweetest of voices.

'I've no time to talk to every gadabout. We want no strangers here. Be off, or you may find a dog at your heels.'

Holmes leaned forward and whispered something in the trainer's ear. He started violently and flushed to the temples.

'It's a lie!' he shouted. 'An infernal lie!'

'Very good! Shall we argue about it here in public, or talk it over in your parlour?'

'Oh, come in if you wish to.'

Holmes smiled. 'I shall not keep you more than a few minutes, Watson,' he said. 'Now, Mr Brown, I am quite at your disposal.'

It was quite twenty minutes, and the reds had all faded into greys before Holmes and the trainer reappeared. Never have I seen such a change as had been brought about in Silas Brown in that short time. His face was ashy pale, beads of perspiration shone upon his brow, and his hands shook until the hunting-crop wagged like a branch in the wind. His bullying, overbearing manner was all gone too, and he cringed along at my companion's side like a dog with its master.

'Your instructions will be done. It shall be done,' said he.

'There must be no mistake,' said Holmes, looking round at him. The other winced as he read the menace in his eyes.

'Oh, no, there shall be no mistake. It shall be there. Should I change it first or not?'

Holmes thought a little and then burst out laughing. 'No, don't,' said he. 'I shall write to you about it. No tricks now or –'

'Oh, you can trust me, you can trust me!'

'Yes, I think I can. Well, you shall hear from me to-morrow.' He turned upon his heel, disregarding the trembling hand which the other held out to him, and we set off for King's Pyland.

'A more perfect compound of the bully, coward and sneak than Master Silas Brown I have seldom met with,' remarked Holmes, as we trudged along together.

'He has the horse, then?'

'He tried to bluster out of it, but I described to him so exactly what his actions had been upon that morning, that he is convinced that I was watching him. Of course, you observed the peculiarly square toes in the impressions, and that his own boots exactly corresponded to them. Again, of course, no subordinate would have dared to have done such a thing. I described to him how when, according to his custom, he was the first down, he perceived a strange horse wandering over the moor; how he went out to it, and his astonishment at recognizing from the white forehead which has given the favourite its name that chance had put in his power the only horse which could beat the one upon which he had put his money. Then I described how his first impulse had been to lead him back to King's Pyland, and how the devil had shown him how he could hide the horse until the race was over, and how he had led it back and concealed it at Mapleton. When I told him every detail he gave it up, and thought only of saving his own skin.'

'But his stables had been searched.'

'Oh, an old horse-faker like him has many a dodge.'

'But are you not afraid to leave the horse in his power now, since he has every interest in injuring it?'

'My dear fellow, he will guard it as the apple of his eye. He knows that his only hope of mercy is to produce it safe.'

'Colonel Ross did not impress me as a man who would be likely to show much mercy in any case.'

'The matter does not rest with Colonel Ross. I follow my own methods, and tell as much or as little as I choose. That is the advantage of being unofficial. I don't know whether you observed it, Watson, but the Colonel's manner has been just a trifle cavalier to me. I am inclined now to have a little amusement at his expense. Say nothing to him about the horse.'

'Certainly not, without your permission.'

'And, of course, this is all quite a minor point compared to the question of who killed John Straker.'

'And you will devote yourself to that?'

'On the contrary, we both go back to London by the night train.'

I was thunderstruck by my friend's words. We had only been a few hours in Devonshire, and that he should give up an investigation which he had begun so brilliantly was quite incomprehensible to me. Not a word more could I draw from him until we were back at the trainer's house. The Colonel and the Inspector were awaiting us in the parlour.

'My friend and I return to town by the midnight express,' said Holmes. 'We have had a charming little breath of your beautiful Dartmoor air.'

The Inspector opened his eyes, and the Colonel's lip curled in a sneer.

'So you despair of arresting the murderer of poor Straker,' said he.

Holmes shrugged his shoulders. 'There are certainly grave difficulties in the way,' said he. 'I have every hope, however, that your horse will start upon Tuesday, and I beg that you will have your jockey in readiness. Might I ask for a photograph of Mr John Straker?'

The Inspector took one from an envelope in his pocket and handed it to him.

'My dear Gregory, you anticipate all my wants. If I might ask you to wait here for an instant, I have a question which I should like to put to the maid.'

'I must say that I am rather disappointed in our London consultant,' said Colonel Ross, bluntly, as my friend left the room. 'I do not see that we are any further than when he came.'

'At least, you have his assurance that your horse will run,' said I.

'Yes, I have his assurance,' said the Colonel, with a shrug of his shoulders. 'I should prefer to have the horse.'

I was about to make some reply in defence of my friend, when he entered the room again.

'Now, gentlemen,' said he, 'I am quite ready for Tavistock.'

As we stepped into the carriage one of the stable-lads held the door open for us. A sudden idea seemed to occur to Holmes, for he leaned forward and touched the lad upon the sleeve.

'You have a few sheep in the paddock,' he said. 'Who attends to them?'

'I do, sir.'

'Have you noticed anything amiss with them of late?'

'Well, sir, not of much account; but three of them have gone lame, sir.'

I could see that Holmes was extremely pleased, for he chuckled and rubbed his hands together.

'A long shot, Watson; a very long shot!' said he, pinching my arm. 'Gregory, let me recommend to your attention this singular epidemic among the sheep. Drive on, coachman!'

Colonel Ross still wore an expression which showed the poor opinion which he had formed of my companion's ability, but I saw by the Inspector's face that his attention had been keenly aroused.

'You consider that to be important?' he asked.

'Exceedingly so.'

'Is there any other point to which you would wish to draw my attention?'

'To the curious incident of the dog in the night-time.'

'The dog did nothing in the night-time.'

'That was the curious incident,' remarked Sherlock Holmes.

Four days later Holmes and I were again in the train bound for Winchester, to see the race for the Wessex Cup. Colonel Ross met us, by appointment, outside the station, and we drove in his drag to the course beyond the town. His face was grave and his manner was cold in the extreme.

'I have seen nothing of my horse,' said he.

'I suppose that you would know him when you saw him?' asked Holmes.

The Colonel was very angry. 'I have been on the turf for twenty years, and never was asked such a question as that before,' said he. 'A child would know Silver Blaze with his white forehead and his mottled off fore leg.'

'How is the betting?'

'Well, that is the curious part of it. You could have got fifteen to one yesterday, but the price has become shorter and shorter, until you can hardly get three to one now.'

'Hum!' said Holmes. 'Somebody knows something, that is clear!'

As the drag drew up in the inclosure near the grand stand, I glanced at the card to see the entries. It ran: –

Wessex Plate. 50 sovs. each, h ft, with 1,000 sovs. added, for four and five-year-olds. Second £300. Third £200. New course (one mile and five furlongs).

1. Mr Heath Newton's The Negro (red cap, cinnamon jacket).
2. Colonel Wardlaw's Pugilist (pink cap, blue and black jacket).
3. Lord Backwater's Desborough (yellow cap and sleeves).
4. Colonel Ross's Silver Blaze (black cap, red jacket).
5. Duke of Balmoral's Iris (yellow and black stripes).
6. Lord Singleton's Rasper (purple cap, black sleeves).

'We scratched our other one and put all hopes on your word,' said the Colonel. 'Why, what is that? Silver Blaze favourite?'

'Five to four against Silver Blaze!' roared the ring. 'Five to four against Silver Blaze! Fifteen to five against Desborough! Five to four on the field!'

'There are the numbers up,' I cried. 'They are all six there.'

'All six there! Then my horse is running,' cried the Colonel, in great agitation. 'But I don't see him. My colours have not passed.'

'Only five have passed. This must be he.'

As I spoke a powerful bay horse swept out from the weighing inclosure and cantered past us, bearing on its back the well-known black and red of the Colonel.

'That's not my horse,' cried the owner. 'That beast has not a white hair upon its body. What is this that you have done, Mr Holmes?'

'Well, well, let us see how he gets on,' said my friend,

imperturbably. For a few minutes he gazed through my field-glass. 'Capital! An excellent start!' he cried suddenly. 'There they are, coming round the curve!'

From our drag we had a superb view as they came up the straight. The six horses were so close together that a carpet could have covered them, but half way up the yellow of the Mapleton stable showed to the front. Before they reached us, however, Desborough's bolt was shot, and the Colonel's horse, coming away with a rush, passed the post a good six lengths before its rival, the Duke of Balmoral's Iris making a bad third.

'It's my race anyhow,' gasped the Colonel, passing his hand over his eyes. 'I confess that I can make neither head nor tail of it. Don't you think that you have kept up your mystery long enough, Mr Holmes?'

'Certainly, Colonel. You shall know everything. Let us all go round and have a look at the horse together. Here he is,' he continued, as we made our way into the weighing inclosure where only owners and their friends find admittance. 'You have only to wash his face and his leg in spirits of wine and you will find that he is the same old Silver Blaze as ever.'

'You take my breath away!'

'I found him in the hands of a faker, and took the liberty of running him just as he was sent over.'

'My dear sir, you have done wonders. The horse looks very fit and well. It never went better in its life. I owe you a thousand apologies for having doubted your ability. You have done me a great service by recovering my horse. You would do me a greater still if you could lay your hands on the murderer of John Straker.'

'I have done so,' said Holmes, quietly.

The Colonel and I stared at him in amazement. 'You have got him! Where is he, then?'

'He is here.'

'Here! Where?'

'In my company at the present moment.'

The Colonel flushed angrily. 'I quite recognize that I am under obligations to you, Mr Holmes,' said he, 'but I must regard what you have just said as either a very bad joke or an insult.'

Sherlock Holmes laughed. 'I assure you that I have not associated you with the crime, Colonel,' said he; 'the real murderer is standing immediately behind you!'

He stepped past and laid his hand upon the glossy neck of the thoroughbred.

'The horse!' cried both the Colonel and myself.

'Yes, the horse. And it may lessen his guilt if I say that it was done in self-defence, and that John Straker was a man who was entirely unworthy of your confidence. But there goes the bell; and as I stand to win a little on this next race, I shall defer a more lengthy explanation until a more fitting time.'

We had the corner of a Pullman car to ourselves that evening as we whirled back to London, and I fancy that the journey was a short one to Colonel Ross as well as to myself, as we listened to our companion's narrative of the events which had occurred at the Dartmoor training stables upon that Monday night, and the means by which he had unravelled them.

'I confess,' said he, 'that any theories which I had formed from the newspaper reports were entirely erroneous. And yet there were indications there, had they not been overlaid by other details which concealed their true import. I went to Devonshire with the conviction that Fitzroy Simpson was the true culprit, although, of course, I saw that the evidence against him was by no means complete.

'It was while I was in the carriage, just as we reached the

trainer's house, that the immense significance of the curried mutton occurred to me. You may remember that I was distrait, and remained sitting after you had all alighted. I was marvelling in my own mind how I could possibly have overlooked so obvious a clue.'

'I confess,' said the Colonel, 'that even now I cannot see how it helps us.'

'It was the first link in my chain of reasoning. Powdered opium is by no means tasteless. The flavour is not disagreeable, but it is perceptible. Were it mixed with any ordinary dish, the eater would undoubtedly detect it, and would probably eat no more. A curry was exactly the medium which would disguise this taste. By no possible supposition could this stranger, Fitzroy Simpson, have caused curry to be served in the trainer's family that night, and it is surely too monstrous a coincidence to suppose that he happened to come along with powdered opium upon the very night when a dish happened to be served which would disguise the flavour. That is unthinkable. Therefore Simpson becomes eliminated from the case and our attention centres upon Straker and his wife, the only two people who could have chosen curried mutton for supper that night. The opium was added after the dish was set aside for the stable-boy, for the others had the same for supper with no ill effects. Which of them, then, had access to that dish without the maid seeing them?

'Before deciding that question I had grasped the significance of the silence of the dog, for one true inference invariably suggests others. The Simpson incident had shown me that a dog was kept in the stables, and yet, though someone had been in and had fetched out a horse, he had not barked enough to arouse the two lads in the loft. Obviously the midnight visitor was someone whom the dog knew well.

'I was already convinced, or almost convinced, that John

Straker went down to the stables in the dead of the night and took out Silver Blaze. For what purpose? For a dishonest one, obviously, or why should he drug his own stable-boy? And yet I was at a loss to know why. There have been cases before now where trainers have made sure of great sums of money by laying against their own horses, through agents, and then preventing them from winning by fraud. Sometimes it is a pulling jockey. Sometimes it is some surer and subtler means. What was it here? I hoped that the contents of his pockets might help me to form a conclusion.

'And they did so. You cannot have forgotten the singular knife which was found in the dead man's hand, a knife which certainly no sane man would choose for a weapon. It was, as Dr Watson told us, a form of knife which is used for the most delicate operations known in surgery. And it was to be used for a delicate operation that night. You must know with your wide experience of turf matters, Colonel Ross, that it is possible to make a slight nick upon the tendons of a horse's ham, and to do it subcutaneously so as to leave absolutely no trace. A horse so treated would develop a slight lameness which would be put down to a strain in exercise or a touch of rheumatism, but never to foul play.'

'Villain! Scoundrel!' cried the Colonel.

'We have here the explanation of why John Straker wished to take the horse out on to the moor. So spirited a creature would have certainly roused the soundest of sleepers when it felt the prick of the knife. It was absolutely necessary to do it in the open air.'

'I have been blind!' cried the Colonel. 'Of course, that was why he needed the candle, and struck the match.'

'Undoubtedly. But in examining his belongings, I was fortunate enough to discover, not only the method of the crime, but even its motives. As a man of the world, Colonel, you know that men do not carry other people's bills about in their pockets. We have most of us quite enough to do to settle our own. I at once concluded that Straker was leading a double life, and keeping a second establishment. The nature of the bill showed that there was a lady in the case, and one who had expensive tastes. Liberal as you are with your servants, one hardly expects that they can buy twenty-guinea walking dresses for their women. I questioned Mrs Straker as to the dress without her knowing it, and having satisfied myself that it had never reached her, I made a note of the milliner's address, and felt that by calling there with Straker's photograph, I could easily dispose of the mythical Darbyshire.

'From that time on all was plain. Straker had led out the horse to a hollow where his light would be invisible. Simpson, in his flight, had dropped his cravat, and Straker had picked it up with some idea, perhaps, that he might use it in securing the horse's leg. Once in the hollow he had got behind the horse, and had struck a light, but the creature, frightened at the sudden glare, and with the strange instinct of animals feeling that some mischief was intended, had lashed out, and the steel shoe had struck Straker full on the forehead. He had already, in spite of the rain, taken off his overcoat in order to do his delicate task, and so, as he fell, his knife gashed his thigh. Do I make it clear?'

'Wonderful!' cried the Colonel. 'Wonderful! You might have been there.'

'My final shot was, I confess, a very long one. It struck me that so astute a man as Straker would not undertake this delicate tendon-nicking without a little practice. What could he practise on? My eyes fell upon the sheep, and I asked a question which, rather to my surprise, showed that my surmise was correct.'

'You have made it perfectly clear, Mr Holmes.'

'When I returned to London I called upon the milliner, who at once recognized Straker as an excellent customer, of the name of Darbyshire, who had a very dashing wife with a strong partiality for expensive dresses. I have no doubt that this woman had plunged him over head and ears in debt, and so led him into this miserable plot.'

'You have explained all but one thing,' cried the Colonel. 'Where was the horse?'

'Ah, it bolted and was cared for by one of your neighbours. We must have an amnesty in that direction, I think. This is Clapham junction, if I am not mistaken, and we shall be in Victoria in less than ten minutes. If you care to smoke a cigar in our rooms, Colonel, I shall be happy to give you any other details which might interest you.'

D. H. LAWRENCE

THE ROCKING-
HORSE WINNER

THERE WAS A WOMAN who was beautiful, who started with all the advantages, yet she had no luck. She married for love, and the love turned to dust. She had bonny children, yet she felt they had been thrust upon her, and she could not love them. They looked at her coldly, as if they were finding fault with her. And hurriedly she felt she must cover up some fault in herself. Yet what it was that she must cover up she never knew. Nevertheless, when her children were present, she always felt the centre of her heart go hard. This troubled her, and in her manner she was all the more gentle and anxious for her children, as if she loved them very much. Only she herself knew that at the centre of her heart was a hard little place that could not feel love, no, not for anybody. Everybody else said of her: 'She is such a good mother. She adores her children.' Only she herself, and her children themselves, knew it was not so. They read it in each other's eyes.

There were a boy and two little girls. They lived in a pleasant house, with a garden, and they had discreet servants, and felt themselves superior to anyone in the neighborhood.

Although they lived in style, they felt always an anxiety in the house. There was never enough money. The mother had a small income, and the father had a small income, but not nearly enough for the social position which they had to keep up. The father went into town to some office. But though he had good prospects, these prospects never materialized. There was always the grinding sense of the shortage of money, though the style was always kept up.

At last the mother said: 'I will see if *I* can't make something.' But she did not know where to begin. She racked her brains, and tried this thing and the other, but could not find anything successful. The failure made deep lines come into her face. Her children were growing up, they would have to go to school. There must be more money, there must be more money. The father, who was always very handsome and expensive in his tastes, seemed as if he never *would* be able to do anything worth doing. And the mother, who had a great belief in herself, did not succeed any better, and her tastes were just as expensive.

And so the house came to be haunted by the unspoken phrase: *There must be more money! There must be more money!* The children could hear it all the time, though nobody said it aloud. They heard it at Christmas, when the expensive and splendid toys filled the nursery. Behind the shining modern rocking-horse, behind the smart doll's house, a voice would start whispering: 'There *must* be more money! There *must* be more money!' And the children would stop playing, to listen for a moment. They would look into each other's eyes, to see if they had all heard. And each one saw in the eyes of the other two that they too had heard. 'There *must* be more money! There *must* be more money!'

It came whispering from the springs of the still-swaying rocking-horse, and even the horse, bending his wooden, champing head, heard it. The big doll, sitting so pink and smirking in her new pram, could hear it quite plainly, and seemed to be smirking all the more self-consciously because of it. The foolish puppy, too, that took the place of the teddy-bear, he was looking so extraordinarily foolish for no other reason but that he heard the secret whisper all over the house: 'There *must* be more money!'

Yet nobody ever said it aloud. The whisper was everywhere, and therefore no one spoke it. Just as no one ever says: 'We are breathing!' in spite of the fact that breath is coming and going all the time.

'Mother,' said the boy Paul one day, 'why don't we keep a car of our own? Why do we always use uncle's, or else a taxi?'

'Because we're the poor members of the family,' said the mother.

'But why *are* we, mother?'

'Well – I suppose,' she said slowly and bitterly, 'it's because your father had no luck.'

The boy was silent for some time.

'Is luck money, mother?' he asked, rather timidly.

'No, Paul. Not quite. It's what causes you to have money.'

'Oh!' said Paul vaguely. 'I thought when Uncle Oscar said *filthy lucker*, it meant money.'

'*Filthy lucre* does mean money,' said the mother. 'But it's lucre, not luck.'

'Oh!' said the boy. 'Then what *is* luck, mother?'

'It's what causes you to have money. If you're lucky you have money. That's why it's better to be born lucky than rich. If you're rich, you may lose your money. But if you're lucky, you will always get more money.'

'Oh! Will you? And is father not lucky?'

'Very unlucky, I should say,' she said bitterly.

The boy watched her with unsure eyes.

'Why?' he asked.

'I don't know. Nobody ever knows why one person is lucky and another unlucky.'

'Don't they? Nobody at all? Does *nobody* know?'

'Perhaps God. But He never tells.'

'He ought to, then. And aren't you lucky either, mother?'

'I can't be, if I married an unlucky husband.'

'But by yourself, aren't you?'

'I used to think I was, before I married. Now I think I am very unlucky indeed.'

'Why?'

'Well – never mind! Perhaps I'm not really,' she said.

The child looked at her to see if she meant it. But he saw, by the lines of her mouth, that she was only trying to hide something from him.

'Well, anyhow,' he said stoutly, 'I'm a lucky person.'

'Why?' said his mother, with a sudden laugh.

He stared at her. He didn't even know why he had said it.

'God told me,' he asserted, brazening it out.

'I hope He did, dear!' she said, again with a laugh, but rather bitter.

'He did, mother!'

'Excellent!' said the mother, using one of her husband's exclamations.

The boy saw she did not believe him; or rather, that she paid no attention to his assertion. This angered him somewhere, and made him want to compel her attention.

He went off by himself, vaguely, in a childish way, seeking for the clue to 'luck'. Absorbed, taking no heed of other people, he went about with a sort of stealth, seeking inwardly for luck. He wanted luck, he wanted it, he wanted it. When the two girls were playing dolls in the nursery, he would sit on his big rocking-horse, charging madly into space, with a frenzy that made the little girls peer at him uneasily. Wildly the horse careered, the waving dark hair of the boy tossed, his eyes had a strange glare in them. The little girls dared not speak to him.

When he had ridden to the end of his mad little journey, he climbed down and stood in front of his rocking-horse, staring fixedly into its lowered face. Its red mouth was slightly open, its big eye was wide and glassy-bright.

'Now!' he would silently command the snorting steed. 'Now, take me to where there is luck! Now take me!'

And he would slash the horse on the neck with the little whip he had asked Uncle Oscar for. He *knew* the horse could take him to where there was luck, if only he forced it. So he would mount again and start on his furious ride, hoping at last to get there. He knew he could get there.

'You'll break your horse, Paul!' said the nurse.

'He's always riding like that! I wish he'd leave off!' said his elder sister Joan.

But he only glared down on them in silence. Nurse gave him up. She could make nothing of him. Anyhow, he was growing beyond her.

One day his mother and his Uncle Oscar came in when he was on one of his furious rides. He did not speak to them.

'Hallo, you young jockey! Riding a winner?' said his uncle.

'Aren't you growing too big for a rocking-horse? You're not a very little boy any longer, you know,' said his mother.

But Paul only gave a blue glare from his big, rather close-set eyes. He would speak to nobody when he was in full tilt. His mother watched him with an anxious expression on her face.

At last he suddenly stopped forcing his horse into the mechanical gallop and slid down.

'Well, I got there!' he announced fiercely, his blue eyes still flaring, and his sturdy long legs straddling apart.

'Where did you get to?' asked his mother.

'Where I wanted to go,' he flared back at her.

'That's right, son!' said Uncle Oscar. 'Don't you stop till you get there. What's the horse's name?'

'He doesn't have a name,' said the boy.

'Gets on without all right?' asked the uncle.

'Well, he has different names. He was called Sansovino last week.'

'Sansovino, eh? Won the Ascot. How did you know this name?'

'He always talks about horse-races with Bassett,' said Joan.

The uncle was delighted to find that his small nephew was posted with all the racing news. Bassett, the young gardener, who had been wounded in the left foot in the war and had got his present job through Oscar Cresswell, whose batman he had been, was a perfect blade of the 'turf'. He lived in the racing events, and the small boy lived with him.

Oscar Cresswell got it all from Bassett.

'Master Paul comes and asks me, so I can't do more than tell him, sir,' said Bassett, his face terribly serious, as if he were speaking of religious matters.

'And does he ever put anything on a horse he fancies?'

'Well – I don't want to give him away – he's a young sport, a fine sport, sir. Would you mind asking him himself? He sort of takes a pleasure in it, and perhaps he'd feel I was giving him away, sir, if you don't mind.'

Bassett was serious as a church.

The uncle went back to his nephew and took him off for a ride in the car.

'Say, Paul, old man, do you ever put anything on a horse?' the uncle asked.

The boy watched the handsome man closely.

'Why, do you think I oughtn't to?' he parried.

'Not a bit of it! I thought perhaps you might give me a tip for the Lincoln.'

The car sped on into the country, going down to Uncle Oscar's place in Hampshire.

'Honour bright?' said the nephew.

'Honour bright, son!' said the uncle.

'Well, then, Daffodil.'

'Daffodil! I doubt it, sonny. What about Mirza?'

'I only know the winner,' said the boy. 'That's Daffodil.'

'Daffodil, eh?'

There was a pause. Daffodil was an obscure horse comparatively.

'Uncle!'

'Yes, son?'

'You won't let it go any further, will you? I promised Bassett.'

'Bassett be damned, old man! What's he got to do with it?'

'We're partners. We've been partners from the first. Uncle, he lent me my first five shillings, which I lost. I promised him, honour bright, it was only between me and him; only you gave me that ten-shilling note I started winning with, so I thought you were lucky. You won't let it go any further, will you?'

The boy gazed at his uncle from those big, hot, blue eyes, set rather close together. The uncle stirred and laughed uneasily.

'Right you are, son! I'll keep your tip private. Daffodil, eh? How much are you putting on him?'

'All except twenty pounds,' said the boy. 'I keep that in reserve.'

The uncle thought it a good joke.

'You keep twenty pounds in reserve, do you, you young romancer? What are you betting, then?'

'I'm betting three hundred,' said the boy gravely. 'But it's between you and me, Uncle Oscar! Honour bright?'

The uncle burst into a roar of laughter.

'It's between you and me all right, you young Nat Gould,' he said, laughing. 'But where's your three hundred?'

'Bassett keeps it for me. We're partners.'

'You are, are you! And what is Bassett putting on Daffodil?'

'He won't go quite as high as I do, I expect. Perhaps he'll go a hundred and fifty.'

'What, pennies?' laughed the uncle.

'Pounds,' said the child, with a surprised look at his uncle. 'Bassett keeps a bigger reserve than I do.'

Between wonder and amusement Uncle Oscar was silent. He pursued the matter no further, but he determined to take his nephew with him to the Lincoln races.

'Now, son,' he said, 'I'm putting twenty on Mirza, and I'll put five on for you on any horse you fancy. What's your pick?'

'Daffodil, uncle.'

'No, not the fiver on Daffodil!'

'I should if it was my own fiver,' said the child.

'Good! Good! Right you are! A fiver for me and a fiver for you on Daffodil.'

The child had never been to a race-meeting before, and his eyes were blue fire. He pursed his mouth tight and watched. A Frenchman just in front had put his money on Lancelot. Wild with excitement, he flayed his arms up and down, yelling '*Lancelot! Lancelot!*' in his French accent.

Daffodil came in first, Lancelot second, Mirza third. The child, flushed and with eyes blazing, was curiously serene. His uncle brought him four five-pound notes, four to one.

'What am I to do with these?' he cried, waving them before the boy's eyes.

'I suppose we'll talk to Bassett,' said the boy. 'I expect I have fifteen hundred now; and twenty in reserve; and this twenty.'

His uncle studied him for some moments.

'Look here, son!' he said. 'You're not serious about Bassett and that fifteen hundred, are you?'

'Yes, I am. But it's between you and me, uncle. Honour bright?'

'Honour bright all right, son! But I must talk to Bassett.'

'If you'd like to be a partner, uncle, with Bassett and me, we could all be partners. Only, you'd have to promise, honour bright, uncle, not to let it go beyond us three. Bassett and I are lucky, and you must be lucky, because it was your ten shillings I started winning with . . .'

Uncle Oscar took both Bassett and Paul into Richmond Park for an afternoon, and there they talked.

'It's like this, you see, sir,' Bassett said. 'Master Paul would get me talking about racing events, spinning yarns, you know, sir. And he was always keen on knowing if I'd made or if I'd lost. It's about a year since, now, that I put five shillings on Blush of Dawn for him: and we lost. Then the luck turned, with that ten shillings he had from you: that we put on Singhalese. And since that time, it's been pretty steady, all things considering. What do you say, Master Paul?'

'We're all right when we're sure,' said Paul. 'It's when we're not quite sure that we go down.'

'Oh, but we're careful then,' said Bassett.

'But when are you *sure*?' smiled Uncle Oscar.

'It's Master Paul, sir,' said Bassett in a secret, religious voice. 'It's as if he had it from heaven. Like Daffodil, now, for the Lincoln. That was as sure as eggs.'

'Did you put anything on Daffodil?' asked Oscar Cresswell.

'Yes, sir. I made my bit.'

'And my nephew?'

Bassett was obstinately silent, looking at Paul.

'I made twelve hundred, didn't I, Bassett? I told uncle I was putting three hundred on Daffodil.'

'That's right,' said Bassett, nodding.

'But where's the money?' asked the uncle.

'I keep it safe locked up, sir. Master Paul he can have it any minute he likes to ask for it.'

'What, fifteen hundred pounds?'

'And twenty! And *forty*, that is, with the twenty he made on the course.'

'It's amazing!' said the uncle.

'If Master Paul offers you to be partners, sir, I would, if I were you: if you'll excuse me,' said Bassett.

Oscar Cresswell thought about it.

'I'll see the money,' he said.

They drove home again, and, sure enough, Bassett came round to the garden-house with fifteen hundred pounds in notes. The twenty pounds reserve was left with Joe Glee, in the Turf Commission deposit.

'You see, it's all right, uncle, when I'm *sure*! Then we go strong, for all we're worth. Don't we, Bassett?'

'We do that, Master Paul.'

'And when are you sure?' said the uncle, laughing.

'Oh, well, sometimes I'm *absolutely* sure, like about Daffodil,' said the boy; 'and sometimes I have an idea; and sometimes I haven't even an idea, have I, Bassett? Then we're careful, because we mostly go down.'

'You do, do you! And when you're sure, like about Daffodil, what makes you sure, sonny?'

'Oh, well, I don't know,' said the boy uneasily. 'I'm sure, you know, uncle; that's all.'

'It's as if he had it from heaven, sir,' Bassett reiterated.

'I should say so!' said the uncle.

But he became a partner. And when the Leger was coming

on Paul was 'sure' about Lively Spark, which was a quite inconsiderable horse. The boy insisted on putting a thousand on the horse, Bassett went for five hundred, and Oscar Cresswell two hundred. Lively Spark came in first, and the betting had been ten to one against him. Paul had made ten thousand.

'You see,' he said, 'I was absolutely sure of him.'

Even Oscar Cresswell had cleared two thousand.

'Look here, son,' he said, 'this sort of thing makes me nervous.'

'It needn't, uncle! Perhaps I shan't be sure again for a long time.'

'But what are you going to do with your money?' asked the uncle.

'Of course,' said the boy, 'I started it for mother. She said she had no luck, because father is unlucky, so *I* thought if I was lucky, it might stop whispering.'

'What might stop whispering?'

'Our house. I *hate* our house for whispering.'

'What does it whisper?'

'Why – why' – the boy fidgeted – 'why, I don't know. But it's always short of money, you know, uncle.'

'I know it, son, I know it.'

'You know people send mother writs, don't you, uncle?'

'I'm afraid I do,' said the uncle.

'And then the house whispers, like people laughing at you behind your back. It's awful, that is! I thought if I was lucky –'

'You might stop it,' added the uncle.

The boy watched him with big blue eyes, that had an uncanny cold fire in them, and he said never a word.

'Well, then!' said the uncle. 'What are we doing?'

'I shouldn't like mother to know I was lucky,' said the boy.

'Why not, son?'

'She'd stop me.'

'I don't think she would.'

'Oh!' – and the boy writhed in an odd way – 'I *don't* want her to know, uncle.'

'All right, son! We'll manage it without her knowing.'

They managed it very easily. Paul, at the other's suggestion, handed over five thousand pounds to his uncle, who deposited it with the family lawyer, who was then to inform Paul's mother that a relative had put five thousand pounds into his hands, which sum was to be paid out a thousand pounds at a time, on the mother's birthday, for the next five years.

'So she'll have a birthday present of a thousand pounds for five successive years,' said Uncle Oscar. 'I hope it won't make it all the harder for her later.'

Paul's mother had her birthday in November. The house had been 'whispering' worse than ever lately, and, even in spite of his luck, Paul could not bear up against it. He was very anxious to see the effect of the birthday letter, telling his mother about the thousand pounds.

When there were no visitors, Paul now took his meals with his parents, as he was beyond the nursery control. His mother went into town nearly every day. She had discovered that she had an odd knack of sketching furs and dress materials, so she worked secretly in the studio of a friend who was the chief 'artist' for the leading drapers. She drew the figures of ladies in furs and ladies in silk and sequins for the newspaper advertisements. This young woman artist earned several thousand pounds a year, but Paul's mother only made several hundreds, and she was again dissatisfied. She so wanted to be first in something, and she did not succeed, even in making sketches for drapery advertisements.

She was down to breakfast on the morning of her birthday. Paul watched her face as she read her letters. He knew the lawyer's letter. As his mother read it, her face hardened and became more expressionless. Then a cold, determined look came on her mouth. She hid the letter under the pile of others, and said not a word about it.

'Didn't you have anything nice in the post for your birthday, mother?' said Paul.

'Quite moderately nice,' she said, her voice cold and absent.

She went away to town without saying more.

But in the afternoon Uncle Oscar appeared. He said Paul's mother had had a long interview with the lawyer, asking if the whole five thousand could not be advanced at once, as she was in debt.

'What do you think, uncle?' said the boy.

'I leave it to you, son.'

'Oh, let her have it, then! We can get some more with the other,' said the boy.

'A bird in the hand is worth two in the bush, laddie!' said Uncle Oscar.

'But I'm sure to *know* for the Grand National; or the Lincolnshire; or else the Derby. I'm sure to know for *one* of them,' said Paul.

So Uncle Oscar signed the agreement, and Paul's mother touched the whole five thousand. Then something very curious happened. The voices in the house suddenly went mad, like a chorus of frogs on a spring evening. There were certain new furnishings, and Paul had a tutor. He was *really* going to Eton, his father's school, in the following autumn. There were flowers in the winter, and a blossoming of the luxury Paul's mother had been used to. And yet the voices in the house, behind the sprays of mimosa and almond-blossom, and from under the piles of iridescent cushions, simply trilled and screamed in a sort of ecstasy: 'There *must* be more money! Oh-h-h; there *must* be more money. Oh, now, now-w! Now-w-w – there *must* be more money! – more than ever! More than ever!'

It frightened Paul terribly. He studied away at his Latin and Greek with his tutor. But his intense hours were spent with Bassett. The Grand National had gone by; he had not 'known', and had lost a hundred pounds. Summer was at hand. He was in agony for the Lincoln. But even for the Lincoln he didn't 'know', and he lost fifty pounds. He became wild-eyed and strange, as if something were going to explode in him.

'Let it alone, son! Don't you bother about it!' urged Uncle Oscar. But it was as if the boy couldn't really hear what his uncle was saying.

'I've got to know for the Derby! I've got to know for the Derby!' the child reiterated, his big blue eyes blazing with a sort of madness.

His mother noticed how overwrought he was.

'You'd better go to the seaside. Wouldn't you like to go now to the seaside, instead of waiting? I think you'd better,' she said, looking down at him anxiously, her heart curiously heavy because of him.

But the child lifted his uncanny blue eyes.

'I couldn't possibly go before the Derby, mother!' he said. 'I couldn't possibly!'

'Why not?' she said, her voice becoming heavy when she was opposed. 'Why not? You can still go from the seaside to see the Derby with your Uncle Oscar, if that's what you wish. No need for you to wait here. Besides, I think you care too much about these races. It's a bad sign. My family has been a gambling family, and you won't know till you grow up how much damage it has done. But it has done damage. I shall have to send Bassett away, and ask Uncle Oscar not to talk racing to you, unless you promise to be reasonable about it: go away to the seaside and forget it. You're all nerves!'

'I'll do what you like, mother, so long as you don't send me away till after the Derby,' the boy said.

'Send you away from where? Just from this house?'

'Yes,' he said, gazing at her.

'Why, you curious child, what makes you care about this house so much, suddenly? I never knew you loved it.'

He gazed at her without speaking. He had a secret within a secret, something he had not divulged, even to Bassett or to his Uncle Oscar.

But his mother, after standing undecided and a little bit sullen for some moments, said:

'Very well, then! Don't go to the seaside till after the Derby, if you don't wish it. But promise me you won't let your nerves go to pieces. Promise you won't think so much about horse-racing, and *events*, as you call them!'

'Oh no,' said the boy casually. 'I won't think much about them, mother. You needn't worry. I wouldn't worry, mother, if I were you.'

'If you were me and I were you,' said his mother, 'I wonder what we *should* do!'

'But you know you needn't worry, mother, don't you?' the boy repeated.

'I should be awfully glad to know it,' she said wearily.

'Oh, well, you *can*, you know. I mean, you *ought* to know you needn't worry,' he insisted.

'Ought I? Then I'll see about it,' she said.

Paul's secret of secrets was his wooden horse, that which

had no name. Since he was emancipated from a nurse and a nursery-governess, he had had his rocking-horse removed to his own bedroom at the top of the house.

'Surely you're too big for a rocking-horse!' his mother had remonstrated.

'Well, you see, mother, till I can have a *real* horse, I like to have *some* sort of animal about,' had been his quaint answer.

'Do you feel he keeps you company?' she laughed.

'Oh yes! He's very good, he always keeps me company, when I'm there,' said Paul.

So the horse, rather shabby, stood in an arrested prance in the boy's bedroom.

The Derby was drawing near, and the boy grew more and more tense. He hardly heard what was spoken to him, he was very frail, and his eyes were really uncanny. His mother had sudden strange seizures of uneasiness about him. Sometimes, for half an hour, she would feel a sudden anxiety about him that was almost anguish. She wanted to rush to him at once, and know he was safe.

Two nights before the Derby, she was at a big party in town, when one of her rushes of anxiety about her boy, her first-born, gripped her heart till she could hardly speak. She fought with the feeling, might and main, for she believed in common sense. But it was too strong. She had to leave the dance and go downstairs to telephone to the country. The children's nursery-governess was terribly surprised and startled at being rung up in the night.

'Are the children all right, Miss Wilmot?'

'Oh yes, they are quite all right.'

'Master Paul? Is he all right?'

'He went to bed as right as a trivet. Shall I run up and look at him?'

'No,' said Paul's mother reluctantly. 'No! Don't trouble.

It's all right. Don't sit up. We shall be home fairly soon.'
She did not want her son's privacy intruded upon.

'Very good,' said the governess.

It was about one o'clock when Paul's mother and father drove up to their house. All was still. Paul's mother went to her room and slipped off her white fur cloak. She had told her maid not to wait up for her. She heard her husband downstairs, mixing a whisky and soda.

And then, because of the strange anxiety at her heart, she stole upstairs to her son's room. Noiselessly she went along the upper corridor. Was there a faint noise? What was it?

She stood, with arrested muscles, outside his door, listening. There was a strange, heavy, and yet not loud noise. Her heart stood still. It was a soundless noise, yet rushing and powerful. Something huge, in violent, hushed motion. What was it? What in God's name was it? She ought to know. She felt that she knew the noise. She knew what it was.

Yet she could not place it. She couldn't say what it was. And on and on it went, like a madness.

Softly, frozen with anxiety and fear, she turned the door-handle.

The room was dark. Yet in the space near the window, she heard and saw something plunging to and fro. She gazed in fear and amazement.

Then suddenly she switched on the light, and saw her son, in his green pyjamas, madly surging on the rocking-horse. The blaze of light suddenly lit him up, as he urged the wooden horse, and lit her up, as she stood, blonde, in her dress of pale green and crystal, in the doorway.

'Paul!' she cried. 'Whatever are you doing?'

'It's Malabar!' he screamed in a powerful, strange voice. 'It's Malabar!'

His eyes blazed at her for one strange and senseless second, as he ceased urging his wooden horse. Then he fell with a crash to the ground, and she, all her tormented motherhood flooding upon her, rushed to gather him up.

But he was unconscious, and unconscious he remained, with some brain-fever. He talked and tossed, and his mother sat stonily by his side.

'Malabar! It's Malabar! Bassett, Bassett, I *know*! It's Malabar!'

So the child cried, trying to get up and urge the rocking-horse that gave him his inspiration.

'What does he mean by Malabar?' asked the heart-frozen mother.

'I don't know,' said the father stonily.

'What does he mean by Malabar?' she asked her brother Oscar.

'It's one of the horses running for the Derby,' was the answer.

And, in spite of himself, Oscar Cresswell spoke to Bassett, and himself put a thousand on Malabar: at fourteen to one.

The third day of the illness was critical: they were waiting for a change. The boy, with his rather long, curly hair, was tossing ceaselessly on the pillow. He neither slept nor regained consciousness, and his eyes were like blue stones. His mother sat, feeling her heart had gone, turned actually into a stone.

In the evening, Oscar Cresswell did not come, but Bassett sent a message, saying could he come up for one moment, just one moment? Paul's mother was very angry at the intrusion, but on second thoughts she agreed. The boy was the same. Perhaps Bassett might bring him to consciousness.

The gardener, a shortish fellow with a little brown moustache and sharp little brown eyes, tiptoed into the room, touched his imaginary cap to Paul's mother, and stole to the bedside, staring with glittering, smallish eyes at the tossing, dying child.

'Master Paul!' he whispered. 'Master Paul! Malabar came in first all right, a clean win. I did as you told me. You've made over seventy thousand pounds, you have; you've got over eighty thousand. Malabar came in all right, Master Paul.'

'Malabar! Malabar! Did I say Malabar, mother? Did I say Malabar? Do you think I'm lucky, mother? I knew Malabar, didn't I? Over eighty thousand pounds! I call that lucky, don't you, mother? Over eighty thousand pounds! I knew, didn't I know I knew? Malabar came in all right. If I ride my horse till I'm sure, then I tell you, Bassett, you can go as high as you like. Did you go for all you were worth, Bassett?'

'I went a thousand on it, Master Paul.'

'I never told you, mother, that if I can ride my horse, and *get there*, then I'm absolutely sure – oh, absolutely! Mother, did I ever tell you? I *am* lucky!'

'No, you never did,' said his mother.

But the boy died in the night.

And even as he lay dead, his mother heard her brother's voice saying to her: 'My God, Hester, you're eighty-odd thousand to the good, and a poor devil of a son to the bad. But, poor devil, poor devil, he's best gone out of a life where he rides his rocking-horse to find a winner.'

JOHN O'HARA

WE'LL HAVE FUN

IT WAS OFTEN said of Tony Costello that there was nothing he did not know about horses. No matter whom he happened to be working for – as coachman, as hostler, as blacksmith – he would stop whatever he was doing and have a look at an ailing horse and give advice to the owner who had brought the horse to Tony. His various employers did not object; they had probably sometime in the past gotten Tony's advice when he was working for someone else, and they would do so again sometime in the future. A year was a long time for Tony to stay at a job; he would quit or he would get the sack, find something else to do, and stay at that job until it was time to move on. He had worked for some employers three or four times. They would rehire him in spite of their experience with his habits, and if they did not happen to have a job open for him, they would at least let him bed down in their haylofts. He did not always ask their permission for this privilege, but since he knew his way around just about every stable in town – private and livery – he never had any trouble finding a place to sleep. He smoked a pipe, but everybody knew he was careful about matches and emptying the pipe and the kerosene heaters that were in most stables. And even when he was not actually in the service of the owner of a stable, he more than earned his sleeping privilege. An owner would go out to the stable in the morning and find that the chores had been done. 'Oh, hello, Tony,' the owner would say. 'Since when have you been back?'

'I come in last night.'

'I don't have job for you,' the owner would say.

'That's all right. Just a roof over me head temporarily. You're giving that animal too much oats again. Don't give him no oats at night, I told you.'

'Oh, all right. Go in the kitchen and the missus will give you some breakfast. That is, if you want any breakfast. You smell like a saloon.'

'Yes, this was a bad one, a real bad one. All I want's a cup of coffee, if that's all right?'

'One of these nights you'll walk in front of a yard engine.'

'If I do I hope I'll have the common sense to get out of the way. And if I don't it'll be over pretty quick.'

'Uh-huh. Well, do whatever needs to be done and I'll pay you two dollars when I get back this evening.'

The owner could be sure that by the end of the day Tony would have done a good cleaning job throughout the stable, and would be waiting in patient agony for the money that would buy the whiskey that cured the rams. 'I got the rams so bad I come near taking a swig of the kerosene,' he would say. He would take the two dollars and half walk, half run to the nearest saloon, but he would be back in time to feed and bed down the owner's horse.

It would take a couple of days for him to get back to good enough shape to go looking for a steady job. If he had the right kind of luck, the best of luck, he would hear about a job as coachman. The work was not hard, and the pay was all his, not to be spent on room and board. The hardest work, though good pay, was in a blacksmith's shop. He was not young any more, and it took longer for his muscles to get reaccustomed to the work. Worst of all, as the newest blacksmith he was always given the job of shoe-ing mules, which were as treacherous as a rattlesnake and as frightening. He hated to shoe a mule or a Shetland pony. There were two shops in town where a mule could be tied up in the stocks, the apparatus that held the animal so securely that it could not kick; but a newly shod mule, released from the stocks, was likely to go crazy and kill a man. If he was going to die that way, Tony wanted his executioner to be a horse, not a goddamn mule. And if he was going to lose a finger or a chunk of his backside, let it be a horse that bit him and not a nasty little bastard ten hands high. Blacksmithing paid the best and was the job he cared the least for, and on his fiftieth birthday Tony renounced it forever. 'Not for fifty dollars a week will I take another job in a blacksmith's,' he swore.

'You're getting pretty choosy, if you ask me,' said his friend Murphy. 'Soon there won't be no jobs for you of any kind, shape, or form. The ottomobile is putting an end to the horse. Did you ever hear tell of the Squadron A in New York City?'

'For the love of Jesus, did I ever hear tell of it? Is that what you're asking me? Well, if I was in New York City I could lead you to it blindfolded, Ninety-something-or-other and Madison Avenue, it is, on the right-hand side going up. And before I come to this miserable town the man I worked for's son belonged to it. Did I ever hear tell of the Squadron A!'

'All right. What is it now?' said Murphy.

'It's the same as it always was – a massive brick building on the right-hand side –'

'The organ-i-zation, I'm speaking of,' said Murphy.

'Well, the last I seen in the papers, yesterday or the day before, this country was ingaged in mortal combat with Kaiser Wilhelm the Second. I therefore hazard the guess that the organ-i-zation is fighting on our side against the man with the withered arm.'

'Fighting how?'

'Bravely, I'm sure.'

'With what for weapons?'

'For weapons? Well, being a cavalry regiment I hazard the guess that they're equipped with sabre and pistol.'

'There, you see? You're not keeping up to date with current happenings. Your Squadron A that you know so much about don't have a horse to their name. They're a machine-gun outfit.'

'Well, that of course is a God damn lie, Murphy.'

'A lie, is it? Well how much would you care to bet me – in cash?'

'Let me take a look and see how much I have on me?' said Tony. He placed his money on the bar. 'Eighteen dollars and ninety-four cents. Is this even money, or do I have to give you odds?'

Murphy placed nineteen dollars on the bar. 'Even money'll be good enough for me, bein's it's like taking the money off a blind man.'

'And how are we to settle who's right?' said Tony.

'We'll call up the newspaper on the telephone.'

'What newspaper? There's no newspaper here open after six p.m.'

'We'll call the New York *World*,' said Murphy.

'By long distance, you mean? Who's to pay for the call?'

'The winner of the bet,' said Murphy.

'The winner of the bet? Oh, all right. I'll be magnanimous. How do you go about it? You can't put that many nickels in the slot.'

'We'll go over to the hotel and get the operator at the switchboard, Mary McFadden. She's used to these long-distance calls.'

'Will she be on duty at this hour?'

'Are you trying to back out? It's only a little after eight,' said Murphy.

'Me back out? I wished I could get the loan of a hundred dollars and I'd show you who's backing out,' said Tony.

In silence they marched to the hotel, and explained their purpose to Mary McFadden. Within fifteen minutes they were connected with the office of *The World*, then to the newspaper library. 'Good evening, sir,' said Murphy. 'This is a long-distance call from Gibbsville, Pennsylvania. I wish to request the information as to whether the Squadron A is in the cavalry or a machine-gun organ-i-zation.' He repeated the question and waited. 'He says to hold the line a minute.'

'Costing us a fortune,' said Tony.

'Hello? Yes, I'm still here. Yes? Uh-huh. Would you kindly repeat that information?' Murphy quickly handed the receiver to Tony Costello, who listened, nodded, said 'Thank you,' and hung up.

'How much do we owe you for the call, Mary?' said Murphy.

'Just a minute,' said the operator. 'That'll be nine dollars and fifty-five cents.'

'Jesus,' said Tony. 'Well, one consolation. It's out of your profit, Murphy.'

'But the profit is out of your pocket,' said Murphy. 'Come on, we'll go back and I'll treat you. Generous in victory, that's me. Like Ulysses S. Grant. He give all them Confederates their horses back, did you ever know that, Costello?'

'I did not, and what's more I don't believe it.'

'Well, maybe you'd care to bet on that, too? Not this evening, however, bein's you're out of cash. But now will you believe that the ottomobile is putting an end to the horse?'

'Where does the ottomobile come into it? The machine gun is no ottomobile.'

'No, and I didn't say it was, but if they have no use for the cavalry in a war, they'll soon have no use for them anywhere.'

'If you weren't such a pinch of snuff I'd give you a puck in the mouth. But don't try my patience too far, Mr Murphy. I'll take just so much of your impudence and no more. With me one hand tied behind me I could put you in hospital.'

'You're kind of a hard loser, Tony. You oughtn't to be that way. There's more ottomobiles in town now than horses. The fire companies are all motorizing. The breweries. And the rich, you don't see them buying a new pair of cobs no more. It's the Pierce-Arrow now. Flannagan the undertaker is getting rid of his blacks, he told me so himself. Ordered a Cunningham 8.'

'We'll see where Flannagan and his Cunningham 8 ends up next winter, the first time he has to bring a dead one down from the top of Fairview Street. Or go up it, for that matter. There's hills in this town no Cunningham 8 will negotiate, but Flannagan's team of blacks never had the least trouble. Flannagan'll be out of business the first winter, and it'll serve him right.'

'And here I thought he was a friend of yours. Many's the time you used his stable for a boudoir, not to mention the funerals you drove for him. Two or three dollars for a half a day's work.'

'There never was no friendship between him and I. You never saw me stand up to a bar and have a drink with him. You never saw me set foot inside his house, nor even his kitchen for a cup of coffee. The rare occasions that I slept in his barn, he was never the loser, let me tell you. Those blacks that he's getting rid of, I mind the time I saved the off one's life from the colic. Too tight-fisted to send for Doc McNary, the vet, and he'd have lost the animal for sure if I wasn't there.

Do you know what he give me for saving the horse? Guess what he give me.'

'Search me,' said Murphy.

'A pair of gloves. A pair of gauntlets so old that the lining was all wore away. Supposed to be fleece-lined, but the fleece was long since gone. "Here, you take these, Tony," said Mr Generous Flannagan. I wanted to say "Take them and do what with them?" But I was so dead tired from being up all night with the black, all I wanted to do was go up in his hay-loft and lie down exhausted. Which I did for a couple of hours, and when I come down again there was the black, standing on his four feet and give me a whinny. A horse don't have much brains, but they could teach Flannagan gratitude.'

After the war the abandonment of horses became so general that even Tony Costello was compelled to give in to it. The small merchants of the town, who had kept a single horse and delivery wagon (and a carriage for Sunday), were won over to Ford and Dodge trucks. The three-horse hitches of the breweries disappeared and in their place were big Macks and Garfords. The fire companies bought American LaFrances and Whites. The physicians bought Franklins and Fords, Buicks, and Dodges. (The Franklin was air-cooled; the Buick was supposed to be a great hill climber.) And private citizens who had never felt they could afford a horse and buggy, now went into debt to purchase flivvers. Of the three leading harness shops in the town, two became luggage shops and one went out of business entirely. Only two of the seven blacksmith shops remained. Gone were the Fleisch-mann's Yeast and Grand Union Tea Company wagons, the sorrels and greys of the big express companies. The smooth-surface paving caused a high mortality rate among horses, who slipped and broke legs and had to be shot and carried away to the fertilizer plant. The horse was retained only by the rich and the poor; saddle horses for the rich, and sway-backed old nags for the junk men and fruit peddlers. For Tony Costello it was not so easy as it once had been to find a place to sleep. The last livery stable closed in 1922, was converted into a public garage, and neither the rats nor Tony Costello had a home to go to, he said. 'No decent, self-respecting rat will live in a garridge,' he said. 'It's an inhuman smell, them gazzoline fumes. And the rats don't have any more to eat there than I do meself.'

The odd jobs that he lived on made no demands on his skill with horses, but all his life he had known how to take proper care of the varnish and the brightwork of a Brewster brougham, the leather and the bits and buckles of all kinds of tack. He therefore made himself useful at washing cars and polishing shoes. Nobody wanted to give him a steady job, but it was more sensible to pay Tony a few dollars than to waste a good mechanic on a car wash. He had a flexible arrangement with the cooks at two Greek restaurants who, on their own and without consulting the owners, would give him a meal in exchange for his washing dishes. 'There ain't a man in the town has hands any cleaner than mine. Me hands are in soapy water morning, noon, and night,' he said.

'It's too bad the rest of you don't get in with your hands,' said Murphy. 'How long since you had a real bath, Tony?'

'Oh, I don't know.'

'As the fellow says, you take a bath once a year whether you need it or not,' said Murphy. 'And yet I never seen you need a shave, barring the times you were on a three-day toot.'

'Even then I don't often let her grow more'n a couple days. As long as I can hold me hand steady enough so's I don't cut me throat. That's a temptation, too, I'll tell you. There's days I just as soon take the razor in me hand and let nature take its course.'

'What stops you?' said Murphy.

'That I wonder. Mind you, I don't wonder too much or the logical conclusion would be you-know-what. My mother wasn't sure who my father was. She didn't keep count. She put me out on the streets when I was eight or nine years of age. "You can read and write," she said, which was more than she could do. With my fine education I was able to tell one paper from another, so I sold them.'

'You mean she put you out with no place to sleep?'

'Oh, no. She let me sleep there, providing she didn't have a customer. If I come home and she had a customer I had to wait outside.'

'I remember you telling me one time your father worked for a man that had a son belonged to the Squadron A. That time we had the bet.'

'That was a prevarication. A harmless prevarication that I thought up on the spur of the moment. I ought to know better by this time. Every time I prevaricate I get punished for it. That time I lost the bet. I should have said I knew about the Squadron A and let it go at that, but I had to embellish it. I always knew about the Squadron A. From selling newspapers in the Tenderloin I got a job walking hots at the race track, and I was a jock till I got too big. I couldn't make the weight any more, my bones were too heavy regardless of how much I starved myself and dried out. That done something to me, those times I tried to make a hundred and fifteen pounds and my bones weighed more than that. As soon as I quit trying to be a jock my weight jumped up to a hundred and fifty, and that's about what I am now.'

'What do you mean it done something to you?' said Murphy.

'Be hard for you to understand, Murphy. It's a medical fact.'

'Oh, go ahead, Doctor Costello.'

'Well, if you don't get enough to eat, the blood thins out and the brain don't get fed properly. That changes your whole outlook on life, and if the brain goes too long without nourishment, you get so's you don't care any more.'

'Where did you get that piece of information?'

'I trained for a doctor that owned a couple trotters over near Lancaster. Him and I had many's the conversation on the subject.'

'I never know whether to believe you or call you a liar. Did you get so's you didn't care any more?'

'That's what I'm trying to get through your thick skull, Murphy. That's why I never amounted to anything. That's why poor people stay poor. The brain don't get enough nourishment from the blood. Fortunately I know that, you see: I don't waste my strength trying to be something I ain't.'

'Do you know what I think, Tony? I think you were just looking for an excuse to be a bum.'

'Naturally! I wasn't looking for an excuse, but I was looking for some reason why a fellow as smart as I am never amounted to anything. If I cared more what happened to me, I'd have cut my throat years ago. Jesus! The most I ever had in my life was eight hundred dollars one time a long shot came in, but I don't care. You know, I'm fifty-five or -six years of age, one or the other. I had my first woman when I was fifteen, and I guess a couple hundred since then. But I never saw one yet that I'd lose any sleep over. Not a single one, out of maybe a couple hundred. One is just like the other, to me. Get what you want out of them, and so long. So long till you want another. And I used to be a pretty handsome fellow when I was young. Not all whores, either. Once when I was wintering down in Latonia – well, what the hell. It don't bother me as much as it used to do. I couldn't go a week without it, but these days I just as soon spend the money on the grog. I'll be just as content when I can do without them altogether.'

One day Tony was washing a brand-new Chrysler, which was itself a recent make of car. He was standing off, hose in hand, contemplating the design and colors of the car, when a young woman got out of a plain black Ford coupe. She was wearing black and white saddle shoes, bruised and spotted, and not liable to be seriously damaged by the puddles of dirty water on the garage floor, but Tony cautioned her. 'Mind where you're walking, young lady,' he said.

'Oh, it won't hurt these shoes,' she said. 'I'm looking for Tony Costello. I was told he worked here.'

'Feast your eyes, Miss. You're looking right at him,' he said.

'You're Tony Costello? I somehow pictured an older man,' she said.

'Well, maybe I'm older than I look. What is there I can do for you?'

She was a sturdily built young woman, past the middle twenties, handsome if she had been a man, but it was no man inside the grey pullover. 'I was told that you were the best man in town to take care of a sick horse,' she said.

'You were told right,' said Tony Costello. 'And I take it you have a sick horse! What's the matter with him, if it's a him, or her if it's a her?'

'It's a mare named Daisy. By the way, my name is Esther Wayman.'

'Wayman? You're new here in town,' said Tony.

'Just this year. My father is the manager of the bus company.'

'I see. And your mare Daisy, how old?'

'Five, I think, or maybe six,' said Esther Wayman.

'And sick in what way? What are the symptoms?'

'She's all swollen up around the mouth. I thought I had the curb chain on too tight; but that wasn't it. I kept her in the stable for several days, with a halter on, and instead of going away the swelling got worse.'

'Mm. The swelling, is it accompanied by, uh, a great deal of saliva?'

'Yes, it is.'

'You say the animal is six years old. How long did you own her, Miss Wayman?'

'Only about a month. I bought her from a place in Philadelphia.'

'Mm-hmm. Out Market Street, one of them horse bazaars?'

'Yes.'

'Is this your first horse? In other words, you're not familiar with horses?'

'No, we've always lived in the city – Philadelphia, Cleveland, Ohio, Denver, Colorado. I learned to ride in college, but I never owned a horse before we came here.'

'You wouldn't know a case of glanders if you saw it, would you?'

'No. Is that a disease?' she said.

'Unless I'm very much mistaken, it's the disease that ails your mare Daisy. I'll be done washing this car in two shakes, and then you can take me out to see your mare. Where do you stable her?'

'We have our own stable. My father bought the Henderson house.'

'Oh, to be sure, and I know it well. Slept in that stable many's the night.'

'I don't want to take you away from your work,' she said.

'Young woman, you're taking me *to* work. You're not taking me away from anything.'

He finished with the Chrysler, got out of his gum boots, and put on his shoes. He called to the garage foreman, 'Back sometime in the morning,' and did not wait for an answer. None came.

On the way out to the Wayman-Henderson house he let the young woman do all the talking. She had the flat accent of the Middle West and she spoke from deep inside her mouth. She told him how she had got interested in riding at cawlidge, and was so pleased to find that the house her father bought included a garage that was not really a garage but a real stable. Her father permitted her to have a horse on condition that she took complete care of it herself. She had seen the ad in a Philadelphia paper, gone to one of the weekly sales, and paid $300 for Daisy. She had not even looked at any other horse. The bidding for Daisy had started at $100; Esther raised it to $150; someone else went to $200; Esther jumped it to $300 and the mare was hers.

'Uh-huh,' said Tony. 'Well, maybe you got a bargain, and maybe not.'

'You seem doubtful,' she said.

'We learn by experience, and you got the animal you wanted. You'll be buying other horses as you get older. This is only your first one.'

They left the car at the stable door. 'I guess she's lying down,' said Esther.

Tony opened the door of the box stall. 'She is that, and I'm sorry to tell you, she's never getting up.'

'She's dead? How could she be? I only saw her a few hours ago.'

'Let me go in and have a look at her. You stay where you are,' he said. He had taken command and she obeyed him.

In a few minutes, three or four, he came out of the stall and closed the door behind him.

'Glanders, it was. Glanders and old age. Daisy was more like eleven than five or six.'

'But how could it happen so quickly?'

'It didn't, exactly. I'm not saying the animal had glanders when you bought her. I do say they falsified her age, which they all do. Maybe they'll give you your money back, maybe they won't. In any case, Miss Wayman, you're not to go in there. Glanders is contagious to man and animal. If you want me to, I'll see to the removal of the animal. A telephone call to the fertilizer plant, and they know me there. Then I'll burn the bedding for you and fumigate the stable. You might as well leave the halter on, it wouldn't be fair to put it on a well horse.'

The young woman took out a pack of cigarettes and offered him one. He took it, lit hers and his. 'I'm glad to see you take it so calmly. I seen women go into hysterics under these circumstances,' he said.

'I don't get hysterics,' she said. 'But that's not to say I'm not in a turmoil. If I'd had her a little while longer I *might* have gotten hysterical.'

'Then be thankful that you didn't have her that much longer. To tell you the truth, you didn't get a bargain. There was other things wrong with her that we needn't go into. I wouldn't be surprised if she was blind, but that's not what I was thinking of. No, you didn't get a bargain this time, but keep trying. Only, next time take somebody with you that had some experience with horses and horse dealers.'

'I'll take you, if you'll come,' she said. 'Meanwhile, will you do those other things you said you would?'

'I will indeed.'

'And how much do I owe you?' she said.

He smiled. 'I don't have a regular fee for telling people that a dead horse is dead,' he said. 'A couple dollars for my time.'

'How about ten dollars?'

'Whatever you feel is right, I'll take,' he said. 'The state of my finances is on the wrong side of affluence.'

'Is the garage where I can always reach you?' she said.

'I don't work there steady.'

'At home, then? Can you give me your telephone number?' she said.

'I move around from place to place.'

'Oh. Well, would you like to have a steady job? I could introduce you to my father.'

'I couldn't drive a bus, if that's what you had in mind. I don't have a license, for one thing, and even if I did they have to maintain a schedule. That I've never done, not that strict kind of a schedule. But thanks for the offer.'

'He might have a job for you washing buses. I don't know how well it would pay, but I think they wash and clean those buses every night, so it would be steady work. Unless you're not interested in steady work. Is that it?'

'Steady pay without the steady work, that's about the size of it,' he said.

She shook her head. 'Then I don't think you and my father would get along. He lives by the clock.'

'Well, I guess he'd have to, running a bus line,' said Tony. He looked about him. 'The Hendersons used to hang their cutters up there. They had two cutters and a bob. They were great ones for sleighing parties. Two – three times a winter they'd load up the bob and the two cutters and take their friends down to their farm for a chicken-and-waffle supper. They had four horses then. A pair of sorrels, Prince and Duke. Trixie, a bay mare, broke to saddle. And a black gelding named Satan, Mr Henderson drove himself to work in.

They were pretty near the last to give up horses, Mr and Mrs Henderson.'

'Did you work for them?'

'Twice I worked for them. Sacked both times. But he knew I used to come here and sleep. They had four big buffalo robes, two for the bob and one each for the cutters. That was the lap of luxury for me. Sleep on two and cover up with one. Then he died and she moved away, and the son Jasper only had cars. There wasn't a horse stabled in here since Mrs moved away, and Jasper wouldn't let me sleep here. He put in that gazzoline pump and he said it wasn't safe to let me stop here for the night. It wasn't me he was worried about. It was them ottomobiles. Well, this isn't getting to the telephone.'

During the night he fumigated the stable. The truck from the fertilizer plant arrived at nine o'clock and he helped the two men load the dead mare, after which he lit the fumigating tablets in the stalls and closed the doors and windows. Esther Wayman came up from the house at ten o'clock or so, just as he was closing the doors of the carriage house. 'They took her away?' she said.

'About an hour ago. Then I lit candles for her,' he said.

'You what?'

'That's my little joke, not in the best of taste perhaps. I don't know that this fumigating does any good, but on the other hand it can't do much harm. It's a precaution you take, glanders being contagious and all that. You have to think of the next animal that'll be occupying that stall, so you take every precaution – as much for your own peace of mind as anything else, I guess.'

'Where did you get the fumigating stuff?'

'I went down to the drugstore, Schlicter's Pharmacy, Six-teenth and Market. I told them to charge it to your father. They know me there.'

'They know you everywhere in this town, don't they?'

'Yes, I guess they do, now that I stop to think of it.'

'Can I take you home in my car?'

'Oh, I guess I can walk it.'

'Why should you when I have my car? Where do you live?'

'I got a room on Canal Street. That's not much of a neighborhood for you to be driving around in after dark.'

'I'm sure I've been in worse, or just as bad,' she said.

'That would surprise me,' he said.

'I'm not a sheltered hothouse plant,' she said. 'I can take care of myself. Let's go. I'd like to see that part of town.'

When they got to Canal Street she said, 'It isn't eleven o'clock yet. Is there a place where we can go for a drink?'

'Oh, there's places aplenty. But I doubt if your Dad would approve of them for you.'

'Nobody will know me,' she said. 'I hardly know anybody in this town. I don't get to know people very easily. Where shall we go?'

'Well, there's a pretty decent place that goes by the name of the Bucket of Blood. Don't let the name frighten you. It's just a common ordinary saloon. I'm not saying you'll encounter the Ladies Aid Society there, but if it didn't have that name attached to it – well, you'll see the kind of place it is.'

It was a quiet night in the saloon. They sat at a table in the back room. A man and woman were at another table, drinking whiskey by the shot and washing it down with beer chasers. They were a solemn couple, both about fifty, with no need to converse and seemingly no concern beyond the immediate appreciation of the alcohol. Presently the man stood up and headed for the street door, followed by the woman. As she went out she slapped Tony Costello lightly on the shoulder. 'Goodnight, Tony,' she said.

'Goodnight, Marie,' said Tony Costello.

When they were gone Esther Wayman said, 'She knew you, but all she said was goodnight. She never said hello.'

'Him and I don't speak to one another,' said Tony. 'We had some kind of a dispute there a long while back.'

'Are they husband and wife?'

'No, but they been going together ever since I can remember.'

'She's a prostitute, isn't she?'

'That's correct,' said Tony.

'And what does he do? Live off her?'

'Oh, no. No, he's a trackwalker for the Pennsy. One of the few around that ain't an I-talian. But she's an I-talian.'

'Are you an Italian? You're not, are you?'

'Good Lord, no. I'm as Irish as they come.'

'You have an Italian name, though.'

'It may sound I-talian to you, but my mother was straight from County Cork. My father could be anybody, but most likely he was an Irishman, the neighborhood I come from. I'm pretty certain he wasn't John Jacob Astor or J. Pierpont Morgan. My old lady was engaged in the same occupation as Marie that just went out.'

'Doesn't your church – I mean; in France and Italy I suppose the prostitutes must be Catholic, but I never thought of Irish prostitutes.'

'There's prostitutes wherever a woman needs a dollar and doesn't have to care too much how she gets it. It don't even have to be a dollar. If they're young enough they'll do it for a stick of candy, and the dollar comes later. This is an elevating conversation for a young woman like yourself.'

'You don't know anything about myself, Mr Costello,' she said.

'I do, and I don't,' he said. 'But what I don't know I'm learning. I'll make a guess that you were disappointed in love.'

She laughed. 'Very.'

'What happened? The young man give you the go-by?'

'There was no young man,' she said. 'I have never been interested in young men or they in me.'

'I see,' he said.

'Do you?'

'Well, to be honest with you, no. I don't. I'd of thought you'd have yourself a husband by this time. You're not at all bad looking, you know, and you always knew where your next meal was coming from.'

'This conversation *is* beginning to embarrass me a little,' she said. 'Sometime I may tell you all about myself. In fact, I have a feeling I will. But not now, not tonight.'

'Anytime you say,' said Tony. 'And one of these days we'll go looking for a horse for you.'

'We'll have fun,' she said.

JOHN STEINBECK

THE GIFT

AT DAYBREAK Billy Buck emerged from the bunkhouse and stood for a moment on the porch looking up at the sky. He was a broad, bandy-legged little man with a walrus mustache, with square hands, puffed and muscled on the palms. His eyes were a contemplative, watery grey and the hair which protruded from under his Stetson hat was spiky and weathered. Billy was still stuffing his shirt into his blue jeans as he stood on the porch. He unbuckled his belt and tightened it again. The belt showed, by the worn shiny places opposite each hole, the gradual increase of Billy's middle over a period of years. When he had seen to the weather, Billy cleared each nostril by holding its mate closed with his forefinger and blowing fiercely. Then he walked down to the barn, rubbing his hands together. He curried and brushed two saddle horses in the stalls, talking quietly to them all the time; and he had hardly finished when the iron triangle started ringing at the ranch house. Billy stuck the brush and currycomb together and laid them on the rail, and went up to breakfast. His action had been so deliberate and yet so wasteless of time that he came to the house while Mrs Tiflin was still ringing the triangle. She nodded her grey head to him and withdrew into the kitchen. Billy Buck sat down on the steps, because he was a cowhand, and it wouldn't be fitting that he should go first into the dining room. He heard Mr Tiflin in the house, stamping his feet into his boots.

The high jangling note of the triangle put the boy Jody in

motion. He was only a little boy, ten years old, with hair like dusty yellow grass and with shy polite grey eyes, and with a mouth that worked when he thought. The triangle picked him up out of sleep. It didn't occur to him to disobey the harsh note. He never had: no one he knew ever had. He brushed the tangled hair out of his eyes and skinned his nightgown off. In a moment he was dressed – blue chambray shirt and overalls. It was late in the summer, so of course there were no shoes to bother with. In the kitchen he waited until his mother got from in front of the sink and went back to the stove. Then he washed himself and brushed back his wet hair with his fingers. His mother turned sharply on him as he left the sink. Jody looked shyly away.

'I've got to cut your hair before long,' his mother said. 'Breakfast's on the table. Go on in, so Billy can come.'

Jody sat at the long table which was covered with white oilcloth washed through to the fabric in some places. The fried eggs lay in rows on their platter. Jody took three eggs on his plate and followed with three thick slices of crisp bacon. He carefully scraped a spot of blood from one of the egg yolks.

Billy Buck clumped in. 'That won't hurt you,' Billy explained. 'That's only a sign the rooster leaves.'

Jody's tall stern father came in then and Jody knew from the noise on the floor that he was wearing boots, but he looked under the table anyway, to make sure. His father turned off the oil lamp over the table, for plenty of morning light now came through the windows.

Jody did not ask where his father and Billy Buck were riding that day, but he wished he might go along. His father was a disciplinarian. Jody obeyed him in everything without questions of any kind. Now, Carl Tiflin sat down and reached for the egg platter.

'Got the cows ready to go, Billy?' he asked.

'In the lower corral,' Billy said. 'I could just as well take them in alone.'

'Sure you could. But a man needs company. Besides your throat gets pretty dry.' Carl Tiflin was jovial this morning.

Jody's mother put her head in the door. 'What time do you think to be back, Carl?'

'I can't tell. I've got to see some men in Salinas. Might be gone till dark.'

The eggs and coffee and big biscuits disappeared rapidly. Jody followed the two men out of the house. He watched them mount their horses and drive six old milk cows out of the corral and start over the hill toward Salinas. They were going to sell the old cows to the butcher.

When they had disappeared over the crown of the ridge Jody walked up the hill in back of the house. The dogs trotted around the house corner hunching their shoulders and grinning horribly with pleasure. Jody patted their heads – Doubletree Mutt with the big thick tail and yellow eyes, and Smasher, the shepherd, who had killed a coyote and lost an ear in doing it. Smasher's one good ear stood up higher than a collie's ear should. Billy Buck said that always happened. After the frenzied greeting the dogs lowered their noses to the ground in a businesslike way and went ahead, looking back now and then to make sure that the boy was coming. They walked up through the chicken yard and saw the quail eating with the chickens. Smasher chased the chickens a little to keep in practice in case there should ever be sheep to herd. Jody continued on through the large vege-table patch where the green corn was higher than his head. The cow pumpkins were green and small yet. He went on to the sagebrush line where the cold spring ran out of its pipe and fell into a round wooden tub. He leaned over and drank close to the green mossy wood where the water tasted best. Then he turned and looked back on the ranch, on the low, whitewashed house girded with red geraniums, and on the long bunkhouse by the cypress tree where Billy Buck lived alone. Jody could see the great black kettle under the cypress tree. That was where the pigs were scalded. The sun was coming over the ridge now, glaring on the whitewash of the houses and barns, making the wet grass blaze softly. Behind him, in the tall sagebrush, the birds were scampering on the ground, making a great noise among the dry leaves; the squirrels piped shrilly on the sidehills. Jody looked along at the farm buildings. He felt an uncertainty in the air, a feeling of change and of loss and of the gain of new and unfamiliar things. Over the hillside two big black buzzards sailed low to the ground and their shadows slipped smoothly and quickly ahead of them. Some animal had died in the vicinity. Jody knew it. It might be a cow or it might be the remains of a rabbit. The buzzards overlooked nothing. Jody hated them as all decent things hate them, but they could not be hurt because they made away with carrion.

After a while the boy sauntered downhill again. The dogs had long ago given him up and gone into the brush to do things in their own way. Back through the vegetable garden he went, and he paused for a moment to smash a green muskmelon with his heel, but he was not happy about it. It was a bad thing to do, he knew perfectly well. He kicked dirt over the ruined melon to conceal it.

Back at the house his mother bent over his rough hands, inspecting his fingers and nails. It did little good to start him clean to school for too many things could happen on the way. She sighed over the black cracks on his fingers, and then gave him his books and his lunch and started him on the mile walk to school. She noticed that his mouth was working a good deal this morning.

Jody started his journey. He filled his pockets with little pieces of white quartz that lay in the road, and every so often he took a shot at a bird or at some rabbit that had stayed sunning itself in the road too long. At the crossroads over the bridge he met two friends and the three of them walked to school together, making ridiculous strides and being rather silly. School had just opened two weeks before. There was still a spirit of revolt among the pupils.

It was four o'clock in the afternoon when Jody topped the hill and looked down on the ranch again. He looked for the saddle horses, but the corral was empty. His father was not back yet. He went slowly, then, toward the afternoon chores. At the ranch house, he found his mother sitting on the porch, mending socks.

'There's two doughnuts in the kitchen for you,' she said. Jody slid to the kitchen, and returned with half of one of the doughnuts already eaten and his mouth full. His mother asked him what he had learned in school that day, but she didn't listen to his doughnut-muffled answer. She interrupted, 'Jody, tonight see you fill the wood box clear full. Last night you crossed the sticks and it wasn't only about half full. Lay the sticks flat tonight. And Jody, some of the hens are hiding eggs, or else the dogs are eating them. Look about in the grass and see if you can find any nests.'

Jody, still eating, went out and did his chores. He saw the quail come down to eat with the chickens when he threw out the grain. For some reason his father was proud to have them come. He never allowed any shooting near the house for fear the quail might go away.

When the wood box was full, Jody took his twenty-two

rifle up to the cold spring at the brush line. He drank again and then aimed the gun at all manner of things, at rocks, at birds on the wing, at the big black pig kettle under the cypress tree, but he didn't shoot for he had no cartridges and wouldn't have until he was twelve. If his father had seen him aim the rifle in the direction of the house he would have put the cartridges off another year. Jody remembered this and did not point the rifle down the hill again. Two years was enough to wait for cartridges. Nearly all of his father's presents were given with reservations which hampered their value somewhat. It was good discipline.

The supper waited until dark for his father to return. When at last he came in with Billy Buck, Jody could smell the delicious brandy on their breaths. Inwardly he rejoiced, for his father sometimes talked to him when he smelled of brandy, sometimes even told things he had done in the wild days when he was a boy.

After supper, Jody sat by the fireplace and his shy polite eyes sought the room corners, and he waited for his father to tell what it was he contained, for Jody knew he had news of some sort. But he was disappointed. His father pointed a stern finger at him.

'You'd better go to bed, Jody. I'm going to need you in the morning.'

That wasn't so bad. Jody liked to do the things he had to do as long as they weren't routine things. He looked at the floor and his mouth worked out a question before he spoke it. 'What are we going to do in the morning, kill a pig?' he asked softly.

'Never you mind. You better get to bed.'

When the door was closed behind him, Jody heard his father and Billy Buck chuckling and he knew it was a joke of some kind. And later, when he lay in bed, trying to make words out of the murmurs in the other room, he heard his father protest, 'But, Ruth, I didn't give much for him.'

Jody heard the hoot owls hunting mice down by the barn, and he heard a fruit tree limb tap-tapping against the house. A cow was lowing when he went to sleep.

When the triangle sounded in the morning, Jody dressed more quickly even than usual. In the kitchen, while he washed his face and combed back his hair, his mother addressed him irritably. 'Don't you go out until you get a good breakfast in you.'

He went into the dining room and sat at the long white table. He took a steaming hotcake from the platter, arranged two fried eggs on it, covered them with another hotcake, and squashed the whole thing with his fork.

His father and Billy Buck came in. Jody knew from the sound on the floor that both of them were wearing flat-heeled shoes, but he peered under the table to make sure. His father turned off the oil lamp, for the day had arrived, and he looked stern and disciplinary, but Billy Buck didn't look at Jody at all. He avoided the shy questioning eyes of the boy and soaked a whole piece of toast in his coffee.

Carl Tiflin said crossly, 'You come with us after breakfast!'

Jody had trouble with his food then, for he felt a kind of doom in the air. After Billy had tilted his saucer and drained the coffee which had slopped into it, and had wiped his hands on his jeans, the two men stood up from the table and went out into the morning light together, and Jody respect-fully followed a little behind them. He tried to keep his mind from running ahead, tried to keep it absolutely motionless.

His mother called, 'Carl! Don't you let it keep him from school.'

They marched past the cypress, where a singletree hung

from a limb to butcher the pigs on, and past the black iron kettle, so it was not a pig killing. The sun shone over the hill and threw long, dark shadows of the trees and buildings. They crossed a stubble field to shortcut to the barn. Jody's father unhooked the door and they went in. They had been walking toward the sun on the way down. The barn was black as night in contrast and warm from the hay and from the beasts. Jody's father moved over toward the one box stall. 'Come here!' he ordered. Jody could begin to see things now. He looked into the box stall and then stepped back quickly.

A red pony colt was looking at him out of the stall. Its tense ears were forward and a light of disobedience was in its eyes. Its coat was rough and thick as an airedale's fur and its mane was long and tangled. Jody's throat collapsed in on itself and cut his breath short.

'He needs a good currying,' his father said, 'and if I ever hear of you not feeding him or leaving his stall dirty, I'll sell him off in a minute.'

Jody couldn't bear to look at the pony's eyes any more. He gazed down at his hands for a moment, and he asked very shyly, 'Mine?' No one answered him. He put his hand out toward the pony. Its grey nose came close, sniffing loudly, and then the lips drew back and the strong teeth closed on Jody's fingers. The pony shook its head up and down and seemed to laugh with amusement. Jody regarded his bruised fingers. 'Well,' he said with pride – 'Well, I guess he can bite all right.' The two men laughed, somewhat in relief. Carl Tiflin went out of the barn and walked up a sidehill to be by himself, for he was embarrassed, but Billy Buck stayed. It was easier to talk to Billy Buck. Jody asked again – 'Mine?'

Billy became professional in tone. 'Sure! That is, if you look out for him and break him right. I'll show you how. He's just a colt. You can't ride him for some time.'

240

Jody put out his bruised hand again, and this time the red pony let his nose be rubbed. 'I ought to have a carrot,' Jody said. 'Where'd we get him, Billy?'

'Bought him at a sheriff's auction,' Billy explained. 'A show went broke in Salinas and had debts. The sheriff was selling off their stuff.'

The pony stretched out his nose and shook the forelock from his wild eyes. Jody stroked the nose a little. He said softly, 'There isn't a – saddle?'

Billy Buck laughed. 'I'd forgot. Come along.'

In the harness room he lifted down a little saddle of red morocco leather. 'It's just a show saddle,' Billy Buck said disparagingly. 'It isn't practical for the brush, but it was cheap at the sale.'

Jody couldn't trust himself to look at the saddle either, and he couldn't speak at all. He brushed the shining red leather with his fingertips, and after a long time he said, 'It'll look pretty on him though.' He thought of the grandest and prettiest things he knew. 'If he hasn't a name already, I think I'll call him Gabilan Mountains,' he said.

Billy Buck knew how he felt. 'It's a pretty long name. Why don't you just call him Gabilan? That means hawk. That would be a fine name for him.' Billy felt glad. 'If you will collect tail hair, I might be able to make a hair rope for you sometime. You could use it for a hackamore.'

Jody wanted to go back to the box stall. 'Could I lead him to school, do you think – to show the kids?'

But Billy shook his head. 'He's not even halter-broke yet. We had a time getting him here. Had to almost drag him. You better be starting for school though.'

'I'll bring the kids to see him here this afternoon,' Jody said.

*   *   *

Six boys came over the hill half an hour early that afternoon, running hard, their heads down, their forearms working, their breath whistling. They swept by the house and cut across the stubble field to the barn. And then they stood self-consciously before the pony, and then they looked at Jody with eyes in which there was a new admiration and a new respect. Before today Jody had been a boy, dressed in overalls and a blue shirt – quieter than most, even suspected of being a little cowardly. And now he was different. Out of a thousand centuries they drew the ancient admiration of the footman for the horseman. They knew instinctively that a man on a horse is spiritually as well as physically bigger than a man on foot. They knew that Jody had been miraculously lifted out of equality with them, and had been placed over them. Gabilan put his head out of the stall and sniffed them.

'Why'n't you ride him?' the boys cried. 'Why'n't you braid his tail with ribbons like in the fair?'

'When you going to ride him?'

Jody's courage was up. He too felt the superiority of the horseman. 'He's not old enough. Nobody can ride him for a long time. I'm going to train him on the long halter. Billy Buck is going to show me how.'

'Well, can't we even lead him around a little?'

'He isn't even halter-broke,' Jody said. He wanted to be completely alone when he took the pony out the first time. 'Come and see the saddle.'

They were speechless at the red morocco saddle, completely shocked out of comment. 'It isn't much use in the brush,' Jody explained. 'It'll look pretty on him though. Maybe I'll ride bareback when I go into the brush.'

'How you going to rope a cow without a saddle horn?'

'Maybe I'll get another saddle for every day. My father might want me to help him with the stock.' He let them feel the red saddle, and showed them the brass chain throatlatch on the bridle and the big brass buttons at each temple where the headstall and brow band crossed. The whole thing was too wonderful. They had to go away after a little while, and each boy, in his mind, searched among his possessions for a bribe worthy of offering in return for a ride on the red pony when the time should come.

Jody was glad when they had gone. He took brush and currycomb from the wall, took down the barrier of the box stall, and stepped cautiously in. The pony's eyes glittered, and he edged around into kicking position. But Jody touched him on the shoulder and rubbed his high arched neck as he had always seen Billy Buck do, and he crooned, 'So-o-o Boy,' in a deep voice. The pony gradually relaxed his tenseness. Jody curried and brushed until a pile of dead hair lay in the stall and until the pony's coat had taken on a deep red shine. Each time he finished he thought it might have been done better. He braided the mane into a dozen little pigtails, and he braided the forelock, and then he undid them and brushed the hair out straight again.

Jody did not hear his mother enter the barn. She was angry when she came, but when she looked in at the pony and at Jody working on him, she felt a curious pride rise up in her. 'Have you forgot the wood box?' she asked gently. 'It's not far off from dark and there's not a stick of wood in the house, and the chickens aren't fed.'

Jody quickly put up his tools. 'I forgot, ma'am.'

'Well, after this do your chores first. Then you won't forget. I expect you'll forget lots of things now if I don't keep an eye on you.'

'Can I have carrots from the garden for him, ma'am?'

She had to think about that. 'Oh – I guess so, if you only take the big tough ones.'

'Carrots keep the coat good,' he said, and again she felt the curious rush of pride.

Jody never waited for the triangle to get him out of bed after the coming of the pony. It became his habit to creep out of bed even before his mother was awake, to slip into his clothes and to go quietly down to the barn to see Gabilan. In the grey quiet mornings when the land and the brush and the houses and the trees were silver-grey and black like a photograph negative, he stole toward the barn, past the sleeping stones and the sleeping cypress tree. The turkeys, roosting in the tree out of coyotes' reach, clicked drowsily. The fields glowed with a grey frostlike light and in the dew the tracks of rabbits and of field mice stood out sharply. The good dogs came stiffly out of their little houses, hackles up and deep growls in their throats. Then they caught Jody's scent, and their stiff tails rose up and waved a greeting – Doubletree Mutt with the big thick tail, and Smasher, the incipient shepherd – then went lazily back to their warm beds.

It was a strange time and a mysterious journey, to Jody – an extension of a dream. When he first had the pony he liked to torture himself during the trip by thinking Gabilan would not be in his stall, and worse, would never have been there. And he had other delicious little self-induced pains. He thought how the rats had gnawed ragged holes in the red saddle, and how the mice had nibbled Gabilan's tail until it was stringy and thin. He usually ran the last little way to the barn. He unlatched the rusty hasp of the barn door and stepped in, and no matter how quietly he opened the door, Gabilan was always looking at him over the barrier of the box stall and Gabilan whinnied softly and stamped his front foot, and his eyes had big sparks of red fire in them like oak-wood embers.

Sometimes, if the work horses were to be used that day, Jody found Billy Buck in the barn harnessing and currying. Billy stood with him and looked long at Gabilan and he told Jody a great many things about horses. He explained that they were terribly afraid for their feet, so that one must make a practice of lifting the legs and patting the hooves and ankles to remove their terror. He told Jody how horses love conversation. He must talk to the pony all the time, and tell him the reasons for everything. Billy wasn't sure a horse could understand everything that was said to him, but it was impossible to say how much was understood. A horse never kicked up a fuss if someone he liked explained things to him. Billy could give examples, too. He had known, for instance, a horse nearly dead beat with fatigue to perk up when told it was only a little farther to his destination. And he had known a horse paralyzed with fright to come out of it when his rider told him what it was that was frightening him. While he talked in the mornings, Billy Buck cut twenty or thirty straws into neat three-inch lengths and stuck them into his hatband. Then during the whole day, if he wanted to pick his teeth or merely to chew on something, he had only to reach up for one of them.

Jody listened carefully, for he knew and the whole country knew that Billy Buck was a fine hand with horses. Billy's own horse was a stringy cayuse with a hammer head, but he nearly always won the first prizes at the stock trials. Billy could rope a steer, take a double half-hitch about the horn with his riata, and dismount, and his horse would play the steer as an angler plays a fish, keeping a tight rope until the steer was down or beaten.

Every morning, after Jody had curried and brushed the pony, he let down the barrier of the stall, and Gabilan thrust past him and raced down the barn and into the corral.

Around and around he galloped, and sometimes he jumped forward and landed on stiff legs. He stood quivering, stiff ears forward, eyes rolling so that the whites showed, pretending to be frightened. At last he walked snorting to the water trough and buried his nose in the water up to the nostrils. Jody was proud then, for he knew that was the way to judge a horse. Poor horses only touched their lips to the water, but a fine-spirited beast put his whole nose and mouth under, and only left room to breathe.

Then Jody stood and watched the pony, and he saw things he had never noticed about any other horse, the sleek, sliding flank muscles and the cords of the buttocks, which flexed like a closing fist, and the shine the sun put on the red coat. Having seen horses all his life, Jody had never looked at them very closely before. But now he noticed the moving ears which gave expression and even inflection of expression to the face. The pony talked with his ears. You could tell exactly how he felt about everything by the way his ears pointed. Sometimes they were stiff and upright and sometimes lax and sagging. They went back when he was angry or fearful, and forward when he was anxious and curious and pleased; and their exact position indicated which emotion he had.

Billy Buck kept his word. In the early fall the training began. First there was the halter-breaking, and that was the hardest because it was the first thing. Jody held a carrot and coaxed and promised and pulled on the rope. The pony set his feet like a burro when he felt the strain. But before long he learned. Jody walked all over the ranch leading him. Gradually he took to dropping the rope until the pony followed him unled wherever he went.

And then came the training on the long halter. That was slower work. Jody stood in the middle of a circle, holding the long halter. He clucked with his tongue and the pony started to walk in a big circle, held in by the long rope. He clucked again to make the pony trot, and again to make him gallop. Around and around Gabilan went thundering and enjoying it immensely. Then he called, 'Whoa,' and the pony stopped. It was not long until Gabilan was perfect at it. But in many ways he was a bad pony. He bit Jody in the pants and stomped on Jody's feet. Now and then his ears went back and he aimed a tremendous kick at the boy. Every time he did one of these bad things, Gabilan settled back and seemed to laugh to himself.

Billy Buck worked at the hair rope in the evenings before the fireplace. Jody collected tail hair in a bag, and he sat and watched Billy slowly constructing the rope, twisting a few hairs to make a string and rolling two strings together for a cord, and then braiding a number of cords to make the rope. Billy rolled the finished rope on the floor under his foot to make it round and hard.

The long halter work rapidly approached perfection. Jody's father, watching the pony stop and start and trot and gallop, was a little bothered by it.

'He's getting to be almost a trick pony,' he complained. 'I don't like trick horses. It takes all the – dignity out of a horse to make him do tricks. Why, a trick horse is kind of like an actor – no dignity, no character of his own.' And his father said, 'I guess you better be getting him used to the saddle pretty soon.'

Jody rushed for the harness room. For some time he had been riding the saddle on a sawhorse. He changed the stirrup length over and over, and could never get it just right. Sometimes, mounted on the sawhorse in the harness room, with collars and hames and tugs hung all about him, Jody rode out beyond the room. He carried his rifle across the pommel.

He saw the fields go flying by, and he heard the beat of the galloping hooves.

It was a ticklish job, saddling the pony the first time. Gabilan hunched and reared and threw the saddle off before the cinch could be tightened. It had to be replaced again and again until at last the pony let it stay. And the cinching was difficult, too. Day by day Jody tightened the girth a little more until at last the pony didn't mind the saddle at all.

Then there was the bridle. Billy explained how to use a stick of licorice for a bit until Gabilan was used to having something in his mouth. Billy explained, 'Of course we could force-break him to everything, but he wouldn't be as good a horse if we did. He'd always be a little bit afraid, and he wouldn't mind because he wanted to.'

The first time the pony wore the bridle he whipped his head about and worked his tongue against the bit until the blood oozed from the corners of his mouth. He tried to rub the headstall off on the manger. His ears pivoted about and his eyes turned red with fear and with general rambunctiousness. Jody rejoiced, for he knew that only a mean-souled horse does not resent training.

And Jody trembled when he thought of the time when he would first sit in the saddle. The pony would probably throw him off. There was no disgrace in that. The disgrace would come if he did not get right up and mount again. Sometimes he dreamed that he lay in the dirt and cried and couldn't make himself mount again. The shame of the dream lasted until the middle of the day.

Gabilan was growing fast. Already he had lost the long-leggedness of the colt; his mane was getting longer and blacker. Under the constant currying and brushing his coat lay as smooth and gleaming as orange-red lacquer. Jody oiled the hooves and kept them carefully trimmed so they would not crack.

The hair rope was nearly finished. Jody's father gave him an old pair of spurs and bent in the side bars and cut down the strap and took up the chainlets until they fitted. And then one day Carl Tiflin said:

'The pony's growing faster than I thought. I guess you can ride him by Thanksgiving. Think you can stick on?'

'I don't know,' Jody said shyly. Thanksgiving was only three weeks off. He hoped it wouldn't rain, for rain would spot the red saddle.

Gabilan knew and liked Jody by now. He nickered when Jody came across the stubble field, and in the pasture he came running when his master whistled for him. There was always a carrot for him every time.

Billy Buck gave him riding instructions over and over. 'Now when you get up there, just grab tight with your knees and keep your hands away from the saddle, and if you get throwed, don't let that stop you. No matter how good a man is, there's always some horse can pitch him. You just climb up again before he gets to feeling smart about it. Pretty soon, he won't throw you no more, and pretty soon he can't throw you no more. That's the way to do it.'

'I hope it don't rain before,' Jody said.

'Why not? Don't want to get throwed in the mud?'

That was partly it, and also he was afraid that in the flurry of bucking Gabilan might slip and fall on him and break his leg or his hip. He had seen that happen to men before, had seen how they writhed on the ground like squashed bugs, and he was afraid of it.

He practiced on the sawhorse how he would hold the reins in his left hand and a hat in his right hand. If he kept his hands thus busy, he couldn't grab the horn if he felt himself going off. He didn't like to think of what would happen if he did grab the horn. Perhaps his father and Billy Buck would never speak to him again, they would be so ashamed. The news would get about and his mother would be ashamed too. And in the school yard – it was too awful to contemplate.

He began putting his weight in a stirrup when Gabilan was saddled, but he didn't throw his leg over the pony's back. That was forbidden until Thanksgiving.

Every afternoon he put the red saddle on the pony and cinched it tight. The pony was learning already to fill his stomach out unnaturally large while the cinching was going on, and then to let it down when the straps were fixed. Sometimes Jody led him up to the brush line and let him drink from the round green tub, and sometimes he led him up through the stubble field to the hilltop from which it was possible to see the white town of Salinas and the geometric fields of the great valley, and the oak trees clipped by the sheep. Now and then they broke through the brush and came to little cleared circles so hedged in that the world was gone and only the sky and the circle of brush were left from the old life. Gabilan liked these trips and showed it by keeping his head very high and by quivering his nostrils with interest. When the two came back from an expedition they smelled of the sweet sage they had forced through.

Time dragged on toward Thanksgiving, but winter came fast. The clouds swept down and hung all day over the land and brushed the hilltops, and the winds blew shrilly at night. All day the dry oak leaves drifted down from the trees until they covered the ground, and yet the trees were unchanged.

Jody had wished it might not rain before Thanksgiving, but it did. The brown earth turned dark and the trees glistened. The cut ends of the stubble turned black with mildew;

the haystacks greyed from exposure to the damp, and on the roofs the moss, which had been all summer as grey as lizards, turned a brilliant yellow-green. During the week of rain, Jody kept the pony in the box stall out of the dampness, except for a little time after school when he took him out for exercise and to drink at the water trough in the upper corral. Not once did Gabilan get wet.

The wet weather continued until little new grass appeared. Jody walked to school dressed in a slicker and short rubber boots. At length one morning the sun came out brightly. Jody, at his work in the box stall, said to Billy Buck, 'Maybe I'll leave Gabilan in the corral when I go to school today.'

'Be good for him to be out in the sun,' Billy assured him. 'No animal likes to be cooped up too long. Your father and me are going back on the hill to clean the leaves out of the spring.' Billy nodded and picked his teeth with one of his little straws.

'If the rain comes, though –' Jody suggested.

'Not likely to rain today. She's rained herself out.' Billy pulled up his sleeves and snapped his arm bands. 'If it comes on to rain – why a little rain don't hurt a horse.'

'Well, if it does come on to rain, you put him in, will you, Billy? I'm scared he might get cold so I couldn't ride him when the time comes.'

'Oh sure! I'll watch out for him if we get back in time. But it won't rain today.'

And so Jody, when he went to school, left Gabilan standing out in the corral.

Billy Buck wasn't wrong about many things. He couldn't be. But he was wrong about the weather that day, for a little after noon the clouds pushed over the hills and the rain began to pour down. Jody heard it start on the schoolhouse roof. He considered holding up one finger for permission to go to the outhouse and, once outside, running for home to put the pony in. Punishment would be prompt both at school and at home. He gave it up and took ease from Billy's assurance that rain couldn't hurt a horse. When school was finally out, he hurried home through the dark rain. The banks at the sides of the road spouted little jets of muddy water. The rain slanted and swirled under a cold and gusty wind. Jody dogtrotted home, slopping through the gravelly mud of the road.

From the top of the ridge he could see Gabilan standing miserably in the corral. The red coat was almost black, and streaked with water. He stood head down with his rump to the rain and wind. Jody arrived running and threw open the barn door and led the wet pony in by his forelock. Then he found a gunnysack and rubbed the soaked hair and rubbed the legs and ankles. Gabilan stood patiently, but he trembled in gusts like the wind.

When he had dried the pony as well as he could, Jody went to the house and brought hot water down to the barn and soaked the grain in it. Gabilan was not very hungry. He nibbled at the hot mash, but he was not very much interested in it, and he still shivered now and then. A little steam rose from his damp back.

It was almost dark when Billy Buck and Carl Tiflin came home. 'When the rain started we put up at Ben Herche's place, and the rain never let up all afternoon,' Carl Tiflin explained. Jody looked reproachfully at Billy Buck and Billy felt guilty.

'You said it wouldn't rain,' Jody accused him.

Billy looked away. 'It's hard to tell, this time of year,' he said, but his excuse was lame. He had no right to be fallible, and he knew it.

'The pony got wet, got soaked through.'

'Did you dry him off?'

'I rubbed him with a sack and I gave him hot grain.'

Billy nodded in agreement.

'Do you think he'll take cold, Billy?'

'A little rain never hurt anything,' Billy assured him.

Jody's father joined the conversation then and lectured the boy a little. 'A horse,' he said, 'isn't any lapdog kind of thing.' Carl Tiflin hated weakness and sickness, and he held a violent contempt for helplessness.

Jody's mother put a platter of steaks on the table and boiled potatoes and boiled squash, which clouded the room with their steam. They sat down to eat. Carl Tiflin still grumbled about weakness put into animals and men by too much coddling.

Billy Buck felt bad about his mistake. 'Did you blanket him?' he asked.

'No. I couldn't find any blanket. I laid some sacks over his back.'

'We'll go down and cover him up after we eat, then.' Billy felt better about it then. When Jody's father had gone in to the fire and his mother was washing dishes, Billy found and lighted a lantern. He and Jody walked through the mud to the barn. The barn was dark and warm and sweet. The horses still munched their evening hay. 'You hold the lantern!' Billy ordered. And he felt the pony's legs and tested the heat of the flanks. He put his cheek against the pony's grey muzzle and then he rolled up the eyelids to look at the eyeballs and he lifted the lips to see the gums, and he put his fingers inside the ears. 'He don't seem so chipper,' Billy said. 'I'll give him a rubdown.'

Then Billy found a sack and rubbed the pony's legs violently and he rubbed the chest and the withers. Gabilan was strangely spiritless. He submitted patiently to the rubbing.

At last Billy brought an old cotton comforter from the saddle room, and threw it over the pony's back and tied it at neck and chest with string.

'Now he'll be all right in the morning,' Billy said.

Jody's mother looked up when he got back to the house. 'You're late up from bed,' she said. She held his chin in her hard hand and brushed the tangled hair out of his eyes and she said, 'Don't worry about the pony. He'll be all right. Billy's as good as any horse doctor in the country.'

Jody hadn't known she could see his worry. He pulled gently away from her and knelt down in front of the fireplace until it burned his stomach. He scorched himself through and then went in to bed, but it was a hard thing to go to sleep. He awakened after what seemed a long time. The room was dark but there was a greyness in the window like that which precedes the dawn. He got up and found his overalls and searched for the legs, and then the clock in the other room struck two. He laid his clothes down and got back into bed. It was broad daylight when he awakened again. For the first time he had slept through the ringing of the triangle. He leaped up, flung on his clothes, and went out of the door still buttoning his shirt. His mother looked after him for a moment and then went quietly back to her work. Her eyes were brooding and kind. Now and then her mouth smiled a little but without changing her eyes at all.

Jody ran on toward the barn. Halfway there he heard the sound he dreaded, the hollow rasping cough of a horse. He broke into a sprint then. In the barn he found Billy Buck with the pony. Billy was rubbing its legs with his strong thick hands. He looked up and smiled gaily. 'He just took a little cold,' Billy said. 'We'll have him out of it in a couple of days.'

Jody looked at the pony's face. The eyes were half closed

and the lids thick and dry. In the eye corners a crust of hard mucus stuck. Gabilan's ears hung loosely sideways and his head was low. Jody put out his hand, but the pony did not move close to it. He coughed again and his whole body constricted with the effort. A little stream of thin fluid ran from his nostrils.

Jody looked back at Billy Buck. 'He's awful sick, Billy.'

'Just a little cold, like I said,' Billy insisted. 'You go get some breakfast and then go back to school. I'll take care of him.'

'But you might have to do something else. You might leave him.'

'No, I won't. I won't leave him at all. Tomorrow's Saturday. Then you can stay with him all day.' Billy had failed again, and he felt badly about it. He had to cure the pony now.

Jody walked up to the house and took his place listlessly at the table. The eggs and bacon were cold and greasy, but he didn't notice it. He ate his usual amount. He didn't even ask to stay home from school. His mother pushed his hair back when she took his plate. 'Billy'll take care of the pony,' she assured him.

He moped through the whole day at school. He couldn't answer any questions nor read any words. He couldn't even tell anyone the pony was sick, for that might make him sicker. And when school was finally out he started home in dread. He walked slowly and let the other boys leave him. He wished he might continue walking and never arrive at the ranch.

Billy was in the barn, as he had promised, and the pony was worse. His eyes were almost closed now, and his breath whistled shrilly past an obstruction in his nose. A film covered that part of the eyes that was visible at all. It was doubtful whether the pony could see any more. Now and then he snorted, to clear his nose, and by the action seemed to plug it tighter. Jody looked dispiritedly at the pony's coat.

The hair lay rough and unkempt and seemed to have lost all of its old luster. Billy stood quietly beside the stall. Jody hated to ask, but he had to know.

'Billy, is he – is he going to get well?'

Billy put his fingers between the bars under the pony's jaw and felt about. 'Feel here,' he said and he guided Jody's fingers to a large lump under the jaw. 'When that gets bigger, I'll open it up and then he'll get better.'

Jody looked quickly away, for he had heard about that lump. 'What is it the matter with him?'

Billy didn't want to answer, but he had to. He couldn't be wrong three times. 'Strangles,' he said shortly, 'but don't you worry about that. I'll pull him out of it. I've seen them get well when they were worse than Gabilan is. I'm going to steam him now. You can help.'

'Yes,' Jody said miserably. He followed Billy into the grain room and watched him make the steaming bag ready. It was a long canvas nose bag with straps to go over a horse's ears. Billy filled it one-third full of bran and then he added a couple of handfuls of dried hops. On top of the dry substance he poured a little carbolic acid and a little turpentine. 'I'll be mixing it all up while you run to the house for a kettle of boiling water,' Billy said.

When Jody came back with the steaming kettle, Billy buckled the straps over Gabilan's head and fitted the bag tightly around his nose. Then through a little hole in the side of the bag he poured the boiling water on the mixture. The pony started away as a cloud of strong steam rose up, but then the soothing fumes crept through his nose and into his lungs, and the sharp steam began to clear out the nasal passages. He breathed loudly. His legs trembled in an ague, and his eyes closed against the biting cloud. Billy poured in more water and kept the steam rising for fifteen minutes. At last he set down the kettle and took the bag from Gabilan's nose. The pony looked better. He breathed freely, and his eyes were open wider than they had been.

'See how good it makes him feel,' Billy said. 'Now we'll wrap him up in the blanket again. Maybe he'll be nearly well by morning.'

'I'll stay with him tonight,' Jody suggested.

'No. Don't you do it. I'll bring my blankets down here and put them in the hay. You can stay tomorrow and steam him if he needs it.'

The evening was falling when they went to the house for their supper. Jody didn't even realize that someone else had fed the chickens and filled the wood box. He walked up past the house to the dark brush line and took a drink of water from the tub. The spring water was so cold that it stung his mouth and drove a shiver through him. The sky above the hills was still light. He saw a hawk flying so high that it caught the sun on its breast and shone like a spark. Two blackbirds were driving him down the sky, glittering as they attacked their enemy. In the west, the clouds were moving in to rain again.

Jody's father didn't speak at all while the family ate supper, but after Billy Buck had taken his blankets and gone to sleep in the barn, Carl Tiflin built a high fire in the fireplace and told stories. He told about the wild man who ran naked through the country and had a tail and ears like a horse, and he told about the rabbit-cats of Moro Cojo that hopped into the trees for birds. He revived the famous Maxwell brothers who found a vein of gold and hid the traces of it so carefully that they could never find it again.

Jody sat with his chin in his hands; his mouth worked nervously and his father gradually became aware that he wasn't listening very carefully. 'Isn't that funny?' he asked.

Jody laughed politely and said, 'Yes, sir.' His father was angry and hurt, then. He didn't tell any more stories. After a while, Jody took a lantern and went down to the barn. Billy Buck was asleep in the hay, and, except that his breath rasped a little in his lungs, the pony seemed to be much better. Jody stayed a little while, running his fingers over the red rough coat, and then he took up the lantern and went back to the house. When he was in bed, his mother came into the room.

'Have you enough covers on? It's getting winter.'

'Yes, ma'am.'

'Well, get some rest tonight.' She hesitated to go out, stood uncertainly. 'The pony will be all right,' she said.

Jody was tired. He went to sleep quickly and didn't awaken until dawn. The triangle sounded, and Billy Buck came up from the barn before Jody could get out of the house.

'How is he?' Jody demanded.

Billy always wolfed his breakfast. 'Pretty good. I'm going to open that lump this morning. Then he'll be better maybe.'

After breakfast, Billy got out his best knife, one with a needle point. He whetted the shining blade a long time on a little carborundum stone. He tried the point and the blade again and again on his callused thumb-ball, and at last he tried it on his upper lip.

On the way to the barn, Jody noticed how the young grass was up and how the stubble was melting day by day into the new green crop of volunteer. It was a cold sunny morning.

As soon as he saw the pony, Jody knew he was worse. His eyes were closed and sealed shut with dried mucus. His head hung so low that his nose almost touched the straw of his bed. There was a little groan in each breath, a deep-seated, patient groan.

Billy lifted the weak head and made a quick slash with the

knife. Jody saw the yellow pus run out. He held up the head while Billy swabbed out the wound with weak carbolic acid salve.

'Now he'll feel better,' Billy assured him. 'That yellow poison is what makes him sick.'

Jody looked unbelieving at Billy Buck. 'He's awful sick.'

Billy thought a long time what to say. He nearly tossed off a careless assurance, but he saved himself in time. 'Yes, he's pretty sick,' he said at last. 'I've seen worse ones get well. If he doesn't get pneumonia, we'll pull him through. You stay with him. If he gets worse, you can come and get me.'

For a long time after Billy went away, Jody stood beside the pony, stroking him behind the ears. The pony didn't flip his head the way he had done when he was well. The groaning in his breathing was becoming more hollow.

Doubletree Mutt looked into the barn, his big tail waving provocatively, and Jody was so incensed at his health that he found a hard black clod on the floor and deliberately threw it. Doubletree Mutt went yelping away to nurse a bruised paw.

In the middle of the morning, Billy Buck came back and made another steam bag. Jody watched to see whether the pony improved this time as he had before. His breathing eased a little, but he did not raise his head.

The Saturday dragged on. Late in the afternoon Jody went to the house and brought his bedding down and made up a place to sleep in the hay. He didn't ask permission. He knew from the way his mother looked at him that she would let him do almost anything. That night he left a lantern burning on a wire over the box stall. Billy had told him to rub the pony's legs every little while.

At nine o'clock the wind sprang up and howled around the barn. And in spite of his worry, Jody grew sleepy. He got into his blankets and went to sleep, but the breathy groans of the pony sounded in his dreams. And in his sleep he heard a crashing noise which went on and on until it awakened him. The wind was rushing through the barn. He sprang up and looked down the lane of stalls. The barn door had blown open, and the pony was gone.

He caught the lantern and ran outside into the gate, and he saw Gabilan weakly shambling away into the darkness, head down, legs working slowly and mechanically. When Jody ran up and caught him by the forelock, he allowed himself to be led back and put into his stall. His groans were louder, and a fierce whistling came from his nose. Jody didn't sleep any more then. The hissing of the pony's breath grew louder and sharper.

He was glad when Billy Buck came in at dawn. Billy looked for a time at the pony as though he had never seen him before. He felt the ears and flanks. 'Jody,' he said, 'I've got to do something you won't want to see. You run up to the house for a while.'

Jody grabbed him fiercely by the forearm. 'You're not going to shoot him?'

Billy patted his hand. 'No. I'm going to open a little hole in his windpipe so he can breathe. His nose is filled up. When he gets well, we'll put a little brass button in the hole for him to breath through.'

Jody couldn't have gone away if he had wanted to. It was awful to see the red hide cut, but infinitely more terrible to know it was being cut and not to see it. 'I'll stay right here,' he said bitterly. 'You sure you got to?'

'Yes. I'm sure. If you stay, you can hold his head. If it doesn't make you sick, that is.'

The fine knife came out again and was whetted again just as carefully as it had been the first time. Jody held the pony's head up and the throat taut, while Billy felt up and down for the right place. Jody sobbed once as the bright knife point disappeared into the throat. The pony plunged weakly away and then stood still, trembling violently. The blood ran thickly out and up the knife and across Billy's hand and into his shirtsleeve. The sure square hand sawed out a round hole in the flesh, and the breath came bursting out of the hole, throwing a fine spray of blood. With the rush of oxygen, the pony took a sudden strength. He lashed out with his hind feet and tried to rear, but Jody held his head down while Billy mopped the new wound with carbolic salve. It was a good job. The blood stopped flowing and the air puffed out the hole and sucked it in regularly with a little bubbling noise.

The rain brought in by the night wind began to fall on the barn roof. Then the triangle rang for breakfast. 'You go up and eat while I wait,' Billy said. 'We've got to keep this hole from plugging up.'

Jody walked slowly out of the barn. He was too dispirited to tell Billy how the barn door had blown open and let the pony out. He emerged into the wet grey morning and sloshed up to the house, taking a perverse pleasure in splashing through all the puddles. His mother fed him and put dry clothes on. She didn't question him. She seemed to know he couldn't answer questions. But when he was ready to go back to the barn she brought him a pan of steaming meal. 'Give him this,' she said.

But Jody did not take the pan. He said, 'He won't eat anything,' and ran out of the house. At the barn, Billy showed him how to fix a ball of cotton on a stick, with which to swab out the breathing hole when it became clogged with mucus.

Jody's father walked into the barn and stood with them in front of the stall. At length he turned to the boy. 'Hadn't you better come with me? I'm going to drive over the hill.' Jody shook his head. 'You better come on, out of this,' his father insisted.

Billy turned on him angrily. 'Let him alone. It's his pony, isn't it?'

Carl Tiflin walked away without saying another word. His feelings were badly hurt.

All morning Jody kept the wound open and the air passing in and out freely. At noon the pony lay wearily down on his side and stretched his nose out.

Billy came back. 'If you're going to stay with him tonight, you better take a little nap,' he said. Jody went absently out of the barn. The sky had cleared to a hard thin blue. Everywhere the birds were busy with worms that had come to the damp surface of the ground.

Jody walked to the brush line and sat on the edge of the mossy tub. He looked down at the house and at the old bunkhouse and at the dark cypress tree. The place was familiar, but curiously changed. It wasn't itself any more, but a frame for things that were happening. A cold wind blew out of the east now, signifying that the rain was over for a little while. At his feet Jody could see the little arms of new weeds spreading out over the ground. In the mud about the spring were thousands of quail tracks.

Doubletree Mutt came sideways and embarrassed up through the vegetable patch, and Jody, remembering how he had thrown the clod, put his arm about the dog's neck and kissed him on his wide black nose. Doubletree Mutt sat still, as though he knew some solemn thing was happening. His big tail slapped the ground gravely. Jody pulled a swollen tick out of Mutt's neck and popped it dead between his thumbnails. It was a nasty thing. He washed his hands in the cold spring water.

Except for the steady swish of the wind, the farm was very

quiet. Jody knew his mother wouldn't mind if he didn't go in to eat his lunch. After a little while he went slowly back to the barn. Mutt crept into his own little house and whined softly to himself for a long time.

Billy Buck stood up from the box and surrendered the cotton swab. The pony still lay on his side and the wound in his throat bellowsed in and out. When Jody saw how dry and dead the hair looked, he knew at last that there was no hope for the pony. He had seen the dead hair before on dogs and on cows, and it was a sure sign. He sat heavily on the box and let down the barrier of the box stall. For a long time he kept his eyes on the moving wound, and at last he dozed, and the afternoon passed quickly. Just before dark his mother brought a deep dish of stew and left it for him and went away. Jody ate a little of it, and, when it was dark, he set the lantern on the floor by the pony's head so he could watch the wound and keep it open. And he dozed again until the night chill awakened him. The wind was blowing fiercely, bringing the north cold with it. Jody brought a blanket from his bed in the hay and wrapped himself in it. Gabilan's breathing was quiet at last; the hole in his throat moved gently. The owls flew through the hayloft, shrieking and looking for mice. Jody put his hands down on his head and slept. In his sleep he was aware that the wind had increased. He heard it slamming about the barn.

It was daylight when he awakened. The barn door had swung open. The pony was gone. He sprang up and ran out into the morning light.

The pony's tracks were plain enough, dragging through the frostlike dew on the young grass, tired tracks with little lines between them where the hoofs had dragged. They headed for the brush line halfway up the ridge. Jody broke into a run and followed them. The sun shone on the sharp white quartz that stuck through the ground here and there. As he followed the plain trail, a shadow cut across in front of him. He looked up and saw a high circle of black buzzards, and the slowly revolving circle dropped lower and lower. The solemn birds soon disappeared over the ridge. Jody ran faster then, forced on by panic and rage. The trail entered the brush at last and followed a winding route among the tall sage bushes.

At the top of the ridge Jody was winded. He paused, puffing noisily. The blood pounded in his ears. Then he saw what he was looking for. Below, in one of the little clearings in the brush, lay the red pony. In the distance, Jody could see the legs moving slowly and convulsively. And in a circle around him stood the buzzards, waiting for the moment of death they know so well.

Jody leaped forward and plunged down the hill. The wet ground muffled his steps and the brush hid him. When he arrived, it was all over. The first buzzard sat on the pony's head and its beak had just risen dripping with dark eye fluid. Jody plunged into the circle like a cat. The black brotherhood arose in a cloud, but the big one on the pony's head was too late. As it hopped along to take off, Jody caught its wing tip and pulled it down. It was nearly as big as he was. The free wing crashed into his face with the force of a club, but he hung on. The claws fastened on his leg and the wing elbows battered his head on either side. Jody groped blindly with his free hand. His fingers found the neck of the struggling bird. The red eyes looked into his face, calm and fearless and fierce; the naked head turned from side to side. Then the beak opened and vomited a stream of putrefied fluid. Jody brought up his knee and fell on the great bird. He held the neck to the ground with one

264

hand while his other found a piece of sharp white quartz. The first blow broke the beak sideways and black blood spurted from the twisted, leathery mouth corners. He struck again and missed. The red fearless eyes still looked at him, impersonal and unafraid and detached. He struck again and again, until the buzzard lay dead, until its head was a red pulp. He was still beating the dead bird when Billy Buck pulled him off and held him tightly to calm his shaking.

Carl Tiflin wiped the blood from the boy's face with a red bandana. Jody was limp and quiet now. His father moved the buzzard with his toe. 'Jody,' he explained, 'the buzzard didn't kill the pony. Don't you know that?'

'I know it,' Jody said wearily.

It was Billy Buck who was angry. He had lifted Jody in his arms, and had turned to carry him home. But he turned back on Carl Tiflin. ''Course he knows it,' Billy said furiously, 'Jesus Christ! man, can't you see how he'd feel about it?'

WILLIAM SAROYAN

THE SUMMER OF
THE BEAUTIFUL
WHITE HORSE

ONE DAY BACK there in the good old days when I was nine and the world was full of every imaginable kind of magnificence, and life was still a delightful and mysterious dream, my cousin Mourad, who was considered crazy by everybody who knew him except me, came to my house at four in the morning and woke me up by tapping on the window of my room.

Aram, he said.

I jumped out of bed and looked out the window.

I couldn't believe what I saw.

It wasn't morning yet, but it was summer and with daybreak not many minutes around the corner of the world it was light enough for me to know I wasn't dreaming.

My cousin Mourad was sitting on a beautiful white horse.

I stuck my head out of the window and rubbed my eyes.

Yes, he said in Armenian. It's a horse. You're not dreaming. Make it quick if you want a ride.

I knew my cousin Mourad enjoyed being alive more than anybody else who had ever fallen into the world by mistake, but this was more than even I could believe.

In the first place, my earliest memories had been memories of horses and my first longings had been longings to ride.

This was the wonderful part.

In the second place, we were poor.

This was the part that wouldn't permit me to believe what I saw.

We were poor. We had no money. Our whole tribe was poverty-stricken. Every branch of the Garoghlanian family was living in the most amazing and comical poverty in the world. Nobody could understand where we ever got money enough to keep us with food in our bellies, not even the old men of the family. Most important of all, though, we were famous for our honesty. We had been famous for our honesty for something like eleven centuries, even when we had been the wealthiest family in what we liked to think was the world. We were proud first, honest next, and after that we believed in right and wrong. None of us would take advantage of anybody in the world, let alone steal.

Consequently, even though I could see the horse, so magnificent; even though I could *smell* it, so lovely; even though I could *hear* it breathing, so exciting; I couldn't *believe* the horse had anything to do with my cousin Mourad or with me or with any of the other members of our family, asleep or awake, because I *knew* my cousin Mourad couldn't have *bought* the horse, and if he couldn't have bought it he must have *stolen* it, and I refused to believe he had stolen it.

No member of the Garoghlanian family could be a thief.

I stared first at my cousin and then at the horse. There was a pious stillness and humor in each of them which on the one hand delighted me and on the other frightened me.

Mourad, I said, where did you steal this horse?

Leap out of the window, he said, if you want a ride.

It was true, then. He *had* stolen the horse. There was no question about it. He had come to invite me to ride or not, as I chose.

Well, it seemed to me stealing a horse for a ride was not the same thing as stealing something else, such as money. For all I knew, maybe it wasn't stealing at all. If you were crazy about horses the way my cousin Mourad and I were, it wasn't stealing. It wouldn't become stealing until we offered to sell the horse, which of course I knew we would never do.

Let me put on some clothes, I said.

All right, he said, but hurry.

I leaped into my clothes.

I jumped down to the yard from the window and leaped up onto the horse behind my cousin Mourad.

That year we lived at the edge of town, on Walnut Avenue. Behind our house was the country: vineyards, orchards, irrigation ditches, and country roads. In less than three minutes we were on Olive Avenue, and then the horse began to trot. The air was new and lovely to breathe. The feel of the horse running was wonderful. My cousin Mourad who was considered one of the craziest members of our family began to sing. I mean, he began to roar.

Every family has a crazy streak in it somewhere, and my cousin Mourad was considered the natural descendant of the crazy streak in our tribe. Before him was our uncle Khosrove, an enormous man with a powerful head of black hair and the largest mustache in the San Joaquin Valley, a man so furious in temper, so irritable, so impatient that he stopped anyone from talking by roaring, *It is no harm; pay no attention to it.*

That was all, no matter what anybody happened to be talking about. Once it was his own son Arak running eight blocks to the barber shop where his father was having his mustache trimmed to tell him their house was on fire. The man Khosrove sat up in the chair and roared, It is no harm; pay no attention to it. The barber said, But the boy says your house is on fire. So Khosrove roared, Enough, it is no harm, I say.

My cousin Mourad was considered the natural descendant of this man, although Mourad's father was Zorab, who was practical and nothing else. That's how it was in our tribe.

A man could be the father of his son's flesh, but that did not mean that he was also the father of his spirit. The distribution of the various kinds of spirit of our tribe had been from the beginning capricious and vagrant.

We rode and my cousin Mourad sang. For all anybody knew we were still in the old country where, at least according to our neighbors, we belonged. We let the horse run as long as it felt like running.

At last my cousin Mourad said, Get down. I want to ride alone.

Will you let me ride alone? I said.

That is up to the horse, my cousin said. Get down.

The *horse* will let me ride, I said.

We shall see, he said. Don't forget that I have a way with a horse.

Well, I said, any way you have with a horse, I have also.

For the sake of your safety, he said, let us hope so. Get down.

All right, I said, but remember you've got to let me try to ride alone.

I got down and my cousin Mourad kicked his heels into the horse and shouted, *Vazire*, run. The horse stood on its hind legs, snorted, and burst into a fury of speed that was the loveliest thing I had ever seen. My cousin Mourad raced the horse across a field of dry grass to an irrigation ditch, crossed the ditch on the horse, and five minutes later returned, dripping wet.

The sun was coming up.

Now it's my turn to ride, I said.

My cousin Mourad got off the horse.

Ride, he said.

I leaped to the back of the horse and for a moment knew the awfulest fear imaginable. The horse did not move.

Kick into his muscles, my cousin Mourad said. What are you waiting for? We've got to take him back before everybody in the world is up and about.

I kicked into the muscles of the horse. Once again it reared and snorted. Then it began to run. I didn't know what to do. Instead of running across the field to the irrigation ditch the horse ran down the road to the vineyard of Dikran Halabian where it began to leap over vines. The horse leaped over seven vines before I fell. Then it continued running.

My cousin Mourad came running down the road.

I'm not worried about you, he shouted. We've got to get that horse. You go this way and I'll go this way. If you come upon him, be kindly. I'll be near.

I continued down the road and my cousin Mourad went across the field toward the irrigation ditch.

It took him half an hour to find the horse and bring him back.

All right, he said, jump on. The whole world is awake now.

What will we do? I said.

Well, he said, we'll either take him back or hide him until tomorrow morning.

He didn't sound worried and I knew he'd hide him and not take him back. Not for a while, at any rate.

Where will you hide him? I said.

I know a place, he said.

How long ago did you steal this horse? I said.

It suddenly dawned on me that he had been taking these early morning rides for some time and had come for me this morning only because he knew how much I longed to ride.

Who said anything about stealing a horse? he said.

Anyhow, I said, how long ago did you begin riding every morning?

Not until this morning, he said.

Are you telling the truth? I said.

Of course not, he said, but if we are found out, that's what you're to say. I don't want both of us to be liars. All you know is that we started riding this morning.

All right, I said.

He walked the horse quietly to the barn of a deserted vineyard which at one time had been the pride of a farmer named Fetvajian. There were some oats and dry alfalfa in the barn.

We began walking home.

It wasn't easy, he said, to get the horse to behave so nicely. At first it wanted to run wild, but as I've told you, I have a way with a horse. I can get it to want to do anything *I* want it to do. Horses understand me.

How do you do it? I said.

I have an understanding with a horse, he said.

Yes, but what sort of an understanding? I said.

A simple and honest one, he said.

Well, I said, I wish I knew how to reach an understanding like that with a horse.

You're still a small boy, he said. When you get to be thirteen you'll know how to do it.

I went home and ate a hearty breakfast.

That afternoon my uncle Khosrove came to our house for coffee and cigarettes. He sat in the parlor, sipping and smoking and remembering the old country. Then another visitor arrived, a farmer named John Byro, an Assyrian who, out of loneliness, had learned to speak Armenian. My mother brought the lonely visitor coffee and tobacco and he rolled a cigarette and sipped and smoked, and then at last, sighing sadly, he said, My white horse which was stolen last month is still gone. I cannot understand it.

My uncle Khosrove became very irritated and shouted, It's

274

no harm. What is the loss of a horse? Haven't we all lost the homeland? What is this crying over a horse?

That may be all right for you, a city dweller, to say, John Byro said, but what of my surrey? What good is a surrey without a horse?

Pay no attention to it, my uncle Khosrove roared.

I walked ten miles to get here, John Byro said.

You have legs, my uncle Khosrove shouted.

My left leg pains me, the farmer said.

Pay no attention to it, my uncle Khosrove roared.

That horse cost me sixty dollars, the farmer said.

I spit on money, my uncle Khosrove said.

He got up and stalked out of the house, slamming the screen door.

My mother explained.

He has a gentle heart, she said. It is simply that he is homesick and such a large man.

The farmer went away and I ran over to my cousin Mourad's house.

He was sitting under a peach tree, trying to repair the hurt wing of a young robin which could not fly. He was talking to the bird.

What is it? he said.

The farmer, John Byro, I said. He visited our house. He wants his horse. You've had it a month. I want you to promise not to take it back until I learn to ride.

It will take you a *year* to learn to ride, my cousin Mourad said.

We could keep the horse a year, I said.

My cousin Mourad leaped to his feet.

What? he roared. Are you inviting a member of the Garoghlanian family to steal? The horse must go back to its true owner.

When? I said.

In six months at the latest, he said.

He threw the bird into the air. The bird tried hard, almost fell twice, but at last flew away, high and straight.

Early every morning for two weeks my cousin Mourad and I took the horse out of the barn of the deserted vineyard where we were hiding it and rode it, and every morning the horse, when it was my turn to ride alone, leaped over grape-vines and small trees and threw me and ran away. Nevertheless, I hoped in time to learn to ride the way my cousin Mourad rode.

One morning on the way to Fetvajian's deserted vineyard we ran into the farmer John Byro who was on his way to town.

Let me do the talking, my cousin Mourad said. I have a way with farmers.

Good morning, John Byro, my cousin Mourad said to the farmer.

The farmer studied the horse eagerly.

Good morning, sons of my friends, he said. What is the name of your horse?

My Heart, my cousin Mourad said in Armenian.

A lovely name, John Byro said, for a lovely horse. I could swear it is the horse that was stolen from me many weeks ago. May I look into its mouth?

Of course, Mourad said.

The farmer looked into the mouth of the horse.

Tooth for tooth, he said. I would swear it is my horse if I didn't know your parents. The fame of your family for honesty is well known to me. Yet the horse is the twin of my horse. A suspicious man would believe his eyes instead of his heart. Good day, my young friends.

Good day, John Byro, my cousin Mourad said.

Early the following morning we took the horse to John Byro's vineyard and put it in the barn. The dogs followed us around without making a sound.

The dogs, I whispered to my cousin Mourad. I thought they would bark.

They would at somebody else, he said. I have a way with dogs.

My cousin Mourad put his arms around the horse, pressed his nose into the horse's nose, patted it, and then we went away.

That afternoon John Byro came to our house in his surrey and showed my mother the horse that had been stolen and returned.

I do not know what to think, he said. The horse is stronger than ever. Better-tempered, too. I thank God.

My uncle Khosrove, who was in the parlor, became irritated and shouted, Quiet, man, quiet. Your horse has been returned. Pay no attention to it.

LYDIA PEELLE

SWEETHEARTS OF THE RODEO

LATELY I'VE BEEN thinking about that summer. We barely ever got off those ponies' backs. We painted war paint across their foreheads and pinned wild turkey feathers in our hair, whooped and raced across the back field, hanging on their necks. Some days they were a pair of bucking broncos, or unicorns, or circus horses, or burros on a narrow mountain pass. Other days they were regal as the ladies' horses, and we were two queens, veiled sultanas crossing the Sahara under a burning sky. We were the kidnapped maidens or the masked heroes. We braided flowers in their matted tails, dandelions and oxeye daisies that got lost in the snarls, wilted, and turned brown. We tore across the back field, our heels dug into their sides. We pulled them up short and did somersaults off their backs. We did handstands in the saddle. We turned on a dime. We jumped the triple oxer, the coop, the wall, the ditch. We were fearless. It was the summer we smoked our first cigarettes, the summer you broke your arm. It was the last summer, the last one before boys.

Our mothers drop us off every morning at seven. We grab two pitchforks and fly through our chores. For four dollars an hour we shovel loads of manure and wet shavings out of the stalls, scrub the water buckets, and fill the hayracks, the hay sticking to our wet T-shirts, falling into our shoes, our pockets, our hair. We race to see who can finish first. When we are thirsty, we run to the hose and drink. Late in the morning Curt comes out to the barn and leans against the massive sliding door. He wears sandals and baggy shorts, and under his thick, dark eyelashes, his eyes are rimmed with red. He tells us what other jobs there are to be done, that we must pick stones out of the riding ring, or refill the water troughs in the pasture with the long, heavy hose. We whine and stamp our feet. He is the caretaker, after all, and supposed to do these things himself.

We were just about to go riding, we say.

Girls, he says, winking. *Come on now.*

He looks over his shoulder and whistles for his dog. You stick your tongue out at his back. Some mornings he stays in his little house and doesn't come out until much later, when the ladies' expensive cars start pulling in the long driveway. They get out and lean against their shiny hoods, smoking cigarettes and talking to Curt in low voices. Sometimes only one or two of them show up, and other times they all come at once, a half-dozen of them with identical beige breeches and high boots that we dream of at night. They never once get a streak of manure across their foreheads or a water bucket sloshed across their shirts. We turn down the volume of the paint-splattered barn radio to hear what they're saying, but we can't make it out. In the afternoon we eat the sandwiches our mothers packed for us and throw our apple cores over the fence to the ponies. They chew carefully and sigh in the hot midday sun. Their eyes close and they let their pink-and-gray mottled penises dangle. We go to them with soapy water and a sponge in a bucket and clean the built-up crust from their sheaths, reaching our arms far up inside. The ladies see us doing this and pay us five dollars to do their geldings, then stand by and watch us, wrinkling their perfect noses.

The ladies' horses all have brass name plates on their stall doors, etched in fancy script, with the names of their sires and dams in parentheses underneath. They are called Curator, Excelsior, Hadrian. The ponies' names change daily, depending on the game. The ponies don't even have stalls. They live out in the field where they eat all day under a cloud of flies. Nobody remembers who they belong to. For the summer, they are ours. They are round and close to the ground, wheezy and spoiled with bad habits. One is brown and dulled by dust. The other is a pinto, bay with white splashes, white on half his face, one eye blue, the other eye brown. The blue eye is blind. We sneak up on this side when we go out to the pasture to catch them, a green halter hidden behind your back, a red one behind mine. The ponies let us get just close enough, then toss their heads and trot away. Peppermints and buckets of grain don't fool them. After a while, we learn to leave their halters on.

The grass in the pasture is knee-high, full of ticks and chiggers, mouse tunnels, quicksilver snakes that scare the ladies' horses into a frenzy. But not the ponies. They are unspookable. Bombproof. When we cinch up their girths they twist their necks to bite our arms. They leave bruises like sunset-colored moons. As the summer gets hotter, we stop bothering with saddles altogether. We clip two lead lines to their halters, grab a hank of mane, and vault on.

We trot through the field and down the hill to the pine woods. We scramble up steep ridges. The ponies are barn sour, much faster coming home than going. We get as far away as we can and then give them their heads to race home through the woods, spruce limbs and vines whipping our faces. We know we are close when we can smell the manure pile. When we come up the hill it is looming like a dark mountain beside the barn. You make a telescope with your thumb and forefinger. Your fingernails are black to the quick.

Land ho! you say. Crows land on the peak of the pile and send avalanches of dirty shavings down its sides. The ladies' little dogs jump out of the open windows of their cars and come running to us, tags jingling.

The ladies hardly ever ride. All day their horses stand out in the sun, their muscles like silk-covered stone. Sometimes they bring them in to the barn and tie them up in the cross-ties, then wander into Curt's house and don't come out again. The horses wait patiently for an hour or so and then begin to paw and weave their heads. They can't reach the flies settling on their withers, the itches on their faces they want to rub against their front legs. They dance and swivel in the aisle, and still the ladies won't come out. Finally we unhook them from the ties and turn them back out in the pasture, where they spin and kick out a leg before galloping back to the herd. When the ladies come out of the little house, late in the afternoon, they squint in the light like they are coming out of a cave and don't ever seem to notice that their horses are not where they left them.

We do everything we can think of to torture Curt. Before he goes out to work on the electric fence, he switches off the fuse in the big breaker box in the barn. We sneak around and flip it back on, then hide and wait to hear his curses when he touches the wire. You slap me five. He comes back into the barn and flicks a lunge whip at us, and we giggle and jump. When he turns away we whisper, *I hate him.* With pitchforks we fling hard turds of manure in his direction, and he hooks his big arms around our waists and dumps us headfirst into the sawdust pile. We squeal and throw handfuls at him when he walks away. Oh, how we hate him! We pretend we've forgotten his name.

In the afternoon we ride our ponies close to the little house to spy on him. Their hooves make marks in the lawn like fingerprints in fresh bread. We ride as close as we dare and see things we don't see in our parents' houses: dirty laundry heaped in the hall, a cluster of dark bottles on top of the refrigerator, ashtrays and half-filled glasses crowding the kitchen table, which is just a piece of plywood on two sawhorses. Your pony eats roses from the bushes under the windows. He wears a halo of mosquitoes. From the bedroom we hear voices, Curt's and a lady's, but it is the only room in which the blinds have been pulled. We try to peer through the cracks, but the ponies yank at their bits and dance in the rosebushes, and we don't really want to see, anyway. *Come on*, you say, and we head out to the back field to play circus acrobats, cops and robbers, cowboys and Indians, whatever mood happens to strike us this day.

The ponies bear witness to dozens of pacts and promises. We make them in the grave light of late day, with every intention of keeping them. We cross our hearts and hope to die on the subjects of horses, husbands, and each other. We dare each other to do near-impossible things. You dare me to jump from the top of the manure pile, and I do, and land on my feet, with manure in my shoes. I double-dare you to take the brown pony over the triple oxer, which is higher than his ears. You ride hell-bent for it but the pony stops dead, throwing you over his head, and you sail through the air and land in the rails, laughing. We are covered in scrapes and bruises, splinters buried so deep in our palms that we don't know they are there. Our bodies forgive us our risks, and the ponies do, too. We have perfected the art of falling.

We know every corner of the barn, every loose board, every shadow, every knot in the wood. It is old and full of holes, home to many things: bats and lizards and voles, spiders that

285

hang cobwebs in the corners like hammocks, house sparrows that build nests in the drainpipes with beakfuls of hay until one day a dead pink baby bird drops to the feet of one of the ladies, who screams and clutches her hair. You scoop it up and toss it on the manure pile, and Curt comes out with the long ladder and pours boiling water down the pipe, and that is the end of the sparrows. Curt laughs at the lady, and rolls his eyes behind her back, and winks at us. We wink back. There is a fly strip in the corner that quivers with dying flies. When it is black with bodies and bits of wing, it is our job to replace it, and we hold our breath when we take it down, praying it won't catch in our hair. And then there are the rats, so many rats that we rip from glue boards and smash with shovels, or pull from snap traps and fling into the woods, or find floating in water troughs where they've dragged themselves, bellies distended with poison and dying of thirst.

In the basement is the workbench where Curt never works; above it, rusty nails sit in a line of baby food jars with lids screwed into a low beam. The manure spreader is parked down there in the dark, like a massive shamed beast. When we open the trap door in the floor above to dump loads from our wheelbarrows, a rectangle of light illuminates the mound of dirty shavings and manure, and we see mice scurry over it like currents of electricity. The ladies never go down to the basement. It is there that we sometimes sit to discuss them, comparing their hair, their mouths, the size of their breasts. *Did you see that one throw up behind the barn Friday afternoon? Did you see this one's diamond ring? Did you see that one slip those pills into Curt's shirt pocket, smiling at him? What were they?*

We hear them call their husbands' offices on the barn telephone and say they are calling from home. We watch two or three go into the little house together, shutting the door behind them. We see Curt stagger from the house and fall over in the yard and stay where he falls, very still, until one of the ladies comes out and helps him up, laughing, and takes him back inside. The ladies hang around when the farrier comes, a friend of Curt's with blond hair and a cowboy hat, watching as he beats a shoe to the shape of a hoof with his hammer. He swears as he works and we stand in the shadows by the grain room and listen carefully, cataloguing every new word. When he leaves, one or two ladies ride off with him in his truck and return an hour or so later and go back to what they had been doing, as if they had never left. They lock themselves in the tack room and fill it with strange-smelling smoke. When we sit in the hayloft we hear their voices below us, high and excited, like small children. The ladies wear lipstick in the morning that is gone by the afternoon. They wear their sunglasses on cloudy days. Some mornings we see that the oil drum we use for empty grain bags is filled to the top with beer bottles. We watch them, and the rules that have been strung in our heads like thick cables fray and unravel in a dazzling arc of sparks. Then we climb on the ponies' backs and ride away down the hill.

One afternoon Curt gives us each a cigarette, and laughs as we try to inhale. *Look, girls!* he says, striking a match on the sole of his boot and lighting his own. *Like this.* We watch his face as he takes a drag, his jaw shadowed with a three-day beard. Later we steal two more from his pack and ride into the woods to practice, watching each other and saying, *No, like this! Like this!* We put Epsom salts in Curt's coffee and lock the tack room door from the inside. We steal his baseball cap and manage to get it hooked on the weathervane. *Ha!* we say, and spit on the ground. *Take that!* He throws one of his flip-flops at us. He drags us shrieking to the courtyard and sprays us with the hose. He tells us we stink. We tell him we don't care.

There is one horse worth more money than the rest put together – it was brought over on a plane, all the way from England. One day we are sitting up in the hayloft, sucking through a bag of peppermints and discussing all the horses we will own someday when we hear an animal's scream from below. The horse, left tied and standing in the aisle, has spooked and broken its halter, gashed its head open on a beam. Blood drips off its eyelashes to a pool by its hooves and it sways like a suspension bridge. We grab saddle pads from the tack room, the ladies' expensive fleece ones, and press them to the wound. They grow hot and heavy with blood. It runs down our arms, into our hair. The horse shakes its head, gnashes its teeth at us. We look over at the little house, all the blinds drawn tight. Who will knock on the door? Who will go? We flip a coin. I don't remember if you won or lost, but you are the one who cuts through the flower bed, who stands on the step and knocks and knocks, and after a long time Curt comes out in jeans and bare feet, no shirt. I hide in the bushes and watch. *What?* he says, frown-ing. You point at his crotch and say, *XYZ!* Without looking down he zips his fly in one motion, like flipping on a light switch. And then in the shadow of the doorway is the lady who the horse belongs to, scowling, her blond hair undone, looking at you like she is having a hard time understanding why you are covered in blood. After the vet comes and stitches up the wound she looks at us suspiciously and whis-pers to Curt. Later, he makes sure she is within earshot before scolding us. When the vet has left and they have gone back into the house, we knock down a paper wasps' nest and toss it through the back window of her car.

There is a pond in the back pasture where the horses go to drink, half hidden by willows and giant honeysuckle bushes that shade it from the noonday sun. On the hottest days we swim the ponies out to the middle, and when their hooves leave the silty bottom, it feels like we are flying. The water is brown and rafts of manure float past us as we swim, but we don't care. We pretend the ponies are Pegasus. And as they swim, we grow quiet thinking about the same thing. We think about Curt – his arms, the curve of his hat brim, the way he smells when he gets off the tractor in the afternoon. You trail your hand in the water and say, *What are you thinking about?* And I say, *Nothing.* When we come out of the water the insides of our thighs are streaked with wet horsehair, as if we are turning into centaurs or wild beasts. The ponies shake themselves violently and we jump off as they drop to their knees to roll in the dust. Other days it is too hot to even swim, to move at all. We lie on the ponies' necks as they graze in the pasture, our arms hanging straight down. The heat drapes across our shoulders and thighs. School is as incomprehensible as snow.

Rodeo is our favorite game, because it is the fastest and most reckless, involving many feats of speed and bravery, quick turns, trick riding. One day late in July, out in the back field, we decide to elect a rodeo clown and a rodeo queen. The ponies stamp out their impatience while we argue over who will be what. Finally the games begin. There is barrel racing and bucking broncos and the rodeo parade. We discover that we can make the ponies rear on command by pushing them forward with our heels while we hold the reins in tight. *Yee haw!* we say, throwing one arm up in the air. The ponies chew the bit nervously as we do it over and over again. We must lean far forward on their necks, or we will slip off. Then the pinto pony goes up and you start to lose your balance. I am doubled over laughing until I see you grope for the reins as the pony goes high, and you grab them with too much effort, and yank his head back too far. He hangs suspended for a moment before falling backward like a tree on his spine. You disappear as he rolls to his side, and reappear when he scrambles to his feet, the reins dangling from the bit. I jump off my pony and run to you. Your arm, from the looks of it, is broken. *Oh shit*, I say. You squint up at me through a veil of blood. *Doesn't hurt.*

Curt was the one who rescued you. He drove his pickup through the tall grass of the back pasture, lifted you onto the bench seat, made you a pillow with his shirt. And when he couldn't get ahold of your parents, he was the one who drove you to the emergency room. I rode in the truck bed, and watched through the window as you stretched your legs across his lap, your bare feet on his thighs. I could see his arms, your face, his tanned hand as he brushed the hair, or maybe tears, from your eyes. I sat across from him at the hospital, waiting while they stitched the gash on your forehead and put your left arm in a cast, and I came in with him to check on you. I hung back in the corner when he leaned over the table, and I heard you whisper to him in a high, helpless voice. I watched your hand grope out from under the blanket, reaching towards his. And I saw him hold it. He held it with both hands. Of course I was jealous, and still am. You must still have that scar to remind you of that summer. I have nothing I can point to, nothing I can touch.

It was early in August when the brown pony died. It happened overnight, and no one knew how: whether he colicked and twisted his gut, or had a heart attack, or caught a hind foot in his halter while tending an itch and broke his own neck. When we found the body, we didn't cry. I remember that we weren't even very sad. We went to find Curt, who lit a cigarette and told us not to tell the ladies. Then we went back and looked at the pony's still body, his velvety muzzle, his open eye, his lips pulled back from his big domino teeth. We touched his side, already cold. Later we rode the pinto pony double out to the pond, your arms around my waist, your cast knocking against my hipbone. Behind us the tractor coughed as Curt pulled the pony's body to the manure pile with heavy chains. We slipped off the pinto, letting him wander away, and sprawled out in the grass. You scratched inside your cast with a stick. Grasshoppers sprang around us. We lay there all afternoon and into the evening, your head on my stomach, our fingers in the clover, trying to think up games we could play with only one pony.

Weeks later we were alone in the barn. We were sweeping the long center aisle, pressing push brooms towards one another from opposite ends, the radio flickering on and off, like it always did. When it faded out completely, we heard the squabbling of dogs out back. We dropped our brooms and ran to see what they'd got. Through a cloud of dust in the paddock we could make out Curt's dog, his butt to us, bracing himself with his tail in the air and growling at one of the ladies' fierce little dogs, who was shaking his head violently, his eyes squeezed shut. Between them, they had the brown pony's head. It took awhile to recognize it. It was mostly bone, yellow teeth and gaping eye sockets, except for a few bits of brown hair that hung on the forehead, some cheek muscle and stringy tendon clinging to the left side. And then we saw the little scrap of green against the white: the pony still had his halter on. This was what the dogs had got their teeth around. Curt had never bothered to take it off. With a final shake of his jaws, the little dog managed to snatch the pony's head away, and he dragged it around the corner of the barn, Curt's dog bounding after.

We stood in the slanting September light and watched this. We listened to the dogs' whines and rumblings, the scrape of the skull against the ground. Then we picked up our brooms, and when we were done sweeping we went and got the pinto pony and rode double down the hill and didn't think much about it again. Death was familiar that summer. It was in the road, in the woods, in the holes of the foundation of the barn; it was the raccoon rotting in the ditch, and the crows that settled there to pick at it until they, too, were flattened by cars, and their bodies swelled and stank in the heat; it was the half-decayed doe we found in the woods with maggots stitching in and out of its flesh, the stillborn foal wrapped in a rotting amniotic sac in the pasture where the vultures perched. We caught a whiff of it, sniffed it out, didn't flinch, touched it with our bare hands, ate lunch immediately afterwards. We weren't frightened of death.

And a few summers later, spinning out of control on a loose gravel road in a car full of boys and beer, we weren't scared of it then, either, and we laughed and said to the boy at the wheel, *Do it again*. We only learned to fear it later, much later, when we realized it knew our names and, worse, the name of everyone we loved. At the height of the summer, in the very dog days, I would have said that we loved the ponies, but I realize now we never did. They were only everything we asked them to be, and that summer, that was enough. I don't know. Lately I've been thinking someone should write an elegy for those ponies. But not me.

PAM HOUSTON

WHAT SHOCK
HEARD

IT WAS LATE SPRING, but the dry winds had started already, and we were trying to load Shock into the horse trailer for a trip to the vet and the third set of X rays on her fetlock. She's just barely green-broke, and after months of being lame she was hot as a pistol and not willing to come within twenty yards of the trailer. Katie and Irwin, who own the barn, and know a lot more than me, had lip chains out, and lunge ropes and tranquilizer guns, but for all their contraptions they couldn't even get close enough to her to give her the shot. Crazy Billy was there too, screaming about two-by-fours and electric prods, and women being too damned ignorant to train a horse right. His horses would stand while he somersaulted in and out of the saddle. They'd stand where he ground-tied them, two feet from the train tracks, one foot off the highway. He lost a horse under a semi once, and almost killed the driver. All the women were afraid of him, and the cowboys said he trained with Quaaludes. I was watching him close, trying to be patient with Katie and Irwin and my brat of a horse, but I didn't want Billy within ten feet of Shock, no matter how long it took to get her in the trailer.

That's when the new cowboy walked up, like out of nowhere with a carrot in his hands, whispered something in Shock's ear, and she walked right behind him into the trailer. He winked at me and I smiled back and poor Irwin and Katie were just standing there all tied up in their own whips and chains.

The cowboy walked on into the barn then, and I got into the truck with Katie and Irwin and didn't see him again for two months when Shock finally got sound and I was starting to ride her in short sessions and trying to teach her some of the things any five-year-old horse should know.

It was the middle of prairie summer by then and it was brutal just thinking about putting on long pants to ride, but I went off Shock so often I had to. The cowboy told me his name was Zeke, short for Ezekiel, and I asked him if he was religious and he said only about certain things.

I said my name was Raye, and he said that was his mother's name and her twin sister's name was Faye, and I said I could never understand why people did things like that to their children. I said that I was developing a theory that what people called you had everything to do with the person you turned out to become, and he said he doubted it 'cause that was just words, and was I going to stand there all day or was I going to come riding with him. He winked at Billy then and Billy grinned and I pretended not to see and hoped to myself that they weren't the same kind of asshole.

I knew Shock wasn't really up to the kind of riding I'd have to do to impress this cowboy, but it had been so long since I'd been out on the meadows I couldn't say no. There was something about the prairie for me – it wasn't where I had come from, but when I moved there it just took me in and I knew I couldn't ever stop living under that big sky. When I was a little girl driving with my family from our cabin in Montana across Nebraska to all the grandparents in Illinois, I used to be scared of the flatness because I didn't know what was holding all the air in.

Some people have such a fear of the prairie it makes them crazy, my ex-husband was one, and they even have a word for it: 'agoraphobia.' But when I looked it up in Greek it said 'fear of the marketplace,' and that seems like the opposite kind of fear to me. He was afraid of the high wind and the big storms that never even came while he was alive. When he shot himself, people said it was my fault for making him move here and making him stay, but his chart only said *acute agoraphobia* and I think he did it because his life wasn't as much like a book as he wanted it to be. He taught me about literature and language, and even though he used language in a bad way – to make up worlds that hurt us – I learned about its power and it got me a job, if nothing else, writing for enough money to pay off his debts.

But I wasn't thinking about any of that when I set off across the meadow at an easy hand gallop behind Zeke and his gelding Jesse. The sun was low in the sky, but it wasn't too long after solstice and in the summer the sun never seemed to fall, it seeped toward the horizon and then melted into it. The fields were losing heat, though, and at that pace we could feel the bands of warmth and cool coming out of the earth like it was some perfectly regulated machine. I could tell Zeke wasn't a talker, so I didn't bother riding up with him; I didn't want Shock to try and race on her leg. I hung back and watched the way his body moved with the big quarter horse: brown skin stretched across muscle and horseflesh, black mane and sandy hair, breath and sweat and one dust cloud rose around them till there was no way to separate the rider from the ride.

Zeke was a hunter. He made his living as a hunter's guide, in Alaska, in places so remote, he said, that the presence of one man with a gun was insignificant. He invited me home for moose steaks, and partly because I loved the way the two words sounded together, I accepted.

It was my first date in almost six years and once I got that into my head it wouldn't leave me alone. It had been almost two years since I'd been with a man, two years almost to the day that Charlie sat on our front-porch swing and blew his brains out with a gun so big the stains splattered three sets of windows and even wrapped around the corner of the house. I thought I had enough reason to swear off men for a while, and Charlie wasn't in the ground three months when I got another one.

It was in October of that same year, already cold and getting dark too early, and Shock and I got back to the barn about an hour after sunset. Katie and Irwin were either in town or in bed and the barn was as dark as the house. I walked Shock into her stall and was starting to take off her saddle when Billy stepped out of the shadows with a shoeing tool in his hand. Women always say they know when it's going to happen, and I did, as soon as he slid the stall door open. I went down when the metal hit my shoulder and I couldn't see anything but I could feel his body shuddering already and little flecks of spit coming out of his mouth. The straw wasn't clean and Shock was nervous and I concentrated on the sound her hooves made as they snapped the air searchingly behind her. I imagined them connecting with Billy's skull and how the blood on the white wall would look like Charlie's, but Shock was much too honest a horse to aim for impact. Billy had the arm that wasn't numb pinned down with one knee through the whole thing, but I bit him once right on the jawline and he's still got that scar; a half-moon of my teeth in his face.

He said he'd kill me if I told, and the way my life was going it seemed reasonable to take him at his word. I had a hard time getting excited about meeting men after that. I'd learned to live without it, but not very well.

* * *

Shock had pitched me over her head twice the day that Zeke asked me to dinner, and by the time I got to his house my neck was so stiff I had to turn my whole body to look at him.

'Why don't you just jump in the hot tub before dinner,' he said, and I swung my head and shoulders around from him to the wood-heated hot tub in the middle of the living room and I must have gone real white then because he said, 'But you know, the heater's messing up and it's just not getting as hot as it should.'

While he went outside to light the charcoals I sat on a hard wooden bench covered with skins facing what he called the trophy wall. A brown-and-white speckled owl stared down its pointed beak at me from above the doorway, its wings and talons poised as if ready for attack, a violence in its huge yellow eyes that is never so complete in humans.

He came back in and caught me staring into the face of the grizzly bear that covered most of the wall. 'It's an eight-foot-square bear,' he said, and then explained, by rubbing his hand across the fur, that it was eight feet long from the tip of its nose to the tip of its tail, and from the razor edge of one outstretched front claw to the other. He smoothed the fur back down with strong even strokes. He picked something off one of its teeth.

'It's a decent-sized bear,' he said, 'but they get much bigger.'

I told him about the time I was walking with my dogs along the Salmon River and I saw a deer carcass lying in the middle of an active spawning ground. The salmon were deeper than the water and their tails slapped the surface as they clustered around the deer. One dog ran in to chase them, and they didn't even notice, they swam around her ankles till she got scared and came out.

He laughed and reached towards me and I thought *for* me,

but then his hand came down on the neck of a six-point mule deer mounted on the wall behind me. 'Isn't he beautiful?' he asked. His hands rubbed the short hair around the deer's ears. It was hanging closer to me than I realized, and when I touched its nose it was warmer than my hands.

He went back outside then and I tried to think of more stories to tell him but I got nervous all over and started fidgeting with something that I realized too late was the foot of a small furry animal. The thing I was sitting on reminded me a little too much of my dog to allow me to relax.

The moose steaks were lean and tender and it was easy to eat them until he started telling me about their history, about the bull that had come to the clearing for water, and had seen Zeke there, had seen the gun even, and trusted him not to fire. I couldn't look right at him then, and he waited awhile and he said, 'Do you have any idea what they do to cows?'

We talked about other things after that, horses and the prairie and the mountains we had both left for it. At two I said I should go home, and he said he was too tired to take me. I wanted him to touch me the way he touched the mule deer but he threw a blanket over me and told me to lift up for the pillow. Then he climbed up and into a loft I hadn't even noticed, and left me down there in the dark under all those frightened eyes.

The most remarkable thing about him, I guess, was his calm: his hands were quieter on Jesse's mane even than mine were on Shock's. I never heard him raise his voice, even in laughter. There wasn't an animal in the barn he couldn't turn to putty, and I knew it must be the same with the ones he shot.

On our second ride he talked more, even about himself

some, horses he'd sold, and ex-lovers; there was a darkness in him I couldn't locate.

It was the hottest day of that summer and it wouldn't have been right to run the horses, so we let them walk along the creek bank all afternoon, clear into the next county, I think.

He asked me why I didn't move to the city, why I hadn't, at least, while Charlie was sick, and I wondered what version of my life he had heard. I told him I needed the emptiness and the grasses and the storm threats. I told him about my job and the articles I was working on and how I knew if I moved to the city, or the ocean, or even back to the mountains, I'd be paralyzed. I told him that it seemed as if the right words could only come to me out of the perfect semicircular space of the prairie.

He rubbed his hands together fist to palm and smiled, and asked if I wanted to rest. He said he might nap, if it was quiet, and I said I knew I always talked too much, and he said it was okay because I didn't mind if he didn't always listen.

I told him words were all we had, something that Charlie had told me, and something I had believed because it let me fall into a vacuum where I didn't have to justify my life.

Zeke was stretching his neck in a funny way, so without asking I went over and gave him a back rub and when I was finished he said, 'For a writer lady you do some pretty good communicating without words,' but he didn't touch me even then, and I sat very still while the sun melted, embarrassed and afraid to even look at him.

Finally, he stood up and stretched.

'Billy says you two go out sometimes.'

'Billy lies,' I said.

'He knows a lot about you,' he said.

'No more than everyone else in town,' I said. 'People talk.

It's just what they do. I'll tell you all about it if you want to know.'

'We're a long way from the barn,' he said, in a way that I couldn't tell if it was good or bad. He was rubbing one palm against the other so slowly it was making my skin crawl.

'Shock's got good night vision,' I said, as evenly as I could.

He reached for a strand of Shock's mane and she rubbed her whole neck against him. I pulled her forelock out from under the brow band. She nosed his back pockets, where the carrots were. She knocked his cap off his head and scratched her nose between his shoulder blades. He put both hands up on her withers and rubbed little circles. She stretched her neck out long and low.

'Your horse is a whore, Raye,' he said.

'I want to know what you said to her to make her follow you into the trailer,' I said.

'What I said to her?' he said. 'Christ, Raye, there aren't any words for that.'

Then he was up and in the saddle and waiting for me to get back on Shock. He took off when I had only one foot in the stirrup, and I just hung around Shock's neck for the first quarter mile till he slowed up.

The creek trail was narrow and Shock wanted to race, so I got my stirrup and let her fly past him on the outside, the wheat so high it whipped across Shock's shoulder and my thigh. Once we were in the lead, Shock really turned it on and I could feel her strength and the give of her muscles and the solidity of the healed fetlock every time it hit the ground. Then I heard Jesse coming on the creek side, right at Shock's flank, and I knew we were coming to the big ditch, and I knew Shock would take it if Jesse did, but neither of us wanted to give up the lead. Shock hit the edge first and sailed over it and I came way up on her neck and held my breath when her front legs hit, but then we were down on the other side and she was just as strong and as sound as ever. Jesse edged up again and I knew we couldn't hold the lead for much longer. I felt Zeke's boots on my calf and our stirrups locked once for an instant and then he pulled away. I let Shock slow then, and when Jesse's dust cleared, the darkening sky opened around me like an invitation.

It wasn't light enough to run anymore and we were still ten miles from the barn. Jupiter was up, and Mars. There wasn't any moon.

Zeke said, 'Watching you ride made me almost forget to beat you.' I couldn't see his face in the shadows.

He wanted silence but it was too dark not to talk, so I showed him the constellations. I told him the stories I knew about them: Cassiopeia weeping on the King's shoulder while the great winged Pegasus carries her daughter off across the eastern sky. Cygnus, the swan, flying south along the milky way, the Great Bear spinning slowly head over tail in the north. I showed him Andromeda, the galaxy closest to our own. I said, 'It's two hundred million light-years away. Do you know what that means?' And when he didn't answer I said, 'It means the light we see left that galaxy two hundred million years ago.' And then I said, 'Doesn't that make you feel insignificant?'

And he said, 'No.'

'How does it make you feel?' I said.

'Like I've gotten something I might not deserve,' he said.

Then he went away hunting in Montana for six weeks. I kept thinking about him up there in the mountains I had come from and wondering if he saw them the way I did, if he saw how they held the air. He didn't write or call once, and I didn't either, because I thought I was being tested and

303

I wanted to pass. He left me a key so I could water his plants and keep chemicals in his hot tub. I got friendly with the animals on the wall, and even talked to them sometimes, like I did to the plants. The only one I avoided was the Dall sheep. Perfect in its whiteness, and with a face as gentle and wise as Buddha. I didn't want to imagine Zeke's hands pulling the trigger that stained the white neck with blood the taxidermist must have struggled to remove.

He asked me to keep Jesse in shape for him too, and I did. I'd work Shock in the ring for an hour and then take Jesse out on the trails. He was a little nervous around me, being used to Zeke's uncanny calm, I guess, so I sang the songs to him that I remembered from Zeke's records: 'Angel from Montgomery,' 'City of New Orleans,' 'L.A. Freeway,' places I'd never been or cared to go. I didn't know any songs about Montana.

When we'd get back to the barn I'd brush Jesse till he shone, rubbing around his face and ears with a chamois cloth till he finally let down his guard a little and leaned into my hands. I fed him boxes full of carrots while Shock looked a question at me out of the corner of her eye.

One night Jesse and I got back late from a ride and the only car left at the barn was Billy's. I walked Jesse up and down the road twice before I thought to look in Zeke's saddlebags for the hunting knife I should have known would be there all along. I put it in the inside pocket of my jean jacket and felt powerful, even though I hadn't thought ahead as far as using it. When I walked through the barn door I hit the breaker switch that turned on every light and there was Billy leaning against the door to Jesse's stall.

'So now she's riding his horse,' he said.

'You want to open that door?' I said. I stood as tall as I could between him and Jesse.

'Does that mean you're going steady?'

'Let me by,' I said.

'It'd be a shame if he came back and there wasn't any horse to ride,' he said, and I grabbed for Jesse's reins but he moved forward faster, spooking Jesse, who reared and spun and clattered out the open barn door. I listened to his hooves on the stone and then outside on the hard dirt till he got so far away I only imagined it.

Billy shoved me backwards into a wheelbarrow and when my head hit the manure I reached for the knife and got it between us and he took a step backwards and wiped the spit off his mouth.

'You weren't that much fun the first time,' he said, and ran for the door. I heard him get into his car and screech out the driveway, and I lay there in the manure, breathing horse piss and praying he wouldn't hit Jesse out on the hard road. I got up slow and went into the tack room for a towel and I tried to clean my hair with it but it was Zeke's and it smelled like him and I couldn't understand why my timing had been so bad all my life. I wrapped my face in it so tight I could barely breathe and sat on his tack box and leaned into the wall, but then I remembered Jesse and put some grain in a bucket and went out into the darkness and whistled.

It was late September and almost midnight and all the stars I'd shown Zeke had shifted a half turn to the west. Orion was on the horizon, his bow drawn back, aimed across the Milky Way at the Great Bear, I guess, if space curves the way Earth does. Jesse wasn't anywhere, and I walked half the night looking for him. I went to sleep in my truck and at dawn Irwin and Jesse showed up at the barn door together.

'He got spooked,' I told Irwin. 'I was too worried to go home.'

Irwin looked hard at me. 'Hear anything from Zeke?' he said.

I spent a lot of time imagining his homecoming. I'd make up the kind of scenes in my head I knew would never happen, the kind that never happen to anyone, where the man gets out of the car so fast he tears his jacket, and when he lifts the woman up against the sky she is so light that she thinks she may be absorbed into the atmosphere.

I had just come back from a four-hour ride when his truck did pull up to the barn, six weeks to the day from when he left. He got out slow as ever, and then went around back to where he kept his carrots. From the tackroom window I watched him rub Jesse and feed him, pick up one of his front hooves, run his fingers through his tail.

I wanted to look busy but I'd just got done putting everything away so I sat on the floor and started oiling my tack and then wished I hadn't because of what I'd smell like when he saw me. It was fifteen minutes before he even came looking, and I had the bridle apart, giving it the oil job of its life. He put his hands on the doorjamb and smiled big.

'Put that thing back together and come riding with me,' he said.

'I just got back,' I said. 'Jesse and I've been all over.'

'That'll make it easier for you to beat me on your horse,' he said. 'Come on, it's getting dark earlier every night.'

He stepped over me and pulled his saddle off the rack, and I put the bridle back together as fast as I could. He was still ready before I was and he stood real close while I tried to make Shock behave and get tacked up and tried not to let my hands shake when I fastened the buckles.

Then we were out in the late sunshine and it was like he'd

never left, except this time he was galloping before he hit the end of the driveway.

'Let's see that horse run,' he called to me, and Jesse shot across the road and the creek trail and plunged right through the middle of the wheat field. The wheat was so tall I could barely see Zeke's head, but the footing was good and Shock was gaining on him. I thought about the farmer who'd shoot us if he saw us, and I thought about all the hours I'd spent on Jesse keeping him in shape so that Zeke could come home and win another race. The sky was black to the west and coming in fast, and I tried to remember if I'd heard a forecast and to feel if there was any direction to the wind. Then we were out in a hay field that had just been cut and rolled, and it smelled so strong and sweet it made me light-headed and I thought maybe we weren't touching ground at all but flying along above it, buoyed up by the fragrance and the swirl of the wind. I drove Shock straight at a couple of bales that were tied together and made her take them, and she did, but by the time we hit the irrigation ditch we'd lost another couple of seconds on Zeke.

I felt the first drops of rain and tried to yell up to Zeke, but the wind came up suddenly and blasted my voice back into my mouth. I knew there was no chance of catching him then, but I dug my heels in and yipped a little and Shock dug in even harder, but then I felt her front hoof hit a gopher hole and the bottom dropped out and she went down and I went forward over her neck and then she came down over me. My face hit first and I tasted blood and a hoof came down on the back of my head and I heard reins snap and waited for another hoof to hit, but then it was quiet and I knew she had cleared me. At least I'm not dead, I thought, but my head hurt too bad to even move.

I felt the grit inside my mouth and thought of Zeke galloping on across the prairie, enclosed in the motion, oblivious to my fall. It would be a mile, maybe two, before he slowed down and looked behind him, another before he'd stop, aware of my absence, and come back for me.

I opened one eye and saw Shock grazing nearby, broken reins hanging uneven below her belly. If she'd re-pulled the tendon in her fetlock it would be weeks, maybe months, before I could ride with him again. My mouth was full of blood and my lips were swelling so much it was running out the sides, though I kept my jaw clamped and my head down. The wind was coming in little gusts now, interrupted by longer and longer periods of calm, but the sky was getting darker and I lifted my head to look for Zeke. I got dizzy, and I closed my eyes and tried to breathe regularly. In what seemed like a long time I started to hear a rhythm in my head and I pressed my ear into the dust and knew it was Zeke coming back across the field at a gallop, balanced and steady, around the holes and over them. Then I heard his boots hit ground. He tied Jesse first, and then caught Shock, which was smart, I guess, and then he knelt next to my head and I opened the eye that wasn't in the dirt and he smiled and put his hands on his knees.

'Your mouth,' he said, without laughing, but I knew what I must've looked like, so I raised up on one elbow and started to tell him I was okay and he said.

'Don't talk. It'll hurt.'

And he was right, it did, but I kept on talking and soon I was telling him about the pain in my mouth and the back of my head and what Billy had done that day in the barn, and the ghosts I carry with me. Blood was coming out with the words and pieces of tooth, and I kept talking till I told him everything, but when I looked at his face I knew all I'd

308

done was make the gap wider with the words I'd picked so carefully that he didn't want to hear. The wind started up again and the rain was getting steady.

I was crying then, but not hard, and you couldn't tell through all the dirt and blood, and the rain and the noise the wind was making. I was crying, I think, but I wanted to laugh because he would have said there weren't any words for what I didn't tell him, and that was that I loved him and even more I loved the prairie that wouldn't let you hide anything, even if you wanted to.

Then he reached across the space my words had made around me and put his long brown finger against my swollen lips. I closed my eyes tight as his hand wrapped up my jaw and I fell into his chest and whatever it was that drove him to me, and I held myself there unbreathing, like waiting for the sound of hooves on the sand, like waiting for a tornado.

MARGARET ATWOOD

WHITE HORSE

IN THEIR SECOND YEAR at the farm, Nell and Tig acquired a white horse. They didn't buy this horse, or even seek her out. But suddenly, there she was.

In those days they picked up animals the way they picked up burrs. Creatures adhered to them. In addition to the sheep, cows, chickens, and ducks, they'd gathered in a dog they called Howl – a blue tick hound, possibly even a thoroughbred: he'd been wearing an expensive collar, though no name tag. He'd wandered in off the side road – dumped there by whoever had mistreated him so badly that he rolled over on his back and peed if anyone spoke a harsh word to him. There was no point in trying to train him, said Tig: he was too easily frightened.

Howl slept in the kitchen, sometimes, where he barked in the middle of the night for no reason. At other times he went on excursions and wasn't seen for days. He would come back with injuries: porcupine quills in his nose, sore paws, flesh wounds from encounters with – possibly – raccoons. Once, a scattering of birdshot pellets from a trespassing hunter. Though he was a coward, he had no discretion.

They'd also sprouted a number of cats, offspring of the single cat that had been transported to the farm from the city, and was supposed to have been spayed. Obviously there had been a mistake, because this cat kittened underneath a corner of the house. The kittens were quite wild. They ran away, and plunged into their burrow if Nell even tried to get near them. Then they would peer out, hissing and trying to look ferocious. When they were older they moved to the barn, where they hunted mice and had secrets. Once in a while, a gizzard – squirrel, Nell suspected – or else a tail, or some other chewed-up body-part offering, would appear on the back-door threshold, where Nell would be sure to step on it, especially if her feet happened to be bare, as they often were in summer. The cats had a vestigial memory of civilization and its rituals, it seemed. They knew they were supposed to pay rent, but they were confused about the details.

They ate out of the dog's dish, which was kept outside the back door. Howl didn't bark at them or chase them: they were too terrifying for him. Sometimes they slept on the cows. It was suspected that they had dealings in the hen house – eggshells had been found – but nothing could be proved.

The white horse – the white mare – had a name, unlike the cats. Her name was Gladys. She had been installed with Tig and Nell because of Nell's friend Billie, who was a horse-lover from childhood but who lived in the city now, leaving her no outlets. Billie had seen the white horse (or mare) standing in a damp field, all by herself, hanging her head disconsolately. She was in a sad condition. Her mane was tangled, her white coat was muddy, and her hooves had not been dealt with for so long that her toes were turned up at the ends like Turkish slippers. Any more time in that swamp, said Billie, and she'd develop foot rot, and once a horse had that, it would soon go lame and that was pretty much game over. Billie had been so outraged by such callous neglect that she'd bought Gladys from a drunken and (she'd said) no doubt insane farmer, for a hundred dollars, which was a good deal more than poor Gladys was worth in her decrepit state.

But then Billie'd had no place to put her.

Nell and Tig had a place, however. They had lots of room

– acres of it! What could be more perfect for Gladys (who was past her prime, who was too fat, who had something wrong with her wind so that she wheezed and coughed) than to come and stay at the farm? Just – of course – until something else could be found for her.

How could Nell say no? She could have said she had enough to do without adding a horse to her long, long list. She could have said she wasn't running a retirement home for rejected quadrupeds. But she hadn't wanted to sound selfish and cruel. Also, Billie was quite tall and determined, and had a convincing manner.

'I don't know anything about horses,' Nell had said weakly. She didn't add that she was afraid of them. They were large and jumpy, and they rolled their eyes too much. She thought of them as unstable and prone to rages.

'Oh, it's easy. I'll teach you,' said Billie. 'There's nothing to it once you get the hang of it. You'll love Gladys! She has such a sweet nature! She's just a cupcake!'

When he heard about Gladys, Tig was reserved. He said that horses needed a lot of care. They also needed a lot of feed. But he'd accumulated all of the other animals – the ones that had been chosen and paid for, rather than just straying onto the property or being spawned on it or dumped on it – and Nell had had no say in those choices. She found herself defending the advent of Gladys as if she herself had made a deliberate and principled decision to take her in, even though she was already regretting her own slackness and lack of spine.

Gladys arrived in a rented horse car, and was backed out of it easily enough. 'Come on, you old sweetie pie,' Billie said. 'There! Isn't she gorgeous?' Gladys turned around obediently and let herself be viewed. She had a round thick body, with legs that were too short for her bulk. She was part

Welsh pit pony, part Arab, said Billie. That accounted for her odd shape. It also meant she would want to eat a lot. Welsh ponies were like that. Billie had made the trip in the horse car with her; she'd bought her a new bridle.

Nell was expected to pay for this bridle, and also for the horse-car rental: Gladys was now hers, it appeared. Surely that had not been the original understanding, but Billie thought it had been. She seemed to feel she was doing Nell a favour – had given her a priceless gift. She didn't charge for the original hundred dollars, nor for her own time. She'd taken a week off work to set Gladys up with Nell. She made a point of mentioning that.

Gladys regarded Nell through her long, frowsy forelock. She had the weary, blank, but calculating look of a carnival con artist: she was sizing Nell up, figuring her out, estimating how to get round her. Then she ducked her head and snatched at a tuft of grass.

'None of that, you naughty girl,' said Billie, jerking Gladys's head up by the bridle. 'You can't let them get away with anything,' she told Nell. She led Gladys to the end of the drive shed, where there was a fenced-in space originally intended for goats – Nell had fought off the goat idea – and tied her up to one of the posts. 'We'll put her in here for now,' she said.

Billie volunteered to stay at the farm until Gladys was settled in, so Nell made up the recently acquired pullout couch in the former back parlour. The previous summer, Nell and Tig had tried to incubate some eggs in there, turning them and sprinkling them with water as per the instructions in the booklet that came with the incubator, but something went wrong and the chicks emerged with goggling eyes and swollen, blue-veined, unfinished stomachs, and had to be hit with a shovel and buried in the back field.

Howl dug them up again, several times, after which the cats got into them, with unpleasant results. Nell kept finding tiny claws in unexpected places, as if the chicks were growing up through the barnyard dirt like disagreeable weeds.

Nell had taken to keeping tomato plants under a grow light in the back parlour, but she'd moved them to the upstairs landing in preparation for Billie's week-long stay.

Much had to be done for Gladys. Equipment was needed. Billie contributed some of her old horse things – a brush, a curry comb, a hoof pick – but the saddle had to be bought. It was second-hand, but still – thought Nell – breathtakingly expensive.

'You need the English, not the Western,' Billie had said. 'That way you'll learn to be a real rider.' What she meant, it turned out, was that with the English saddle you had to grip with your knees or else you would fall off. Nell would rather have had the Western saddle – she had no interest in plummeting off a horse – but at least with Gladys it wasn't very far down to the ground, because of her stumpy little legs.

Saddle soap had to be applied to the saddle and worked in, metal items on the tackle had to be polished. A horse blanket was needed too, and a crop, and some old towels, for rubbing Gladys down. Gladys would have to be rubbed down like a boxer after every session of exercise, said Billie, because horses were delicate creatures, and the number of diseases or conditions they could get was staggering.

After the tackle had been brought up to scratch, Gladys herself had to be gone over, inch by inch. Nell did the work – because she had to learn how, didn't she? – with supervision by Billie. Dust and old hair came off Gladys in clouds, long white horsehairs from her mane and tail detached themselves and floated onto Nell. Gladys bore all this patiently, and might even have enjoyed it. Billie said she was enjoying it –

317

she seemed to have a pipeline to Gladys's mind. She spent some time patiently explaining that mind to Nell so Nell wouldn't do anything that might spook Gladys and cause her to panic and bolt. The hens were a potential danger; so was the laundry. Nell had strung a clothesline between two of the apple trees out at the front of the house, which was therefore a no-go zone. 'They hate flapping,' Billie said. 'They see a different picture out of each eye, so they don't like surprises. Life comes at them from all sides. It's unsettling for them. You can imagine.'

A farrier was called in – luckily Billie knew one – and Gladys had her hooves trimmed, and sparkling new horse-shoes applied. She was looking friskier now, she was taking more of an interest. Her ears swivelled around at the sound of Nell, who always had a carrot with her, or a sugar cube – this because of a hot tip from Billie.

'She has to bond with you,' said Billie. 'Breathe into her nose.'

Then Nell had to try digging the stones out of Gladys's hooves. This needed to be done at least twice a day, said Billie, and also before riding Gladys, and after riding Gladys, because you never knew when she might pick up a stone. Nell was afraid of being kicked, but Gladys didn't mind having her feet picked out. 'She knows it's for her own good,' said Billie, whacking Gladys on the rump. 'Don't you, you big lump?' Gladys was on a diet, despite the carrots. Being thinner – Billie claimed – would help with the wheezing problems. It would be necessary to ride Gladys every day: she needed the exercise, and also the excitement. Horses were easily bored, said Billie.

At last it was time to try Gladys out. The saddle was lifted onto her, the girths tightened. Gladys put her ears back and gave a crafty sideways look. Billie swung up into the saddle and kicked Gladys in the flanks, and Gladys cantered off down the road to the back field. They looked quite funny – top-heavy. Tall Billie astride fat Gladys, with Gladys's stumpy little legs whirring away underneath her like an eggbeater.

After a while Billie and Gladys came back. Gladys was wheezing, Billie pink in the face. 'She's been ridden by too many people,' said Billie. 'She has a hard mouth. I bet she was used for kiddie rides.'

'What do you mean?' said Nell.

'She has a whole bagful of tricks,' said Billie. 'Bad habits. She'll try them out on you, so look out.'

'Tricks?'

'You just have to stay on,' said Billie grimly, dismounting. 'Once she knows you're on to her, she'll cut out the monkey business. You're a bad girl,' she said to Gladys. Gladys coughed.

Nell found out what the tricks were the first time she tried to ride Gladys. Billie ran alongside, shouting instructions. 'Don't let her get near the fence, she'll try to scrape you off! Keep her away from the trees! Don't let her stop, give her a kick! Pull her head up, she's not allowed to eat that! Don't pay any attention to that cough, she's doing it on purpose!'

Though Gladys wasn't going very fast, Nell clung on, resisting the impulse to lean forward and clutch Gladys by the mane. She had a vision of Gladys rearing up on her two back legs or else her two front legs, as in films, with the same result in either case – Nell shooting off into the bushes, head-first. But nothing like that happened. At the end of the track, Gladys halted, wheezing and panting, and Nell actually got her to turn around. Then – after Gladys had glanced back over her shoulder with an incredulous but resigned stare – they repeated their odd merry-go-round motion, back to their starting point.

'Well done!' said Billie. 'Good girl!' The praise was for Gladys. 'See? You just have to be strict,' she said to Nell.

When the week was over, Billie left, in a sullen mood, because Gladys had not been sufficiently grateful for having been rescued – she'd nipped Billie on the bum when having her head tied to a post as part of her diet procedure. Once Billie was no longer in the picture, Gladys and Nell came to an understanding. True, every time Nell approached with the bridle Gladys would start wheezing, but once the saddle was on she'd remember she might get a carrot at the end of her ordeal, and she would settle down, and off they would go, down to the back field – always the same track. They avoided the gravel side road – neither of them liked trucks – and the front of the house as well, because of the laundry; they didn't ride across the fields, because of hidden groundhog holes. During these rides Nell spent most of the time trying to make Gladys behave and the rest of it letting her do what she wanted, because Nell was curious about what that might be.

Sometimes Gladys wanted to stop in mid-canter to see if Nell would fall off. Sometimes she wanted to stand still, swishing her tail and sighing as if extremely tired. Sometimes she wanted to revolve slowly in a circle. Sometimes she wanted to eat weeds and wayside clover – Nell drew the line at that. Sometimes she wanted to go over to the barnyard fence and watch the sheep and cows, and also the cats, which had taken to sleeping on her broad, comfortable back.

Between the two of them, Nell and Gladys passed their riding time pleasantly enough. It was a conspiracy, a double impersonation: Nell pretending to be a person who was riding a horse, Gladys pretending to be a horse that was being ridden.

Sometimes they didn't bother cantering or trotting. They

ambled along in the sunlight, lazily and without purpose. At these times Nell would talk to Gladys, which was better than talking to Howl, who was an idiot, or to the hens or cats. Gladys had to listen: she couldn't get away. 'What do you think, Gladys?' Nell would say. 'Should I have a baby?' Gladys, trudging along, sighing, would swivel an ear back in the direction of the voice. 'Tig isn't sure. He says he isn't ready. Should I just do it? Would he get angry? Would it ruin everything? What do you think?'

Gladys would cough.

Nell would have preferred to have had this conversation with her mother, but her mother wasn't available. Anyway she probably wouldn't have said much more than Gladys. She too would have coughed, because she would have disapproved. Nell and Tig were – after all – not married. How could they possibly be married, when Tig couldn't manage to get himself divorced?

But if Nell's mother knew about Gladys, maybe she would come up to the farm. Her mother had been a devoted horse person once, a long time ago. She'd had two horses of her own. Was it conceivable that, with Gladys dangled like a lure in front of her, she might overcome her reservations – about Tig, about Nell, about their unorthodox living arrangements? Wouldn't she be tempted? Wouldn't she long to have one small idyllic canter out to the back field, for old times' sake, with Gladys's pony-sized legs going like an eggbeater? Wouldn't she want to know that Nell now loved – improbably, and at last – one of the same activities she herself had once loved?

Perhaps. But Nell had no way of knowing. She and her mother weren't exactly speaking. They weren't exactly not speaking, either. The silence that had taken the place of speech between them had become its own form of speech.

In this silence, language was held suspended. It contained many questions, though no definite answers.

As spring turned into summer, Tig and Nell had more and more visitors, especially on the weekends. These visitors would just happen to be driving by, on a little outing from the city, and they'd drop in to say hello, and then they'd be invited for lunch – Tig loved cooking big impromptu lunches, featuring huge vats of soup and giant wads of cheese, and Nell's home-baked bread – and then the day would wear on and the visitors would stroll out to the back field for a walk. They were not allowed to ride Gladys, because of her bad manners with strangers, said Nell, though really she'd become possessive about her, she wanted to keep Gladys all to herself. Then Tig would say they might as well stay for dinner, and then it would be too dark or too late or they would be too drunk to drive back to the city, and they'd end up on the pullout couch in the back parlour, and – if there were a lot of them – dispersed here and there, some of them on foam mattresses or sofas.

In the mornings they would sit around after breakfast – stacks of Tig's wheat-germ pancakes were featured – saying how restful it was in the country, while Nell and Tig tidied up the dishes. They might stand around with their arms dangling at their sides, asking if there was anything they could do – Nell could remember when she herself was like that – and Nell might send them out to the hen-house with a basket padded with tea towels, to collect eggs, which gave them a thrill. Or she would put them to work weeding the garden. They would say how therapeutic it was to get dirt on their fingers; then they would breathe deeply as if they'd just discovered air; then they would have lunch again. After they'd left, Nell would wash their sheets and towels and hang them up on the outside line to flap in the sunshine between the apple trees.

Usually these visitors to the farm were couples, but Nell's baby sister, Lizzie, would come up by herself. The frequency of her visits was connected with the troubles in her life: if there were lots of troubles she would visit, if there weren't many troubles she wouldn't.

The troubles were about men, of which there had already been a number in her life. The men behaved badly. Nell listened to the accounts of their thoughtlessness, their contrariness, and their betrayals, coupled with descriptions of Lizzie's own shortcomings, flaws, and mistakes. She joined in the task of deciphering the men's casual remarks – remarks that usually had a mean and hurtful undertone, it was decided. Then Nell would take Lizzie's side and denounce the men as unworthy. At this point Lizzie would turn around and defend them. These men were exceptional – they were smart, talented, and sexy. In fact, they were perfect, except that they didn't love Lizzie enough. Nell sometimes wondered how much *enough* would be.

Lizzie had been born when Nell was eleven. She'd been an anxious baby and then an anxious child and then an anxious teenager, but now she was twenty-three. Nell hoped the anxiety would begin to wear off soon.

It was her anxiety that caused Lizzie to pick away at the men, peeling them down through their callous and blemished outer layers to get at their pristine cores – at the good, kind hearts she believed were hidden inside them somewhere, like truffles or oil wells. The men didn't seem to relish the process of being peeled, not in the long run. But no one could stop Lizzie from doing it. This would go on until some other man would come along, and then the former man would be archived.

Lizzie and Nell had the same noses. They both bit their fingers. Other than that, there were differences. Nell looked the age she was, but Lizzie could have been mistaken for a fourteen-year-old. She was thin, delicate-looking, with big eyes the colour of blue-green hydrangeas. Hydrangeas were a flower she favoured; she had a list of other favourite flowers. She liked the ones with small petals.

She thought Nell and Tig should plant some hydrangeas at the farm. She had other planting suggestions as well.

Lizzie loved the farm. Certain of its aspects enraptured her – the apple blossoms, the wild plum trees along the fence-lines, the swallows dipping over the pond. One beautiful day, Nell and Lizzie were sitting outside the back door making ice cream. The inner ice cream canister was turned by electricity; they'd run an extension cord into the house. The outer canister was packed with chipped ice and rock salt. Some of the cats were watching from a distance: they knew there was cream involved. Howl had been over to investigate but had been alarmed by the whirring noise the machine was making and had backed away, whimpering.

As for Gladys, she was keeping an eye on them from the other side of the barnyard fence. She lived inside the barnyard now, because Nell had decided the sheep and cows would be company for her. After a short period of terrorizing the sheep by stampeding them around the barnyard, teeth bared, tail fully erect, she'd turned them into a herd of what she must have decided were dwarfish, woolly horses, and now bossed them around. They in turn had accepted her as a giant balding sheep, and followed her everywhere. She dealt with the cows and their lumbering attempts to monopolize the food supply by sneaking up on them and biting them; Nell had even witnessed a kick. These activities and the chance they gave her to express herself had improved her frame of mind immeasurably. She was now quite perky, like a housebound drudge recently widowed and in the process of discovering the pleasures of nail polish, hair salons, and bingo. Her diet was a thing of the past, Nell having been proven too feeble to enforce it.

'Isn't this *normal?*' said Nell, meaning the ice cream, the cats, the dog, Gladys looking over the fence – the whole bucolic scene. What she meant was *domestic*.

'This air's so great,' said Lizzie, breathing in. 'You should stay here forever. You shouldn't even bother going in to the city. When are you going to get rid of that rusty old machinery?'

'It's lawn sculpture. That would suit *them*,' said Nell. 'They'd never have to see me again.'

'They'll get over it,' said Lizzie. 'Anyway they live in the Middle Ages. Is it a harrow?'

'They might like Gladys,' said Nell hopefully.

'Gladys is beside the point,' said Lizzie.

Nell thought about that. 'Not to herself,' she said. 'I think it's actually a disker. The other one's a drag harrow.'

'They wouldn't like Howl,' said Lizzie. 'He's too craven for them. What you need is a rusty old car.'

'We've got one, we're driving it,' said Nell. 'He's mentally deficient. I can see their point though. Everything's different now. They aren't used to it.'

'That's their problem,' said Lizzie, who despite her fragility could be tough when it came to other people, and especially other people who were doing wounding things to Nell.

When Lizzie and Nell spoke together, they often left out the middle terms of thought sequences because they knew the other one would fill them in. *Them* meant their parents, in whose books – outdated, prudish books, according to

Lizzie – only cheap, trashy women did things like living with married men.

Lizzie was the messenger. She took it as her mission to assure their parents that Nell was not dying of any fatal disease, and to report to Nell that it was not yet time for the parents to meet Tig, of whom Lizzie approved, with reservations. First the parents would have to enter the twentieth century. Lizzie herself would be the judge of when that had happened.

It's fun for her to be the judge, thought Nell. She's been on the judged end enough times. She probably has discussions with them about me. Me and my bad behaviour. Now I'm the problem child, for a change.

'How's Claude?' she said. Claude was Lizzie's current man. He'd been away a lot, on trips, and had been offhand about his dates of return. He was away right now, and a week overdue.

'There's something wrong with my digestive system,' said Lizzie. What she meant was, I am feeling very anxious, because of Claude. 'I think I have irritable bowel syndrome. I have to see a doctor about it.'

'He just needs to grow up,' said Nell.

'I mean, he might be dead or something,' said Lizzie. 'He doesn't get that part.'

'What are you talking about?' said Tig, coming around the corner of the house. 'Is the ice cream ready?'

'You,' said Nell.

Lizzie came up the next weekend. 'What about your irritable bowel syndrome?' Nell asked her.

'The doctor couldn't find anything,' Lizzie said. 'He referred me to a shrink. He thinks it's psychological.'

Nell didn't think this was a totally bad idea. Maybe the

326

shrink could do something about the anxiety, the crises, the troubles with men. Help Lizzie get some perspective.

'Are you going to go?' she asked. 'To the shrink?'

'I've already been,' said Lizzie.

A few weeks later, Lizzie came up again. She didn't say much and seemed preoccupied. It was hard to wake her in the mornings. She was tired a lot of the time.

'The shrink's put me on a pill,' she said. 'It's supposed to help the anxiety.'

'And has it?' said Nell.

'I'm not sure,' said Lizzie.

She hadn't been to see their parents lately, she said. She hadn't got around to it. She no longer seemed to care what the parents thought of Nell and her immoral lifestyle, a subject that had once been of much interest to her.

Claude had departed, possibly for good. Lizzie expressed anger with him, but in a curiously detached way. There was no new man on the scene. She didn't seem to care about that, either. She appeared to have shelved the plans she'd had – just a few weeks earlier – for going back to school in the fall. She'd been quite excited about it then, and hopeful. It was going to be a whole new chapter.

Nell was concerned, but decided to wait and see.

The weekend after that Lizzie was back again. She was walking stiffly and drooling a little. Her face lacked expression. She said she felt weak. Also she'd quit her temporary job, which had been in a sportswear store.

'There's something really wrong with Lizzie,' Nell said to Tig. She wondered if some malign influence in the back parlour – the same influence that had wreaked such havoc with the incubating chicks – was affecting Lizzie. The neighbourhood farmers had let it drop, almost casually, that the farmhouse was haunted: that was why it had been on the market for so long before Tig and Nell had bought it, as everyone with any sense had always known.

Nell didn't entirely believe in this haunting phenomenon and had seen no direct evidence of it. Still, Howl the dog wouldn't go into that room, and sometimes barked at it. But this in itself proved nothing, as his phobias were numerous. Mrs Roblin from up the road said some kids had once stolen a marble tombstone from the cemetery and used it for making pull taffy in that house, which had been a bad idea: the ghost might have got in that way. Mrs Roblin was considered to be an authority on such matters: she always took care never to have thirteen to dinner, and was said to be able to smell blood on the stairs whenever there was to be a violent death – a car crash, a lightning strike, a tractor rolling over and squashing its driver.

Mrs Roblin had told Nell to leave a meal on the table overnight, to let the ghost know it was welcome. (Nell, feeling foolish, had actually done this, in the middle of the previous winter, during a blizzard, when things had got a little too dark and foreboding. A slice of ham and some mashed potatoes were what she thought such a spirit might like. But Howl had snuck in somehow and eaten this food offering, and tipped over the glass of milk Nell had placed beside it, so leaving out the meal might not have accomplished much.)

Could the rumoured haunting entity have got into Lizzie? But such a thought was ridiculous. Anyway, now that it was summer, the house did not seem very haunted after all.

'It must be the pills,' said Tig.

Neither of them knew much about pills. Nell decided to phone the shrink, whose name was Dr Hobbs. She left a message with the secretary. After a few days, Dr Hobbs phoned back.

The conversation was very disturbing.

Dr Hobbs said that Lizzie was a schizophrenic, and that he had therefore put her on an antipsychotic drug. That would control the symptoms of her mental illness, which were many. He himself would see her once a week, though she would have to call ahead to set the time, as he was very busy and he would have to make a special effort to fit her in. Lizzie could drive into the city for these sessions, which would deal with her inability to adjust to real life. Meanwhile, said Dr Hobbs, Lizzie would be incapable of holding down a job, going to school, or functioning independently. She would have to live with Nell and Tig.

Why not with Nell's parents? Nell asked, once she had caught her breath.

'It's her preference to live with you,' said Dr Hobbs.

Nell knew nothing about schizophrenia. Lizzie hadn't ever seemed crazy to Nell, just sometimes very sorrowful and despondent, but maybe that was because Nell was used to her. She remembered that she and Lizzie had some odd uncles, so it might be genetic. But then, everyone had odd uncles. Or a lot of people did.

'How do you know Lizzie's a schizophrenic?' Nell said. She wanted to sit down – she felt sick to her stomach – but the telephone was on the wall and the cord was too short.

Dr Hobbs laughed in a condescending way. *I'm the professional*, his tone said. 'It's the word salad,' he said.

'What is word salad?' said Nell.

'She doesn't make any sense when she talks,' said the doctor. Nell had never noticed this.

'Are you sure?' she said.

'Sure about what?' said Dr Hobbs.

'That she's – what you say she is.'

The doctor laughed again. 'If she wasn't a schizophrenic,

these drugs she's on would kill her,' he said. He then said that Nell should not say anything to Lizzie about the diagnosis. That was a delicate matter, and needed to be handled with care.

Nell called him back the next week. She had trouble getting through – she left several messages – but she persisted, because Lizzie's state was becoming more and more alarming. 'What about the way she's walking?' she asked. Lizzie's hands were beginning to shake, she'd noticed. Dr Hobbs said that the stiffness and the drooling and shaking were symptoms of Lizzie's disease – all schizophrenics had those symptoms. Lizzie was just the age at which this disease manifested itself. A person could seem perfectly normal, and then in their late teens or early twenties, out came the schizophrenia, like some malignant blossom.

'How long is this going to go on?' said Nell.

'The rest of her life,' said Dr Hobbs.

Nell felt cold all over. Though Lizzie'd had some bad times in the past, Nell had never suspected anything like this.

She discussed the situation with Tig after Lizzie had gone to bed. How would he feel, being saddled with a mad relative?

'We'll cope,' he said. 'Maybe she'll snap out of it.' Nell felt so grateful to him she almost wept.

There were a lot of other things Nell needed to know over the next few months. How could Lizzie be trusted with driving a car – Tig's old Chevy – back and forth to the city, with her body so stiff and her hands shaking like that? But Dr Hobbs – whose tone was becoming more and more hostile, as if he felt Nell was pestering him – said that was fine, Lizzie was perfectly capable of driving.

He also said he hadn't told Lizzie the truth about her condition yet because she wasn't ready for that news. She was hallucinating about some man called Claude, he said; she was convinced Claude was dead. Also she'd been suicidal when she'd come to him. But he could guarantee that she wouldn't commit suicide any time soon.

'Why not?' said Nell. She'd thought that *I'm going to kill myself* was a figure of speech for Lizzie, as it was for her. Now it appeared she'd been wrong; nevertheless she felt preternaturally calm. She was getting used to these fragments of nightmare that kept coming at her out of the mouth of Dr Hobbs.

But Dr Hobbs appeared to be confused about who she was: he seemed to think that she and Tig were Lizzie's parents. Nell carefully explained the actual relationship, but every time she spoke with him she had to remind him about it.

Meanwhile, Lizzie's real parents – Nell's parents – had gone into shock. But they were talking to Nell again, or at least her mother was. 'I don't know what to do,' she would say. It was a plea – *Don't send her back here!* It was as if Lizzie had committed some shameful, unmentionable act – something in between a social gaffe and a crime.

Then Nell's mother would ask plaintively, 'When is she going to get better?' As if Nell had any special insights.

'I'm sure the doctor knows what's right,' Nell would say. She still believed that anyone with a medical degree must know what he was talking about. She needed to believe that: she put some effort into it. 'You should come up to the farm and see my horse,' she added. 'You like horses. Her name is Gladys. You could go for a ride.' But her mother was too distressed by Lizzie's plight.

Nell herself hadn't been riding Gladys much, because she was pregnant. She didn't want to be thrown off a horse and lose the baby, as happened in novels. She hadn't yet shared her knowledge with Tig, however.

331

What would it be like if the baby arrived and Lizzie was still like this? How could she manage?

By now it was September. Nell tried to get Lizzie to help her with the preserving, but it was no use: Lizzie was too tired. Nell set a bowl of red currants in front of her and asked her to pick off the stems – that wouldn't be too hard – but Lizzie couldn't seem to manage it. She sat at the table, gazing into space, with her pathetic little mound of picked-over currants shoved to one side.

'He doesn't like me,' she said. 'The doctor.'

'Why wouldn't he like you?' said Nell.

'Because I'm not getting better,' said Lizzie.

Tig had been doing some research of his own. 'This guy isn't making any sense,' he said. 'Those pills won't kill you if you aren't schizophrenic – how could they? You'd have a lot of corpses to explain.'

'But why would he tell us that?' said Nell.

'Because he's a fraud,' said Tig.

'I think we need a second opinion,' said Nell.

The new doctor they found was an expert in antipsychotic drugs. 'Lizzie shouldn't have been put on this,' she told Nell. 'I'm taking her off it.' The stiffness, the trembling, the weakness – all those were by no means the symptoms of a disease. They were produced by the drug itself, and once the stuff was out of Lizzie's system they would go away.

Not only that, Lizzie should never have been allowed to drive a car while so heavily medicated, said the new doctor. Her life had been in danger every minute she'd been behind the wheel.

'If I ever met that creep on the street I'd shoot him,' Nell said to Tig. 'If I had a gun.'

'Lucky you don't know what he looks like,' said Tig.

'I bet he thought we were hillbillies,' said Nell. 'Because we live on a farm. I bet he thought he could tell us any old thing, and we'd believe it.' Which had in fact been the case, they had believed it. 'He must've thought we were dumb as a sack of hammers. I wonder if he believed any of it himself? If so, he's a lunatic!'

'Hillbillies?' said Tig. 'Where did you dig up *that* word? Though we've got the farm machinery for it!' Then they both started to laugh, and hugged each other, and Nell told him about the baby, and it was all fine.

Nell felt tremendous relief at the new turn of events – she wouldn't have to look after a drooling, shambling Lizzie for the rest of her life – but she also felt a shiver of fear. Lizzie would not go back to being the way she was before Dr Hobbs got hold of her: her interlude as a zombie would have changed her. She would now be someone else, someone as yet unknown. Also, Nell was well aware that Lizzie would consider her own actions a betrayal. And Lizzie would be right – they were a betrayal. If Nell had been the supposed schizophrenic, Lizzie wouldn't have put up with Dr Hobbs and his toxic gobbledegook for two seconds.

'Why didn't you tell me what he thought?' Lizzie said to Nell, once she was no longer tranquillized. Now, instead, she was furious. 'You should have asked me! I could have told you I wasn't a schizophrenic!'

Useless for Nell to say that once you think someone's unhinged you don't trust their word, especially on the subject of their own mental health. So she didn't say it.

'He told me you had word salad,' Nell said weakly.

'He told you I had what?'

'He said you didn't make sense.'

'Oh for fuck's sake! I talked to him the same way I talk to

you!' said Lizzie. 'We skip the middles of sentences, you know that. He just had trouble *following* me. He couldn't get from A to C! I had to spell things out for him. He was just plain, ordinary stupid!'

'He must have been having a nervous breakdown, or something,' said Nell. 'To be so – so unprofessional.' And malevolent, she felt like adding. It was Tig's opinion that Dr Hobbs had been doing secret drug experiments for the CIA, an idea that had seemed far-fetched, at the time.

'Well, he's fucked up my life,' said Lizzie grimly. 'I've *lost* a big chunk of it. What an asshole!'

'Not that much,' said Nell soothingly. She meant the big chunk of life.

'Fine for you to say,' said Lizzie. 'You weren't there.'

It was decided that Lizzie would stay on at the farm until some plan could be formulated. For one thing, she didn't have any money. It was too late for her to go back to school this year, as she'd intended doing before the catastrophe of Dr Hobbs.

She was seeing her new doctor once a week. The subject was family issues. She went for long walks around the farm, and dug vigorous holes in the garden. She wasn't saying much to Tig and Nell, though she made friends with Gladys. She didn't ride her, but she would run around in the barnyard with her, the cows moving aside to let them past, the sheep following behind. Her lassitude of the summer had been replaced by a ferocious energy.

Nell, who was now swelling visibly, watched through the window, a little envious: she wouldn't be able to gallop around like that for a while. Then she went back to kneading the bread, letting herself settle into the soft curves, the soothing warmth, the peaceful rhythm. She thought they were all out of danger now; she thought Lizzie was.

Then, one crisp October night, Lizzie attached the vacuum cleaner hose to the exhaust pipe of the car, ran it in through the window, and turned on the motor.

Tig heard the motor running and went outside. By the time he got to her, he said, Lizzie had turned the motor off and was just sitting there. He said this was a good sign. He'd had to wake Nell up to tell her this. How could she have been asleep at such a time?

After getting herself under control, Nell came downstairs in her nightgown, with an old sweater of Tig's thrown on top of it. She felt cold all over. Her teeth were chattering.

By then Lizzie and Tig were sitting at the kitchen table having hot chocolate. 'Why did you do that?' Nell said to Lizzie, once she could speak. She was trembling with fright, and with what she would much later come to discover had been rage.

'I don't want to discuss it,' said Lizzie.

'No. I mean, why did you do that, *to me?*'

'You'd cope with it,' said Lizzie. 'You cope with everything.'

It wasn't the same night that Gladys ran away, but Nell remembers it as the same night. She can't seem to separate the two events. She remembers Howl barking, though it's unlikely he would have done anything so appropriate. She also remembers a full moon – a chilly, white, autumnal moon – another atmospheric detail she herself may well have supplied. But a full moon would have been fitting, because animals are more active then.

It was the cows who'd set the tragedy in motion, on one of their periodic jailbreaks. They'd got the fence down again and had taken off for the nearest herd of other cows. Gladys, on the other hand, had made for the paved highway two miles away. She must have been bored with her little kingdom, she must have been tired of ruling over the sheep. Also, Nell hadn't been paying enough attention to her. She'd wanted an adventure.

She was hit by a car and killed. The driver had been drinking, and was going fast. It must have been a shock to him to have flown over the top of the hill and seen a white horse standing right in front of him, lit up by the moonlight. He himself was only shaken, but his car was a mess.

Nell felt terrible about Gladys. She felt guilty and sad. But she didn't want to indulge these feelings because they would cause upsetting chemicals to circulate through her bloodstream, and that might affect the baby. She listened to a lot of Mozart string quartets in an attempt to stay cheerful.

The next fall she planted a patch of daffodils at the front of the property, in memory of Gladys. The daffodils came up every year, and grew well, and spread.

They are still there. Nell knows that, because she drove past the farm a few years ago just to see it again. When was that, exactly? Shortly after Lizzie got married, and went in for home cooking, and gave up sorrow. Whenever it was, it was in the spring, and there were the daffodils, hundreds of them by now.

The farmhouse itself had lost its ramshackle appearance. It looked serene and welcoming, and somewhat suburban. Laundry no longer flapped between the apple trees. The rusting farm machinery had gone. The siding on the house had been freshly painted, a fashionable colour of pioneer blue. On either side of the front door was a planter with a shrub in it – rhododendrons, thought Nell. Whoever was living there now preferred things tidier.

TED HUGHES

THE RAIN HORSE

AS THE YOUNG MAN came over the hill the first thin blowing of rain met him. He turned his coat-collar up and stood on top of the shelving rabbit-riddled hedgebank, looking down into the valley.

He had come too far. What had set out as a walk along pleasantly-remembered tarmac lanes had turned dreamily by gate and path and hedge-gap into a cross-ploughland trek, his shoes ruined, the dark mud of the lower fields inching up the trouser legs of his grey suit where they rubbed against each other. And now there was a raw, flapping wetness in the air that would be downpour again at any minute. He shivered, holding himself tense against the cold.

This was the view he had been thinking of. Vaguely, without really directing his walk, he had felt he would get the whole thing from this point. For twelve years, whenever he had recalled this scene, he had imagined it as it looked from here. Now the valley lay sunken in front of him, utterly deserted, shallow, bare fields, black and sodden as the bed of an ancient lake after the weeks of rain.

Nothing happened. Not that he had looked forward to any very transfiguring experience. But he had expected something, some pleasure, some meaningful sensation, he didn't quite know what.

So he waited, trying to nudge the right feelings alive with the details – the surprisingly familiar curve of the hedges, the stone gate-pillar and iron gatehook let into it that he had used as a target, the long bank of the rabbit-warren on which he stood and which had been the first thing he ever noticed about the hill when twenty years ago, from the distance of the village, he had said to himself 'That looks like rabbits'.

Twelve years had changed him. This land no longer recognized him, and he looked back at it coldly, as at a finally visited home-country, known only through the stories of a grandfather; felt nothing but the dullness of feeling nothing. Boredom. Then, suddenly, impatience, with a whole exasperated swarm of little anxieties about his shoes, and the spitting rain and his new suit and that sky and the two-mile trudge through the mud back to the road.

It would be quicker to go straight forward to the farm a mile away in the valley and behind which the road looped. But the thought of meeting the farmer – to be embarrassingly remembered or shouted at as a trespasser – deterred him. He saw the rain pulling up out of the distance, dragging its grey broken columns, smudging the trees and the farms.

A wave of anger went over him: anger against himself for blundering into this mud-trap and anger against the land that made him feel so outcast, so old and stiff and stupid. He wanted nothing but to get away from it as quickly as possible. But as he turned, something moved in his eye-corner. All his senses startled alert. He stopped.

Over to his right a thin, black horse was running across the ploughland towards the hill, its head down, neck stretched out. It seemed to be running on its toes like a cat, like a dog up to no good.

From the high point on which he stood the hill dipped slightly and rose to another crested point fringed with the tops of trees, three hundred yards to his right. As he watched it, the horse ran up to that crest, showed against the sky –

for a moment like a nightmarish leopard – and disappeared over the other side.

For several seconds he stared at the skyline, stunned by the unpleasantly strange impression the horse had made on him. Then the plastering beat of icy rain on his bare skull brought him to himself. The distance had vanished in a wall of grey. All around him the fields were jumping and streaming.

Holding his collar close and tucking his chin down into it he ran back over the hilltop towards the town-side, the lee-side, his feet sucking and splashing, at every stride plunging to the ankle.

This hill was shaped like a wave, a gently rounded back lifting out of the valley to a sharply crested, almost concave front hanging over the river meadows towards the town. Down this front, from the crest, hung two small woods separated by a fallow field. The near wood was nothing more than a quarry, circular, full of stones and bracken, with a few thorns and nondescript saplings, foxholes and rabbit holes. The other was rectangular, mainly a planting of scrub oak trees. Beyond the river smouldered the town like a great heap of blue cinders.

He ran along the top of the first wood and finding no shelter but the thin, leafless thorns of the hedge, dipped below the crest out of the wind and jogged along through thick grass to the wood of oaks. In blinding rain he lunged through the barricade of brambles at the wood's edge. The little crippled trees were small choice in the way of shelter, but at a sudden fierce thickening of the rain he took one at random and crouched down under the leaning trunk.

Still panting from his run, drawing his knees up tightly, he watched the bleak lines of rain, grey as hail, slanting through the boughs into the clumps of bracken and bramble. He felt hidden and safe. The sound of the rain as it rushed and lulled

341

in the wood seemed to seal him in. Soon the chilly sheet lead of his suit became a tight, warm mould, and gradually he sank into a state of comfort that was all but trance, though the rain beat steadily on his exposed shoulders and trickled down the oak trunk on to his neck.

All around him the boughs angled down, glistening, black as iron. From their tips and elbows the drops hurried steadily, and the channels of the bark pulsed and gleamed. For a time he amused himself calculating the variation in the rainfall by the variations in a dribble of water from a trembling twig-end two feet in front of his nose. He studied the twig, bringing dwarfs and continents and animals out of its scurfy bark. Beyond the boughs the blue shoal of the town was rising and falling, and darkening and fading again, in the pale, swaying backdrop of rain.

He wanted this rain to go on forever. Whenever it seemed to be drawing off he listened anxiously until it closed in again. As long as it lasted he was suspended from life and time. He didn't want to return to his sodden shoes and his possibly ruined suit and the walk back over that land of mud.

All at once he shivered. He hugged his knees to squeeze out the cold and found himself thinking of the horse. The hair on the nape of his neck prickled slightly. He remembered how it had run up to the crest and showed against the sky.

He tried to dismiss the thought. Horses wander about the countryside often enough. But the image of the horse as it had appeared against the sky stuck in his mind. It must have come over the crest just above the wood in which he was now sitting. To clear his mind, he twisted around and looked up the wood between the tree stems, to his left.

At the wood top, with the silvered grey light coming in behind it, the black horse was standing under the oaks, its head high and alert, its ears pricked, watching him.

342

A horse sheltering from the rain generally goes into a sort of stupor, tilts a hind hoof and hangs its head and lets its eyelids droop, and so it stays as long as the rain lasts. This horse was nothing like that. It was watching him intently, standing perfectly still, its soaked neck and flank shining in the hard light.

He turned back. His scalp went icy and he shivered. What was he to do? Ridiculous to try driving it away. And to leave the wood, with the rain still coming down full pelt, was out of the question. Meanwhile the idea of being watched became more and more unsettling until at last he had to twist around again, to see if the horse had moved. It stood exactly as before.

This was absurd. He took control of himself and turned back deliberately, determined not to give the horse one more thought. If it wanted to share the wood with him, let it. If it wanted to stare at him, let it. He was nestling firmly into these resolutions when the ground shook and he heard the crash of a heavy body coming down the wood. Like lightning his legs bounded him upright and about face. The horse was almost on top of him, its head stretching forwards, ears flattened and lips lifted back from the long yellow teeth. He got one snapshot glimpse of the red-veined eyeball as he flung himself backwards around the tree. Then he was away up the slope, whipped by oak twigs as he leapt the brambles and brushwood, twisting between the close trees till he tripped and sprawled. As he fell the warning flashed through his head that he must at all costs keep his suit out of the leaf-mould, but a more urgent instinct was already rolling him violently sideways. He spun around, sat up and looked back, ready to scramble off in a flash to one side. He was panting from the sudden excitement and effort. The horse had disappeared. The wood was empty except for the drumming, slant grey rain, dancing the bracken and glittering from the branches.

343

He got up, furious. Knocking the dirt and leaves from his suit as well as he could he looked around for a weapon. The horse was evidently mad, had an abscess on its brain or something of the sort. Or maybe it was just spiteful. Rain sometimes puts creatures into queer states. Whatever it was, he was going to get away from the wood as quickly as possible, rain or no rain.

Since the horse seemed to have gone on down the wood, his way to the farm over the hill was clear. As he went, he broke a yard length of wrist-thick dead branch from one of the oaks, but immediately threw it aside and wiped the slime of rotten wet bark from his hands with his soaked handkerchief. Already he was thinking it incredible that the horse could have meant to attack him. Most likely it was just going down the wood for better shelter and had made a feint at him in passing – as much out of curiosity or playfulness as anything. He recalled the way horses menace each other when they are galloping around in a paddock.

The wood rose to a steep bank topped by the hawthorn hedge that ran along the whole ridge of the hill. He was puffing himself up to a thin place in the hedge by the bare stem of one of the hawthorns when he ducked and shrank down again. The swelling gradient of fields lay in front of him, smoking in the slowly crossing rain. Out in the middle of the first field, tall as a statue, and a ghostly silver in the under-cloud light, stood the horse, watching the wood.

He lowered his head slowly, slithered back down the bank and crouched. An awful feeling of helplessness came over him. He felt certain the horse had been looking straight at him. Waiting for him? Was it clairvoyant? Maybe a mad animal can be clairvoyant. At the same time he was ashamed to find himself acting so inanely, ducking and creeping about in this way just to keep out of sight of a horse. He tried to imagine how anybody in their senses would just walk off home. This cooled him a little, and he retreated farther down the wood. He would go back the way he had come, along under the hill crest, without any more nonsense.

The wood hummed and the rain was a cold weight, but he observed this rather than felt it. The water ran down inside his clothes and squelched in his shoes as he eased his way carefully over the bedded twigs and leaves. At every instant he expected to see the prick-eared black head looking down at him from the hedge above.

At the woodside he paused, close against a tree. The success of this last manoeuvre was restoring his confidence, but he didn't want to venture out into the open field without making sure that the horse was just where he had left it. The perfect move would be to withdraw quietly and leave the horse standing out there in the rain. He crept up again among the trees to the crest and peeped through the hedge.

The grey field and the whole slope were empty. He searched the distance. The horse was quite likely to have forgotten him altogether and wandered off. Then he raised himself and leaned out to see if it had come in close to the hedge. Before he was aware of anything the ground shook. He twisted around wildly to see how he had been caught. The black shape was above him, right across the light. Its whinnying snort and the spattering whack of its hooves seemed to be actually inside his head as he fell backwards down the bank, and leapt again like a madman, dodging among the oaks, imagining how the buffet would come and how he would be knocked headlong. Half-way down the wood the oaks gave way to bracken and old roots and stony rabbit diggings. He was well out into the middle of this before he realized that he was running alone.

Gasping for breath now and cursing mechanically, without a thought for his suit he sat down on the ground to rest his shaking legs, letting the rain plaster the hair down over his forehead and watching the dense flashing lines disappear abruptly into the soil all around him as if he were watching through thick plate glass. He took deep breaths in the effort to steady his heart and regain control of himself. His right trouser turn-up was ripped at the seam and his suit jacket was splashed with the yellow mud of the top field.

Obviously the horse had been farther along the hedge above the steep field, waiting for him to come out at the woodside just as he had intended. He must have peeped through the hedge – peeping the wrong way – within yards of it.

However, this last attack had cleared up one thing. He need no longer act like a fool out of mere uncertainty as to whether the horse was simply being playful or not. It was definitely after him. He picked up two stones about the size of goose eggs and set off towards the bottom of the wood, striding carelessly.

A loop of the river bordered all this farmland. If he crossed the little level meadow at the bottom of the wood, he could follow the three-mile circuit, back to the road. There were deep hollows in the river-bank, shoaled with pebbles, as he remembered, perfect places to defend himself from if the horse followed him out there.

The hawthorns that choked the bottom of the wood – some of them good-sized trees – knitted into an almost impassable barrier. He had found a place where the growth thinned slightly and had begun to lift aside the long spiny stems, pushing himself forward, when he stopped. Through the bluish veil of bare twigs he saw the familiar shape out in the field below the wood.

But it seemed not to have noticed him yet. It was looking out across the field towards the river. Quietly, he released himself from the thorns and climbed back across the clearing towards the one side of the wood he had not yet tried. If the horse would only stay down there he could follow his first and easiest plan, up the wood and over the hilltop to the farm.

Now he noticed that the sky had grown much darker. The rain was heavier every second, pressing down as if the earth had to be flooded before nightfall. The oaks ahead blurred and the ground drummed. He began to run. And as he ran he heard a deeper sound running with him. He whirled around. The horse was in the middle of the clearing. It might have been running to get out of the terrific rain except that it was coming straight for him, scattering clay and stones, with an immensely supple and powerful motion. He let out a tearing roar and threw the stone in his right hand. The result was instantaneous. Whether at the roar or the stone the horse reared as if against a wall and shied to the left. As it dropped back on its fore-feet he flung his second stone, at ten yards' range, and saw a bright mud blotch suddenly appear on the glistening black flank. The horse surged down the wood, splashing the earth like water, tossing its long tail as it plunged out of sight among the hawthorns.

He looked around for stones. The encounter had set the blood beating in his head and given him a savage energy. He could have killed the horse at that moment. That this brute should pick him and play with him in this malevolent fashion was more than he could bear. Whoever owned it, he thought, deserved to have its neck broken for letting the dangerous thing loose.

He came out at the woodside, in open battle now, still searching for the right stones. There were plenty here, piled and scattered where they had been ploughed out of the field.

He selected two, then straightened and saw the horse twenty yards off in the middle of the steep field, watching him calmly. They looked at each other.

'Out of it!' he shouted, brandishing his arm. 'Out of it! Go on!' The horse twitched its pricked ears. With all his force he threw. The stone soared and landed beyond with a soft thud. He rearmed and threw again. For several minutes he kept up his bombardment without a single hit, working himself into a despair and throwing more and more wildly, till his arm began to ache with the unaccustomed exercise. Throughout the performance the horse watched him fixedly. Finally he had to stop and ease his shoulder muscle. As if the horse had been waiting for just this, it dipped its head twice and came at him.

He snatched up two stones and roaring with all his strength flung the one in his right hand. He was astonished at the crack of the impact. It was as if he had struck a tile – and the horse actually stumbled. With another roar he jumped forward and hurled his other stone. His aim seemed to be under superior guidance. The stone struck and re-bounded straight up into the air, spinning fiercely, as the horse swirled away and went careering down towards the far bottom of the field, at first with great, swinging leaps, then at a canter, leaving deep churned holes in the soil.

It turned up the far side of the field, climbing till it was level with him. He felt a little surprise of pity to see it shaking its head, and once it paused to lower its head and paw over its ear with its fore-hoof as a cat does.

'You stay there!' he shouted. 'Keep your distance and you'll not get hurt.'

And indeed the horse did stop at that moment, almost obediently. It watched him as he climbed to the crest.

The rain swept into his face and he realized that he was

freezing, as if his very flesh were sodden. The farm seemed miles away over the dreary fields. Without another glance at the horse – he felt too exhausted to care now what it did – he loaded the crook of his left arm with stones and plunged out on to the waste of mud.

He was half-way to the first hedge before the horse appeared, silhouetted against the sky at the corner of the wood, head high and attentive, watching his laborious retreat over the three fields.

The ankle-deep clay dragged at him. Every stride was a separate, deliberate effort, forcing him up and out of the sucking earth, burdened as he was by his sogged clothes and load of stone and limbs that seemed themselves to be turning to mud. He fought to keep his breathing even, two strides in, two strides out, the air ripping his lungs. In the middle of the last field he stopped and looked around. The horse, tiny on the skyline, had not moved.

At the corner of the field he unlocked his clasped arms and dumped the stones by the gatepost, then leaned on the gate. The farm was in front of him. He became conscious of the rain again and suddenly longed to stretch out full-length under it, to take the cooling, healing drops all over his body and forget himself in the last wretchedness of the mud. Making an effort, he heaved his weight over the gate-top. He leaned again, looking up at the hill.

Rain was dissolving land and sky together like a wet water-colour as the afternoon darkened. He concentrated raising his head, searching the skyline from end to end. The horse had vanished. The hill looked lifeless and desolate, an island lifting out of the sea, awash with every tide.

Under the long shed where the tractors, plough, binders and the rest were drawn up, waiting for their seasons, he sat on a sack thrown over a petrol drum, trembling, his lungs heaving. The mingled smell of paraffin, creosote, fertilizer, dust – all was exactly as he had left it twelve years ago. The ragged swallows' nests were still there tucked in the angles of the rafters. He remembered three dead foxes hanging in a row from one of the beams, their teeth bloody.

The ordeal with the horse had already sunk from reality. It hung under the surface of his mind, an obscure confusion of fright and shame, as after a narrowly-escaped street accident. There was a solid pain in his chest, like a spike of bone stabbing, that made him wonder if he had strained his heart on that last stupid burdened run. Piece by piece he began to take off his clothes, wringing the grey water out of them, but soon he stopped that and just sat staring at the ground, as if some important part had been cut out of his brain.

RAYMOND CARVER

CALL IF YOU NEED ME

WE HAD BOTH BEEN involved with other people that spring, but when June came and school was out we decided to let our house for the summer and move from Palo Alto to the north coast country of California. Our son, Richard, went to Nancy's grandmother's place in Pasco, Washington, to live for the summer and work toward saving money for college in the fall. His grandmother knew the situation at home and had begun working on getting him up there and locating him a job long before his arrival. She'd talked to a farmer friend of hers and had secured a promise of work for Richard baling hay and building fences. Hard work, but Richard was looking forward to it. He left on the bus in the morning of the day after his high school graduation. I took him to the station and parked and went inside to sit with him until his bus was called. His mother had already held him and cried and kissed him goodbye and given him a long letter that he was to deliver to his grandmother upon his arrival. She was at home now finishing last-minute packing for our own move and waiting for the couple who were to take our house. I bought Richard's ticket, gave it to him, and we sat on one of the benches in the station and waited. We'd talked a little about things on the way to the station.

'Are you and Mom going to get a divorce?' he'd asked. It was Saturday morning, and there weren't many cars.

'Not if we can help it,' I said. 'We don't want to. That's why we're going away from here and don't expect to see

353

anyone all summer. That's why we've rented our house for the summer and rented the house up in Eureka. Why you're going away, too, I guess. One reason anyway. Not to mention the fact that you'll come home with your pockets filled with money. We don't want to get a divorce. We want to be alone for the summer and try to work things out.'

'You still love Mom?' he said. 'She told me she loves you.'

'Of course I do,' I said. 'You ought to know that by now. We've just had our share of troubles and heavy responsibilities, like everyone else, and now we need time to be alone and work things out. But don't worry about us. You just go up there and have a good summer and work hard and save your money. Consider it a vacation too. Get in all the fishing you can. There's good fishing around there.'

'Water-skiing too,' he said. 'I want to learn to water-ski.'

'I've never been water-skiing,' I said. 'Do some of that for me too, will you?'

We sat in the bus station. He looked through his yearbook while I held a newspaper in my lap. Then his bus was called and we stood up. I embraced him and said, 'Don't worry, don't worry. Where's your ticket?'

He patted his coat pocket and then picked up his suitcase. I walked him over to where the line was forming in the terminal, then I embraced him again and kissed him on the cheek and said goodbye.

'Goodbye, Dad,' he said, and turned from me so I wouldn't see his tears.

I drove home to where our boxes and suitcases were waiting in the living room. Nancy was in the kitchen drinking coffee with the young couple she'd found to take our house for the summer. I'd met the couple, Jerry and Liz, graduate students in math, for the first time a few days before, but we shook hands again, and I drank a cup of coffee that Nancy poured. We sat around the table and drank coffee while Nancy finished her list of things they should look out for or do at certain times of the month, the first and last of each month, where they should send any mail, and the like. Nancy's face was tight. Sun fell through the curtain onto the table as it got later in the morning.

Finally, things seemed to be in order and I left the three of them in the kitchen and began loading the car. It was a furnished house we were going to, furnished right down to plates and cooking utensils, so we wouldn't need to take much with us from this house, only the essentials.

I'd driven up to Eureka, 350 miles north of Palo Alto, on the north coast of California, three weeks before and rented us the furnished house. I went with Susan, the woman I'd been seeing. We stayed in a motel at the edge of town for three nights while I looked in the newspaper and visited realtors. She watched me as I wrote out a check for the three months' rent. Later, back at the motel, in bed, she lay with her hand on her forehead and said, 'I envy your wife. I envy Nancy. You hear people talk about "the other woman" always and how the incumbent wife has the privileges and the real power, but I never really understood or cared about those things before. Now I see. I envy her. I envy her the life she'll have with you in that house this summer. I wish it were me. I wish it were us. Oh, how I wish it were us. I feel so crummy,' she said. I stroked her hair.

Nancy was a tall, long-legged woman with brown hair and eyes and a generous spirit. But lately we had been coming up short on generosity and spirit. The man she'd been seeing was one of my colleagues, a divorced, dapper, three-piece-suit-and-tie fellow with graying hair who drank too much and whose hands, some of my students told me, sometimes shook in the classroom. He and Nancy had drifted into their affair at a party during the holidays, not too long after Nancy had discovered my own affair. It all sounds boring and tacky now – it is boring and tacky – but during that spring it was what it was, and it consumed all of our energies and concentration to the exclusion of everything else. Sometime in late April we began to make plans to rent our house and go away for the summer, just the two of us, and try to put things back together, if they could be put back together. We each agreed we would not call or write or otherwise be in touch with the other parties. So we made arrangements for Richard, found the couple to look after our house, and I had looked at a map and driven north from San Francisco and found Eureka, and a realtor who was willing to rent a furnished house to a respectable middle-aged married couple for the summer. I think I even used the phrase 'second honeymoon' to the realtor, God forgive me, while Susan smoked a cigarette and read tourist brochures out in the car.

I finished storing the suitcases, bags, and cartons in the trunk and backseat and waited while Nancy said a final goodbye on the porch. She shook hands with each of them and turned and came toward the car. I waved to the couple, and they waved back. Nancy got in and shut the door. 'Let's go,' she said. I put the car in gear and we headed for the freeway. At the light just before the freeway we saw a car ahead of us come off the freeway trailing a broken muffler, the sparks flying. 'Look at that,' Nancy said. 'It might catch fire.' We waited and watched until the car managed to pull off the road onto the shoulder.

We stopped at a little café off the highway near Sebastopol. Eat and Gas, the sign read. We laughed at the sign. I pulled up in front of the café and we went inside and took a table near a window in the back. After we ordered coffee and sandwiches, Nancy touched her forefinger to the table and began tracing lines in the wood. I lit a cigarette and looked outside. I saw rapid movement, and then I realized I was looking at a hummingbird in the bush beside the window. Its wings moved in a blur of motion and it kept dipping its beak into a blossom on the bush.

'Nancy, look,' I said. 'There's a hummingbird.'

But the hummingbird flew at this moment and Nancy looked and said, 'Where? I don't see it.'

'It was just there a minute ago,' I said. 'Look, there it is. Another one, I think. It's another hummingbird.'

We watched the hummingbird until the waitress brought our order and the bird flew at the movement and disappeared around the building.

'Now that's a good sign, I think,' I said. 'Hummingbirds. Hummingbirds are supposed to bring luck.'

'I've heard that somewhere,' she said. 'I don't know where I heard that, but I've heard it. Well,' she said, 'luck is what we could use. Wouldn't you say?'

'They're a good sign,' I said. 'I'm glad we stopped here.'

She nodded. She waited a minute, then she took a bite of her sandwich.

We reached Eureka just before dark. We passed the motel on the highway where Susan and I had stayed and had spent the three nights two weeks before, then turned off the highway and took a road up a hill overlooking the town. I had the house keys in my pocket. We drove over the hill and for a mile or so until we came to a little intersection with a service station and a grocery store. There were wooded mountains ahead of us in the valley, and pastureland all around. Some cattle were grazing in a field behind the service station. 'This is pretty country,' Nancy said. 'I'm anxious to see the house.'

'Almost there,' I said. 'It's just down this road,' I said, 'and over that rise.' 'Here,' I said in a minute, and pulled into a long driveway with hedge on either side. 'Here it is. What do you think of this?' I'd asked the same question of Susan when she and I had stopped in the driveway.

'It's nice,' Nancy said. 'It looks fine, it does. Let's get out.'

We stood in the front yard a minute and looked around. Then we went up the porch steps and I unlocked the front door and turned on the lights. We went through the house. There were two small bedrooms, a bath, a living room with old furniture and a fireplace, and a big kitchen with a view of the valley.

'Do you like it?' I said.

'I think it's just wonderful,' Nancy said. She grinned. 'I'm glad you found it. I'm glad we're here.' She opened the refrigerator and ran a finger over the counter. 'Thank God, it looks clean enough. I won't have to do any cleaning.'

'Right down to clean sheets on the beds,' I said. 'I checked. I made sure. That's the way they're renting it. Pillows even. And pillowcases too.'

'We'll have to buy some firewood,' she said. We were standing in the living room. 'We'll want to have a fire on nights like this.'

'I'll look into firewood tomorrow,' I said. 'We can go shopping then, too, and see the town.'

She looked at me and said, 'I'm glad we're here.'

'So am I,' I said. I opened my arms and she moved to me. I held her. I could feel her trembling. I turned her face up and kissed her on either cheek. 'Nancy,' I said.

'I'm glad we're here,' she said.

*   *   *

We spent the next few days settling in, taking trips into Eureka to walk around and look in store windows, and hiking across the pastureland behind the house all the way to the woods. We bought groceries and I found an ad in the newspaper for firewood, called, and a day or so afterwards two young men with long hair delivered a pickup truckload of alder and stacked it in the carport. That night we sat in front of the fireplace after dinner and drank coffee and talked about getting a dog.

'I don't want a pup,' Nancy said. 'Something we have to clean up after or that will chew things up. That we don't need. But I'd like to have a dog, yes. We haven't had a dog in a long time. I think we could handle a dog up here,' she said.

'And after we go back, after summer's over?' I said. I rephrased the question. 'What about keeping a dog in the city?'

'We'll see. Meanwhile, let's look for a dog. The right kind of dog. I don't know what I want until I see it. We'll read the classifieds and we'll go to the pound, if we have to.' But though we went on talking about dogs for several days, and pointed out dogs to each other in people's yards we'd drive past, dogs we said we'd like to have, nothing came of it, we didn't get a dog.

Nancy called her mother and gave her our address and telephone number. Richard was working and seemed happy, her mother said. She herself was fine. I heard Nancy say, 'We're fine. This is good medicine.'

One day in the middle of July we were driving the highway near the ocean and came over a rise to see some lagoons that were closed off from the ocean by sand spits. There were some people fishing from shore, and two boats out on the water.

I pulled the car off onto the shoulder and stopped. 'Let's see what they're fishing for,' I said. 'Maybe we could get some gear and go ourselves.'

'We haven't been fishing in years,' Nancy said. 'Not since that time Richard was little and we went camping near Mount Shasta. Do you remember that?'

'I remember,' I said. 'I just remembered, too, that I've missed fishing. Let's walk down and see what they're fishing for.'

'Trout,' the man said, when I asked. 'Cutthroats and rainbow trout. Even some steelhead and a few salmon. They come in here in the winter when the spit opens and then when it closes in the spring, they're trapped. This is a good time of the year for them. I haven't caught any today, but last Sunday I caught four, about fifteen inches long. Best eating fish in the world, and they put up a hell of a fight. Fellows out in the boats have caught some today, but so far I haven't done anything.'

'What do you use for bait?' Nancy asked.

'Anything,' the man said. 'Worms, salmon eggs, whole-kernel corn. Just get it out there and leave it lay on the bottom. Pull out a little slack and watch your line.'

We hung around a little longer and watched the man fish and watched the little boats *chat-chat* back and forth the length of the lagoon.

'Thanks,' I said to the man. 'Good luck to you.'

'Good luck to you,' he said. 'Good luck to the both of you.'

We stopped at a sporting goods store on the way back to town and bought licenses, inexpensive rods and reels, nylon line, hooks, leaders, sinkers, and a creel. We made plans to go fishing the next morning.

But that night, after we'd eaten dinner and washed the

dishes and I had laid a fire in the fireplace, Nancy shook her head and said it wasn't going to work.

'Why do you say that?' I asked. 'What is it you mean?'

'I mean it isn't going to work. Let's face it.' She shook her head again. 'I don't think I want to go fishing in the morning, either, and I don't want a dog. No, no dogs. I think I want to go up and see my mother and Richard. Alone. I want to be alone. I miss Richard,' she said and began to cry. 'Richard's my son, my baby,' she said, 'and he's nearly grown and gone. I miss him.'

'And Del, do you miss Del Shraeder too?' I said. 'Your boyfriend. Do you miss him?'

'I miss everybody tonight,' she said. 'I miss you too. I've missed you for a long time now. I've missed you so much you've gotten lost somehow, I can't explain it. I've lost you. You're not mine any longer.'

'Nancy,' I said.

'No, no,' she said. She shook her head. She sat on the sofa in front of the fire and kept shaking her head. 'I want to fly up and see my mother and Richard tomorrow. After I'm gone you can call your girlfriend.'

'I won't do that,' I said. 'I have no intention of doing that.'

'You'll call her,' she said.

'You'll call Del,' I said. I felt rubbishy for saying it.

'You can do what you want,' she said, wiping her eyes on her sleeve. 'I mean that. I don't want to sound hysterical. But I'm going up to Washington tomorrow. Right now I'm going to go to bed. I'm exhausted. I'm sorry. I'm sorry for both of us, Dan. We're not going to make it. That fisherman today. He wished us good luck.' She shook her head. 'I wish us good luck too. We're going to need it.'

She went into the bathroom and I heard water running in the tub. I went out and sat on the porch steps and smoked a

361

cigarette. It was dark and quiet outside. I looked toward town and could see a faint glow of lights in the sky and patches of ocean fog drifting in the valley. I began to think of Susan. A little later, Nancy came out of the bathroom and I heard the bedroom door close. I went inside and put another block of wood on the grate and waited until the flames began to move up the bark. Then I went into the other bedroom and turned the covers back and stared at the floral design on the sheets. Then I showered, dressed in my pajamas, and went to sit near the fireplace again. The fog was outside the window now. I sat in front of the fire and smoked. When I looked out the window again, something moved in the fog and I saw a horse grazing in the front yard.

I went to the window. The horse looked up at me for a minute, then went back to pulling up grass. Another horse walked past the car into the yard and began to graze. I turned on the porch light and stood at the window and watched them. They were big white horses with long manes. They'd gotten through a fence or an unlocked gate from one of the nearby farms. Somehow they'd wound up in our front yard. They were larking it, enjoying their breakaway immensely. But nervous, too; I could see the whites of their eyes from where I stood behind the window. Their ears kept rising and falling as they tore out clumps of grass. A third horse wandered into the yard, and then a fourth. It was a herd of white horses, and they were grazing in our front yard.

I went into the bedroom and woke Nancy. Her eyes were red and the skin around the eyes was swollen. She had her hair up in curlers, and a suitcase lay open on the floor near the foot of the bed.

'Nancy,' I said. 'Honey, come and see what's in the front yard. Come and see this. You must see this. You won't believe it. Hurry up.'

362

'What is it?' she said. 'Don't hurt me. What is it?'

'Honey, you must see this. I'm not going to hurt you. I'm sorry if I scared you. But you must come out here and see something.'

I went back into the other room and stood in front of the window, and in a few minutes Nancy came in tying her robe. She looked out the window and said, 'My God, they're beautiful. Where'd they come from, Dan? They're just beautiful.'

'They must have gotten loose from around here somewhere,' I said. 'One of these farm places. I'll call the sheriff's department pretty soon and let them locate the owners. But I wanted you to see this first.'

'Will they bite?' she said. 'I'd like to pet that one there, the one that just looked at us. I'd like to pat that one's shoulder. But I don't want to get bitten. I'm going outside.'

'I don't think they'll bite,' I said. 'They don't look like the kind of horses that'll bite. But put a coat on if you're going out there; it's cold.'

I put my coat on over my pajamas and waited for Nancy. Then I opened the front door and we went outside and walked into the yard with the horses. They all looked up at us. Two of them went back to pulling up grass. One of the other horses snorted and moved back a few steps, and then it, too, went back to pulling up grass and chewing, head down. I rubbed the forehead of one horse and patted its shoulder. It kept chewing. Nancy put out her hand and began stroking the mane of another horse. 'Horsey, where'd you come from?' she said. 'Where do you live and why are you out tonight, Horsey?' she said, and kept stroking the horse's mane. The horse looked at her and blew through its lips and dropped its head again. She patted its shoulder.

'I guess I'd better call the sheriff,' I said.

'Not yet,' she said. 'Not for a while yet. We'll never see

363

anything like this again. We'll never, never have horses in our front yard again. Wait a while yet, Dan.'

A little later, Nancy was still out there moving from one horse to another, patting their shoulders and stroking their manes, when one of the horses moved from the yard into the driveway and walked around the car and down the driveway toward the road, and I knew I had to call.

In a little while the two sheriff's cars showed up with their red lights flashing in the fog and a few minutes later a fellow in a sheepskin coat driving a pickup with a horse trailer behind it. Now the horses shied and tried to get away, and the man with the horse trailer swore and tried to get a rope around the neck of one horse.

'Don't hurt it!' Nancy said.

We went back in the house and stood behind the window and watched the deputies and the rancher work on getting the horses rounded up.

'I'm going to make some coffee,' I said. 'Would you like some coffee, Nancy?'

'I'll tell you what I'd like,' she said. 'I feel high, Dan. I feel like I'm loaded. I feel like, I don't know, but I like the way I'm feeling. You put on some coffee and I'll find us some music to listen to on the radio and then you can build up the fire again. I'm too excited to sleep.'

So we sat in front of the fire and drank coffee and listened to an all-night radio station from Eureka and talked about the horses and then talked about Richard, and Nancy's mother. We danced. We didn't talk about the present situation at all. The fog hung outside the window and we talked and were kind with one another. Toward daylight I turned off the radio and we went to bed and made love.

The next afternoon, after her arrangements were made and her suitcases packed, I drove her to the little airport where she would catch a flight to Portland and then transfer to another airline that would put her in Pasco late that night.

'Tell your mother I said hello. Give Richard a hug for me and tell him I miss him,' I said. 'Tell him I send love.'

'He loves you too,' she said. 'You know that. In any case you'll see him in the fall, I'm sure.'

I nodded.

'Goodbye,' she said and reached for me. We held each other. 'I'm glad for last night,' she said. 'Those horses. Our talk. Everything. It helps. We won't forget that,' she said. She began to cry.

'Write me, will you?' I said. 'I didn't think it would happen to us,' I said. 'All those years. I never thought so for a minute. Not us.'

'I'll write,' she said. 'Some big letters. The biggest you've ever seen since I used to send you letters in high school.'

'I'll be looking for them,' I said.

Then she looked at me again and touched my face. She turned and moved across the tarmac toward the plane.

Go, dearest one, and God be with you.

She boarded the plane and I stayed around until its jet engines started, and in a minute the plane began to taxi down the runway. It lifted off over Humboldt Bay and soon became a speck on the horizon.

I drove back to the house and parked in the driveway and looked at the hoofprints of the horses from last night. There were deep impressions in the grass, and gashes, and there were piles of dung. Then I went into the house and, without even taking off my coat, went to the telephone and dialed Susan's number.

ACKNOWLEDGMENTS

MARGARET ATWOOD: 'White Horse', copyright © 2006 by O. W. Toad, Ltd, from *Moral Disorder and Other Stories* by Margaret Atwood. Used by permission of Nan A. Talese/ Doubleday, a division of Random House, Inc. © Margaret Atwood, 2006, 'White Horse' from *Moral Disorder & Other Stories*, by permission of Bloomsbury Publishing Plc.

ISAAC BABEL: 'The Story of a Horse' from *Complete Works of Isaac Babel* by Isaac Babel, edited by Nathalie Babel, translated by Peter Constantine. Copyright © 2002 by Peter Constantine. Used by permission of W. W. Norton & Company, Inc.

RAYMOND CARVER: From *Call If You Need Me* by Raymond Carver. Published by Harvill Secker. Reprinted by permission of The Random House Group Limited and The Wylie Agency.

PAM HOUSTON: 'What Shock Heard' from *Cowboys are My Weakness* by Pam Houston. Copyright © 1992 by Pam Houston. Used by permission of W. W. Norton & Company, Inc.

TED HUGHES: 'The Rain Horse' from *Difficulties of a Bridegroom* by Ted Hughes. Used by permission of Faber and Faber Limited. 'The Rain Horse' from *Difficulties of a Bridegroom* by Ted Hughes. Copyright © 1995 by Ted Hughes. Reprinted by permission of Picador, an imprint of St. Martin's Press LLC.